Praise for the W...

"The forecast calls for . . .

"[As] swift, sassy, and sexy as Laurell K. Hamilton . . .
Rachel Caine takes the Weather Wardens to places the
Weather Channel never imagined!"   —Mary Jo Putney

"A fast-paced thrill ride [that] brings new meaning to
stormy weather."   —*Locus*

"An appealing heroine, with a wry sense of humor that
enlivens even the darkest encounters."   —SF Site

"Fans of Laurell K. Hamilton and the Dresden Files by Jim
Butcher are going to love this fast-paced, action-packed, romantic urban fantasy."   —*Midwest Book Review*

"A kick-butt heroine who will appeal strongly to fans of
Tanya Huff, Kelley Armstrong, and Charlaine Harris."
     —*Romantic Times*

"A neat, stylish, and very witty addition to the genre, all
wrapped up in a narrative voice to die for. Hugely enter-
taining."   —SF Crowsnest

"Chaos has never been so intriguing as when Rachel Caine
shapes it into the setting of a story. Each book in this series
has built in intensity and fascination. Secondary characters
blossom as Joanne meets them anew, and twists are revealed that will leave you gasping."
     —Huntress Book Reviews

"The Weather Warden series is fun reading . . . more en-
gaging than most TV."   —*Booklist*

"If for some absurd reason you haven't tucked in to this
series, now's a good time. Get cracking."   —Purple Pens

"I dare you to put this book down."
     —*University City Review* (Philadelphia)

"Overall, the fast pace, intense emotion, cool magics, and a
sense of hurtling momentum toward some planet-sized con-
clusion to the overarching story are keeping me a fan of the
Weather Warden series. I continue to enjoy Joanne's girly-
girl yet kick-ass nature."   —Romantic & Fantasy Novels

Also by Rachel Caine

THE WEATHER WARDEN SERIES

Rachel Caine

UNDONE

OUTCAST SEASON, BOOK ONE

A ROC BOOK

ROC
Published by New American Library, a division of
Penguin Group (USA) Inc., 375 Hudson Street,
New York, New York 10014, USA
Penguin Group (Canada), 90 Eglinton Avenue East, Suite 700, Toronto,
Ontario M4P 2Y3, Canada (a division of Pearson Penguin Canada Inc.)
Penguin Books Ltd., 80 Strand, London WC2R 0RL, England
Penguin Ireland, 25 St. Stephen's Green, Dublin 2,
Ireland (a division of Penguin Books Ltd.)
Penguin Group (Australia), 250 Camberwell Road, Camberwell, Victoria 3124,
Australia (a division of Pearson Australia Group Pty. Ltd.)
Penguin Books India Pvt. Ltd., 11 Community Centre, Panchsheel Park,
New Delhi - 110 017, India
Penguin Group (NZ), 67 Apollo Drive, Rosedale, North Shore 0632,
Auckland, New Zealand (a division of Pearson New Zealand Ltd.)
Penguin Books (South Africa) (Pty.) Ltd., 24 Sturdee Avenue,
Rosebank, Johannesburg 2196, South Africa

Penguin Books Ltd., Registered Offices:
80 Strand, London WC2R 0RL, England

First published by Roc, an imprint of New American Library,
a division of Penguin Group (USA) Inc.

First Printing, February 2009
10 9 8 7 6 5 4 3 2 1

To Jean Stuntz, my dear and patient friend,
who sat with me in a humid bar
in Oklahoma City and helped me figure out
what made *Outcast Season* a halfway good idea.
You, my dear, rock.

ACKNOWLEDGMENTS

To Cynthia Clarke, for services above and beyond!
My friends P. N. Elrod, Sharon Sams-Adams, and the Time Turners for extraordinary support.

To beta readers Brooke Carleton, Sonya Volkhardt, and Jesse L. Cairns for masterful commentary and guidance.

To the Victory dealership in Arlington, Texas, and the Smart Car dealership in Dallas.

Chapter 1

IT ONLY TOOK one word to destroy me, after millennia of living in peace and security, and the word was *No*.

I knew as I made my answer that it would not come without consequences. Had I known just how vast those would be, and how far they would ripple, I doubt I would have had the courage.

Humans say that ignorance is bliss, and perhaps that's true, even for Djinn.

For a moment, it seemed that my act of outright defiance brought with it no reaction. Ashan, the Djinn facing me—one of the oldest of the Old Ones—was a swirl of brilliance without form, a being without the trap of flesh, just as I was.

I thought that perhaps, this time, my defiance might go unpunished, and then I felt a ripple in the aetheric currents surrounding me. The aetheric was the world in which I lived, a plane of light and energy, heat and fire. It had little in common with the lower planes, the ones tied to dirt and death. I lived in heaven, and a ripple in heaven was ominous indeed.

I watched as Ashan—brother, father, god of my existence, newly made Conduit from Mother Earth to the Djinn—took on form and substance. It required power to do such a thing here, in this place; I had not bothered with form in so many turnings of the world

I didn't think I could even remember the shapes, and even if I did, I had not the raw force necessary to manipulate things here.

Ashan's aetheric form became ominously solid and dark, and I felt the ripples grow stronger, rocking the reality around us. The bands and currents of colors, pastel and perfect, took on sharp edges. Rainbows bled and wept.

"No?" He repeated it from a mouth that was almost human form, giving me the chance to change my answer. To save myself.

"I cannot. No."

This time, the rainbows burned. Another ripple hit me in a wave, hot and thick with menace, and I felt a strange pulling sensation that quickly became . . . pain, as much as one could feel pain without physical form. I was in danger; every instinct screamed it.

"Last chance," Ashan said. "Cassiel, don't test me. I can't allow your rebellion. Not now. Do as you are ordered."

What I was doing wasn't rebellion, but he couldn't see this so clearly, and I could not explain. I had never been known for my reasonable nature, and I never explained myself.

I stayed silent.

"Then you chose this. Remember that."

I felt the tugging inside of me turn white-hot, searing in its intensity. I felt the exact moment when Ashan ripped away my connection to the aetheric, to him, to the mother of us all, the Earth.

Beyond that, the vast and unknowable God.

I felt the exact moment when I died as a Djinn, and fell, screaming. I crashed through all the planes of heaven, shattering each in turn, a bright white star burning as it fell. I took on form.

Solidity.

Pain.

I landed facedown in the mud and dirt.
Destroyed.

"Cassiel."

The voice was a whisper, but it burned in my ears
like acid. The slightest sound—even my own name—
was agonizing. I had never been hurt before, and I
was drowning in the sensations, the agony of it. The
humiliating fury of helplessness, of being trapped in
flesh. Of being mutilated and emptied and cut off.

The worst of it was that it was my own fault.

I rolled away from the sound of my name being
called again, and from the gentle brushing touch of a
hand. My fresh-born nerves screamed, outraged by
every hint of pressure. I couldn't separate my thoughts
from the overwhelming, crushing burden of senses I
had never bothered to master before, because I had
never bothered to be human.

"Cassiel, it's David. Can you hear me?"

David. Yes. David was Djinn, a Conduit like Ashan.
He would understand. He could help. He could sense
the echoing emptiness inside me where my power had
once been; he could tell how badly damaged I was.
He could make it *stop*.

"Help," I whispered, or tried to. I don't know if he
understood me. The sounds that came from my mouth
sounded less like words than the raw whimpering of a
wounded animal. There was no elegance to my plea, no
eloquence. I had no grace. I was trapped in a prison of
heavy, uncooperative flesh, and everything hurt. I tried
to get away from the pain, but no matter how I writhed,
changing my skin, changing inside it, the burn was constant. The agony of being *alone* never went away.

His voice grew louder, more urgent. "Cassiel. Listen
to me. You're shifting too fast. You have to choose a
shape and hold on to it, do you understand? You're
killing yourself. Stop shifting!"

I didn't understand. It was all flesh, and nothing felt right, nothing felt true. I kept blindly changing my form—the shape of my face, the length of my legs and arms, my height, my weight. I abandoned human templates altogether for something smaller, something catlike, but that felt wrong, too, worse than wrong, and I clawed back into human flesh and fell on my side again, panting and exhausted. I blinked my eyes—oh, so limited, these eyes, seeing such a narrow spectrum of light—and saw that my exhausted body had settled into a female form, long-limbed, pale. The hair that straggled across my field of vision was very pale, as well—white, with a touch of ice blue. It matched the devastating cold inside of me.

I was shivering. Frozen. I had never known what it was really like, nerves rasping on each other in such a way. It felt horrific and humiliating, being so exposed, so raw and badly formed.

Something warm fell across my naked body, and I rolled into it, groaning uncontrollably. I felt myself lifted up and embraced in David's arms, weak as a newborn child.

I fixed my gaze on his face. *So different.* He was not the bright, burning flame I had known from the aetheric; here, he was in the form of a human man. Still, there was a touch of the Djinn in the hot coppery color of his eyes, and in the gleam of his skin.

David had always loved abiding among mortals, while I'd avoided them, shunned the idea of taking flesh at all. We had never been friends, even so much as Djinn might be; allies from time to time, when the occasion suited. Never more. Ironic we should find ourselves at the same destination, by such different roads.

"Cassiel," he said again, and brushed hair back from my face as he braced my head against his chest. "What happened to you?" He sounded genuinely concerned, although I was none of his responsibility—but David had always had a touch of the human about him, because of his origins. False-born, a Djinn only in power and not in lineage, bred from humans and brought up to the Djinn only through the catastrophic deaths of thousands. They called themselves the New Djinn. Not like Ashan. Not like *me*. We were the True Djinn, born of the power of the Earth. These others were merely late-coming pretenders.

"Can you hear me? What *happened*?"

Even had I been in command of my new lips, lungs, and tongue, I couldn't confess what had brought me down to this terrible state, not without revealing more than even David should know.

I *would not* tell.

He must have seen that, because I felt his attention focus on me, warm and liquid, passing over and through me. It was . . . soothing. Like his hand, which was stroking my hair, avoiding contact with my fragile, newborn skin.

His expression changed, eyes widening. I didn't have enough experience with human faces to know what that meant. "You've been cut off. Cassiel, you're *dying*. Why has Ashan done this to you?"

He was right; I was dying. I sensed my hunger, a dark core of desperation inside that was growing worse with each labored breath I took. Djinn don't need human food; we sustain ourselves from the aetheric . . . but I could no longer reach it. The life of the Djinn, the very breath of it, was closed to me.

No wonder it all hurt so badly.

I felt David lifting me, felt the drag of gravity heavy on my flesh. What if he dropped me? I imagined the impact, the pain, and felt a horrible surge of terror. I huddled in his arms, helpless and furious with inadequacy.

Cassiel the great. Cassiel the terrible.

Cassiel the undone.

I forced my senses outward, away from my raw flesh, to focus on the world around me. I was in a human home of some type, with no memory of how I'd found it, or how David had found me. Everything seemed too bright, too sharp, too *flat*. I couldn't sense my surroundings as I should have been able to, as a Djinn would have known them; the bed on which he carefully laid me felt cool against my skin, and blissfully soft, but it was just nerves responding to pressure and temperature. Human senses, blunt and awkward.

As a Djinn, I should have been able to know this room at a glance—know its history, know where and how everything in it had originated. I should have been able to unspool the history of each small thing back through time, if I wished. I should know it all down to its smallest particles, and be able to make and unmake it at will, with enough power and ability.

But instead I sensed it as a human might, in surfaces, interpreted in light and smell and touch and sound. And taste. There was a foul metallic coating in my mouth. Blood. I swallowed it, and felt a twinge of nausea. I could *bleed*. The thought made me feel even more fragile.

The bed sagged on one side as David seated himself next to me. "Cassiel," he said again. "Try to speak."

I licked my lips with a clumsy, thick tongue, and squeezed air from my lungs to mumble, "David." Just his name, but it was a triumph of a kind. And his smile was a reward.

"Good," he said. "Before we do anything else, let me give you some power. You're badly injured. I won't overload you—just enough to stabilize you. All right?"

He took my hands in his—gently, but still my nerves screamed in protest at the unfamiliar touch. I rattled inside, and realized that what I felt was anxiety, channeled through human instincts.

The fear mounted as I felt the warmth David granted cascade into me . . . and pass right through me. I couldn't hold on to what he was trying to give. It was maddening, like watching life-giving water flow by in a tunnel, while dying of thirst.

David let go and sat back. Behind him, the sun was rising through an open window, a fierce ball of fire draped in oranges and reds and pinks, barely filtered by the thin white curtains. I turned my face away from its burning, unable to feel its energy the way I had as a Djinn. The rumpled sheets smelled of human musk. The table beyond the bed held some kind of mechanical device with hard-burning red characters, an abstract thing that only gradually made sense to me as a type of clock for marking hours. So slow, this way of understanding. So pitifully, painfully slow.

A closet on the far side of the room was open, revealing a dizzying rainbow of cloth and color. The room smelled sharply of perfumes, soaps, and sex.

"This is Joanne's room," David said. "She'll be back soon. Cassiel, can you try to tell me what happened?"

I shook my head, or tried—that was the currently accepted negative gesture, or so I thought. Even though I had never taken flesh before, there were things the Djinn knew, things they absorbed. Human languages. Human habits. We could not avoid them, not even those who held ourselves strictly apart; the knowledge seeped through the aetheric, into our unwilling awareness.

That was the fault of the New Djinn, who had never shed their human beginnings, and gave us connection to these tiny, brief lives.

David looked at me soberly for a moment, then put his hand flat against my forehead. A kind of benediction, very light and gentle.

"You're in pain," he said. "I'm sorry that I can't help you, but you're not one of my people. You're

Ashan's. I can't touch you, and I can't undo what he's done."

Ashan. Ah yes, I was Ashan's. I was one of the Old Djinn, the First Djinn, who came before any human walked the Earth. I was a spirit of fire and air, and Ashan had cast me down to this heavy, crippling flesh.

I struggled to hold to that knowledge. Already, the aetheric seemed so far away. So unattainable.

"I'll speak with him," David said, and tried to rise. I forced my muscles to my will, and grabbed his wrist. It was a weak hold, hardly even strong enough to restrain a human child, much less a Djinn, but David understood the gesture. He paused, and I felt his pulse of alarm before I matched it to the frown of his expression. "You don't want me to go to Ashan? You're sure?"

"I'm sure," I whispered. I had just doubled my output of human words. It felt ridiculously cheering. "He won't listen."

I was tired from the effort of saying it, and closed my eyes, but the blackness within terrified me, and I opened them again. David was still frowning at me. He began to ask a question, then stopped himself, shook his head, and smoothed my hair again.

"Rest," he said. "I'll try to find a way to help."

I struggled with a pitiful feeling of gratitude, and the ghost of an old, imperious wave of contempt. Contempt for him, for caring for me at all. Contempt for my own appalling weakness.

"Rest," David repeated, and despite everything, I found myself burrowing beneath the warm covers, into the smell of another human's skin, and darkness slipped over my eyes. I didn't want to let go. I fought.

But it won.

I woke up to a woman's voice, dry and lightly amused. "Okay, David, I'm sure there's a perfectly reasonable explanation for why there's a naked girl in

my bed. No, really, I'm sure. And you have about—
oh—five seconds to come up with it."

I blinked, turned clumsily in my cocoon of sheets
and blankets, and saw the woman standing over me,
arms folded. She was tall, slender, with long dark hair
and eyes like sapphires. Skin like fine porcelain, lightly
dusted with gold.

Even as unfamiliar as I was with the subtleties of
human facial expressions, she didn't look happy.

I heard David stir on the other side of the room,
where he'd taken a seat in a wing chair. He put aside
a book he was holding and stood up to come to the
woman and put his arms around her. "Her name is
Cassiel. Djinn. She's only here until I can help her get
her strength back," he said. "Something happened to
her. I can't tell what it was, but I'm trying to find out."

"One of yours?"

"Actually, no. One of Ashan's."

"Ashan's? Oh, that's great. Perfect." With a shock,
I realized that the woman must be Joanne Baldwin. I
knew who she was, of course. All of the Djinn knew
of the Weather Warden, and her love affair with one
of the two leaders of the Djinn world. She was both
one of the more warily respected of the billions of
humans crawling the face of the planet . . . and one
of the most hated, in many quarters, including Ashan's. "And why isn't she in his bed, then, instead of
mine?"

"Good question," David said. "I don't know. She
isn't saying much. She can't."

Joanne wasn't angry, I realized, despite her words.
She was looking at me with what I thought was vague
kindness. "Cassiel," she said. "David—you're sure
she's really a Djinn? I mean—"

That frightened me. How could she not be certain
of that? Had I fallen so low that I could be mistaken
for a *human*?

"Old Djinn," I managed to say. "Ashan's."

Her next question came right to me. "I've never met you before, have I?"

"No." Because I had never worn flesh before. Never craved it.

She nodded slowly, and a slight frown grooved itself between her eyebrows. "David says you're hurt." Her blue eyes unfocused, and her black pupils expanded. She was looking into the aetheric, I knew, and seeing my damaged soul. "My God. You really *are* hurt. Can you draw power at all?"

I managed to shake my head in the negative. Joanne turned to David. "What the hell is that bastard doing, dumping her out here on us? Is he trying to kill her, or just interfere with what we're doing? We need to get out there, dammit! We're supposed to be *bait* for the Sentinels, not—General Hospital for Wayward Djinn."

They exchanged a look, a long one, that contained information I could not understand. David touched her gently, a stroke of fingers along the skin of her arm.

"I don't know what he intends, but if we can't figure out a way to get her access to the aetheric, this will kill her, no question about it," David said. "She's very weak. She could barely settle into this form. No chance she can shift again, at this point. She's living on whatever she has in reserve right now, and what I try to give her just bleeds away. I think because she's Ashan's creature, I can't really touch her. Not even to save her."

Joanne pulled up a chair and sat, elbows on her knees. She was wearing a close-fitting red top and rough blue woven pants, and there was a glitter of gold on her left hand with a fire-red ruby in its center. "Want me to try?" she asked, cutting her eyes toward David. He crossed his arms, frowning deeply. "C'mon, it's worth a shot. You already tried. Ashan's clearly left the clue phone off the hook. Let me have a go. Better than just letting her up and die on us, right?"

He gave her one sharp nod, but said, "If anything happens, I'm cutting the connection. Careful. Cassiel's strong, and she's not herself."

I wanted to be offended by such presumption from a mere New Djinn—even one such as David—but I couldn't deny the truth. I was not myself. I no longer even knew, truly, what portion of myself I'd lost, or what remained.

I felt that I was losing more of myself with every beat of my all-too-human heart.

Joanne took a deep breath, reached out, and folded her long, carefully manicured fingers around my strange pale ones.

And power snapped a connection tight between us, like lightning leaping to ground, and I felt my whole body convulse with the impact. Such *power*, rolling like red-hot lava through veins and nerves, feeding and filling the dark hollows of my bones. I almost wept in relief, so strong was it, so great was my need, and I greedily pulled power from her vast, rich store, bathing in it, glorying in it. . . .

. . . Until a sharp, heavy, black force slammed between us, and the flow of energy disappeared.

David stood between us, and he pushed me back down, one hand solidly on my chest. He held me on the bed as I struggled, panting, but his attention was on Joanne Baldwin. She was standing against the far wall, and the chair in which she'd been sitting was lying overturned on the floor. As I watched, she slid slowly down the wall and hid her face in shaking hands.

"Jo?" David sounded alarmed and angry. "Are you all right?"

She waved vaguely without looking up. "Okay," she said. "Give me a minute. Not fun."

He pulled in a breath and turned his focus back to me.

"Be still," he snapped, and I stopped struggling, suddenly aware how desperate I seemed—how primeval—and of the anger in his eyes. I stilled myself, except for fast, panting breaths, and nodded to let him know I had control of myself again. He reluctantly let me go. I sat up, but slowly, making no sudden moves to trigger his defenses.

"I'm sorry," I said, forming the words more easily now. "I did not mean to hurt her."

"Well, that makes it all better," Joanne said, and groaned. "And also, by the way, *ow.* Crap, that hurt." Her blue eyes were bloodshot and vague, as if she'd taken a blow to the head. "Right. Maybe I'm not cut out for being Florence Nightingale to the Djinn."

I felt better. Steadier, if nowhere near normal. At least my human form seemed to be working properly— that was a start. I pushed the covers back and swung my legs off the bed, but it took a long, agonizing moment before I could drag myself upright and find my balance.

David didn't help me. In fact, both he and Joanne kept a wary, watchful distance.

"She's stuck in that form?" Joanne said.

"As far as I can tell." He was looking at me with a kind of clinical interest, and I put one foot carefully in front of the other, taking my first trembling steps as a human, until I arrived at the mirror on the closet door.

Tall, this body. Thin. For a female form, it was narrow, barely rounded at the breast and hip. Long arms and legs, all of my skin very pale. My hair was a white puffball around my head, frail and ethereal, and my eyes . . .

. . . My eyes were the cool green of arctic ice. No shine of Djinn to them, despite the color. I had no power to spare for that sort of display.

"Too bad, really," Joanne said as she levered herself back to her feet, staggering only a little. "Because I'm pretty sure the albino look will limit your fashion choices. And it does make you stand out. Then again, there's always spray tanning."

This was the form I'd chosen, out of instinct. It must have had some truth to it. I shrugged, watching the play of muscles beneath the flawless white skin.

David cocked his head, watching me as I inspected my new body.

Joanne noticed. "Uh, honey? Unless you're planning to start stuffing dollars in her nonexistent G-string, a robe might be nice."

He smiled, and retrieved a garment from the back of her closet door. It was a long, pale pink fall of silken cloth, and it settled cold against my skin but began to warm almost immediately. My first clothing. The color reminded me of disjointed things: primroses in the spring, cherry blossoms fluttering in the wind, sunrise. And it reminded me most strongly of the shifting, ethereal colors of a Djinn's aura on the aetheric, so pale as to be transparent.

I smoothed the fabric, belted it, and looked up at the two of them. David had moved to Joanne's side, both of them staring at me with identical expressions that were not quite welcoming, not quite mistrustful. Cautious. "Thank you," I said. "I am better now."

I had not, in a thousand years, said a word of gratitude to a New Djinn, let alone to a human. Humans were lesser beings, and I felt nothing for them but contempt, when I bothered to feel anything for them at all.

So it cost me to speak the words, and I still felt a core of anger that I had been brought so low. I knew she heard the resonance of it. The arrogance. But is it arrogance if one is truly superior?

"Don't thank me yet. You're feeling better, but that's not going to last," Joanne said. "The power you pulled from me is going to dry up on you, and it'll go faster the more you try to use your powers. Best I can tell, you can't access the aetheric at all yourself; you can only do it when touching a human. A Warden." Her eyes grew narrow and very dark. "Which makes you a kind of Ifrit. One who preys on humans instead of other Djinn. I can't even tell you how much that doesn't make me happy."

Ifrit. It was the dark dream of all Djinn, that existence—too damaged to be healed, yet existing nevertheless. Endlessly consuming the power and vital essences of other Djinn to survive. I wasn't an Ifrit, not quite, but she was right. . . . It was a close thing. And Wardens were vulnerable to me.

Wardens, I realized with a startled flash, were *food.*

It required some kind of statement. Some promise. "I will not prey on you," I said, and somehow it sounded, to my ears, as if I found the whole concept distasteful. "You need not fear me."

"Oh, I don't," Joanne said, and crossed her arms. "If I feared you, believe me, this would be a very different conversation. But I'm not letting you wander off to grab a snack off any Warden who crosses your path, either. What you did to me would have killed most of them."

I felt my whole body stiffen, and power tingled in my fingertips. I wondered if my eyes had taken on that metallic shine, like David's. "How will you stop me?" I asked, very softly. "I will not be caged. Nor bottled, *Warden.* My kind has seen quite enough of that."

I had never in my life been a slave to the humans. Unlike many of my fellows, who had been tricked or suborned into service by the Wardens over many thousands of years, I had never been captured, never made their property. I had no love of mortals, and no fear of them, either. And I would not *ever* be owned.

We stood there, the three of us, in a peculiar triangle, in such a human-seeming, normal home. David, fierce and powerful, but with little hold over me because I was a different kind of Djinn altogether. Joanne, just as fierce, but fragile and mortal, therefore of no more consequence to me than any of her kind.

But . . . what was I?

I didn't know. I was neither human, nor was I Djinn, and it terrified me. I said, very quietly, "Where can I go? If not here, where?"

Even to my ears, it sounded strangely empty and weak. Joanne exchanged a long look with David, some silent communication in their own language I couldn't share.

"She's got a point," he said.

Joanne sighed. "You can stay," she said. "For a couple of days, no more. But one wrong move, Cassiel, and you're going to wish we'd let you dry up and fade away."

Chapter 2

THE REST OF the day passed. I learned more of my human body, and the more I learned, the less I liked. Its machinery was too fragile and required too much maintenance. Food. Breathing. Finally, sleeping. The humiliating process of waste elimination was enough to make me wish fondly for oblivion.

Joanne, distantly compassionate through this, assured me that I would soon adjust. And I did, out of necessity. By the next day, I even began to enjoy some of the tastes of the food and drink she offered me, and learn which were better avoided. *Coffee* was strongly flavored and good. *Garlic* was not, until she showed me that it was best used to season other things and not eaten in large pieces. (I tried seasoning my food with coffee, but the results were disappointing.)

Ice cream was a revelation. For the first time in human form, I experienced a warm rush of something that I identified as real pleasure. It must have shown plainly in my expression, because Joanne, seated across from me at the kitchen table, smiled and pointed a spoon at the round container, still frosted and smoking lightly in the warmth of the room.

"Ben and Jerry's," she said. "I figured if anything could teach you to smile, it'd be New York Super Fudge Chunk."

Had I smiled? Surely not. I gazed at her, feeling my

brows pull together in what I'd learned was a forbidding expression, and took another spoonful of the frozen chocolate dessert.

"It's not bad," I said, trying my best to sound indifferent. I spoiled it by closing my eyes to savor the creamy goodness as the ice cream melted in my mouth.

"This is a good sign," Joanne said. "If you didn't like chocolate, I might have to write you off as a lost cause."

I opened my eyes to gaze at her. "Would you?"

She licked the spoon. "For real?"

"Would you consider me a lost cause? Do you?" It was an important question, and I felt I deserved the answer.

Joanne's clear blue eyes studied me unblinkingly as she cleaned the spoon. "Yeah," she said. "Sorry, but I do. If you hang on to being a Djinn, you're never going to make it as a human. I've been there. I know what it feels like, being so close to God and then ending up back here. At least I wasn't born to it, though. You were. So you'd better make your peace and move on, or sooner or later, it'll kill you."

"Or you will," I said.

She tilted her head slightly to the side. It might have been an acknowledgment. It might have simply been an attempt to get to the last bit of chocolate on the spoon.

"We need to get you out of here," she said finally, and I sensed the subject was closed. "There are things going on here in the mortal world. David and me, we're—" She looked for a moment completely blank. "Okay, I have no idea how to explain to you what's going on around here, except that people are out to get us."

I took a spoonful of ice cream. "Is that not usual?" I had heard it from Ashan many times.

"Well, yeah, kinda. But this time—" She shook her head, eyes gone distant and a little dark. "This time David's in real danger. Tell me, do you know anything about antimatter?"

I didn't know the word. I frowned at her. "The anti of matter? Is that not—nothing?"

"You'd think," she said. "But no. It's the opposite of matter. It destroys it."

"Such a thing cannot exist here." Not in any level of the aetheric that I knew.

"Well, it *can*, so long as it's contained in something else. But yeah, I get your point." Joanne waved that away with her spoon. "The thing is, we're in the middle of something, and it's very big. The Djinn—they're not being a lot of help. Not even David's folks. I was hoping you could tell me something."

"I know nothing," I said. That was all too true. "You think this antimatter could harm *David*?" Such a thing seemed impossible. It took another Djinn, or something equivalent in power, to inflict pain on him.

"I think it could destroy him," Joanne said soberly. "And I don't know how to stop it. Yet."

I felt a surge of energy like a close strike of lightning, and came instantly to my feet, spinning to face the doorway. Joanne didn't. She continued to sit, calmly digging her spoon into the ice cream and taking another bite.

But I sensed that under the calm, she was tense and watchful.

"Visitors usually knock," she said. "Cassiel? This a friend of yours? Because if he is, we're really going to have to talk about boundaries."

The Djinn who stood in the doorway was, in fact, familiar to me, although I wasn't sure that the human terms of *friend* and *foe* really applied. Bordan was . . . less well-disposed to me than many. He'd taken on human form, that of a young man with jet-black hair and eyes as dark as oil, but with a blue sheen that gave him an eerie, unsettling stare. He'd chosen skin of a rich, satin gold, and clothed himself in black. So very different from the Djinn I knew, and yet . . . the same. A physical manifestation of all that he was. I could not possibly have mistaken him.

Even though we had rarely been allied, seeing the cold contempt in his human-form eyes was a shock.

He gave me only that single, searing glance, and then he angled toward Joanne, pointedly excluding me.

"Where is David?" Bordan asked. It was clear he wanted nothing to do with Joanne, either—but she was preferable to dealing with me.

I could tell from her smile she read the subtext just as well. "He's out," she said. "Want a cup of coffee while you wait? Some ice cream? Mmmm, Ben and Jerry's? C'mon. Even Djinn have to love a little frozen dessert now and then."

He didn't dignify that with an answer. He simply stood, silent and motionless, staring at her. No human could outstare a Djinn, but Joanne tried. It was an impressive effort. I supposed the fact that she'd actually been one, at least for a short period, had given her a certain immunity.

"Right," she finally said. "So, you're here to take your little lost sheep back where she belongs?"

He looked revolted. "Cassiel? We do not want her back. Do as you wish with her."

I had never been an enemy of Bordan, but at that moment, I felt rage slowly building. "I will not be *given*," I said. "I am not *property*."

Bordan didn't even accord me the respect of having heard my words. "She is no longer one of us. No longer Djinn."

"She's dying," Joanne said. "Did you know that?"

"It's her choice." Bordan's eyes flickered for a moment into the blue of a gas flame. "She knows how to gain Ashan's favor. If she does the thing he asks of her, she will be welcome among us again."

"Oh yeah?" Joanne licked her spoon contemplatively. "What thing would that be?"

Bordan only smiled.

Joanne must have read my expression quite well enough to see my desperate need to avoid this subject. "Cassiel? I'm not going to ask what it is. Just if you want to do it."

"No," I said. My throat felt tight and dry. "No, I do not want to do it."

"Settles that." She turned her attention back to the other Djinn. "So I guess our message to Ashan would be to kiss our pretty human asses, the end. See yourself out, then, unless you change your mind about the ice cream."

Bordan looked as if he didn't know whether to laugh or kill her. "You don't understand," he said. "You don't know Cassiel at all. She is not some stray cat that will befriend you if you feed her."

"Well, true, she's more like a tiger. But I already trust her one hell of a lot more than I ever will Ashan. Because I *do* know him, bucko."

"This is a senseless waste of time," Bordan said. The fire had faded out of his eyes, and he looked a little taken aback. Clearly, he hadn't been among humans much, either—or if he had, he hadn't been prepared for the experience of Joanne Baldwin. I confess, neither was I. "She will die if she doesn't agree to his wishes. She has no choice."

"Bullshit," Joanne said with an indecent amount of cheer. "She's not dying. Not on my watch, she won't. Point of information you can scurry back to Ashan and whisper in his ear: Cassiel can draw power from Wardens, just like any other Djinn. And that makes your blackmail about as effective as a roadblock in the middle of a parking lot, doesn't it? So blow."

"What?" Bordan looked completely confused now.

Her tone chilled. "Get out of my house," she said. "Now. And tell Ashan any future visitors should make appointments with my social secretary. Oh, wait— don't have one. So tell him to just start holding his breath until I get back to him."

Bordan's skin took on a hard glitter, like the ice on the tub of ice cream, and his eyes had an obsidian glitter sharp enough to cut. "You mock me."

"Well, you may not have a sense of humor, but don't let anybody tell you you're not perceptive." He didn't seem to know how to take that response. Joanne rolled her eyes. "*Go away*, or you're going to find out just how much power I really do have. You're annoying me. You really don't want to do that. I've been annoyed all to hell and gone the past few weeks already."

I looked at her, still speechless. She was different to my eyes in that moment—strong, confident, and utterly sure of herself. Not a Djinn, who would never have been so direct. But for a human . . . formidable. Even without access to the aetheric, I felt power stir in the room, and knew it was rising up around her, framing her like a fan of hot, swirling light.

Bordan might have been her superior in raw power, but only if he was allowed to strike. And I could see, from the way he bowed his head, he was far from free to do so. "As you wish," he said. "Keep the traitor. But if you do, know the risk you take. We may not be as forgiving in the future."

"We'll see," Joanne said. "Must be one hell of a dirty job, if you're that intent on making her do it."

I could have told her, but it was a thing I strove to suppress. A shame I couldn't bear to let surface, except in brief, painful surges.

Bordan couldn't answer because he wouldn't know. It was not a thing that Ashan would ever allow to be common knowledge, not to the other Djinn. That was

one advantage I had; my spectacular ejection from the
Djinn would cause doubt and rumors. And Ashan
could not afford that. He might be powerful, but he
had never been loved.

"If this is your decision," Bordan said, "you may
live with it. And, in time, regret it."

Without another look in my direction, Bordan vanished, and took my last lingering hope with him. I
would not be accepted back among the Old Djinn. I
could never be one of David's New Djinn; Ashan had
ensured that by blocking my path to the aetheric levels
of the world.

I could never be truly human, either.

In the lingering silence after, Joanne said, "I don't
know about you, but I think this situation just up-
graded from ice cream to alcohol."

I had never tasted wine before, and the strong smell
of it nauseated me. I wet my lips with it and put it
aside, revolted. Everything seemed wrong suddenly.
My skin felt tight around my body, my borrowed
clothes rough and abrasive as sandpaper. The light
was too harsh, the room cluttered and full of sharp
edges. I reached blindly for a chair and dropped into
it, covering my eyes. I was shaking, and there was a
pressure building inside of me, as if I might somehow
inexplicably burst.

Instead, I felt wetness bleed from my eyes and flow
down my cheeks. I wiped at it in confusion and saw
tears on my pale hands.

"No," I said. "No, I am not human. I do not *cry*
like some helpless . . . animal!"

But I continued to sob, undone before the burning
power of my own despair, and it made me angrier
than ever. When Joanne tried to speak to me, I hit
out at her, shoving her back.

She dealt me a sharp, stinging blow across the face.
I cried out from the surge of pain, clapped my hand
to my burning cheek, and stared at her in astonish-

ment. My nose was running. I felt miserable, and miserably human.

"Stop acting like an ass," she said. "You're alive. You're not lost, and you're not dying. Ashan won't take you back—well, boohoo. I've met the guy, and frankly I consider that a bonus. If you want to survive, you're going to need us. You need the Wardens. *Stop being an idiot.*"

Was I being an idiot? I felt like one, but only because I lacked the power to hit back. I glared at her, willing her to feel my anger. She did not seem impressed, but then, I'd heard the stories. . . . She had faced down Ashan and won. She had defeated Demons.

My feeble anger did not precisely terrify her.

"I don't need your Wardens," I said flatly. "I don't need humans. I will never need them."

"Guess what, Cupcake. You not only need Wardens— you might as well get used to the concept of needing humans, too, because you *are* one," Joanne said. "For all intents and purposes. So I think you'd better reconsider." She reached out, grabbed a box of pop-up tissues, and lobbed it neatly into my lap. I slowly pulled sheets from it and wiped clumsily at my streaming eyes, my dripping nose.

Joanne rolled her eyes. "Here," she said, and grabbed a fresh tissue. She clamped it over my nose. "Blow."

"What?"

"Blow out through your nose. C'mon, you're a bad-ass Djinn—you can manage to blow your nose like a two-year-old."

I blew, feeling humiliated and filthy and desperately angry about it. Then I got another tissue and blew my nose again, by myself, and felt some of the stinging in my eyes subside.

Joanne looked at me in silence for a few seconds. I looked back, utterly unable to find anything to say.

"Ice cream's melting," she said. "Bring the wine."

I suspected later that she deliberately failed to warn me about the effects of the alcohol.

The next day, I left Joanne's house for the first time, as what passed for human. She had found clothes for me—clothes to her own taste, not necessarily mine, although she had acceded gracefully to my request for the color to be light rose instead of the icy blue she originally chose. I had had enough of cold.

The trousers were long, slim, and white, fitting well enough around the contours of my body. She had found me ankle-high boots of a soft white leather, and a white silk shirt under a pale pink jacket, tailored close. My hair remained unusual, but I decided that I liked its fine, drifting, puffball wildness. It suited me. *It's like a bag of feathers,* Joanne had said, and given up trying to tame it into anything like a human style. *At least it's not going to get messed up in the wind.*

Still. "I feel like a fool," I said, as she opened the door of her car.

"Well, you shouldn't," she said. "You do look exotic, but kind of fabulous at it. Besides, you're riding in a sweet vintage Mustang. Enjoy the experience."

I had no idea what that should mean. I understood the automobile was a vehicle for transportation, but the other subtleties escaped me. I folded myself awkwardly into the machine's passenger's seat, fumbling with the safety belts she told me must be worn.

Joanne activated the machine, which rumbled unpleasantly, and the reek of burning metal made me feel trapped and claustrophobic. The windows rolled down, thankfully. I close my eyes as she drove and let the wind play over my skin and in my hair. It had a seductive pleasure to it, this sense of touch. Capable of so many different tones and colors.

"Doing okay?" she asked. I opened my eyes and nodded. The car was moving fast, too fast for me to focus on anything in particular, unless it was at a fair distance. Driving looked complicated. I felt an unexpected stab of nervousness; there was so much I had never done and wasn't sure I could learn. Humans seemed to overcome barriers as easily as breathing. I wasn't sure I had the instinct.

Joanne made no further comment. It wasn't a long drive, wherever she was taking me. We followed the coastline for a while, and the sight of the rolling, sparkling sea made me long to stop this rattling human contraption and take a seat on the sand, watching the surf roll. *The Mother is there*, I thought. *In the water. In the ground. In the air.* I had avoided thinking of how cut off I'd become from the pulse of the Earth, but the sight of that vast, moving ocean brought back the sense of isolation. I could walk her surface, but never know her, not in the way I had once. I was no longer her child; I was far, far less.

I was both glad and disappointed when the road turned away from the sea, and I lost sight of it among cars, streets, and the concrete canyons of the human-built city.

Joanne pulled the car to a covered area in front of a large, towering structure, and stepped out without turning off the engine. A uniformed man handed her a slip of paper, got into the driver's seat, and looked at me in surprise. I stared back.

"Hey." That was Joanne, opening my passenger's-side door. "That's the valet. We're getting out here."

I felt a fool again, and more of one when I realized how many people—strangers—seemed drawn to stare at me once I was out of the vehicle. Many people, men and women alike. I was doing nothing to merit their attention, but still they stared. Most looked quickly away when I glared at them.

Joanne led me inside of the building, and artificially cool, dry air closed around my skin, making me suddenly grateful for the jacket. How did humans cope with such drastic changes? It seemed insane. Why would they not simply accept the temperature as it came?

We went through a narrow hallway, which opened into a huge, soaring open room that lifted toward heaven. I stopped and stared. I knew humans built on a vast scale, but knowing and seeing seemed to be quite different things.

Concentric, gently flowing levels rose, stacked one atop the other, and it took me a moment to realize that each of the squares of metal evenly spaced on each level was, in fact, a door. Doors to rooms. So many separations between humans. It was a bit baffling how it all fit together.

There was a large central column in the center of the atrium, which housed banks of glass-faced rooms. No, not rooms: elevators, devices to move people between floors. Joanne led me into one, pressed a button, and leaned against the wood paneling to give me an interested look. My feet sank deep into richly woven carpets, and around us, music played, as soft as the whisper of the aetheric.

"You're handling it well," she said. "Being out in public for the first time."

Was I? I felt awkward, anxious, and freakish. I decided to stare out into the atrium as the elevator surged upward, carrying us into the air, far up. I pressed close to the glass, fascinated, and was disappointed when we slowed and stopped near the top of the building. The perspective change reminded me of looking down as a Djinn. Of flying. Of the aetheric.

"Coming?" Joanne asked me as she exited the elevator. I wasn't sure I wanted to, but I followed. We walked around the sinuous curve of the level, open to the atrium below, and Joanne paused next to one of the metal doors to knock. Apart from the number engraved on it, the door was identical to every other.

It swung open, and I faced another human, one also known to me, at least by appearance. His name was Lewis, and he was also a Warden. A favorite of Jonathan's, as I remembered. I had never met him, but I had seen him before, on the aetheric.

I looked him over anew with human eyes. We were almost of a height, but that was where our resemblance ended. His hair was a dark chestnut brown, shot through with strands of red and gold. His skin was tanned dark, and his eyes were rich brown, very deep and secret. The current fashion among human men, I thought, was to shave their facial hair; he had clearly not bothered for at least a day or more.

His clothes were plain—a dark shirt, denim pants, blocky, hard-leather boots.

And there was no mistaking the sense of power that clung to him like smoke and shadows.

"Come in," Lewis said, and stood aside to let me enter. I did, followed by Joanne, and found that the room was small but well-appointed, much like Joanne's home. A bed took up most of the space. A couch near the window held two other occupants. One was David, looking more purely human than ever.

I did not know the other person. He was male, of a darker, more coppery skin than Lewis, and he had black, smooth, close-cropped hair. He had shaved, I noticed. He wore a loose shirt and dark trousers, nothing remarkable.

"Right," Lewis said. "Cassiel, have a seat. You know who I am?"

He pointed to a chair at the desk. Joanne settled herself on the couch next to David, and Lewis took a seat on the edge of the bed, facing me.

I slowly lowered myself into the chair. "Lewis," I said. "Leader of the Wardens."

He and Joanne exchanged a quick glance. "For now," he said. "You never know how long those kind of things will last in times like these. You're Cassiel. Until recently, you were a Djinn."

I nodded.

"And now you need the help of the Wardens to draw the energy you need to stay alive."

Nothing to do but nod again, no matter how much I resented it. I had the feeling that Lewis's dark eyes did not miss my reluctance.

Instead of asking me another question, he looked at David. "What's her story?" he asked.

David took his time composing his answer, but he didn't look at me for permission, or apology. "Cassiel has always been on Ashan's side," he said. "A True Djinn, very old. Not exactly an ally to mankind in the past. I can't tell you much about her. Among the Djinn she's known as being stern, unforgiving, and arrogant, but Ashan cutting her off from the other Djinn seems to have mellowed her. A little."

Mellowed? I glowered at him. Of all he had said, that was the most offensive.

"Will she keep her promises?" Lewis asked.

"Don't ask him," I said. "Ask me. They would be my promises."

They all looked at me. David gave me a trace of a smile. "She's right," he said. "But if you don't mind me saying it, Cassiel's never been one to lie. She wouldn't deceive you. It would be"—his eyebrows quirked; such a human gesture—"undignified."

I couldn't disagree with it. I fixed Lewis with a long, challenging look, and got a half-bitter smile from him in response. "You don't exactly come begging, do you?" he said. "Hungry?"

For a moment, I thought he meant hungry for food, but then I knew what he was offering. I didn't look at Joanne or David. I held his stare. "Very," I said evenly.

"Want a taste?"

Lewis held out his hand to me. I stood up, looking down at him, trying to read his expression. It was a test, I knew that. But what kind of test, I couldn't tell.

I slowly reached out and took his hand in mine, as if we were merely shaking hands in the human fashion. A complicated set of emotions sped through me . . . fear, most strangely. Hunger. Longing. An almost irresistible urge to take, and take, and take . . .

I allowed myself to merely touch on his power, drawing a thin thread of it into myself. It flowed through my veins like gold, and despite everything, I could not resist a slow, trembling sigh.

And then I let go, stepped away from him, and settled back in my chair.

Lewis lowered his hand back to rest on his knee. There had been no change in his expression at all, but suddenly I knew what he was thinking and feeling. The power I'd taken from him granted me that kind of access, an intimacy that was startling because it was so different from what I'd experienced with Joanne. It was as if for a moment I *was* Lewis, and I could see all his past . . . his longing for Joanne, never to be truly sated. His solitary life. His discomfort with the responsibility he now held. His deep, abiding wish to simply *be*.

"You should have been a Djinn," I said, surprising myself, and Lewis blinked.

"Probably," he said. "But here we are. So, you obviously have control of what it is you do. I know you could have grabbed for all the power you could hold, but you didn't. Why?"

Because it was a test. That was true, but also not true. "I am not a beast," I said. "I can control my needs, just as you can."

I didn't look toward Joanne, but I saw a spark go through him, a tiny tremble that meant he'd understood precisely what I meant. "How can I be sure of that?" he asked, a little more sharply. He didn't like a stranger knowing his secrets.

"You have my promise," I said. "I will never take more than I need, and I will never deliberately injure or weaken a Warden in the process, unless they are attempting to do harm to me." I had with Joanne, but I'd been new and afraid. I understood better now.

"And you'll ask permission first," Lewis said.

"Yes. I will ask, unless it is an emergency."

"You realize this is a promise," Lewis said. "You sure you can keep it?"

"It's no more than the promises humans make with each other to live in peace together."

"People break those all the time," Joanne murmured.

I knew that far better than she did. "No doubt they do, when they are threatened. I make the same promise, with the same understanding. If I am not threatened, I will live in peace with you. But I won't die quietly." I didn't try to explain or insist. I just waited. They would trust me or not; there was nothing I could do to convince them. Lewis glanced at David, then Joanne. I didn't see them make any obvious signals, but he must have gained some understanding, and I realized with a jealous rush that they were communicating on a level I would never again attain.

They were speaking in the aetheric.

I focused on the silent fourth in the room, who had so far not participated at all. He was watching me, but like Lewis, he guarded his expression well.

Lewis said, "All right," and got up from the bed. I rose, too, automatically taking a step back, as if there were any place to run if he decided to send me away from the Wardens. "You're on a trial basis, and I want you far away from here—we've got way too much to deal with at the moment. I'm assigning you to partner with a Warden. You'll help him do his job, and in return, he'll give you regular access to the aetheric."

The man who'd been sitting unintroduced, on the couch, rose now. Lewis nodded toward him. "This is Manny Rocha," he said. "Manny will be your partner, at least for the first couple of months. If you make it through that, we'll see. If at any time Manny finds you hard to get along with, or if you don't do the job or keep your word, you're cut off, and we don't help you anymore. Deal?"

I didn't know this Warden, this Manny Rocha. He seemed bland and unexceptional to me—shorter than Lewis or David, slender, of no special significance. No Djinn that I knew had ever spoken his name, either in praise or damnation.

"No," I said, and saw a flash of surprise go across every face in the room. "Not so simple as that. The Wardens do not serve for the joy of service. You are paid, are you not?"

Lewis worked it out first, and laughed out loud.

"What the hell?" Joanne asked blankly.

"She wants a job," Lewis said. "Which proves, more than anything else, she's really becoming human. Okay, done, at standard entry-level rates. We'll work out housing and all that crap later. Agreed?"

I had no idea if it was fair, but I did not think Lewis would cheat me. He'd know how important fair dealing was to Djinn. I nodded and held out my hand to Manny Rocha. He hesitated. I thought I understood why.

"I won't take power from you unless you agree," I said. "And I will always ask, unless there is an emergency." After sipping from the wellspring of Lewis's power, I had no need of Manny Rocha at all. He looked just a little relieved, and gave me a brisk, competent sort of handshake. Just the touch of flesh, nothing more.

"Nice to meet you," he said, the first words he'd spoken. He had a neutral voice, with a hint of an accent—calm and soothing. "Don't screw this up. If you do, it won't be just the two of us that suffer. It's all the people we could have helped."

I looked at him for a long moment, frowning. He meant what he'd said. An altruistic Warden? I supposed there must have been a few, but I was shocked that Lewis had been able to turn one up so quickly.

Of course, the worst of them had been weeded out over the past few years, thanks to the Djinn uprising and other factors. Lewis himself had begun to cleanse the ranks of corruption and graft. So perhaps Manny was, as he appeared to be, an honest man.

That would, I thought, be interesting.

I cocked an eyebrow. "I won't *screw it up* if you won't," I said. "Are you sure you want to work with me?"

His grin surprised me. It changed him completely, made him real and full of secrets. "I like a challenge," he said. "That's why they picked me. That, and my work's really pretty boring. You might liven things up a little. Also, I think I was probably the only one insane enough to say yes."

I had never had the impulse to laugh. Smile, yes, but laughter was a new thing, and when it bubbled from me, uncontrolled, I was unsettled. So many odd things about living in this flesh.

But somehow, I felt it might not be as bad as I'd feared.

Chapter 3

I'D NEVER EXPECTED that Manny Rocha didn't live close by. Human distances baffled me, but when he showed me a map of the country—*country*, another thing to learn; I was a citizen of the United States now, according to the paperwork that Lewis had provided me—I discovered that it was far removed from Florida. As Lewis had warned me, he wanted me well away from Joanne, David, himself, and whatever crisis loomed for them—less, I suspected, from any concern for me than a desire not to trip over me in the heat of battle.

Manny pointed to an almost square state near the center of the map. "That's New Mexico," he said. "It's another state. We're in Florida right now, here." He tapped the squiggle of irregular lines on the map. "Going here." His fingers moved a long, long way between the two. "Now, usually I'd fly, but I don't want you freaking out. Last thing I want to do is deal with you and Homeland Security at the same time."

Freaking out, I realized, meant "losing control." I frowned at him. "I will not *freak out.*"

"Yeah, great. I still think I'd rather drive," he said.

I looked again at the map. "How many minutes is this drive?" I was still struggling with the concepts of artificial time, but from the look on Manny's face, I had not struggled hard enough. "Hours?"

"Days," he said. "That's a couple of days, lady."

Days. Trapped in a clanking, stinking metal monster. No. "Is there no other way?"

"Like I said, we could fly, but—"

Flying. I was most comfortable in the air. "Fine."

"You have to understand, there are rules—"

Everything had rules in the human world. Annoying. "I will not freak out."

As Manny had supposed, I was wrong about that.

So many *rules.* I had no baggage, except for a leather bag to carry the identification the Wardens had given me, and a handful of currency that Manny, muttering under his breath, had withdrawn from a machine he'd called an ATM. I had watched the process carefully, then checked the plastic cards that the Wardens provided. I had one with my image imprinted on it that read at the top DRIVER'S LICENSE, which meant I could operate a motor vehicle. Not that I would ever wish to. I had a gold, shimmering card with the image of an ancient goddess on its surface.

"Credit card," Manny explained, when I held it up. We were standing in line at the airport. "For buying things. But don't buy things."

"Then why did I receive one?"

"Because my bosses are crazy?"

I held up the next card.

"Yeah, that's an ATM card. Somewhere in there, you should have information about your PIN number. That's like a code you put into the machine. If you have the right code and the right card, you get money. Money comes to you from the Wardens. It's compensation for the work you do for them." Did my ears deceive me, or did Manny Rocha seem to resent that? "But you have to pay attention. You can't pull out more money than you have in the account."

That seemed straightforward enough. I put the ATM card, credit card, and driver's license back into my purse, and pulled out a small dark blue booklet with pale blue pages. The inside front cover once again held my image. I stared at it for some time, but the image did not move.

"Passport," Manny said before I asked. "You need that. Keep it out, along with your tickets."

All around me, people were waiting. Some stood patiently, some fidgeted, some seethed. Traveling seemed to be a tremendous effort. I began to see why Manny might prefer to drive, despite the horrible, suffocating, noisy box on wheels. The journey would at least be under his control.

I watched the security process with great interest, but despite my study, when it came time for me to copy the actions of those who had gone before me, I found it clumsy and humiliating. I placed my bag in the plastic bin, which rumbled away through the machine—*X-ray machine*, according to Manny—and slipped off my shoes at the impatient motion from the guard and added those to another bin.

But when I walked through the portal, alarms sounded. I froze, frowning, as two large men in matching clothes came toward me.

"Back up," one ordered. "Got any metal on you?"

Metal. I looked down at my clothing. I had a belt, yes, with a metal buckle. I removed it.

Alarms again. I felt an unfamiliar pressure in my chest. Anxiety? It was infuriating. These rules were *infuriating*. I had held power since before the ancestors of these humans had learned to scratch pictographs in rocks, and they were making me feel . . . afraid.

I gritted my teeth and removed my jacket when they ordered it. In my shirtsleeves, with bare feet, I walked through the portal, and no alarms sounded.

The relief was even more humiliating than the anxiety.

Manny Rocha breezed through without a pause, and

stopped next to me to pull on his shoes and pick up
the bags and detritus from his pockets. "Just remember. Flying was *your* choice." He paused a second,
then said without looking directly at me, "I thought
you'd lose your temper."

I almost had. "I did not."

"Yeah. Good. Let's keep it that way."

I had been powerful once. Powerful enough to re-
duce this building to smoking ash. Instead of comforting me, that thought made me feel heavy in my skin,
and helpless. Again.

I put on my shoes, belt, and jacket; grabbed my
single bag; and followed Manny as he set out down
the long, broad, busy hallway.

There were Djinn in the airport.

I don't know why that came as a surprise to me; it
shouldn't have, but I had not thought there were so
many of us walking the earth, much less lingering in
this transient place. I waited for Manny to point them
out to me, but he seemed oblivious, and when we took
our seats in the area designated for our flight, I decided to open the subject.

"Djinn?" he repeated, frowning, and looked around
sharply. "Where?"

Ah. So it was true; even the Wardens could not
identify a Djinn in human form, if the Djinn wished
to remain concealed. That meant that the humans
around me, even those who had some bit of Warden
ability, saw nothing when they looked at me but a tall,
awkward, pale woman with untidy white hair.

No. I *was* nothing but a tall, awkward, pale woman
with untidy white hair. No longer a Djinn. I had to
remember that.

I shifted uncomfortably in the hard seat, and tried
not to breathe too deeply. Public spaces were filthy
with odors, soaked with emotions. It put me on edge.

I pointed to the first Djinn I saw. "There." He was a plain young man in a red T-shirt and jeans, carrying a backpack, but I caught the flare of his aura. When he turned my direction, I saw a flash of opal in his eyes.

Then he disappeared into the crowd.

Manny was looking at me oddly. "Who?"

There was no point in trying. He wouldn't recognize a Djinn, not the way I would. I shook my head and shifted again restlessly. I wanted to move, to walk. To feel less caged.

The thought that I would be trapped inside of a small metal box, surrounded by humans and all their odors and noises and emotions, made me feel a little sick. *Perhaps we should have driven.* I could have opened a window. I understood—Manny had emphasized it to me in forceful language—that I could not do so on the aircraft.

"We got you an apartment," he was saying. "It's your home. You'll stay there when you're not working. It's not far from my place, a couple of blocks. Got you a phone, too. You're on your own for furniture. I'll give you some catalogs; we get a ton of them."

He said *we.* He had said that before. "You don't live alone."

Manny glanced at me, then down at the magazine open in his hands. "No. I've got a wife, Angela, and a daughter. Isabel. Ibby, for short."

"Angela," I repeated. "Isabel. Ibby."

"They've got nothing to do with you." He said it aggressively, as if I had trespassed on something private. "They're not Wardens. They're my family."

Merely humans, then. I would have no interaction with them. "I have no interest in them," I said, which I meant to be reassuring. Manny frowned again. "What?"

"I think I need to send you to school or something. You always this unpleasant?"

I gazed at him for a long moment without blinking. "You don't enjoy flying."

I had surprised him. "What makes you say—"

"It's obvious." I felt my lips curl into a smile. "You strike out at me, but it's not me you fear."

"Doesn't mean you're not a bitch, Cassie."

Cassie? "My name is Cassiel." I glowered at him. That made him smile, and the longer I glared, the wider the smile.

"Okay," he finally said. "No nicknames. Got it."

Our staring match was interrupted by a tinny, crackling voice from overhead. Our flight, it seemed, was ready for boarding. I rose gratefully, clutching my ticket, and began to move toward the uniformed attendant.

"Whoa," Manny said, and grabbed me by the arm. "We're not—"

I turned on him, snarling. "Take your hand off of me!" I couldn't abide being touched so suddenly, with such disrespect.

Manny didn't let go. "Hey. Easy!" His voice was soft, but sharp as a knife. "I told you, no freaking, and I wasn't kidding. You cause a scene in here, and we both end up in trouble. Relax. I was saying that we're not first class, so we have to wait our turn."

There were classes among humans. I'd known there were, of course; I was not totally ignorant of power and structure. But America prided itself on being a free and equal society. I wondered who became first class, and how.

"Money," Manny said, when I asked. He loosened his grip on me. "Sorry about grabbing, but you're going to have to remember not to take my head off, okay?"

"Okay," I said. It wasn't, but I would have to find a way to make allowances for his impulsive actions.

And my own. This body seemed to have its own set of rules and behaviors, and I was not entirely comfortable in controlling its responses.

I waited in silence while the *first class* section boarded—I could see no differences, in truth, between Manny and those others, so perhaps it really was a question of money—and then moved forward when he prompted me.

The hallway was narrow, chilly, and reeked of oil and metal. I coughed and tried not to breathe, but that was not possible.

When I reached the rounded door of the aircraft, I had a curious wave of anxiety. *It's so small.* And so it was, not only the entrance, but the plane itself—smaller than I'd expected, tremendously fragile in its construction. *I am entrusting myself to the care of humans.*

"Hey," Manny said, and put a hand on my shoulder. "Go. You're holding up the line."

I didn't want to do it, but I stepped into the plane.

I'd like to say it wasn't as bad as I expected, but that would be a lie.

I survived the flight in much the same way I'd survived my fall from Djinn grace: by sheer endurance. It was not a pleasant experience. My body was prone to fits of anxiety whenever the plane shuddered in the sky, which was often. My body also constantly complained of aches, pains, discomforts, annoyances, and a persistent need to rid itself of the liquids I compulsively consumed.

When we escaped from the confinement some five hours later, I was unsteady and weak with relief. The air in the jetway seemed clean and refreshing, after breathing the filthy recycled stuff, and the spring of metal and rubber under my feet felt almost joyous.

Leaving the airport was easier by far than I'd expected—we simply walked out, into the hot, dry air. The sun was low on the horizon, and the sky . . .

. . . Oh, the *sky*.

I stopped and stared. I had seen more beautiful

things as a Djinn, but never as a human, through human eyes, and the colors of the sunset woke feelings in me I had never known were possible. It made me feel small and yet, somehow, part of something vast and astonishing.

"Home sweet home," Manny said, and grabbed my arm again. It was a credit to the beautiful display of the sunset that I did not even care. "Let's go, Cassiel."

We were only a few steps out of the building when a small human form ran headlong into Manny and clasped him around the knees. "Papa, Papa, Papa!"

I had not known Manny could smile that way—so full of tenderness. "Hey, Ib," he said, and peeled the child away from his knees to lift her up. She promptly circled his neck with chubby arms, legs wrapping around his waist. A perfectly miniature person, dressed in miniature adult fashion in small blue jeans, an offensively bright shirt, and . . .

Isabel turned her face toward me and smiled, and it was as if the sun had risen new and clean, full of warmth and impartial welcome. She was a lovely child, with skin the color of caramel and eyes of a dark, warm brown. A round little face, surrounded by glossy black curls. "Who's that, Papa?"

"That's Cassiel," he told her. "She's my new friend. Say hello to her."

Isabel studied me for a few seconds, still smiling, and then said, "Hello. My papa's taking me for pizza."

"Oh, your papa is, is he?" Manny shifted her weight to one hip and gave me a look that invited me to share his amusement. "Tell you what: Let me get Cassiel settled, and then we'll see. Where's your mom?"

The child pointed, and there, a few paces away next to a large dark red van, was an older, taller version of Isabel. She had the same long, curling hair, the same smile, but there was a distance to her. She was much more guarded.

She waved. Manny waved back. So did Isabel. "That's Angela," Manny said. "Guess she got off work after all." He stopped for a moment, staring at his wife, and without looking at me, he said, "You understand, I don't want you putting them at risk. I wasn't planning for you to meet them on day one, but I guess that's where we are now."

I didn't understand, but I knew he wanted reassurance. "I will not harm your family," I said stiffly. In truth, they were not Wardens. Their lives meant little to me.

Manny sent me a glance, finally. "All right. Then let's go."

Manny had gone only a few feet when he realized I was not following, and turned back with a frown.

"Well?" he asked. "You coming or not?"

I had no choice. Manny was my Conduit, my only survival. I felt like an imposter, but it was better than being alone.

Manny and his family lived in *Albuquerque*, a town of hills and mountains. Humans had tamed the land, but not subdued it; there was wildness here, and power. I felt the vibration of it in the ancient mountains, in the clear blue sky above.

The structure of their house, on the other hand, was so new as to have no aetheric presence at all. "We just got it about six months ago," Manny told me as he unlocked the door and held it open for his wife and child. Isabel skipped inside, shoes thundering on the wooden floor. "It's small, but we like it." He seemed strangely anxious that I like it, too.

I nodded, unsure what to say. It was a box. Walls, floors, ceilings. Cluttered with bright furniture and toys. Angela picked up some and moved them aside, but not as if she were worried about my opinion; she simply did it automatically. Isabel, seeing her mother's actions, imitated her, picking up a doll and carrying it by one arm to drop it into a primary-colored box in the corner of the room.

I wondered if I would be expected to do that, as well.

I did not know the protocols, so I stood, watching, as Manny put down his bag and turned on a light next to the sofa. "Living room," he said. Which I thought was a curious way to refer to it—did they not live in all the rooms? Was there a dying room? "Bedrooms through there. Kitchen. There's a sunroom on the back, which is nice."

Manny was nervous. Perhaps it was my stare. I looked away and wandered the room, idly trailing my fingertips over the cold, still pictures in frames. Family. Human family.

"That's my brother," he said. "Luis."

He thought I was looking at the picture that my fingers were touching. I picked up the frame and saw that it held the image of a man, handsome, a little younger than Manny. A stronger jaw, but kind eyes.

"He's a Warden, too," Manny said. "You'll meet him later, maybe. He's out in Florida right now."

I put the photo down. "I would like to go now," I said, which I thought was a polite way to request an end to this. Evidently not. Manny frowned at me.

"You want something to eat first? You do want to eat, right?"

Did I? I supposed I did. Djinn in human form seemed to emulate all human functions equally, and my stomach was growling in frustration. I hadn't yet mastered the knack of anticipating its needs.

I nodded.

Angela, who'd said very little, patted her daughter on the head and sent her scampering off to play before turning to me. I was struck by her again—a quiet, controlled woman, strong. So closely guarded. "Manny tells me you're not human," she said. "Is that right?"

I cocked my head. "I was not born human. I seem to be human enough now."

Human enough. A frightening statement.

"All right," Angela said. "I've seen Djinn before. I know they're dangerous. Let me make something clear to you—if you hurt my husband, if you even *think* about hurting my daughter, I'll kill you. Understand?"

Manny looked taken aback. Angela's dark eyes remained steady, fixed on mine, and I sensed nothing from her but sincerity.

"I understand," I said, and searched for something else to say. Human words seemed clumsy to me. Ridiculously inappropriate to what I wanted to communicate. "I will make mistakes. I cannot help that."

Her fierce stare softened a bit. "Mistakes are okay," she said. "But don't make them twice. And don't you dare make them with my daughter."

I inclined my head.

"Now," she said. "How do you feel about enchiladas?"

"Neutral," I said, "since I don't know what they are."

Angela gave me her first real smile. "Then you're in for a treat."

"Or not," Manny said, "if you don't like hot sauce."

She hit him. It was, I realized, a playful blow, not an angry one, and I was surprised at my physical reaction, which was an impulse to reach out and stay her hand.

I had wanted to defend him. Why? Because he was my Conduit. My life source.

I hadn't anticipated that at all.

I did not like hot sauce, which made Isabel laugh until tears rolled down her cheeks. She scooped up spoonfuls of the spice and ate them to show me how silly I was.

I could not be bested by a mere child. I continued

to try, choking on the burn, until at last Angela took pity on me and removed it from the table. Isabel pouted until her father tickled her into laughter again.

It was a quiet meal—quieter than I suspected was their normal case. "When do we begin our duties?" I finally asked, after consuming several glasses of iced tea that Angela provided.

"Tomorrow," Manny said. "Unless there's an emergency, which I hope there isn't." He stood up, picked up his plate and mine, and carried them into the kitchen. "I'll take you home now," he called back.

Isabel ran around the table and—to my shock—crawled up into my lap. The warm, real weight of her was surprising. I looked down at her upturned face, at her smile, and frowned in puzzlement. "What do you want?" I asked her. Angela made a strangled sound of protest and rose from her chair, but I extended a hand to stop her. "Isabel?"

"A hug," Isabel said. "You're funny, lady."

I thought that was quite likely true, from her miniature perspective.

I was unaccustomed to hugs, but she was an adequate instructor. She took my arms and fitted them around her small body. "Tighter!" she commanded. I dutifully squeezed, well aware of how fragile her bones were beneath the skin.

When she began to squirm, I let go. She almost toppled from my lap, and I grabbed her to steady her.

Isabel giggled, and it was as warm as sunlight.

This is a child. A young soul. A blank slate. I had never met one before, and it was oddly . . . freeing.

"That's enough," Angela said, and grabbed Isabel from my lap. "You need to learn some manners, *mija.*"

"She's sad," Isabel protested. "I wanted to make her smile!"

Manny came back from the kitchen. His eyes darted from Angela holding his daughter in a protective embrace, to me sitting quietly in my chair. I was not smiling. In truth, I could have, but I knew it would ring false to the child.

"Not yet, Isabel," I told her. "Maybe later. But— thank you for the hug."

I meant it. She had reached out to me, and although it should not have mattered to me . . . it did.

Manny broke the silence by picking up his car keys from the table and saying, in a carefully bland tone, "Let's get you home."

Home.

It was another box. It was filled with odors, of course—choking detergent where the carpets had been recently cleaned, paint reeking from the newly retouched walls. Aside from the odors, the room was empty save for a single small cot, made up with sheets, blanket, and pillow. A single small folding table. A single small lamp.

I liked the simplicity of it.

"Yeah," Manny said, and juggled keys in his hand for a second before tossing them to me. I snatched them out of the air without looking. "Cozy, I know. Sorry, we didn't have time to get things for you, and I figured you'd want to pick furniture and stuff yourself."

He was apologizing. How odd.

"It's fine," I said. I threw open the nearest window and took in a breath of the air that rolled over the sill, redolent of sage and high mountain spaces.

"I guess—I'll bring over some catalogs tomorrow. You can pick what you want. Clothes, too. You want Angela to go with you to find things?"

I looked down at myself. "What's wrong with what I have?"

He blinked. "Nothing. Uh, you can't wear the same thing all the time."

I knew that. "I bought several copies of the same

clothing. I know clothes must be changed and laundered."

"But—everything you bought is the same?"

"Yes."

He shook his head. "You are not a normal girl."

I was not a *girl*. But I assumed he meant it in a figurative sense, and allowed it to pass.

Manny laid out the contents of a folder on the table. "Checkbook. Remember what I said about the ATM, and how you can only pull out what you have in the account? Same thing here. Just because you have checks left, that doesn't mean you can keep on writing them. Here's your phone number. Rings to this cell phone, so you should memorize it." He pulled a small pink device from his pocket. "Sorry about the color; pink was all I could get. Last-minute."

I liked pink. "It's fine." I took the machine in my hands and felt the energy coursing through it. My Djinn senses were blunted, but in close proximity, I could still feel the broad strokes of its engineering. "How does it work?"

He showed me. I called his home, explained to Angela that we were testing my cell phone, and hung up.

"We usually say good-bye," Manny said dryly.

"Why?"

"Same reason we do most things. Because it's polite."

I was starting to see that. I slid the small pink phone into my pocket. "Manny."

I had not said his name before, and it drew his attention, with a hint of anxiety. "Yes?"

"I—" My throat threatened to close around the words, but how could I survive if I could not acknowledge this? "I need—"

He understood without more being said, and extended his hand to me. I took it, cool fingers closing on warmer ones, and reached out for power.

It flowed through him in a thick golden stream, slow and sweet as honey. Not nearly as powerful as what Lewis had given me, and I sensed that it would not sustain me as long, but good nevertheless. I took in a deep breath as the warmth infused me, as the world flared into auras and a brief, tantalizing glimpse of the worlds beyond, and then steadied back into human terms.

It wasn't easy to do it, but I let go.

Manny staggered. I grabbed his arm and guided him to the cot, where he sat and leaned forward, breathing hard. "I am sorry," I said. "Did I—"

"No." His voice sounded rough, and he didn't look at me directly. "No, I'm fine. You did fine. It's just—it feels—"

"Bad," I supplied soberly. He raised his head, and I was surprised by the glitter in his eyes.

"No. It feels *good.*"

Oh.

That, I realized, could be extraordinarily dangerous for us both.

Manny left quickly after, reminding me to lock the door. I did, flimsy as the barrier was, and wandered through my apartment. It was indeed small—a "living" area, a kitchen, a second empty room, and a bath. I opened all the windows. Humans enjoyed living in boxes. I did not.

For the first time since falling into human flesh, I was alone. Truly alone.

I sat cross-legged on the floor, eyes shut, and tried to remember what it had felt like to be a Djinn. The memories faded so quickly, anchored in skin. The power from Manny resonated inside, a slow and constant rush, and for some time, nothing intruded.

Until I felt the world shift.

Something had happened, subtle and vile, on the

edges of my awareness. It was not in the air—there were Wardens at work, molding the forces there, but all was well. Fire, then? No, I sensed nothing but silence from that quarter.

The vile thing was happening to a living creature, and so it whispered through the power Manny had granted me.

And it was happening *here.*

I shot to my feet, eyes opening, and cast about for any sense of direction. Yes, *there, there,* to my right and not far away . . .

I unlocked and opened the door and stepped out on the landing my apartment shared with two others. The pulse was weak now, the life fading.

I descended the two flights of stairs at a run, arrived at ground level, and turned the corner.

A child lay on the ground, with a knot of other children around him. No one was touching him, and I got no sense of malice. Only confusion, and a dawning awareness of something wrong.

There was a machine next to him—a bicycle.

He had fallen.

"Move," I ordered the children, and they scattered like bright birds. I knelt next to the boy, my hands moving slowly above him, sensing the rightness of his body, and then the wrongness in his skull.

The bone was broken. The brain—

"Get his people," I said, intent on the task before me.

"What?"

"His father! His mother!" My brain struggled to parse words. "Parents."

Two of the children ran, shouting at the top of their lungs. I slid my hand carefully behind the boy's head, and under the feather-soft hair I felt the depression where he'd struck the curb. Blood flooded warm across my fingers.

I needed Manny, but he was away, and I was alone.

The Djinn part of me said, *It is an accident. It is the way of living things.* And the Djinn part of me was content to let it be so.

But the human part, the human part screamed in frustration, too urgent to ignore.

I pulled from the reserve of power inside and poured it through my fingertips. Of all that the Djinn knew, we knew this—the template of things. We could build, we could destroy . . . and we could, on occasion, heal, if we held enough power inside, and the injury was fresh and contained.

I felt the bone shift, and the boy screamed. The sound pierced me like cold metal, but I gritted my teeth and kept focusing on my work, sealing the bone together. I concentrated then on reducing the swelling of his injured brain tissues. The cut in the scalp was stubborn, and continued to leak red despite my commands.

Human hands closed around my shoulders and yanked me away from the shrieking child. I fell backward, surprised.

A human man was looming above me, face dark red with rage, a fist clenched. "What are you doing to my kid?" he shouted.

The boy squirmed away from me, got to his short legs and hurried to his father's protection, wrapping his arms around the man's waist. I remembered Isabel grabbing on to Manny's knees, and the fierce love and protective instinct I'd sensed between them.

"I did not hurt him," I said. I didn't move. Violence hung like a black cloud around the man, and any provocation could unleash the storm. "He fell from his bicycle. He struck his head."

The words had the desired effect, as did my calm tone and direct gaze. The man's posture shifted, his fist relaxed, and he looked down at his child. He lifted the boy in his arms and touched the back of the small head.

His fingers came away bloody. "My God—"

"You should see a doctor," I said. Not that the child needed one, but I thought it sounded like a human thing to say. "I don't think he's hurt badly, but—"

The boy began to cry, wails of pain and fright, and buried his face in his father's chest. The man stared at me for a moment, then nodded once, a dry sort of thanks, before carrying his child away.

One of the other children grabbed the bicycle and wheeled it after them. One wheel wobbled badly.

I sat there breathing hard, blood on my hands, blood cooling in the gutter, and wondered what I had just done. I'd reacted virtually without thinking. I'd spent my precious hoard of energy almost down to the last trickle, and I knew that I would have continued to give until the well ran dry, once I had engaged in the battle for the child's life.

That frightened me. Djinn were not so careless, nor so caring of others. *He was human. Humans die.* That was the Djinn philosophy, and it was *true*.

Yet I had not even once thought of withholding my help.

I got up, sore and tired, and went back to my apartment to wash and sleep, and worry about what was happening to me.

"You *what*?" I had not expected Manny to be angry, but he clearly was; his face was darkening in much the same way as the boy's father's had when he'd been contemplating violence. "How could you be so damn careless? You don't know what you're doing. You're not a healer—you can't just—" He got his temper under control by taking several slow, deep breaths. "How's the kid?"

"I don't know."

"Great. Just great. Do you have any idea how much trouble you could have been in? What if the kid had died on you? Hell, what if he died *later*?"

"I didn't cause his injury," I said, affronted. We were standing in the living area of my apartment, and Manny had brought two cups of coffee—a morning ritual, he'd assured me. It was a kind gesture, but he'd done it before I had told him of the child and my actions.

The coffee sat forgotten on the table now.

"Maybe not, but you could have gotten tied up with all kinds of questions, and the police—" Manny pressed a hand to his forehead. "Damn. What am I saying? It might not have been smart, but I'd have done the same thing. I couldn't have ignored it, either. But I have *training*. You don't, Cassiel. You can't just—jump in. Especially not without me, okay?"

I accepted that without argument. By human standards, it was true enough. "I should not have acted so quickly," I agreed. "I need more power."

I put it bluntly, to see both how it felt on the tongue and how he would react. The taste of it was fine. His reaction was instructive, in that his eyes widened, and I saw a spark of something that might have been excitement, quickly buried.

"All right," he said, and his tone seemed deliberately casual. He held out his hand. I took it, and almost immediately, the beast inside of me, the hungry, desperate part, began to greedily devour what was offered. My sensible mind faded, pushed aside by need.

I felt Manny try to pull away. It sparked instincts in me—not Djinn instincts; the primitive impulses of a ruthless, successful predator.

The human impulse to hunt was complicating my needs.

No!

My distaste of those human instincts was all that

saved him. I let go, wrenching the flow of power shut between us, and backed physically away, arms wrapped around my aching stomach.

Manny collapsed. It was slow, almost graceful, and he was never unconscious; he simply lacked the strength, or the will, to keep on his feet. Or his knees. He fell full length on the carpet and rolled onto his back, eyes dark and wide, gasping for breath.

"I'm sorry," I said. I was. I was also well aware that I should not touch him again, not now. "Did I hurt you?"

"Not—exactly," he said. He groaned and rolled painfully onto his side, then up to a sitting position. I could see the trembling in his muscles, as if he'd received a violent electric shock. "Let's not do that again, okay? You're kind of hard on your friends."

"I said I was sorry."

"You can say it again. It won't offend me." Manny rested his back against the bare wall, pulled up his knees, and rested his forearms on them. "Christ. We've got to work on that. You can't take it out of me like that. If we're in real trouble, you could kill us both, not to mention anybody we're trying to help." He rested his head against the wall and sighed. "And at the risk of sounding like a woman, that hurts when you do it wrong."

I stayed silent. I felt a strange burn of shame, deep down, that wouldn't be smothered. *I hurt him.* I hadn't meant to do so, but that hardly mattered. *If I'd killed him, he leaves behind others.* The interconnectedness of human life had never truly made itself real to me until I had sat at the table, eating food prepared by his wife, watching his daughter laugh and smile.

Manny didn't speak again. I crouched down across from him, eye level, and stared deep into his eyes.

"I can't promise," I said. "I will do my best, but I may not always be able to control this. You must be prepared to defend against me."

His gaze didn't waver. "That's not real comforting."

"It wasn't meant to be." I smiled slightly, but I didn't imagine that was comforting, either. "I assume the Wardens are keeping track of what I do."

He had the grace to look a little embarrassed. "I turn in reports, yeah. They want to make sure you're not—"

"Out of control."

"Exactly."

"Am I?"

It was Manny's turn not to answer. He held the silence, and the stare, and I could not read his impenetrable human eyes at all. So much lost in me. So much that could go wrong.

"Help me up," he said, and held out his square, muscular hand. I did, careful to keep it only to surface touching, although I could sense the power coursing through him even through so light a contact. "Get your coffee. Let's go to work."

Work was a new and interesting concept for me. I understood duty, of course, and using one's skills and powers for a purpose. But *work* was a completely different thing, because it seemed so . . . *dreary*.

Manny Rocha had an office. A small, cheap single room in a building full of such accommodations. The sign on the windowless door read, ROCHA ENVIRON-MENTAL SERVICES. He unlocked the office and stepped inside, gesturing for me to follow as he picked up a scattering of envelopes from the carpeted floor. "Sorry about the mess," he said. "Been meaning to pick up a little."

Whatever Manny's skills might entail, clearly organization was not one of them. Mountains of paper and folders towered on every flat surface, leaning against each other for drunken support. There was not a single spot, other than his chair behind the broad, rectangular desk, that held clear space.

"Yeah," he said, seeing my expression. "Maybe *mess* doesn't really cover it. I've been meaning to get around to it—it's just that—"

"You hate such tasks."

"Filing. You got it."

"How would you prefer it to be filed?"

He stopped in the act of picking up a handful of fallen papers and turned toward me. "What?"

"How would you prefer it to be filed?" I repeated, exercising patience I had not known was available to me until that moment.

"Listen, if you can file this shit, you can do it any way you want." He sounded both hopeful and doubtful, as if I might believe that the filing of papers was beneath me. What he did not seem to understand was that when *everything* humans did was beneath me, a mundane task such as filing made very little difference.

"Very well," I said. I could have done it in a dozen different ways—from subtle to dramatic—but I chose a Djinn-style flourish. The paperwork vanished from every surface with an audible *pop* of displaced air, even the sheafs held in Manny's hands, and I expanded my consciousness to analyze the fundamental structure of every folder, every file. Destroying and re-creating at will, even though it was a ridiculous expense of power. "Open the drawer."

The far wall of his office was a solid block of cabinets with sliding drawers. He hesitated, then opened one at random.

Inside, a neatly ranked system of folders, filed papers.

"I filed them by subject," I said. "I can change that, if you wish, of course."

"You're kidding," he said blankly. "*Dios mio*, you're not kidding. There's a folder here on boundary disputes. On acid levels in the water. On—what the hell is this?" He pulled a folder out and frowned at it. "Boundary adjustments in *Colorado*? That's not supposed to be here. Hell."

Manny closed the file drawer and sat down in his chair. Hard. He looked around at his office as if he'd never seen it before, placing his hands palm down on the empty desktop. "Holy shit," he said. "You—how did you do that?"

I shrugged. "Simple enough. It's only paper and ink, after all." Except that I had expended far too much power in doing it, though I decided I would not tell him that. I sat in the leather armchair across from him. "What else shall we do?"

He was staring, and suddenly he barked out a sound it took me a moment to identify as laughter. "You do windows too, Cassie?"

"Cassiel."

"Right, sorry."

I sensed I might be in danger of becoming too accommodating. "No. I do not do windows."

"Then we can go right to the Warden stuff, I guess." He cleared his throat and reached for the computer keyboard off to the side, sliding it in front of himself. The machine was angled toward him from a corner of the desk. "Can't believe I can actually see the damn screen without moving things around. Let me check e-mail."

"You have forty-seven messages," I said. "Six of them have to do with requests for support from other Wardens. Shall we focus first on those?"

"I never had a Djinn," Manny admitted. "This how it was before? Working with a Djinn?"

I had no idea, but the idea of being compared to one of my kind enslaved to a bottle turned my too-human stomach, and I knew my expression hardened. "I doubt it."

He knew dangerous ground when he stepped upon it. Manny nodded. "I guess you can read the e-mails?"

"Of course."

"Which one is most urgent?"

I gave it a second's thought. "The new instability

Warden Garrity identified in Arizona is classified as a strike/slip fault."

"Garrity, Garrity—" Manny clicked keys and pulled up the e-mail in question. He read it through, nodded, and said, "Yeah, that's a place to start. Okay. Here's what we do—we mark it on the aetheric; we tag it so it's clearly visible. If there's a stress buildup, we bleed that off through surrounding rock in smaller tremors. Otherwise, the spring keeps on coiling, and we get a big shake when it releases. Usually that's no big deal, but it can cause a lot of damage if we don't head it off."

I nodded, familiar with the concepts. It was different as a Djinn, but still similar enough. "How do I assist you?"

He took his gaze from the screen to glance at me for a second. "Don't know. Just follow me and see if you've got any ideas."

I was anchored to human flesh. "I—need to touch you. To rise into the aetheric."

"No biting," he said, and held out his hand. I reached across the desk to take it. It was his left hand, and the metallic gold of his wedding ring felt an odd contrast to the skin and bones. "Ready?"

"Ready," I said. I didn't know if I was, but surely rising into the aetheric was as natural to me as breathing was to a human.

It wasn't. Not anymore. It felt wrong, the way I had to fight free of the heavy, dragging anchor of my body. Only Manny's sure touch kept me from falling back. Even after we had risen, and the spectrums shifted to show us auras and the mysteries of perceptions, I felt the continuing pull to return.

I had not known it was such hard work.

Manny couldn't speak in the aetheric, but he didn't need to. I was pulled along like a child's doll as he arrowed up into the higher plane, leveled out, and looked down on the Earth. It was a dizzying view, all opalescent colors, sparks, whispers. In the aetheric Manny looked startling—younger than in his physical form, slimmer, and almost completely covered with the shifting ghosts of tattoos. I didn't know what they symbolized, but clearly they were important to him.

His aura was a pale blue, tinged and sparked with yellow and gold. Not as powerful as others I had seen, but powerful enough for the work he was doing.

He pointed, and I nodded, bracing myself for the fall. When it came, it was shockingly fast. The ground rushed toward us, and the snap of energy whipped us to a hovering stop above a landscape alive with a twisting line of fire. Not real fire, but energy, stored deep beneath the planet's skin. Building toward explosion.

Had I still been Djinn, I would have simply admired the violence of it, the beauty of the incredible forces at work. But Djinn weren't at risk from such things, and so had nothing to fear. We did not build. We rarely died.

Humans were not so fortunate. For the first time, I found myself wondering about the fates of those milling thousands in their homes, towns, and cities, oblivious to the explosive danger under their feet.

I found myself *caring*.

I wasn't sure whether I found that intriguing or annoying.

Bleeding off the energy through surrounding rock was a delicate, slow process, but gradually the fault's energy faded from a throbbing, urgent red to a pale gold, stable and calm. It would present a constant threat, but with regular maintenance from the Earth Wardens, it would only threaten, not destroy.

When Manny released his grip on me, it was like a giant steel spring snapped tight, and I spun out of control away from him, hurtling through the aetheric, through the oil-slick layers of color. The descent was sickening. *Terrifying*. If I had been able to scream, I would have; how was it humans traveled this way, dragged down by their anchoring bodies?

I slammed back into flesh with a spasmodic jerk that nearly toppled the armchair. Across from me, Manny Rocha barely flinched as he settled into the human world again.

He opened his eyes to look at me, and there was a glow in his eyes that took me by surprise. Power, yes, and something else.

Rapture.

It faded quickly, as if he didn't want me to see it in him. "You okay?" he asked. I shook my head. My mouth was dry, my stomach empty and growling. Worse than that, though, I felt . . . exhausted. Drained again. I felt a soul-deep stab of frustration. *I can't live this way, off of the scraps of others. I am Djinn!*

Ashan had made me a beggar, and in that moment, I hated him for it so bitterly that I felt tears in my eyes. Now I would weep like a human, too. How much more humiliation could I bear?

Manny's hands closed on my shoulders. I drew in a startled breath, and my pale fingers circled his wrists. I had intended it to be defense, to throw off his touch, but the sense of his skin on mine stilled my panic.

"I need—" I couldn't speak. I'd taken so much this morning, and yet it was already spent. I felt on the verge of collapse, horribly exposed.

Manny understood. "Promise you won't take more than I give?"

I nodded.

It was trust, simple and raw, and I did not deserve it.

It took a wrenching, painful effort, but I took what was offered, and nothing more.

Perhaps I could learn to deserve it.

Chapter 4

WE HAD WORKED only a half day at reducing the stress in the fault, but Manny decreed that I needed rest.

"I'm fine," I told him sharply, as he gathered up his keys on the way to the door.

"Yeah, you're fine now," he said, "but you're going to need some sleep. Trust me on this, Cassiel. Wardens go through this when we first start out. It's natural to have to build up your endurance."

Not for a Djinn, I thought but did not say. None of this was natural for a Djinn, after all.

Manny had locked the office door behind us and we were on our way to the elevators when a stranger stepped out to block our path. Clearly one of my kind, to my eyes; he was wreathed in golden smoke, barely in his skin, and his eyes were the color of clear emeralds.

Not a stranger, after all. *Gallan.* He didn't so much as glance at Manny; his stare stayed on me. I came to a halt and reflexively put a hand out for Manny to stay behind me.

"What do you want?" I asked. Gallan—tall in this form, long-legged, with long, dark hair worn loose— seemed to find me amusing in my fragile human form. He leaned against the wall, with his arms folded, still blocking our path.

"I came to see if it was true." His eyebrows slowly lifted. "Apparently, it is. How did you anger him so, Cassiel?"

There was only one *him*, for us. Gallan was, at times, a friend and ally, but first and foremost, he was a Djinn. An *Old* Djinn, one of Ashan's, and I could no longer trust him. "It's not your business." I meant it as a warning. He couldn't have taken it any other way, but something about it amused him.

"Have you seen any others? Since—" His gesture was graceful, vague, and yet all inclusive. *Since this happened.* The event being, of course, too embarrassing and humiliating to mention directly.

"No," I said sharply. I had, but there was no reason to tell him. "Leave, Gallan. I don't want company."

"You never do." He smiled slowly. "Until you do. Tell me that it is completely done between us, and I won't trouble you again."

I felt my pale cheeks heating—a human response. Pulse beating faster. I didn't know if it was fright or something else. Something just as primitive.

"Leave."

"Tell me again." His eyes took on a brilliant gleam, sharp enough to cut.

"Leave."

"Again." He took a step toward me, and I felt the heat of him, the smoke, the fire. "Once more and it's done, Cassiel. Once more and you'll never see me again."

The word locked in my throat. Threes are powerful to us, compelling. I could dismiss him, and he would go.

I could not say it.

Another step brought him even closer to me, close enough to raise a hand that trailed light at the edges of my vision. He stroked my cheek, and I shuddered.

Gallan leaned closer, so close he eclipsed the world, and those eyes were as hungry as gravity.

"Do what he wants," he whispered, barely a breath in my ear, "and come home, Cassiel. Come home."

He melted away into mist. I caught my breath on a cry—rage, loss; I wasn't certain what emotion tore a hole through me, except that it was violent and painful.

Manny put a hand on my elbow. "Who the hell was that?"

I barked out a sound that was not quite a laugh. "A friend." I got a look of utter disbelief in return. "A very old friend."

The human world seemed so limited and lifeless, after the glitter in Gallan's eyes. I felt sick and faint and lost. It must have shown, because Manny's grip tightened on my arm.

"Yeah," he said. "Let's get you home."

Days passed, and Manny was right: I did build up endurance over time. Soon the clumsy process of entering and exiting the aetheric felt natural to me, and I learned to ration my own resources until I could stay with Manny until *he*, not I, tired.

"I couldn't do this before," he admitted to me one afternoon, after a long day of working with a team of Fire Wardens to help contain a major conflagration across the border in Arizona. "Work all day like this, I mean. You help a lot. You're learning fast."

It was surprisingly touching, receiving even such a casual compliment. I nodded carefully, wiping my forehead free of a light beading of sweat. We were outside at the fire, not in the office, and we stood at the boundary of the area in a section deemed safe. I had not seen the Fire Wardens, but that was because (Manny assured me) they were in the thick of the blaze, fighting it from within. That seemed a grim risk to take, but this time, at least, they were successful. The flames were dying.

No doubt the human firefighters around us were a

part of that, as well—they were filthy, exhausted, hunched empty-eyed on camp chairs as they drank cold water or ate what the volunteers had brought for them. Brave, all of them. None of them had to be here, and I was only now beginning to realize *why* they were here. Some of them because it was a job, most certainly, but some because it was a calling. A thing of honor.

I could not help but honor them in turn.

Manny checked the fire again—we had raised fire-breaks of earth and green vegetation, which a faraway Weather Warden had saturated with steady downpours—and said, "I think we're done here. Looks like they're mopping it up now. Come on, I have a stop to make."

Another one? I had been hoping for home, a bath, and bed, but I kept silent as we walked to Manny's battered pickup truck. It wore a new layer of ash and smudged smoke over the old dirt; he shrugged and, with a slight pulse of will, cleared the windshield, leaving the rest of the dirt intact. "Looks strange to have a clean vehicle out here," he told me, when I sent him a questioning look. "You get noticed. Better to blend in."

I was getting used to the stink of the internal combustion engine, but it still seemed wrong after the cleaner organic compounds in the smoke of the forest. I rolled down the window and took in slow, shallow breaths. After a moment, I realized that I was covered with a faint layer of soot, and the need for a bath climbed higher on my priorities. *Just a little,* I thought. *Just enough to make myself clean.*

It was a selfish use of my hoarded power, but I couldn't stand being dirty. I used a light brushing of it to sweep off the soot, just as Manny had cleaned his windshield.

Manny glanced my way. "You okay?"

My power levels were still adequate, if not strong;

I wouldn't need to draw again for some time. "I'm fine," I assured him. "Where are we going?"

"You'll love it," he said, and grinned in a way that convinced me this was one of his attempts at a joke.

"The fire," I said. "I thought there would be more attention put to it by the Wardens."

Manny sent me a cautious glance. "Yeah, usually there would be. There's something going on, on the East Coast. Most of the stronger Wardens are out there, or heading there. So we're on skeleton crew, working with whatever we can." His smile reemerged. "That's why we have to make this stop."

We drove fifteen miles on a rutted dirt road and turned into an equally rutted dirt driveway, crossing a metal grating with bone-jarring thumps. When Manny braked in a cloud of dust, I looked around for landmarks.

There were none, except for a small house and a large storage building—a barn?—still distant. No sign of anyone nearby.

Manny got out of the truck and walked away. I frowned, debating, and then followed without being summoned.

"Where are we going?" I demanded again, more sharply. Manny pointed. *"Where?"*

"Right there," he said, and I heard that tone again, as if this was providing him some subtle amusement. And he kept walking toward the area he'd indicated.

Which was, in fact, a *cattle pen*. Inside of it, the huge beasts milled, bumped against each other, made low sounds of either contentment or distress.

As I walked nearer, I began to perceive the smell. I stopped. "No."

"Part of the job, Cassiel," Manny said without pausing. He vaulted up on the metal bars and over the railing, landing with a thump inside the pen, his boots barely avoiding a thick clump of cattle waste.

The beasts took little notice of his arrival. I held my breath, hovering at the barely acceptable limits of the rich, earthy stench, as Manny touched each creature. He was marking them, I realized, each with a touch that showed in the aetheric. "What are you doing?" I choked, and put my hands over my nose and mouth as the smell threatened to overwhelm my defenses.

"Checking them out," he called back. "We've had some outbreaks of foot-and-mouth disease around here, and even one case of mad cow we were able to cure. But we have to stay on top of it. One scare like what happened in Britain, and the beef industry is in real trouble. Used to be another Earth Warden around here who specialized in this stuff, but he's gone."

"Can't you do it from a distance?"

"Yes." He flashed a grin in my direction. "It just isn't as much fun as seeing the look on your face."

I gave him a long, long stare. I imbued it with all the Djinn haughtiness at my command, which was quite a bit, even now. "I will wait in the truck," I said, and turned to go.

A strange silence fell over the land, a hush that prickled along my nerves like a storm of needles, and I stopped, turning my head, searching for the cause of it. *Something . . .*

"Cassiel!" Manny cried.

I whirled, heart pounding, as I felt the surge of power roar through the air, swirling around the cattle pen.

A whirling, invisible cyclone of energy separated me from Manny.

A cow trumpeted in panic and pain, shook its head, and toppled to its knees. It hit the trampled ground with a thud and thrashed, screaming.

Another.

Another.

"Manny!" I screamed it, and although it was an enormous effort without his help, I launched myself up into the aetheric with all the power I had in reserve.

It didn't help. Djinn senses were beyond me; what was left was inconsistent, confusing, a blur of forces that twisted in on itself like a hurricane, spiraling tighter and tighter. Manny was backing away from it, but there was nowhere to go; the cattle were panicked, as much of a danger to him and each other as the power encircling them. He could have fought through them to the metal fence, but not beyond, with the forces swirling just outside and moving inward.

It was a noose, and the noose was drawing tighter. I did not stop to think. I plunged into the storm.

The force hit me with staggering intensity, whipping my fragile body, punching into my head and soul like red-hot needles. I struggled on and felt cold metal under my searching hands. *The fence.* I wriggled between the bars and fell into soft dirt, bathed in the stench of the cattle and their leavings. That no longer mattered.

I crawled. The pressure against my head eased first, and then my shoulders, as I inched farther into the temporarily safe area inside the cattle pen.

Not so safe as all that. I heard the panicked bellows of the cattle, and massive sharp hooves stomped the ground beside my head. I heaved myself up just as Manny's hands closed around me, whirling me around to face him.

"What the hell are you doing?" he shouted at me, and swung me out of the way as a massive cow charged the rushing band of power edging in over the fence.

The cow entered the wall, wailed an eerie cry, and toppled to its knees, then to its side.

Dead.

I felt the breath stop in my lungs. *I might have died.* It had not occurred to me because Djinn didn't think of such things, of the way fragile bodies could so easily shatter. Suddenly, Manny's anger at me made sense.

The power took on a reddish hue and crept in another foot, forcing the cattle back. Whether we risked the barrier or not, we would eventually be injured, and probably killed, by the panicked beasts.

My once-Djinn nature *might* protect me a second time, but I couldn't rely on it, and I couldn't risk Manny's life.

My hand slipped down his arm to grab his hand. He flinched, then nodded, tight-lipped. "Do it," he said.

"Together," I replied.

Compared with the white-hot geyser of Lewis Orwell's abilities, Manny was weak, but strong enough—and canny enough—to allow me to take his power, *all* his power, amplify it, and feed it back to him. It was, I thought, the reason that humans had made Djinn their servants—our ability to channel, magnify, and refine their powers so completely.

It was trust I required, and trust I received, as Manny let go of his own destiny and put it into my hands.

I shaped his power into a sharp edge, something that gleamed like the blade of a knife on the aetheric. I forced the edges finer, finer still, until it was thin as a whisper, and strong as steel.

Then I threw out my arms and cut through the barrier holding us penned. Not only the storm of force around us, but the iron of the cattle pen itself.

I formed a second sharp-edged plane and slammed it down five feet from the first, through force and metal. The metal fence, chopped at two points, fell in the middle to form an exit, a break in the attack large enough for us to escape.

Except that Manny did not take it. Instead, he began slapping the cattle's thick hides, driving them to the hole I kept open. "Move!" he yelled. The cows, once prodded, saw the clear space and thundered toward it. I could not dodge out of the way. I was transfixed by the crushing load of concentration; the barriers I'd managed to erect were strong, but holding them against the battering attack was like holding a pane of glass against a hurricane—a doomed effort, but one requiring all my attention.

Manny must have realized that just in time. I felt a sudden surge of power from him—just a small amount, because he had little left to give. Just enough to divert the cattle from my unprotected body.

The beasts streamed around me, hot and bellowing, and thundered through the narrow gap. When the last bawling animal was free, Manny hesitated at the edge.

"Go!" I shouted. He plunged through.

I did not think I could keep the barriers in place while moving, but I tried, walking slowly and calmly with my arms outstretched to either side. My fingertips brushed the slick, cool surface of the walls I'd put in place. I felt them shudder.

I felt them shatter when I was still in the middle.

The storm closed around me and shattered me, too.

I came back to consciousness with my eyes full of cloudless blue sky, tasting dust and metal. When I took a breath, it was thick with the smell of cattle.

It was the stench that convinced me. *Ah, then. Not dead, unless the humans are correct about hell.*

For a moment, as pain washed over me, I wished I'd been granted that mercy, but instead, a face loomed close, blocking out the sun. I expected Manny, but no. A cow, blinking its huge brown eyes, watched me with as deep a curiosity as something so primitive could muster. It nudged me with a damp nose.

"Hey!" Manny's sharp voice startled the cow, and it pulled back and away, trotting off to join its fellows placidly cropping the trampled grass. This time Manny's shadow blocked the sun as he leaned over me. "You're okay. Thank God."

I felt strangely . . . light. Empty. I held out my hand to him, and it trembled with the effort.

He looked at it, then past my shaking fingers to focus on my face.

"You saved my life," he said. There was something odd in his voice. "You really did."

I had no strength left to voice my needs. Part of me was already fraying at the edges, and I was afraid, the way I'd been afraid as Ashan ripped me from the world of the Djinn and sent me falling into flesh.

This time, I was falling into darkness. No one, not even the Djinn, knew what came after that. I was empty, and fading.

Manny's hand wrapped around mine in a strong clasp, and he sat down beside me as the power trickled slowly from the wellspring inside him, filling empty spaces inside me. I gasped in relief and pain, and wrapped my other hand around his.

The flow of power seemed intolerably slow. It was all I could do not to rip and tear at his control to get at that life-giving flow, but I forced myself to stay down, stay still, be passive.

And in time, the panic lessened, and the emptiness receded. Well before I was complete, though, Manny's supply of power failed. He could give no more without endangering himself.

"It's enough," I told him, in response to his silent question. He helped me to my feet. I looked down at myself and grimaced, because in my haste to reach him I had crawled through filth. I did not have it to spare, but I used a pulse of power to clean myself.

Manny laughed. "Vanity really is your vice of choice, isn't it?"

"No," I said somberly. "I believe it's pride."

* * *

Manny had no idea who might want to kill him. He was, he said, not a man who made enemies; that might or might not be correct, but I felt he was telling me the truth as he saw it.

This had not felt like an attack from another Warden, though I supposed that was possible. While it had been full of power and energy, there had been a formless sense about it, too. I supposed that it could have been a Djinn, but only if the Djinn was merely toying with us. Testing, perhaps—testing me?

A new thought, and one not entirely comforting. I didn't like having faceless, nameless enemies.

We drove back to town in silence; Manny, I could perceive, was thinking furiously about what had happened. He had walked to the house and spoken to the rancher about the dead cattle; I have no idea what explanation he put to it—perhaps something to do with freak weather or lightning. He kept his thoughts and suspicions—if he had any—to himself.

Instead of taking me to my apartment, or back to our office, he took me to his home. Isabel was in the front yard, playing some elaborate and complicated game involving three dolls, a large number of scattered building blocks, and a much-abused cardboard box large enough to hide in.

"Papa!" She threw the dolls in the dirt and ran to wrap herself around Manny. He lifted her and kissed her dirty face, settled her on his hip, and turned to face the street. There was a large, gleaming black truck with flames painted in an orange blaze along the sides parked there—a flamboyant, obvious sort of vehicle.

There seemed to be conflict in his expression— delight warring with dread. He shook his head. "I see Uncle Luis is here," he said. "Right?"

"Right!" Isabel bubbled, and laughed. She stared at

me over Manny's shoulder, smiling, and I waved wearily in return. "Cassie looks funny."

"Cassiel," I said reflexively. "Not Cassie."

Manny grimaced and nudged his daughter. "It's not polite to say people look funny, Ibby."

"But she does! She's white like snow, and her hair's fluffy. How come she doesn't look like everybody else?"

"Ibby!"

I summoned up the will to laugh a little. "Don't. She's right. I do look odd to her eyes." *And to my own. Definitely to my own . . .*

"Hey, bro." The screen door to the house opened with a creak of hinges, and the man who stood there was a bit shorter than Manny, but far broader in the chest and shoulders. His hair was glossy, straight, and down to his shoulders. He was wearing a gray sleeveless shirt that revealed muscular arms covered with intricate dark tattoos.

Flames.

I had seen his picture, on the mantel.

"You look like hell, man," he said, and held out a sweating brown bottle to Manny. "Bad day at the office?"

"You could say that." Manny let Isabel down, and she scampered back to her playground, gathering up and dusting off her dolls before resuming her games. Manny had a certain guarded distance, and I wondered if it was because of this stranger, or me. "Luis, meet Cassiel. You probably heard about her." He twisted the cap from the bottle Luis had given him, and drank a deep, thirsty mouthful of the beer.

Luis. Brother. Another Warden, and one far stronger than Manny; I could feel his energy like heat against my skin, even from several feet away. An Earth Warden, like his brother. I wondered why he'd gotten tattoos of flames; it seemed an odd sort of choice.

I remembered, too, that when Manny was on the aetheric, he had the ghosts of the same tattoos on his arms. Odd indeed . . . unless his unconscious manifestation on the aetheric wished to be like his brother.

Luis had large brown eyes, and they surveyed me with interest and intensity. He offered a vague salute with his half-empty bottle of beer. "Hey, Cassiel," he said. "You drink beer?"

"Yes," I said. There was a challenge in his question, and I was in no mood to be defeated. Luis nodded, without any change in expression, and reached down inside the door. He held a bottle out to me. I went up the porch steps and took it, twisted the cap as I'd seen Manny do, and took a deep swallow.

The taste was foul. I choked, coughed, and managed not to spew the stuff back on Luis's smirking face. I swallowed and willed myself not to give him more amusement.

The second sip was easier. "Thank you," I said.

"You're an asshole," Manny told his brother. "Inside. What the hell are you doing here, man?"

He shoved Luis on the shoulder. Manny was the weaker of the two, but Luis allowed himself to be pushed, retreating back into the house.

We followed.

Angela was setting the table—four places. When she saw me, she quickly turned away and added another plate, as well as a welcoming silent smile. I thought—though my command of human expressions was not expert—that she looked troubled, despite the smile.

"Seriously, man, have you lost your mind?" Manny demanded as the screen door banged shut behind us with a sound like a thunderclap. "You don't come back to Albuquerque. You know that. You're asking for trouble."

Luis's face set in stubborn lines. "I don't let fear run my life," he said. "You shouldn't either, Manny."

"I got a wife and kid! I got things to lose, bro. You

think about that before you go stirring things up again." Manny shot me a look, excluding me from this strange conversation. I wandered to the screen door to watch Isabel playing in the box, earnestly talking to her dolls as they acted out whatever drama she had constructed. One toppled over into the dust, and Isabel leaned the other two over the fallen, mimicking human concern. Angela moved to the window to check on her child before going back to the kitchen.

I continued to listen to the brothers.

"This is still Norteño territory, and they're not going to miss you rolling up, big as life, in that damn flashy truck," Manny was saying. "You want to visit, you at least let me know before you come. We got our own problems around here without throwing yours on top."

"Love you too, Manny," Luis said. "Look, I'm sorry, but all that crap, that's past, all right? The Norteños have bigger things to worry about than me. I've been out of that a long time now."

"You know how it is: You're never out. I hear they remember." Manny was less angry now, but I could sense the dark undercurrents still in his voice. "Think about Angela and Ibby. I'm planning to move them out of here later in the year, now that I got a raise from the Wardens."

"For taking her on?" *Her* meant, of course, me. I decided that mentioning me included me once more in the conversation, and turned toward the two men. Manny glanced nervously toward me; Luis did not. His eyes were fixed on his brother, and his muscular arms were folded across his chest. "Shit, bro, you sure about this?"

"You mean, is he sure about me?" I deliberately took another shallow sip of the beer. The malty, bitter aftertaste was less prominent this time. "I doubt he is, but I have proved useful to him."

Luis did look at me this time, and I did not care for the expression on his face. It seemed to pass judgment, and I would not be judged by humans. Not even by a Warden as powerful as I suspected Luis to be. "You get yourself in trouble today?" he asked—not me, but Manny. Manny shook his head.

"Not any more than usual."

I wondered why Manny was feeling it necessary to lie, even by omission, to his own brother, but I kept my silence. The two men continued to stare at each other, a contest of wills that left a palpable shiver in the air, and then Luis shrugged and chugged down half of his beer in one long gulp. "You know where I am if you need me."

He didn't wait for Manny to answer, but turned and walked into the kitchen, where Angela was preparing the meal. Isabel banged in through the front door, still clutching her dolls, and ran into the kitchen. Voices rose and fell, punctuated by Isabel's giggles.

Manny sipped his beer in silence, eyes unfocused and distant.

"Your brother," I said.

"Yeah," he answered. "Lucky me."

Chapter 5

I LEARNED A great deal at the meal that night, mainly from the silences and when they fell. Manny loved his brother, but there were secrets between them, things that not even Angela seemed to fully understand. I said little, preferring to observe.

The meal was tamales, Angela explained to me, and went into great detail of how to season the pork that was rolled into the cornmeal. I was grateful that she quickly pointed out that the corn husk skins should be removed before eating, as that had posed a worry for me. The food was a heady mixture of tastes and textures, and Ibby tipped hot sauce freely onto my plate, begging me to try it with the tamales and rice. I haughtily refused. That earned me laughter from the others at the table, but kind laughter. Bright, not dark.

"So," Manny said, "Luis, you staying long?"

"Maybe." He shoveled another bite of food into his mouth. He had not been shy about the hot sauce, and seemed unaffected by it. "Waiting on a transfer out of Florida. I'm kind of on detached service right now."

Manny exchanged a look with his wife, and Angela frowned. "Where's the transfer to?" she asked. "Ibby, stop playing with the rice. You're getting it all over the table."

Isabel glowered at her, but ate the forkful of rice

she had been waving around. Luis took a sip of his beer.

"They tell me they're short of Wardens in Colorado," he said. "So probably there, but it'll be closer than the coast." He nudged Isabel, seated next to him. "You'd like that, right?"

"Right!" She chewed her food noisily and grinned at him.

"Luis—" Manny said, and then shrugged. "It's your life, man. But if I were you, I wouldn't come back here. Not to New Mexico. And not to any place Norteños has a chapter. They don't forget, man. And they never forgive. You know that."

"I know. I just don't care," Luis said. He focused his attention back on his plate. "So what have you guys been up to while I was gone? Ibby?"

Isabel launched into a bubbling, breathless story about everything from the history of her dolls to the horny toad she had found in the backyard. Angela caught my eye and smiled, and I felt . . . warmed. Part of the circle of safety, however much an illusion it might be.

I saved his life, I thought, watching Manny as he talked and laughed with his wife and daughter. *He would not be here tonight if I hadn't.*

There was something curiously strong about that feeling. I didn't know what to name it, or whether or not it would help or harm me—but I couldn't ignore it. As a Djinn, I had never cared about an individual human, other than as a tool to be used and discarded. I had never given a moment's thought to what they had been before or after; I had spent as little time as possible in contact with them, and forgotten them almost immediately. Now I wondered. I thought about all of those faces I had glimpsed through the ages of my life—young, old, male, female—and how I might have helped or harmed them.

It was unsettling.

I realized, with a prickle of alarm, that Luis Rocha was watching me over Isabel's head. I wondered what was in my face, and how much it betrayed my feelings.

He said nothing, only nodded and turned his attention back to Angela, who was asking if he wanted more tamales. With his gaze off of me, I could look at him without feeling intrusive, and I found myself admiring the clean lines of his face, the way the light caught on his dark copper skin. The blue-black shine of his hair.

He was beautiful. Not as beautiful as a Djinn—no human could be—but there was something wild and fiercely lovely about him. I was reminded of eagles, soaring high as they hunted. He had something of the eagle in him.

When Angela began to gather the dishes, I rose to help her. It seemed to be expected, and it gave me a chance to follow her into the kitchen, away from the men and Isabel.

Angela accepted the dishes with a smile of thanks and began running hot water in the sink. "So, what do you think of him?" she asked. "Luis?"

"Interesting," I said. I leaned against the counter, watching as she rinsed dishes in soapy water. "There is tension between him and his brother."

Angela laughed softly. "Little bit, yeah." She glanced at me, eyes veiled under her lashes. "You want to know why?"

I didn't answer. I gathered up pots and pans from the stove and moved them to the area where Angela was rinsing and scrubbing.

"Luis got in trouble a few years ago," Angela said. She pitched her voice low, hardly loud enough to reach my ears. "Gang trouble. He used to be a Norteño when he was young and stupid, until he found out he had the gift and the Wardens came calling.

Saved his life, probably. But the gang didn't want to let him go." She shook her head, mouth set in a grim line. "Still don't."

I cocked my head and asked, "Gang?"

Angela spent a long moment marveling at my ignorance before she shrugged and said, "Like a tribe, only they're not related by blood. They protect each other against other gangs, go to war together, that kind of thing. And they make money, usually selling drugs or stealing. But it's a hard life. People die all the time, and they die real young."

"Were you in a gang?" I asked her. That surprised her, and I got a wide-eyed shake of her head. "Yet you seem—sympathetic."

She sighed. "Not so much sympathetic as understanding. I knew so many of them. Most of them are dead now, but there are always kids, young kids, waiting to step up. I worry, that's all. I worry that no matter what we do, the gangs grow, because we don't make a place for these young ones. We give them good reason to be angry."

I didn't understand. I hardly understood anything of human culture, but it seemed to me that *gangs* were no different than any other cultural grouping—humans banded together for defense and profit. They always had. Sometimes it was by family, sometimes by nation, sometimes by religion, but always they divided and combined themselves.

War was a fact of their lives.

I realized with a chill that the Djinn had done the same, fractured themselves into factions. Were we becoming like the humans? No better than?

Surely not.

"Is Luis in danger?" I asked Angela, handing her a collection of spoons and forks.

"We're all in danger," she said. "As long as Luis is in Norteños territory."

"I'll keep you safe," I said.

Angela sent me a look I could not read. "Will you?"

We finished the dishes in silence.

The next day our small office saw a visit from the Warden local officials—two senior Wardens, one Fire and one Weather. Neither was as impressive in their power signature as Luis Rocha, but they seemed competent enough, and both wielded more ability than Manny.

They wanted a report of the attack we had experienced. Manny had written it in detail, but they ignored the paper and instead asked us to describe the incident, over and over, until I simply saw no reason to answer the questions and stopped responding.

"You're certain you didn't recognize the power signature of the person conducting this attack?" the woman asked. Greta, her name was, and her aura clearly identified her as a Fire Warden. Physically, she was a small woman with reddish, close-cropped hair and large blue eyes. Her skin was a cool, pale beige, marked here and there with spots that looked like burns. She hadn't bothered to have them healed or the scars removed. "You saw nothing on the aetheric?"

"Nothing I could identify," Manny said. "Like I said, it was odd. It really didn't feel like a trained Warden, but there was a lot of power behind it."

"But not a Djinn." Greta's gaze moved to me. "You're sure."

I shrugged. I'd stated it several times; there was no need to continue to speak. They were making me angry. They seemed to doubt not only Manny's word, but my own. I could not truly imagine why they thought we would lie.

"Look, if you made a mistake, if you tried something and it got out of hand, you can admit it," said

the man—Scott, the Weather Warden. He was very
tall, with bushy black hair and a hangdog, heavily
lined face. His voice was sharp and nasal, and ac-
cented to match. "Better to do it now than after we
find out for ourselves."

Manny's face took on a darker hue, and I felt a
pulse of anger from him. "We're not lying."

Greta sent her fellow Warden a quick glance. "We
don't think you are," she said. "I think what Scott is
trying to say is that if there's something you haven't
told us, now is the time to come clean about it.
Okay?"

Manny nodded tightly. "I've told you everything."

"And you, Cassiel?"

"I have told the truth, as well," I said. "Don't call
me a liar again." I was aware of the dangerous edge
to my words, and I found I didn't much care.

It was Scott's turn to turn red with anger. "You're
here because we *let* you be here—don't you forget it!"
he barked. "I didn't want you in our territory. If you
give me cause, I'll ship you back to Florida so fast
you'll get whiplash. I don't like having a rogue Djinn
in the mix, and if I had to bet, I'd bet that whatever
went wrong here, it was your fault. Get me?"

"I could," I said evenly. I let it ring in the silence.

Manny took in a breath, then let it slowly out.
"Yeah," he finally said. "Cassiel, let's all just calm
down. We didn't do anything wrong. Somebody attacked us; we don't know who it was or even if it was
a Warden or a Djinn. But we're on the lookout for
anything like it. Okay?"

Scott's gaze was locked on mine. I allowed a slow,
cool smile across my lips, and saw him flinch from
whatever he saw naked in my eyes. There were virtues
to the Djinn having gone to war with the Wardens,
however briefly. It had taught them to respect us.

"Fine," Greta said. She sounded subdued and a little nervous. "Let's move along. I don't want you out in the field for a couple of days, so stay here and do whatever you can remotely. Watch your backs. If you see anything odd, call for help immediately."

"I hear your brother's in town," Scott said to Manny. "That right?"

"He's staying with us for a few days, yeah."

"I heard he applied for a transfer. I tried to get him, but they tell me we're already fully staffed in this region. He'll probably go to Colorado." Scott's muddy gaze narrowed. "Too bad. He's got real skills. We could use him."

"So could Colorado," Greta said sharply. "Enough. Manny, Cassiel, thank you for your patience. We'll leave you to it."

"Oh," Scott said, and snapped his fingers. "Did you get a report in the mail? Something that should have gone to the Colorado office, maybe?"

There was something odd about the way he broached the subject—too quick, with too ingratiating a smile. Before Manny could answer, I said, "I have filed the papers. I saw nothing like that."

Manny cut a sharp glance at me, but he followed my lead and stayed quiet.

"Okay," Scott said. He stared at me for a few seconds. "Well. If it arrives, just let me know."

Greta rose. Scott seemed reluctant to leave, but he had little choice; she was clearly the senior in the team, and once her course was set, she did not seem the type to be balked. She shook Manny's hand, then—after a slight hesitation—mine. I wondered what she had been told.

Perhaps she'd been told the truth. In that case, no wonder she had hesitated. I was careful to keep the brief contact impersonal, merely surface, and saw a flash of relief in her eyes.

I wasn't so careful with Scott. He pulled free

quickly, wiping his hand against his trousers. I had not made a friend.

I hadn't intended to.

"Manny Rocha is a good Warden," I said. "Don't try to imply otherwise."

I kept my stare on Scott until the door closed between us with a final, soft click.

"You shouldn't antagonize him," Manny said.

"You shouldn't placate him." I turned back to reach for the folders on the desk.

"What was all that about? Why'd you lie to him? We've got a folder of stuff for Colorado, right?"

"I don't know," I said softly. I transferred my gaze back to the closed door and frowned. "I don't know."

Manny yawned. "Screw it. We'll look at it tomorrow. It's probably nothing we need to worry about, anyway. I don't know about you, but getting interrogated by the boss makes me tired."

It made me tired, too, and I allowed him to draw me out of the office and deliver me home.

Djinn do not sleep, unless they take human form. Perhaps that's one of the lures for us, that brief period of oblivion . . . and dreams. Dreams of things beyond our control.

I had never dreamed before, but that night, alone in darkness, I dreamed of Luis Rocha. In my dream he was both the same and different; more and less. A Djinn, not a Warden. His core was bright, burning power, and the tattoos licking his arms were real flames barely contained by their ink outlines. He was a beautiful, wild thing, and in the dream—in the *dream*—I was drawn to him, like water to the sky. His heat melted the ice within me. I knew nothing of bodies, but the dream was of flesh and need and fire, and when I woke I was trembling, aching, and echoing with the aftershocks of pleasure.

I had not dreamed of Manny. I had dreamed of his *brother*.

This seemed oddly significant to me.

I said nothing of the dream to Manny when he came to get me the next morning, to take me to the office. I felt uncomfortable in my skin, acutely aware of the flesh enclosing me. I had always considered it to be a tool, a shell, but the dream had given me new understanding. Human souls were *partnered* with bodies, and at times, it seemed, sensation drove reason.

I was not sure I liked it.

Seeing Luis waiting in the office hallway was a not unpleasant shock, a throwback to the dream that sent hot waves of sensation from the soles of my feet through the top of my head. I averted my eyes from him, eager to keep any hint of what was in my mind from him.

"Something wrong?" Manny asked me as he unlocked the door. I shook my head, pale hair lashing my face. "Yeah, obviously not. Poker face, Cassiel, look it up. . . . Hey, bro. What's up? Isn't this a little bit early for you?"

There was a brief pause, and I saw Luis shift his weight from a casual posture to something more— cautious. "You didn't leave a message?"

"Leave what message?"

"To meet you here at the office."

Manny turned the knob and opened the door. "Like I'd want to see your ugly face first thing in the morning. No, man, I—"

I felt it first, a fraction of a second before either of the Wardens. I shoved Manny into his brother, to one side of the door, and spun in the opposite direction.

Fire exploded out of the open office door in a white-hot jet, rolling like lava to boil against the opposite wall, which immediately blistered, cooked, and began to burn. On the other side of the wall of flame, I saw Manny and Luis scrambling backward. Safe, for the moment.

I was not. By turning the other direction I had saved my flesh, but now I was trapped in an alcove at the end of the hallway, a shallow box with no way out. The air rippled with heat, and smoke began pouring from the flaming walls and ceiling—black and thick in my mouth and nose. My eyes stung and watered, and I found myself pressed back against the farthest wall, gasping in shallow, choking breaths.

I needed to get control of it, but the fire—fire terrified me in ways I had never imagined. It was an instinct erupting from the roots of my body, an atavistic need to retreat from the flames.

I am Djinn. I am born of fire. It can't hurt me.

But it could now, and my flesh knew that all too well. I struggled to control my reactions. I had power; all I needed to do was apply it.

But the power was rooted in Earth, and fire responded little to my feeble attempts.

A shape emerged from the flames—human-formed but made of fire, and that cooled into the dull red of molten metal.

A Djinn.

It looked at me for a long moment, then reached out to me. When I hesitated, it cocked its head to one side, plainly impatient.

I reached out, and my fragile human hand grasped his.

There was no sense of burning.

He pulled me into the fire, and I was surrounded by the flames, enveloped and caressed by them. It was like being a Djinn again, for a brief and euphoric second.

Then I felt a shove and I stumbled on, into air that felt ice-cold after the heat of the blaze. The air was

thick with toxic smoke. I reached out and felt the solid
surface of a wall. I followed it, coughing and choking,
until I ran into a warm body and human hands gripped
my shoulders.

"I've got her!" I recognized the voice, even smoke
roughened. Luis Rocha. "Cassiel. Come on!"

A shadow charged toward us—Manny. He took my
other arm and together the brothers towed me out of
the smoke, to clearer air.

The office building was a chaos of people running,
yelling, talking on cell phones. People carried comput-
ers, purses, files. One man had an equipment dolly
with a file cabinet, though how he imagined he would
get it down the stairs was a mystery.

"Fire Wardens are responding," Manny said, and
coughed. His mouth and nose were black with soot, and
his eyes were bloodshot. I imagined I looked no better.
Luis bent over, hacking and choking, and spat out black.

"There they go," Luis said, and sank down against
a wall to a crouch as we felt the power of the Wardens
sweep past us in a cool wave. The smoke lessened,
and I heard the roar of the fire subside to a dull mutter. "*Fuck.* What the hell was that? Who the fuck did
you piss off, Manny?"

"Me? Somebody told *you* to be here, remember?
Maybe they're not after *me!*"

They glared at each other, red-eyed and belligerent.
I had never seen the blood relationship between them
so clearly.

I cleared my throat and tasted ash. "You're angry
because you're afraid," I said. "So you should be.
Someone wanted to kill us, or at least cared nothing
of killing all of us so long as they achieved their goal.
Someone capable of igniting fire on a massive scale,
which means a Warden—"

"Or a Djinn," Luis finished for me, and both brothers stared in my direction. "No use asking if *you've*
made any enemies lately."

I hadn't told them that there had been a Djinn on-site . . . who'd pulled me out of the fire. It didn't seem the prudent time to do it now. I held my silence. I had recognized the Djinn himself as a New Djinn, one of David's followers, but I didn't know him well, and I didn't think that the New Djinn had any reason to pursue me at the cost of human lives.

Ashan, on the other hand . . . Ashan was one to hold a grudge for generations, and human damage was nothing to him.

The crush at the stairs eased, and firefighters in yellow slickers urgently beckoned us to proceed down and out of the building, as the sirens howled their alarm.

Luis had enemies. So did I. So did Manny.

There was no way to be sure who had been the intended target of the attack, except one: ask the one individual I knew had witnessed it.

I slipped away from Manny and Luis in the confusion downstairs, climbed up on the bed of a flatbed truck in the parking lot, and surveyed the scene. It seemed chaos, but there was purpose at its core—the firefighters seemed to know their business, as did the police and ambulance attendants helping those who needed it.

The Djinn were plain to me, even in human disguise. There were two in the crowd, but neither was the Djinn who'd pulled me from the fire. Still, they would carry a message.

I jumped off the truck, landed heavily—gravity and flesh were an uncomfortable combination—and felt a flash of pain like a knife through my right leg. No broken bones, only a pulled muscle. I forced myself to ignore it as I pushed through the crowd of babbling humans talking excitedly.

When I reached the spot where the first Djinn had been, he was no longer there. No longer in sight at all. I extended my senses cautiously, as limited as they were, but found nothing.

He had seen me coming, and retreated to where I couldn't follow.

The other Djinn was more accommodating. She was in the form of a small human child, with long, silky blond hair and fair skin. Eyes so blue they seemed made of sky. She sat perched on a decorative stone block at the edge of the parking lot, swinging her feet and watching the building belch black smoke toward the sky.

"How are you enjoying your exile?" she asked me, as I crouched down next to her. Like me, she was Old Djinn, and a particular favorite of Ashan's; unlike me, she enjoyed a certain freedom to act as she pleased, because of her age and power.

"I'm not," I said shortly. "Venna, there was a Djinn inside the building, in the fire. Can you tell me who it was?"

"Certainly," she said, and her lips curved into a faint, annoying smile. "I *can*."

"Will you?"

"No."

I held my temper with difficulty. "Then will you convey a message to him, and tell him that I need to ask him what happened?"

Venna continued to drum her patent-leather heels on the stone, and she never looked away from the building. "Ashan's still very angry with you," she said.

"Did he do this?"

"Do what?"

"Set this fire."

That earned me a glance, a dismissive one. "Why would he?"

A fair question, but I couldn't predict what Ashan might or might not do. "Did he order it done?"

"No." That was surprising; I had not expected so

definitive an answer, not from a Djinn as old and canny as Venna. "I'll convey your message to the one who was here. Just this once, Cassiel, as a favor. Don't ask me again, or I'll hurt you."

She said it with no particular heat, but I knew she meant every word. And she was more than capable. For all her little-girl prettiness, Venna was a vast, dangerous being, and if I displeased her . . .

I bent my head in silent acknowledgment.

Venna misted away. I realized that I had made a fatal human error—I hadn't asked how long it would take. Time was measured differently among the Old Djinn, and so was humor; she might fulfill her promise, but take several human lifetimes doing it. That would be inconvenient.

Whatever her motives, Venna took pity on me. It was only a moment before another Djinn faded into view, perched on the same block she had occupied. This one was far taller, an adult male dressed in human-style trousers and a white shirt. Beneath the businesslike clothing, his skin was a rich copper, but still almost within human ranges; only a shade or two redder than Luis's, I thought. His eyes, however, were nothing like human. Colors swirled and merged in them like living opals.

I doubted the people around us could even see him. There was a slight blur to his figure, and when I turned my head away, he disappeared from my peripheral vision altogether.

"You have questions," he said. "I'm not surprised. I'm Quintus." He held out his hand to me, human fashion, and I took it with great care. He felt like a penny left in the sun. "I didn't set the fire, if that's what you wanted to ask."

"I didn't think you had," I said. "My name is—"

"We all know your name, Cassiel. We've all been warned." His voice was deep as a bell but soft, as if

I were a great distance away. "I'm sorry. I would like to help you, if I could."

"You don't even know me."

That earned me an amused quirk of his eyebrows. "I'm not one of your Old Djinn. When I was alive as a man, I never required that I know people to help them," he said. "That's the difference between Old and New Djinn, in a nutshell, I suppose—you only help your own, and then only when the spirit moves you. Well, if you want to know about the fire, I can tell you this: it was a Warden who set it."

"You're sure?"

"Of course." His smile turned dark and bitter. "I'm well acquainted with the Warden in question. I was once her slave."

I let a few seconds of silence pass before I asked the obvious. "Who is it?"

"Why do you think I would tell you?" he asked, and confusion froze me for a long second, while his smile stretched. "I was once her slave; I didn't say I don't like her. The two, you know, are not mutually exclusive."

They were to me. "You won't give me her name."

"No, because I know why she did what she did. It was an act of desperation, Cassiel. You should know all about those." He paused, gaze fixed on the fire. "No one is injured, no one is dead. Let it go."

"It was directed at *me*. Or my Conduit, which is the same thing. I can't ignore it."

"The matter's closed. The Warden won't be coming after either of you again. I swear that to you. I'll see to it personally."

I didn't want to believe Quintus, but there was something so solid and open about him that I finally, grudgingly nodded. "Very well," I said. "But if your Warden mistress breaks her word and comes for either Manny Rocha or me again, I'll break *her*. I'll go through you if I have to. Are we clear on this?"

He didn't smile. "Perfectly clear," he said. "I would do the same, in your position." He offered his hand again, and we clasped firmly. "Call on me if you need help, Cassiel. I find the world isn't as exciting now that I'm not in the thick of the fight."

An odd way to see things. I only wanted out of it, and back to my peaceful existence well away from this world and all its grubby problems.

He nodded, I nodded in return, and Quintus misted away. I had, I thought, made an ally. How reliable of one remained to be seen, but it helped me feel a little less alone, on this day when so much seemed against me.

One of the passing firefighters stopped and frowned at me. "Ma'am? Do you need help?"

"No." The kind of help I needed, I doubted I would get from him.

Manny, after his initial focus on making sure others were safe, was livid over the loss of his office and records. Our floor of the building was a total loss. I doubted one scrap of paper remained unburned.

"I kept telling you, bro, get all that crap archived. You ever listen to me? No." Luis, in the fashion of brothers throughout history, was not being helpful. "When's the last time you cleaned out those files, anyway?"

Manny sent me a don't-you-dare-speak glare. "Few weeks ago," he snapped. "And for your information, I *did* archive some stuff. Last year. Or—yeah, maybe a couple of years ago."

Luis just shook his head. Now that the crisis was past, he seemed to be finding this quite funny. "Look at it this way: You get to start fresh. Replace that crappy furniture that was left over from the Eisenhower administration."

"I *liked* that desk!"

"Nobody ever accused you of having taste, man."

We were making our way, slowly, to Manny's car. Luis had his own truck parked a little farther away. The fire trucks were still here, blocking off rows of cars, but ours seemed unimpeded. The police had taken our statements—or rather, taken Luis and Manny's statements. I had said little, except to support their general protestations of ignorance about the cause.

I wasn't at all sure the police officer had believed any of us. I wouldn't have, in his place. We definitely seemed suspicious.

We were almost to the car when Manny groaned. "Oh, man, just what I need."

"What?"

"The boss."

He meant the Weather Warden, Scott, who'd been so unpleasant during our last encounter. Scott was striding toward our small group, and his hangdog face was mottled red with fury.

I stepped out in front of Manny, taking the focus of his angry eyes, and Scott halted his advance.

"Are you threatening me?" he barked. I didn't respond or move, except for the wind lashing my soft white hair around my face. Somehow I knew that my very stillness would be more intimidating than an answer. "Manny! Call her off!"

"I don't own her," Manny said. "She's a person. Talk to her like one."

Scott clearly didn't want to stoop so low, but he nodded stiffly. "Please step aside, Cassiel."

I held my place for long enough to make him uneasy, then moved back, beside Manny.

Once again, I had acted to protect humans. *It's self-interest,* I told myself. *Nothing but that.*

Some part of me still wondered.

"What the hell happened here?" Scott asked. Manny was nervous; I could feel it coming from him in waves. He managed to keep his face expressionless.

"I don't know," he said. "It looks to me like either a Djinn or Warden attack, but we'll need a Fire Warden to get to the bottom of it. Could have been plain old human arson or some kind of electrical problem, even. Hard to tell."

Whatever Scott thought about that, he let it go. "Greta's out of town, handling a fire around Santa Fe. She'll be back in the morning. She'll do the investigation." He paused for a few seconds, then jerked his head to the side. "Talk to you alone for a minute?"

Manny joined him—again, not eagerly—and the two of them walked a few feet away. In the chaos of the parking lot, that was enough to shield them from human senses, and my own were so blunted that I could only pick out a few words here and there. It was sufficient to tell me that Scott was determined to paint this attack as some kind of shortcoming of Manny's.

"Hey," Luis said, and his hand touched my arm lightly.

"What?" I frowned at him.

"You look like you want to rip Scott's colon out through his nose. Thought I should mention it, in case you didn't want it to be quite that obvious."

It took a moment for his meaning to sink in. I had not been guarding myself as well as I'd thought, and that was cause for concern. How did humans manage all these complicated feelings, so easily betrayed by their faces and bodies? I'd thought I was learning, but obviously, I had far to go.

Luis was watching his brother and Scott with a cool light in his eyes. "That guy's a bureaucratic asshole," he said, "but the biggest danger Manny has from him is a busted performance review. Considering how few Wardens there are walking around these days, that's not exactly a mortal danger." His gaze shifted to me, and once again, I had an unwelcome flash of that vivid, unsettling dream, of the way his dream-skin had felt against mine. "Unless you know something I don't."

"Know something," I repeated.

"About the fire?"

"I know it was caused by a Warden," I said, "but I don't know the Warden's name. I've been assured that it won't happen again."

Whatever Luis had been expecting, it had not been that. "*What?* How do you know that?"

I shrugged. "Djinn."

He opened and closed his mouth, plainly searching for words and finding nothing. It was a satisfying display, which I watched with interest. He finally managed to gather his thoughts. "Listen, I don't care what the Djinn told you—and since when do they talk to you? I thought they threw you out—"

"They did."

He shook that off. "Whatever the Djinn said, somebody wanted both me and Manny standing in front of that door when it opened, and that means they were out to kill us. Call me crazy, but I think that they may not stop at just the one try!"

Quintus had seemed very sure about his former master, but it was possible that he was not in possession of all the facts . . . or that he had lied to me. Djinn did not usually lie to each other, but I was no longer one of them, no longer connected. . . .

I did not like the sick feeling in my stomach that came with these thoughts. *If he lied to me, I couldn't tell.* That was worse than unsettling. That was devastating.

"I don't know," I said, and my voice sounded soft and fragile. "I don't know if I can find out, Luis."

"You want to save Manny, don't you? He's your

meal ticket. Seems like it might be a good idea to keep on asking around." Luis's full lips quirked into something that resembled a smile, but somehow was not. "Even if you don't care if *I* get barbecued."

"I do," I said, and then wished I had not spoken at all, because his eyes widened and he *looked* at me. Saw me as something other than his brother's annoying, impaired partner.

I felt something inside me respond, a stirring I had not known, except in the dream. It was primal and dark and deep, and it felt . . . *good.*

I looked away, studying the ground, willing the feeling to subside. I felt warm, and too much in my skin.

"Good to know," Luis said, his voice carefully neutral. "Looks like my brother's done getting his ass chewed. *Vamanos.*"

Luis opened the passenger's-side door of Manny's car for me, and offered me a hand. I looked at it in confusion, then put my fingers in his palm, very lightly. He guided me into the car, and before he let go, Luis's thumb moved very lightly across my knuckles. It was an impersonal touch, or it should have been, but it traveled through me like a wave of light.

"See you later," he said, and shut the car door.

When I finally did raise my head, he was walking away, hands in his pockets. Another uncontrollable wave of heat flamed through me, and subsided to a banked glow deep inside.

I have no need of this, I told myself. *I need no complications. All I want to do is survive.*

My body, it seemed, thought differently of the matter.

I was so intent on watching Luis that I flinched when Manny opened his driver's-side door, thumped into the seat, and slammed the door with so much violence the car rocked. I looked at him, and his expression was still blank. His hands were rigid as they gripped the steering wheel, and his knuckles turned white from pressure.

"Bastard," he finally said, and turned the key to start the engine. "Let's get the hell out of here."

"Are you all right?" I asked.

The glance he threw me was bitter, black, and wild. "Sure. I'm just perfect. Why the hell wouldn't I be?"

I did not ask again, and we sat in silence as he drove too fast, too recklessly, all the way to his home.

Chapter 6

ANGELA WAS WAITING outside for our arrival—I
didn't think Manny had called, but I supposed that
Luis might have done so. She looked tense but carefully composed, and rose to her feet to embrace
Manny as he came up the front steps. She framed his
face between her hands, gave him a long, loving look,
and said, "Go get cleaned up; you smell like an ashtray."

He kissed her quickly and went inside, which left
the two of us standing together.

"Do I smell like an ashtray?" I asked.

Her lips curled unwillingly into a smile. "I'd guess
you do, but I'm not getting close enough to sniff you."
She cocked her head slightly, studying me. "You do
look more like a scarecrow than usual, *es verdad*.
After Manny gets through, maybe you can shower. I
can find you something to wear."

"No," I said. "I'll wear what I have." The thought
of wearing someone else's clothes made my skin crawl
with horror. "But I would be glad of the shower."

"No problem." Angela opened the screen door for
me as we entered the house. "Keep it down; Ibby's
taking a nap."

Ibby, in fact, was not. The child bounced up from
the couch and jumped in place, face alight with pleasure. "Cassie, Cassie, Cassie!"

I sighed. "*Cassiel*, please." For all the good I sensed it would do. Angela stifled a laugh.

I had no idea of the human protocol for such things, but I knelt down, and the child rushed my arms. Warm, chubby arms around my neck. A moist kiss on my cheek. "Ewwww, you smell like burning things," Ibby said.

"I'm about to wash it away," I said soberly. "Will that be better?"

She nodded vigorously, curls bouncing. "Were you at a fire?"

"Yes, Ibby."

"Were there firemen?"

"Yes, quite a few."

"Was it a big fire?"

"Big enough."

Ibby's dark eyes widened, and she looked around the room. I didn't understand at first, until her eyes filled with tears and she wailed, "Where's Papa?"

I had no experience of crying children, but luckily, Angela quickly encircled her daughter in her arms and patted her on the back. "Hush, *mija*, Papa's fine. Hear that? He's taking a shower right now."

"Was he in the fire?" Her small voice trembled.

"He was there with Cassiel," Angela said, and her gaze touched mine for a moment. "But look, they're both fine. She's fine, and Papa's fine. So what are you crying about, Ibby?"

Ibby's sobs became sniffles. "Nothing. I'm not crying."

"Good girl." Angela kissed her cheek and let her slip back to the floor. "Go play, *mija*."

Ibby wandered down the hall toward her room, pausing at the bathroom door to listen to the fall of water. She looked back at me doubtfully, and I nodded. I was trying to convey that her father was, in fact, fine; I couldn't tell if she believed that, but she went to her room at the end of the hall, and after a few moments I heard music playing.

Angela let out a slow breath. "She gets so anxious when she thinks something's happened. She knows Manny's got a hazardous job. We try to keep it away from her, but she's a smart girl. She knows."

I wanted to tell her that Manny was in no danger, but in truth, I couldn't be sure of that. Luis's words had robbed me of my confidence, made me doubt all my certainties. "I told you, I will watch over him," I offered. It felt awkward, but still, it also felt . . . right. I saw relief spread through her. *She trusts me to keep my word.* That felt oddly important—and also a weight on my shoulders.

"That'll make Ibby feel better," Angela said. She didn't say, *and me,* but I understood that to be true. "You probably need something cold to drink."

I was, in fact, thirsty, and I followed her to the kitchen, where she chatted about meaningless details of the day, as if we were friends. I supposed we were, in a way. I sipped the iced tea she prepared and nibbled at a cookie from a plate on the table.

Manny came in, hair damp and curling from the shower, dressed in fresh clothing. He grabbed a cookie and ate it in two bites. Angela kissed him on the cheek and gave him a glass of iced tea, and the two of them talked in Spanish for a moment. I was content to let the sounds wash over me. There was something oddly calming about such normality, even if it was so very human.

Ibby crawled up into the chair next to me and reached out for a cookie.

"Ibby!" her mother said sharply. The child pulled back and looked abashed. "Ask."

"May I please have a cookie, Mama?"

"Yes, you may have *one.*"

Ibby surveyed the plate and took the largest. I approved of her strategic approach.

"What did Scott say to you, Manny?" I asked. I reached for a second cookie. After all, I was both older and larger than the child. It seemed fair.

"That I should have sent the files off for archiving months ago," he said. "Some kind of regulations. Like we didn't have other things to worry about."

"He blames you?"

"Let's just say it won't come out in my favor in the report."

"Do you think—" I paused, because I realized that this might not be the best moment to pose the question. Still, it needed to be asked. "Do you think someone was aiming for you or Luis, rather than the destruction of the office?"

Manny looked tired. The fine lines around his eyes were etched more deeply than before, and his skin seemed more sallow. "Maybe," he said. "I don't know. I don't know why anybody would come after me."

"And Luis?"

He didn't answer. Angela did. "Lots of people got problems with Luis," she said. "He's the kind of guy who makes enemies, you know? A lot more than Manny."

I understood that, on some instinctive level; Manny was more concerned with his family, and while he had courage and determination, his goals were centered on his wife and child.

Luis was different. I couldn't tell what Luis desired, or what drove him, and that made him dangerous to me.

"Mama, may I have another cookie?"

"No."

"Cassie had two."

I broke my cookie in half and offered it to Isabel. "Cassiel," I said.

She giggled.

The laptop that Manny had provided me with was at my apartment. Upon arrival, I logged in, as Manny

had shown me, to the Warden computer system and
began to research Luis Rocha.

His personnel file was impressive and extensive.
The most recent entry was by someone I knew—
Joanne Baldwin, who commended Luis for his quick
action during a Florida emergency, an earthquake,
shortly before he had left the state to return here to
New Mexico. It must have happened before I had
fallen, though I'd had no hint of it, far above in
the aetheric.

Luis was more powerful than I had thought, and
better regarded among the Wardens. This was not necessarily a badge of honor; many Wardens were cor-
rupt, and no few of them had used their power for
their own enrichment. Power tempts humans in ways
that it does not seem to warp Djinn.

Then again, Djinn seemed to have many shortcom-
ings, as well, now that I was in human flesh.

In the earliest entries, notes were made of Luis's
gang affiliation. It had been a difficult decision, it
seemed, whether or not to bring Luis into the Wardens organization. They had almost decided to go the
opposite direction—use an Earth Warden to remove
his powers permanently. I knew something of that process. It was painful, and it had a significant failure
rate, both in terms of how often it worked and how
often the patients died.

Luis was lucky the Wardens had been too selfish to
give up a strong talent. But they had kept eyes on
him, and still did, from all indications.

Luis Rocha might be well thought-of by his peers,
but he was still not trusted by the administration. Interesting. I wondered if he knew.

I learned nothing more from the files, save what I
already knew: The Wardens regarded Luis as a much
stronger talent than his brother.

When I turned to Manny's personnel records, I

began to understand why. Manny was, without any question, loyal and honest, but he had failings, and they had been ruthlessly documented. Late paperwork. Failure to follow Warden regulations regarding office procedures. Sloppy documentation. These were not major infractions, only a long-standing pattern of behavior that had contributed to Manny being regarded as less than excellent at his job. Coupled with his low level of power, it meant that he would never rise much higher than his current position.

But nothing pointed to a reason anyone might wish him dead. There were no references of enemies, conflicts, *nothing*.

Manny did not make enemies.

Luis, on the other hand, did. He had exceptional successes, but his path was littered with conflict. I began to see a pattern to it, although it was not obvious; Djinn, after all, were students of patterns.

Those Luis had clashed with, both inside and outside of the Wardens, had been dishonest in some way. Like his brother, Luis cared fiercely about such things; unlike Manny, he often took on—and defeated—those who did not. Surprisingly, this had not harmed him as much as I would have expected. His records showed that every investigation of his conduct had been decided in his favor.

Unlike Manny's. No one was likely to be Manny's enemy; he was clearly his own.

I made a note of which Wardens particularly Luis had differed with over the years. There were only two names that appeared more than twice, and both were Fire Wardens: Landry Dent and Molly Magruder.

Molly Magruder was the only female on the list, and the Djinn at the office blaze had clearly referred to the arsonist as *her*.

She was not in New Mexico, but in the adjoining state of Texas, in a town called El Paso. It had an airport.

I decided to go to her.

It was only as I was going through the degrading and tedious process of security checks that I realized that I had not spoken to Manny about this, or asked for his permission to go. *I am not a slave,* I told myself. *I can come and go as I please.*

At my own risk, perhaps. If this came to a fight, I was as ready as possible; Manny had given me an infusion of Earth power before I'd left his house for the evening, and I had used almost none of it.

But I had the very strong feeling that Manny would also not be pleased with me for taking this initiative, and also, that he would be right in some way.

I didn't allow that to stop me.

The flight was short, thankfully, and uneventful; I could feel the energy coursing through the air and clouds, an ocean of power invisible to the humans seated with me in the aircraft. I found myself pressing my hand to the window, straining to touch what I knew I couldn't, and wondering when—if ever—these longings would subside.

El Paso was a desert town, surrounded by ancient, low mountains and capped with an overturned bright bowl of a sky—a blue even clearer than that of Albuquerque. The air was dry and crisp, the city older than I had expected, and more noisy, dirty, and crowded. It sprawled out through the desert in a jumble, even crawling the sides of the mountains.

It came as a surprise to realize that I did not know the simple mechanics of finding an address. I would have asked Manny, of course, but Manny was hundreds of miles away now, and a phone call might not be well received.

At a desk labeled INFORMATION I consulted a man who provided me with a map and explained how to summon a car for hire outside that would take me to the address I wished.

It was all pleasingly simple. Perhaps human life was not as complex as I'd been led to believe. . . . But this was a fantasy, and one that ended as I struggled to understand the terms *fare* and *tip*, and why one was not included in the other.

I had not made a friend when I dismissed the cab, and the problem of how I would return to the airport was still to be solved, but I stood in front of the address of Warden Molly Magruder. The street was called Dungarvin, and the house was a simple affair, only a little larger than the one Manny Rocha called home. It was well kept, with neatly trimmed trees and an edge of dry grass surrounding a desert-appropriate cactus garden near the front door.

It looked exactly as normal as the houses around it.

I walked to the door and knocked.

The woman who opened the door was about Manny's age, tall and heavy in her flesh. She had long blond hair twisted in a sloppy knot at the back of her head, and sharp blue eyes that took me in without much comprehension at first.

Awareness dawned quickly. I slapped a palm against the wooden facing of the door as she tried to slam it in my face.

"Molly Magruder," I said, "I've come to ask you why you tried to kill Luis Rocha."

She stepped back and stared at me as I crossed the threshold and quietly closed and locked the door. I leaned against the wood, arms folded.

"You're Djinn," she said.

"Perceptive," I replied, "but wrong. I am not Djinn. I am human."

She blinked. "Human."

"I am now."

"Well, it must just suck to be you."

I could not have agreed with her more. Molly backed away from me, bumped into a chair behind her, and stopped. I looked around the room. It was clean, spare, and showed nothing of the person who lived in its walls. Molly's furniture was square and serviceable. The artwork she had chosen to display was bland and uninspired. I found myself contrasting it with the vivid joy of Manny's household, or even the feminine strength of Joanne Baldwin's rooms.

Molly Magruder did not really exist here at all.

"Did Luis send you?" she asked.

"No. He doesn't know I've come."

"Then how—"

It was a confession, of a sort. "Quintus," I said. "Although he did not give me your name. But he was your Djinn, was he not?" I moved a tan pillow from one end of the couch and sat, crossing my legs with a whispering creak of leather. "Why do you hate Luis Rocha so bitterly?"

Molly stared at me for a long moment, and then— to my surprise—collapsed in the chair behind her and began to weep in wrenching, frantic sobs, like a desperate child. I had no idea what to do or say to such flagrant emotion, so I simply watched her, unmoving. After long moments, she got control of herself and glared at me through red-rimmed eyes.

"You don't know," she said. "You don't know *anything.*"

"Educate me," I said, and folded my hands.

Molly Magruder, it seemed, had been as much of a pawn in this as a Djinn slave had once been to her. She owed favors to another Warden, and that Warden had wanted two things from her: the destruction of the records filed in Manny's Albuquerque office, and—if possible—the death of Manny and Luis Rocha. Because she was safely removed from the area and had a history with Luis, she had been a logical choice for this task.

"You are willing to kill for a favor," I said. She sent me another glare, but despite the aggressive anger she tried to project, her hands were trembling, even clasped together.

"I didn't want to," she snapped. "It's political, okay? These things happen in the Wardens. People want other people out of the way sometimes. You wouldn't understand."

I understood all too well. Human ambition was a toxic thing, tainting everyone it touched. "Who?"

"I'm not telling you that."

She would, but I understood it would take time to convince her. "Explain to me *why*, then. Why someone would wish them dead."

She hadn't expected me to move away from the question so easily, and, caught off balance, she answered. "There was something in the records he didn't want found, I know that much."

"And the death of the Rocha brothers?"

"Personal," she said. "None of your business. None of mine, either."

"You don't care for Luis much, correct?" I got a bitter smile in response, and no other answer. "I met your Djinn. Quintus. It's a pity you aren't worthy of his trust. He seemed to care for you a great deal."

That wiped away her smile. "Leave Quintus out of this."

"I would like to leave you both out of it," I said. "All you need do is give me the name of the Warden who forced you to do this thing." The Warden had likely not *forced* her, but it seemed a politic way to describe things. She seemed to respond, regardless of the truth of the description.

"I can't do that." Still, despite her words, I sensed the force behind them was lessened.

"Do I need to threaten you?" I asked. I was careful to keep my words steady, my voice soft. Menace, I had found, was more effective delivered in that manner.

"With what?" The flash of scorn was back in her eyes. "You said you weren't a Djinn."

"That's true. I am worse than a Djinn by far." I leaned forward, and saw her flinch backward . . . just a bit. "I am a Djinn with the powers of an Earth Warden. That means I can stop your heart, explode your fragile veins, crush your bones—I can do worse than kill you, Molly Magruder. I can leave you a helpless prisoner inside your own flesh if I wish it. Or I could suck every bit of power from you, and leave you a dying husk."

I would not, of course; it would have meant breaking promises I had made to Lewis Orwell, and to Manny. But she could not know that, and I let no hint of it show in my steady, predatory stare.

Molly dropped her gaze to her trembling hands. "He can't know it came from me."

"He won't."

"How do I know—"

"You have my word."

She glanced up at me, then down. Her hair hid her face, but I did not sense she was tempted to lie to me. "A Weather Warden. His name is Scott."

"Scott," I repeated. "Scott Sands. In Albquerque."

She nodded. I stood up and walked to her side, crouched down, and looked into her face. It bled slowly white under the pressure of my stare.

"Listen to me," I said. "If you lie to me, I will not forgive. Do you understand?"

She did. "I'm not lying. It's Scott."

"On your life."

"On my life."

I rose to my feet with a shadow of my old Djinn grace. "Then you may have your life back," I said, and glanced around the gray, soulless house. "Such as it may be."

The small pink phone Manny had given me rang as I was waiting for a cab to arrive. I had been waiting for some time, and despite the fierce and constant sun, I was considering walking to the airport.

I pulled out the tiny machine and studied it. The small screen on the front was lit with a blue-white glow, and it spelled out MANNY CALLING. I examined the individual buttons and found one that seemed to indicate talking.

I wished, in short order, that I had not.

"Cassiel!" I heard his voice from a great distance, and cautiously put the phone closer to my ear. "*Dios mio*, I've been trying to get you. Where the hell are you?"

"El Paso," I said.

There was a long silence. Had I been born human, it might have seemed ominous.

"El Paso," he repeated slowly, at long last. "*Texas?*"

"It is on the border of New Mexico, as well. And Mexico, which is another country." I had been studying the maps. I was somewhat pleased with my ability to distinguish between *New* Mexico and the Mexico not designated as old.

"I know where it—look, what are—how did you—" He couldn't decide which question was more important, but I understood both.

"I came because I found someone who knew about the fire," I said. "I have spoken with her. I now know who set the fire, and why. As to how, I used an airplane. And a cab. Cabs are for hire."

Manny let loose a torrent of Spanish, which I did not bother to translate because the meaning was clear enough: He was not pleased. In midstream, he switched back to English. "—*solamente!* You don't go anywhere alone—you damn sure don't ditch me and go flying off to *Texas*! What if something had happened, you think of that?"

I was briefly warmed by his concern. Briefly, because he went on to say, "What if we'd had some kind of emergency here, and I needed you?"

"I see." My voice, well beyond my control, had taken on a flat, dark tone. I wondered if the small device was capable of relaying such subtleties. "Of course. I am at your disposal, Warden Rocha. Perhaps, instead of an apartment, you would prefer to furnish me with a bottle from which you could summon me at will."

"I didn't mean—" I heard an explosive rattle of air on the speaker from his end. "All right, maybe I did. You work for us, remember? That means you do what the Wardens tell you to do. And you get paid. If you want to break that agreement and go running off without support or notice—"

"I am sorry. I thought it was the correct course of action."

"And you didn't tell me because . . . ?"

Because Manny would have proceeded cautiously, and I didn't think we could afford such slow progress. "It was an error in judgment," I said. It was difficult to say the words, even if I knew them as false. "I am coming back now."

"Damn straight you are. Look, you okay? Nothing happened, right?"

A yellow car turned the corner and slowed as it came toward me. "Nothing has happened," I said. "I will see you in a few hours."

I pressed the OFF button before he could ask more questions. I was not certain of the security of these devices, and speaking in the open seemed to me to be a risk we could not afford to take. Perhaps it would have been safe, but it was safer still to wait to talk in private, face-to-face.

The cabdriver was a quiet man, which suited me well. I watched the city roll by the car window during the short drive back to the airport, paid him in cash (adding in the tip this time without being instructed) and was getting out of the vehicle when he said, "Hope you're flying out soon."

I paused. "Why?"

He nodded at the eastern horizon. "Storm's coming."

The next flight back to Albuquerque was a three-hour wait, and I spent it watching passersby, looking for Djinn. I spotted two—a male and female traveling together, disguised as college-age humans, complete with backpacks. They gazed at me in turn, for long moments, and then went about their business without comment.

I had known them once, but their reaction only served to tell me again how far I had fallen, and how isolated I was from what had been my family.

I turned my attention outward to the storm. The cabdriver was correct; the city of El Paso had a hot, dry climate, but a few times a year—sometimes only once a year—a storm formed in the normally stable air. The amount of rain it would dump would be, by the standards of most areas, negligible—an inch or two, perhaps.

In El Paso, it would result in deaths, as those unaccustomed to driving on wet streets lost control, or the flood canals went from dry canyons to raging rivers.

The clouds had a velvety darkness to them, a solidity that I could almost feel as they swept across the sky, spreading like spilled ink. The sun flared brightly, then was swallowed and became a pale ghost, barely a bright circle through the clouds. . . . And then it was gone altogether.

The vicious growl of thunder shook the plate glass windows of the lounge where I sat.

An overhead speaker finally announced the boarding of my flight. Mindful of Manny's lessons, I waited until my ticket group was called, walked the jetway with the rest, and then settled myself in the narrow, uncomfortable seat with care. Had I still been able to shift my form, I'd have shortened my legs; as it was, I twisted to one side to avoid having my knees deeply buried in the next row's cushions.

My cell phone rang again. Manny, of course. I started to answer it, but the uniformed attendant told me it was not allowed. I switched the phone off instead, settled back as much as I could, and waited for takeoff.

The fine hairs on my arms began to prickle. I looked down, puzzled by this response from a body I had at least begun to understand, and the muted fragments of Djinn senses that I still possessed screamed a warning.

I had only an instant in which to act, and no real knowledge to guide me—instinct alone would save or damn me.

This was an attack by weather, and since my power flowed from Manny's, I had little dominion over that aspect of things. What I *could* do, however, was insulate the aircraft by sinking the wheels themselves beneath the tarmac, all the way into raw dirt.

Lightning hit the fuselage of the plane with the force of an explosion, blowing out fuses and plunging the interior into muddled darkness. *The fuel,* I thought, and quickly shifted my focus to the massive tanks. It would take only a spark to set it off, and although the plane was now insulated, I could feel the lightning *hunting* for a vulnerability.

This was being directed. Directed by a Weather Warden, without any question.

Chemical reactions came under the aegis of the Fire Wardens, but the petrochemical fuel was, in large part, of the Earth, and I was able to keep it from exploding.

It was a very, very close thing.

When the assault finished, amid the screaming of humans around me, I leaned back in my chair and listened to the sound of the rain hitting the fragile skin of the aircraft. It pounded in fury, expressing the rage of the Warden who had driven it here.

Peace, I thought to it. *I don't want to be here, either.*

I felt sick, weak, and empty, but the people around me were alive. So was I.

It was something, in a world of nothing.

After far too much fuss and bother, we were moved to another plane. By the time the flight finally departed, the brief, violent storm was breaking, and the sun burning away the black clouds.

Manny met me at the Albuquerque airport.

If I had expected a welcome, I would have been disappointed; no smiles for me, only the fiercest of frowns and a hard grip on my arm to march me toward the exit.

"We were delayed," I said. "The first plane was struck by lightning."

"Yeah, I know. Accidentally on purpose. Don't say anything until we're in the van."

The van was idling at the passenger pickup location, and the driver was Luis Rocha. He gave me the smile that Manny had not, as I slid into the seat behind him. Manny climbed into the passenger's side and slammed the door with vicious fury.

"Drive," he told Luis. Luis cocked an eyebrow toward me as he shifted the van into drive and pulled into traffic.

"He's been like this all day," Luis said. "You owe me for putting up with him."

I did not reply. I was watching Manny, trying to determine why he was so angry with me. Granted, I had not asked his permission to travel, but did he truly expect that I would? It seemed difficult to believe. I was not a slave, nor was I a child.

"Who is it?" Manny asked me. "You said you knew who started the fire. Who?"

"I spoke with a Warden in El Paso named Molly Magruder. She is directly responsible."

Luis's reaction was instructive; he flinched, and the van veered until he quickly corrected it. Behind us, someone honked a horn in annoyance. Luis made a rude gesture out the window.

"And?" Manny prodded. He'd noticed his brother's reaction too, but he didn't comment.

"She created the fire, but it was at the request of someone else. Your boss," I said. "Scott. The same Weather Warden who just tried to silence me, and a plane full of innocent people, in El Paso."

That brought a long, thoughtful silence, during which the two brothers exchanged glances. Luis shrugged. Manny, I thought, went from angry to seeming a bit ill.

"You're sure about this?"

"Sure? No. I have the word of Molly Magruder, and the attack on my aircraft. I cannot positively identify a Warden by his actions, unless I'm connected to him."

Luis cleared his throat. "That might be a little tough, then, because we just got a bulletin come over the Warden network. Molly Magruder was killed."

"Killed," I repeated. It did not immediately hit me what this might mean. "Killed how?"

"Murdered," Luis said. "She was found in her house, dead. Somebody had crushed her heart inside her chest." He shifted his gaze from the road to the rearview mirror, and met my eyes. "Somebody like an Earth Warden."

"Or a Djinn," I said.

"Exactly. You got anybody that saw her alive after you left her house? Maybe saw her waving bye-bye to you from the door?"

"No. I did not see her again. The driver picked me up at the curb." I began to understand exactly what he meant, and it was unpleasant. "You mean that they will believe that I killed her."

"Did you?" Manny was looking out the window, not at me. Luis gave me another quick, almost involuntary glance in the mirror.

"No."

"That's all you've got to say about it?"

"I left her alive. I took a cab to the airport. I boarded a plane, which was attacked by a Weather Warden. What more is there to tell?"

"She's got a point," Luis offered. "She can't just make up an alibi out of nothing."

"I'm not asking her to! But there's got to be some way to prove—"

"Find the killer," I said. "It isn't Scott, clearly; he was well capable of attacking me at the airport, but it takes an Earth Warden to crush a heart in the chest."

"Or a Djinn," Manny said.

"Or both."

Manny looked directly at me. "I think you'd better explain why Ashan hates you so bad."

I was wondering just when the subject would arise; I was surprised that it hadn't already, as Manny felt more and more comfortable around me. "I can't," I said.

"Won't," Luis supplied. "That's what she means."

"Yes, *won't*," I said sharply. "It's Djinn business, and none of yours."

"It's our business when we're neck deep in it!"

"That has nothing to do with *this*! This is some petty Warden political—"

"We don't *know* what this is, and neither do you! I'm sick of your damn secrets!" Manny's shout overrode mine. I sank back against the upholstery and turned my attention out the window, shutting him and his brother out for the time being. I crossed my arms, then remembered that humans did that in arguments to indicate they were set in their opinions. I uncrossed them and put my hands in my lap instead—not because I wasn't set in my opinion, but because I did not want to be seen as that human.

Ignoring them quieted things down considerably. The remainder of the conversation occurred between Luis and Manny, and it was in lower tones. I did not pay much attention, watching as the streets and houses of Albuquerque flashed by.

We pulled to a halt in front of Manny's house. Angela and Ibby were in the front yard, and Ibby immediately bounded to the fence to wave as Manny and Luis descended from the van. Manny, in a fit of very human pique, did not open the back sliding door for me. It proved more difficult to manage than I'd thought, and so I was just exiting the vehicle as Manny and Luis crossed the street and entered the front yard gate.

A car started its engine down the block and pulled out into the road, heading toward us—a large black car, with heavily tinted windows. Older. More solidly built than newer models. I did not pay it much mind, save to wait for it to pass so that I could cross the street.

It slowed a little as it approached.

I saw Luis recognize the danger first—a widening of his eyes, a cold shock in his expression. He was closest to Ibby, and he grabbed her and hurled her violently to the ground. Her scream cut the morning like a silver knife, just an instant before the air shattered under the thunder of guns firing.

I saw Angela and Manny fall. Luis dived for the ground, covering Isabel.

Bullets pocked pale holes in the house behind them, shattered windows.

The black car applied speed and screeched around the nearest corner.

I screamed in rage, and the day went red. *They dared. They dared attack those I protected!*

I did not think about my actions. I simply threw myself into pursuit.

Human bodies are not meant for such excesses, but I poured energy recklessly into my tissues, forcing the muscles to extreme efforts, and although the car accelerated away, I began to catch up. I heard yelling inside the black sedan, and a gun appeared from the back right side and fired at me. I dodged and continued to gain on them.

The car took another corner on two wheels. More gunfire opened up, this time from the passenger's side of the vehicle.

It missed.

I gained.

When I sensed my muscles were capable of no more effort without serious damage, I slowed. The sedan pulled away, and I heard whoops of victory from within it.

If they had seen the snarl that formed on my face, they would not have celebrated so quickly.

The paved street rose up to my command, twisting and cracking in an oncoming wave six feet tall. The car slammed into it at killing speed, and the sound of rending metal and shattering glass was louder than gunfire.

I quickly eased the ground back into place. The asphalt topping was broken and pitted, but that could not be helped. I saw the red glow at the edges of my vision sparkle into black, and knew that I was in danger of overextending myself, spending too much power. Not even rage could fuel me past that point.

I walked up to the shattered car. Inside were shattered humans. Some were even alive, though I did not think they would be for long. For a moment, I wondered if I should feel something for them—regret for ending their lives? They were young, but they had fired guns at a child younger still, and that I could not forgive.

I pulled out my cell phone and dialed the emergency number Manny had shown me to report an accident, and began the walk back to the house. After a few moments, I realized how exhausted I was, how much that effort had drained from me. More than I'd expected.

More than I could afford.

Manny will help, I thought, and something flickered inside of me, a pale shadow of a connection. *Manny?*

The connection snapped, a physical sensation that brought with it a white-hot flash of pain. I stopped, panting, and braced myself with my hands on my knees.

Manny?

I forced myself to a jog. People were peering from their windows, looking at the steaming wreckage in the middle of the street; a few noticed me, but there was little to connect me to the event other than proximity. I kept moving. I heard sirens, but the emergency and police response was from behind me.

I turned the corner and slowed to a walk. Manny's house was within view, eerily quiet now that the shooting was done. I could not see anyone. Likely they had all gone inside, which would be a sensible thing to do. . . .

No, I saw Isabel. She was huddled next to the fence, clearly terrified. Her small fists were balled up to cover her mouth.

And then I saw Luis Rocha, on his knees next to two prone human bodies. There was blood on his hands, splashed on his shirt. Thin threads of it on his face. As I watched, he put the palm of his right hand on the chest of the man lying on the ground. He braced it with the left, then pumped, hard, five times.

Leaned forward to tilt the head back and breathe into the open mouth.

He was gasping and sweating with effort. Luis's eyes fixed on me, and all the pieces flew together, took on weight and meaning. It all hit me with the force of a head-on collision.

Manny. Manny was lying on the ground. Manny was bleeding.

He was trying to save Manny's life. Next to Manny, Angela was already dead, with a bullet lodged in her brain. I could sense the inert darkness in her. Her life, her energy, was gone, fled beyond where I could chase.

"Get over here!" Luis screamed at me. I vaulted the fence and ran to his side, knelt beside him, and took his hand. I had no power left, barely enough to continue to nourish my human body, but what I had, I gave.

It was not enough. Luis's Earth powers were already depleted from his efforts, and although I tried to amplify what was left, it was too little, the damage too great.

Manny's heart had been shredded by the force of the bullet. Another had broken his spine.

He was dead. The last wisps of energy faded out of him, left the body empty and dark in front of me.

Luis realized it at the same moment, and as I glanced up at him, I saw the overwhelming horror and loss dawn in his face.

"No," he said. "No. *No!*"

I said nothing. There was too much inside of me, too much to understand, to feel, to process. Manny was *gone.* He would never laugh at me again, or be angry, or take my hand and give me some of his life. He had no life to give. He was no longer in the flesh stretched out before me.

Angela. Angela would never make her child another meal, touch her with love and kindness, wipe away her tears. Angela had made me food in her kitchen, and smiled at me.

They were my friends.

They were *dead*.

I was unprepared for the harsh burn of grief. It made the world unsteady around me, made me tremble deep within, and I could think of nothing, *nothing* to do. Tears stung in my eyes, and I felt them fall, cold as diamonds.

Luis's dark eyes locked on mine, and they ignited not with tears, but with fury. "Where were you?" he screamed, and grabbed me by the shoulders to shake me with brutal force. "You *bitch*, where did you go? They were dying! *They were dying!*"

I understood then. Angela and Manny had fallen as I'd taken up the pursuit of the car. I had left Luis alone with them, with the overwhelming task of trying to save one or the other . . . or neither.

I had spent my energy in vengeance. Would it have made a difference if I had immediately linked with Luis and struggled to heal the damage done? *No,* something inside of me said, but I couldn't be sure of that. If I'd acted for life, instead of death . . .

Luis shook me again, screaming at me in Spanish.

I knocked his hands away with a sharp impact of my forearms against his and took in a steadying breath. My heart was racing, my tears falling in cold streams. I felt dead inside, not merely from the expense of power but from the loss of something I had not even known I could value.

"Isabel," I said. Luis, face still contorted in fury and grief, rocked back on his heels, away from me, and looked at his niece. She was weeping, curled in a ball with a dirty-faced doll clutched to her chest.

"Oh, *mija*," he whispered, and the anger melted from him. "Oh, no."

He got to his feet, moving like a man twice his age, and picked the girl up in his arms. I put a hand on her back—partly to comfort, and partly to sense her physical condition.

She was unharmed, though Luis's hands left streaks of her father's blood on her clothes.

"Take her inside," I said. "Call the police."

He walked up the front steps to the door. Isabel's eyes were open but seeing nothing. She was sucking her thumb.

Luis turned her face away from her parents and me, and sent me a glare that would have quailed even Ashan. "You should have stayed, you Djinn bitch," he told me. "If you'd stayed, they'd be alive."

I knew, as I knelt next to the dead body of the man who had been my Conduit, and my first real friend, that Luis was right.

I should have stayed.

Chapter 7

STRANGE, HOW ONE person's tragedy so quickly becomes someone else's job. The ambulance attendants first, though their efforts were small; they knew well that neither Angela nor Manny would ever rise again. They left the bodies there, in the front yard, for the police. As they walked away, they were talking about stopping for a meal.

As if life went on.

I wanted to destroy them, snuff them out like candles, but I knew that Manny and Angela would not want it so. I didn't have the power to do it, either.

I stood, still and quiet, waiting. *I won't leave you*, I told them. *Not again.*

The police arrived moments later—a marked cruiser, with flashing lights and sirens. One of the officers immediately made a straight line for me; the other began moving back crowds of neighbors and passersby who had gathered to gawk.

"Ma'am?"

I focused away from Manny's bloody, empty face to the smooth expression of the policeman opposite me.

"What's your name?"

"Cassiel," I said. He wrote something down and waited, as if I should have more to say. Ah yes. Last names. Humans had last names, denoting family lineage. "Rose. Cassiel Rose." So read the identification card in my pocket. When he asked, I produced it, and he wrote down more information before handing it back.

"Can you tell me what happened here?"

I did, as best I could. The black sedan approaching, the gunfire. Chasing the car. I stopped short of admitting that I'd caused the crash.

He let several beats of silence go by when I was finished. "You . . . chased them."

"Yes."

"You chased a car full of gang-bangers who'd just shot up a house."

"Yes." I didn't know why he was asking. I didn't think I had been unclear.

"You catch up with them?" he asked.

"The car crashed," I said absently. "I called the ambulance."

"Lady—" He shook his head. "What the hell were you thinking? They could have killed you, too."

Certainly. I wondered why he thought I did not know that, but I remained silent.

"You know these two?"

"Yes," I said softly. "Manny and Angela Rocha. They live here with their daughter, Isabel."

"Isabel," he repeated, scribbling in his notebook. "Where's the daughter?"

"Inside with her uncle Luis. She's five."

He paused, glancing up at me, and made another note. "She was here when it happened?"

"Yes."

"And the uncle?"

"Yes."

"Either one of them injured?"

"No."

"Did you see any of the people shooting?"

I shook my head. "I was on the other side of the street," I said. "Getting out of the van."

He tapped a pencil on his notebook. "How are you connected with all this?"

"What do you mean?"

"Come on, lady. You don't exactly fit in around here."

I supposed that I didn't. It wouldn't have taken a great detective to determine such a thing. "I'm a colleague of Manny Rocha's," I said. "I work with him."

That seemed acceptable. "Where?"

"Rocha Environmental Services."

"And you do—what, exactly?"

I gave him a flat, emotionless stare. "Analysis."

Whether he believed that or not, it didn't seem he was inclined to press. He took down my telephone number and address, and went inside the house to speak with Luis.

Again, I was alone with the dead.

Death, for Djinn, is dissolution—being unmade. Undone, as I'd been undone by Ashan. But this . . . the flesh remained, a constant reminder of what was lost. Manny's eyes were open, the pupils huge and dark, and I wanted awareness to return to his body. I wanted him to look at me once more. I wanted to tell him that I was sorry for my choices.

He is not lost, something told me. *Nothing is lost.*

But my connection to him was gone, and even if Manny's soul had passed on, it had traveled to a place I could not reach and might never reach. There was a hole here, in this world, where he had been.

I was alone. Strange that it should hurt so much.

Next came a rumpled, tired-looking detective, who asked the same questions again. I gave the same answers. He also spoke with Luis, who remained in the house, and then a coroner's van arrived.

I thought it odd that it took almost an hour before Manny and Angela were at last declared dead. I remembered older days, older ways—a priest might have tapped them on the forehead with a small hammer, to claim them for the gods then, but no one would have questioned that they were dead. But in these days, these times, pictures were taken to document their ends, and then they were lifted and sealed into black plastic sheaths.

Taken away.

I watched as their bodies were removed, and felt another pang of loss. Death happened in stages among humans, and with each step another tie severed. How many remained?

You don't have to feel it at all, something in me said. *You could leave. Go back to the Wardens and tell them you want a new posting. You need never see Luis Rocha or Isabel again.*

It was so tempting to walk away, to leave this behind in the human world where it belonged. To start over. I could choose to walk away. It would be easy.

It would be a Djinn thing to do.

Instead, I sat down on the front porch step and waited.

In time, the police cars left, the onlookers dispersed. The phone inside began to ring, and I heard the muted sound of Luis's voice, explaining to callers what had happened. Friends, family, perhaps the Wardens had called, as well.

Isabel cried. She wailed. It was the sound of a child realizing that her world had broken around her. I was not human. I could not give her false promises, and the thought still lingered in me, *I could leave.* Just walk away from all this pain, this senseless, stupid waste.

As night began to fall, the front screen door slammed, and with a creak of wood, Luis settled down next to me on the steps. He smelled of soap and shampoo, freshly laundered clothing. No trace of Manny's death still remained on him.

He did not speak for a while. We watched the sun go down in a bright blaze of colors.

"Isabel wants to see you," he said. "You coming in?"

I turned and looked at him. He did not meet my gaze.

"For the kid," Luis said. "Not for me. I don't care what the hell you do."

I stood up and walked into the house. It smelled like—home. The still-lingering aroma of Angela's last meal on the air. Clean, warm, welcoming. In the kitchen, plates and glasses still remained in the sink, waiting to be washed; I drew hot water and added soap, and scrubbed them sparkling before I went to the child's bedroom.

Luis had tucked her securely in her bed, but she was not asleep. Her thumb was still in her mouth, and her eyes were dark and very wide.

I sat down on the edge of the bed and very carefully stroked her silken dark hair. "Ibby," I said. "I am here."

She didn't speak, but she curled against me. Tears leaked silently from her eyes. I picked her up in my arms, heavy and warm and human, and rocked her until she began to cry in earnest. Chubby arms around my neck, holding tight.

I buried my face in the clean cotton of her nightgown. It was for her comfort, not my own. Djinn did not grieve. Djinn *walked away*.

It took hours, but she fell asleep still in my arms. I tucked her back in her bed and went out into the living room, where Luis sat in the dark.

I crouched down next to his chair, putting our eyes at a level, though he did not look at me.

"I would not ask," I said, "except that Manny is gone. I need—" My tongue didn't want to finish the request. Luis's dark eyes shifted, and the look sent shivers through me.

"You need power," he said. "Yeah?"

I nodded. I held out my thin white hand, and his own large, strong one closed over it in a crushing grip.

"Fine," he said. "Here. Take it."

Power rushed across the link, burning and angry, and I gulped down all I could before finally yanking my hand free of his. He continued to glare at me, and the stolen fire inside me gave me an insight I didn't want.

"You blame me," I said.

"Of course I blame you."

"Yet the men in the car were shooting at you, not at me." I said it calmly, without accusation, but Luis flinched as though struck. "Isn't that true?"

He didn't answer. He looked through me, to some event in his past that I couldn't read. As a Djinn, I could have known; as a human, I would not have even seen the shape of it. This frustrating middle ground made my head ache with possibilities.

"Maybe," he said at last. "The police say it was a car full of Norteños, so maybe they were aiming for me. Why? Does that make you feel better about leaving Manny and Angela alone to die while you played the big, bad Djinn hero?"

It was my turn to flinch, inwardly at least. "Even had I been there, even had I used every ounce of power inside me and destroyed myself in the process, I could not have saved Angela. She was dead the moment the bullet entered her brain. It's not likely I could have repaired the damage to Manny's heart, either."

He knew that. He was an Earth Warden; his analysis would have shown him the same thing, but he could not, would not, accept it.

The night stretched on in silence, and finally Luis said, "Get out. I don't want you in their house."

I rose to my feet, but didn't move to the door. "Isabel—"

"She's my niece. I'll take care of her." His bloodshot eyes fixed on mine. "Go away. Get your free lunch somewhere else. You don't belong here."

No one—human or Djinn—had *ever* spoken to me so, in such words, in such tones. It should have been a death sentence for him, with as much power as tingled in my veins.

Instead, I walked away. I left the house, closing the door quietly behind me, and as I stood out in the dark, I realized that I had no car and no way to get to my home.

I pointed myself in the right direction, and began to walk.

I did not go home. I walked to the building, but there was nothing inside it to draw me. Instead, I walked all night, thinking. The world passed in a blur of lights, noise, distant laughter. None of it mattered. I couldn't leave the prison of my own body, and inside that cage I waited, trapped, for *something*.

In the morning, my cell phone began to ring. Messages from the Wardens organization. Manny had likely been right; they were assuming that I'd had a hand in the death of the Warden in El Paso.

It occurred to me that I did have something I could do. Something to channel this dark need inside of me. Something to lash out at this world that had hurt me.

Manny's superior officer in the Wardens, Scott Sands, lived in an expensive high-rise building in downtown Albuquerque, one that commanded a view of the pine-covered mountains. Once again, I walked; the feeling of movement was important to me, and I was in no great hurry. Not now.

The apartment building had electronic security, which was a simple thing to confound. I took the steps at a run. When there were no more steps, I opened the door to the top level—a quiet, carpeted hall with solid, expensive doors.

I could have knocked, perhaps.

Instead, I blew open the door to 1514, and then I

shattered the the plate glass windows that composed the entire back wall of the apartment. Cold mountain wind shrieked in, sending Scott Sands lurching to his feet in surprise. He was still in his bathrobe and slippers. I was happy to see that he lived alone—I would not have hesitated had he put his family in the line of fire, but neither would I have relished it.

But alone—ah, that was a different thing, and I could take my time about it.

He cowered before me, and then, of course, he remembered he was a Warden, and he counterattacked.

Electricity arced from every power outlet in the apartment, formed a pink-tinged bolt in the palm of his hand, and arrowed toward me.

I dodged it easily. It struck the walls of his apartment and splashed in a burning spray across his carpet, crisping it into stinking slag.

"Is that your best effort?" I asked, and began walking toward him. "I was expecting more from a hardened killer, Scott. Perhaps you should try again."

He scrambled away from me, pale legs flashing beneath his fluffy black bathrobe. The wind pushed at him, sending papers flying in a white storm around us.

He used the wind, whipping the papers into a cutting vortex between us. I had no command of the wind, but because the power I'd taken was Earth power, I had command of the paper, and I sent it hurtling inward to cover him in a choking, smothering cloud. It rammed against his mouth, nose, and eyes, triggering panic.

He lost control of the vortex.

I had my hand around his throat before he could claw the clinging sheets from his eyes, and the Earth power coursing through my veins made me far stronger than a human of my size. It would have been easy to crush him.

I held him still instead, staring into his wide, frightened eyes. Thinking of Manny's open eyes, the last time I had seen them. Open and so empty.

"You hired the Fire Warden to burn Manny Rocha's office," I said. "And to kill Manny and Luis, if possible. Yes?"

He clawed at my hand, but he would have had more luck opening a vise with feathers. "Yes," he choked out. "Yes!"

"Were you responsible for the shooting?" He didn't answer. His pupils were huge, his face growing purple. It occurred to me that he might need breath to speak, and I loosened my grip enough to let a trickle of air into his lungs. "I'm not in a good mood, Warden Sands. Please answer swiftly."

"No," he gasped. "No!"

"Why did you destroy Manny's office, then?"

"I—can't breathe—"

"That is the point of choking you," I pointed out. "Haste, please, if you want to live."

Scott's face was distended, his eyes bulging, and there was true panic in him now. He'd kill me if he could, but I had the upper hand, and it was crushing his throat.

"Orders," he managed to scrape out. "From the Ranch."

"The Ranch," I repeated. It meant nothing to me. "Whose ranch? Where?"

"Mistake," he wheezed. "Papers. Had to kill them, in case they knew."

He wouldn't speak another word, not even when I squeezed tighter. At last, I dropped him semiconscious to the floor and crouched down next to him, staring into his eyes. The terror in him was close to madness.

"You fear your masters more than you fear me," I said. I didn't need his acknowledgment; it was clear enough. "Do you really think that's wise, Warden

Sands? I think you understand how little I care about your pathetic life just now."

He blinked at me and said, "You don't know. You don't understand."

"Clearly, I don't care."

He laughed. *Laughed.* It was a raw, broken sound, and then he rolled over to his hands and knees, the robe loose and dragging as he crawled.

He reached the windowsill and glanced back at me, and I saw the light of madness in his eyes.

"You can't fight her," he said. "I'd like to see you try, bitch."

And then he pitched forward, out into empty space.

I moved to the window and slapped aside the blowing, lashing curtains. Beyond, the fragile blue of the New Mexico sky burned over the mountains, and the sun shone brightly.

There was no sign of Warden Scott Sands on the pavement below. It was as if he had . . . flown away.

Wardens had unique powers, it was true, but even had he been capable of such a feat, he would have still been visible against the clear morning sky.

He was simply . . . gone. As if—and this struck me deep, and badly—as if he had walked away, into the aetheric. Wardens could not. Djinn could . . . but Sands was no Djinn. And there were only a few of my kind capable of carrying humans unharmed through the aetheric. Fewer still who would be at the beck and call of humans.

I stayed where I was for a long moment, staring out at the impossible, and then I walked slowly across the broken glass to the shattered door. I heard the sirens below on the street, likely responding to my explosive entry into this apartment.

Once again, I felt the net drawing tight around me, and I didn't know how to stop it. This was human business, Warden business, and a Djinn had no place in it.

My phone rang. This time, as I took the stairs down to street level, I answered it.

"Hey," a male voice said. "It's Lewis Orwell. And you're in one hell of a lot of trouble."

"I know," I said.

"You kill anybody, Cassiel?"

"No." Not technically. "Possibly the four in the car who shot Manny. Do they count?"

He sighed. "That's a question we don't have time to get into. You kill any Wardens?"

"No."

"Because I've been told you did." He paused for a second. "Manny's dead. Did you have anything to do with it?"

"No," I said. "I was there. I saw it."

Someone was coming up the stairs. I froze on the landing where I was, pressed my shoulders to the concrete, and willed myself invisible. This was an Earth Warden trick, using only a fraction of my power, and it worked beautifully; the police officers jogged past me, heading up. I waited until they had turned two flights before continuing on my way.

"I need your help," I said.

"Can't. We've got big-time problems of our own right now. All the Wardens I can grab are coming with me, out of the country. Most of the Djinn are coming, too. The best I can do for you is to tell you where to find some resources."

"Resources?"

"Money. Identification." I heard the sound of the ocean, strong and rhythmic, through the speaker of the phone. "I need to go. You won't be able to reach me again until I get back, so be careful. Are you ready for the information?"

"Yes," I said. "Ready."

Unexpectedly, what he gave me was not addresses, but coordinates—numbers. I memorized them and repeated them back, and then, just as quickly, Lewis was gone, the phone call ended.

When I tried to call back, the number didn't respond.

The Wardens were facing dangers that had nothing to do with me. Even the Djinn were involved. I had the strong feeling that my survival now rested solely with me, and if I wished to find any kind of justice for Manny Rocha, any kind of justice for his wife and his daughter, then I would need to save myself first.

Alone.

I descended the remaining flights of stairs and slipped out a service entrance. My appearance was no longer simply exotic, but dangerously obvious. I would need *things.*

Luckily, the human world was full of them.

I dyed my hair in the restroom of a gas station. The harsh chemical smell clung to me even after I had wiped away the excess and dried my hair as best I could using the bathroom's blower mechanism. It no longer looked like a white puffball, at least. Instead, it looked like a *pink* puffball, lighter at the ends. I resembled, I realized, one of the unhealthy-looking pink snacking cakes in the convenience store's shop.

With the last of my cash, I bought changes of clothes and makeup. I deliberately chose unusual styles, in garishly colored layers, and made up my face in dramatic neon strokes. I looked young and outrageous, and I noticed that following this transformation most humans avoided eye contact with me.

I was no longer immediately recognizable as the pale albino woman in white who had been spotted at the scene of so many deaths, and that was all I wanted.

Lewis's coordinates led me to the heart of Albuquerque, in Old Town, to a shaded spot next to the blocky tan-and-brown structure of the National

Atomic Museum. It was just a bare patch of earth, and a large flat rock. Humans had scrawled obscure messages on its surface, but time was bleaching them into history, and I wondered for a moment how he expected me to find anything in so empty a place.

One of the obscure messages caught my eye, because it was the glyph of the Wardens—an odd place for it to be lurking, most surely. I traced it with a fingertip, and then lifted the rock.

Beneath it was damp earth, but it formed a slight hollow—as if something had been buried beneath. I dug with my fingers and brushed cool metal—a cylinder, a type of container with a screw-on lid. It was welded shut, in a way that any competent Earth Warden would have been able to unseal but that would resist simple human tampering; I burned my fingertips opening it, but the reward was a folded piece of notepaper and three plastic bags.

The note, although unsigned, was clearly from Lewis Orwell, and it said,

> *If you're holding this, you're an Earth Warden in trouble, and I decided you were worth helping. The bags contain cash, two new credit cards with high limits, and a set of clean ID documents for you to alter. One thing: If you use any of this without my authorization, I'll kill you. Call first. You know the number.*

I presumed that since Lewis had sent me here, there was little need for another phone call. I opened each bag in turn. Cash—several thousand dollars in old bills. Two credit cards, as he'd promised, in the neutral-gender name of Leslie Raine. The identification—a Texas driver's license, birth certificate, and passport—were in the same name. The photograph was of an extremely generic human, androgynous. I concentrated on each of them in turn, adjusting the pigments within the photographs until the image more closely resembled me, including my newly pink hair.

I wrote my name and the date on the back of the note and put it back in the cylinder, sealed it, and buried it beneath the rock again.

Leslie Raine.

It seemed as much my name as any other.

I left Albuquerque on a newly purchased motorcycle. The motor vehicle permit that had come with my new identity, I was told, would not allow me to operate the machine legally until I took the tests necessary, but despite my new disguise I didn't feel comfortable placing myself on police property to achieve that goal. I simply asked to see an example of a motorcycle license, which would allow me to make the necessary alterations to the license I had.

I solemnly lied to the vendor that I would go straight to the appropriate authority to obtain the proper documents. He was less inclined to question me once the credit card purchase went through, and I added a black helmet, white leather jacket, gloves, and chaps. I donned those in the changing room, picked up the helmet, mounted the motorcycle, and taught myself the mechanics of it in a few moments.

"You sure you can handle that?" the salesman asked me as I went over the controls. "That's a lot of motorcycle, lady."

Indeed, it was. The motorcycle was a sleekly designed Victory Vision in gray and steel, and it had cost the Wardens quite a bit of money. Still, I felt it was better than buying a car; I was doubtful that I'd want to be trapped in a steel box for hours on end, but this seemed freeing. Powerful.

I started the engine and savored the shivering purr of power. I pressed the throttle and listened to the finely tuned roar, and for the first time in my human life, it felt entirely natural to smile.

"It's perfect," I said. I put on the helmet, raised the kickstand, and put the machine into gear.

The salesman waved good-bye to me in my rearview mirror. I concentrated on operating the motorcycle. It was a complex dance of balance, intuition, and control, and I felt a rush of excitement I had not felt since falling into flesh. This—this was freedom. I was alone, I had escaped my enemies, and for the moment, at least, I could simply *exist*.

I opened the throttle as I left the city limits, and the motorcycle leaped eagerly into action with a deep-throated roar. The vibration rang through me, clear and clean, and there seemed to be nothing ahead of me but empty, open road. The wind pushed at me like a solid wall, seeking entrance to my clothes, my hair, fanning across my neck in a cooling jet.

In time, my human concerns returned, whispering in the silence. *Manny and Angela are dead. You can't simply run. You owe a debt.*

It was a debt that Luis Rocha did not want me to pay. I could leave, and he would be happy with that outcome.

I decided, with deep regret, that I would not be. I needed answers. I needed to be sure that the child Manny and Angela had left behind knew the truth about her parents—their dedication, their bravery, their kindness to me.

She would need to know the truth about their deaths, as well. I had part of the answer, but not all. Scott Sands had been no normal Warden, and there had been a reason he had gone after Manny.

I could not believe that it would simply end.

The Ranch.

I would need to find what it meant, or it was likely that Luis and Isabel would never really be safe.

*   *   *

The trip from Albuquerque to Sedona, Arizona,
took only about five hours—a remarkably short time,
given the pleasurable experience of riding the motorcycle. It felt like effortless gliding, a reminder of all
that I had once been. Despite the helmet, I felt less
closed-in than I had in either airplanes or cars, and
the sense of the wind passing over me, the sun beating
hot on my back, gave me a kind of peace I hadn't
realized I had missed.

As a Djinn, I had been connected to the Mother
through Conduits—for most of my memory that Conduit had been a Djinn named Jonathan, a mortal who
had died well before recorded human history had
begun. Many thousands of years later—and only a
year ago, if so much—Jonathan had chosen to die so
that his friend David could live on, and that had splintered the Djinn. It had ultimately divided us, made
Ashan the connection for the Old Ones, like me, and
David the Conduit for New Djinn.

But there were other ways to reach the Mother than
the Conduits, and the place I was going was one. I
had chosen the location that was not only closest, but
most likely to welcome me; the Chapel of the Holy
Cross in Sedona was holy to Djinn as well as humans,
and served two purposes. The human worship was un-
important to me, but in that chapel resided an avatar
of the Earth herself—an Oracle.

It was possible this Oracle would speak to me, even
trapped in a lowly human body.

She had, after all, been similarly trapped once.

I had never visited the chapel in human form; this
spot had existed on the aetheric, as well, since time
began, and I had never been forced to interact with
an Oracle with the burden of skin and bone. As I
glided the motorcycle at a low purr into the parking
area, the sun was flaring its last on the red sandstone

rocks, and it was as beautiful a thing as I'd seen since opening human eyes.

And I was afraid that she would not receive me.

I took the long flights of stairs at a run, hoping that the activity would chase away the cold fear; all it accomplished was to bring an ache to my muscles, and sweat to trickle beneath my leather jacket. *A Djinn died here.* I had felt that powerful event even so far away, on the highest levels of the aetheric. Ashan had killed her. He had not reckoned with the consequences of that action, or how very angry Mother Earth had been with him for his crime.

Ashan, too, had almost lost his life. I did not think it had taught him any genuine lessons.

The doors at the top of the landing stood closed and locked. It was after the times posted for visitors, but that was meant for humans, not for me.

Surely, not for me.

I reached out to touch the warm metal of the handle, and I felt an answering stir behind the door, something vast and powerful and intensely old.

The door clicked open without any action from me.

Within, sunset spilled through the huge glass windows, tinting the simple, small church in vivid oranges and dusky reds.

A woman sat on a wooden pew near the back. As I walked toward her, I slowed; I hadn't expected her to be so clearly recognizable. And so much a mirror of her mother.

"Imara," I said. "I am—"

"Cassiel," she said. Her dark hair rippled in a breeze I couldn't feel, as did her brick red dress around her knees and feet. Her face seemed human, but her eyes were immortal, and more than mere Djinn.

I sank down to one knee and bent my head.

"No need for that," Imara said. Her voice seemed to come from a long distance, echoing oddly in the stone walls of the chamber. "Sit. You've come a long way." I didn't know whether she meant now, on the motorcycle, or in a larger sense. . . . From Djinn to what I was now was surely a very long fall.

It didn't seem right to make myself comfortable in her presence, but I eased myself onto the pew at the end, as far from her as I could manage. I could feel the slow, strong pulse of Earth power from her, like the heartbeat of the Mother, and it frightened me. I longed for it, and I was afraid. . . .

. . . Afraid I no longer deserved to feel it. I craved it, though. My hands trembled with the force of it.

Imara said, "It's hard to talk to you in this form. I don't have much time."

I avoided her gaze. "I need—" I couldn't finish the thought. She knew, in any case.

"I can't help you. Ashan is your Conduit. If he chooses to cut you off, there is nothing any Oracle can do."

"I—I know. I don't ask that." I waited until she slowly nodded.

"Your Warden, then," she said. "You want to know why events took the course they did. Why he is dead."

"I know why he's dead." My voice sounded rough and odd to my ears. "Enemies fired guns at him. Bullets ripped his flesh. And I chose revenge over duty."

"Sometimes revenge and duty are the same," Imara said. Her voice was getting even fainter, and the wind tossing her hair stronger. "I'm not connected anymore to the human world, except through my mother, but I can tell you one thing: You couldn't have saved him. I can see all the possible roads, and they all end in the same place for Manny Rocha and his wife."

I expected to feel relief, knowing that it wasn't my fault, but all I could feel, here in this quiet place, was a vast sense of emptiness. "I liked him," I said. It sounded very strange. "I liked Manny. I liked Angela. And they're gone."

Imara studied me, and there was something frightening about being looked on by such a power. There was compassion in it, but at such a vast distance that its warmth couldn't reach me. "I know," she said. "But it's how they live. It has its own power, that frailty."

The injustice of that threatened to overthrow my self-control. "I want justice. I want their killers to pay."

"Those who killed them already paid."

"Not enough."

She didn't answer. She only studied me for so long that it felt like a geologic age was passing.

"You left the child," she finally said.

"I had to. The police—"

"The child misses you. She grieves, and she needs you."

Suddenly, with a strength that shocked me, I remembered the feeling of Isabel's arms around my neck, of her warm body in my arms. *Oh*. It hurt so much that I wrapped my own arms over my stomach and rocked slowly back and forth, trying to drive away the pain.

It only sank deeper, and carried with it a terrible sadness.

I felt tears form hot in my eyes and trickle down my face. My head felt hot and tight, and I gasped for breath.

Imara's hand touched my shoulder. It should have made me hurt less, but instead the grief tightened in on itself in a choking spiral, and I began to sob, as helpless as any human.

"You're learning," she said. "That's good. You can't be a Djinn now, Cassiel. You have to be something else. It hurts, but it's a true thing, what you are. You're bound to the world now."

I had always thought the Djinn more connected to one another—bound by the cords of power. But now

I was seeing that humans were bound to one another, as well, in strange and difficult knots.

It should have felt like a trap. I would have thought it so once.

"You have to go back to them," she told me. "I know it's dangerous, and I know it won't be easy, but your future doesn't lie here with me, or with any Djinn. It's with them. If you want to find the truth about what happened to your friends, you must go back."

"Back," I repeated. "Back to *what*?"

"To Isabel. To Luis." The color of her eyes shifted between embers, flames, the pure gold at the heart of the sun, black, gray. "I know it's difficult to believe, but a power has put you here for a reason, Cassiel."

I sucked in an unsteady breath and wiped tears from my face. "I'm here because of Ashan."

She smiled, very slightly, and raised an eyebrow in an expression so like her mother I almost smiled in return. "Is he not a power?"

Her voice was as faint as a whisper now, and the invisible wind blowing across her had whipped into gale force. Her hand slipped from mine and fell back into her lap.

"Wait," I said. "Please. Tell me about the Ranch. They would have killed to protect it. It must be important."

"It is," she said. "It will be, to you." Her voice faded to a thin ghost. "Go now. Isabel—"

She faded like a candle flame.

I sat for a moment, staring at the growing darkness beyond the windows, and then stood and began the long journey home.

Chapter 8

I WAS TWO miles outside of Sedona when I felt the earth grumble and mutter, and power stir around me.

So. They know where I am. It could have been the Wardens; it could have been the faceless enemy that Scott Sands had so feared. Whoever it might be, they were coming for me, and coming fast.

And I welcomed the opportunity for an open, vicious fight.

I opened the throttle on the Victory and bent low across the handlebars, and the road became a blur of black, yellow, and shifting shadows. No moon yet, and the last rays of sunset were fading into black. There were headlights on the road coming toward me, and they were bright enough to dazzle.

A car suddenly swerved across the line and skidded toward me. I swore under my breath. No time to stop, only a fraction of a second to decide. A Djinn could survive such a crash; I couldn't.

I shifted my weight and steered, heading *for* the oncoming car, trusting instincts I hadn't known I possessed.

The car brushed by me with inches to spare. The wind of its passage battered me, and I heard the thin, enclosed screams of those inside it. Not my enemies, only victims, trapped in a war they didn't comprehend.

I couldn't help them. If I stopped, I was dead. I had

to hope that, having missed me, my enemies would release them to let them continue on their way.

Ahead, a large tractor-trailer shuddered, and the giant metal rack of cars it carried tipped and twisted as it jackknifed into my path. The entire rig crashed onto its side and skidded toward me, shooting dry sparks.

It blocked the whole road. No room to go around, and nothing but loose sand to the sides. If I went off the road, I'd crash, and if that didn't finish me, I'd be on foot and an easy target.

I reached down into the earth and yanked a section of the road upward. The asphalt rose in a ramp, and then I was hurtling forward, leaving the ground in a long, flat arc.

The back tire of the Victory barely cleared the still-skidding wreckage. I couldn't spare a breath for relief; I was coming down now, and I knew my driving skills were not equal to handling that challenge easily. My innate Djinn nature allowed me to learn quickly, but not *completely*.

I pulled at the road on the other side, giving myself a ramp to land on, and even so, the impact of the motorcycle's tires grabbing hold almost overturned me. I controlled the wobbling machine somehow and focused ahead. Nothing could come at me from behind, not now; my enemies themselves had seen to it.

No, the next attack would come from ahead, or . . .

I had almost no warning, only an indefinable sensation on my left side. Just enough time to realize that speed wouldn't save me this time.

I let go of the throttle and jammed on the brakes.

A massive off-road vehicle on tall tires, black as a beetle, roared out of the dark. It had no lights, but there was a glow inside it from the instrument panel, and it reflected off the panicked face of the driver. He was trying to steer, but the wheel was locked.

The giant beast was aimed directly at me.

I couldn't get out of the way. He was too close, coming too fast, and as his front tires bit the gravel at the edge of the road, the truck erupted out of the dust with a roar and accelerated even more.

I flung myself and the motorcycle down, to the right. My side hit the road with a stunning impact, and a broad knife of agony tore through my body as the Victory's weight slammed down on my right leg.

The truck's undercarriage passed over me, reeking with hot metal and oil—a second of black terror, and then gone, spinning out of control off on the other side of the road, flipping in dust-devil showers of pale sand.

I had to get up, but when I tried, agony lanced through my right leg—broken or sprained.

For a precious few seconds, the power arrayed against me had nothing to throw at me. No oncoming vehicles. The ones it had used already were smoking wrecks.

Get up.

The leg, I decided between sobbing gasps, was not broken, only badly bruised and sprained.

Get up!

I struggled out from under the Victory, rolled over, and forced myself to my feet. I had to put most of my weight on my left leg, dragging the near-useless right, and it was an act of torture to pull the motorcycle to its balance point again. What had seemed so effortless and light in motion was cruelly heavy in stillness.

The Victory glittered in a sudden flash of headlights. Another oncoming vehicle. I gritted my teeth and calmed myself as I straddled the motorcycle.

It wouldn't start.

"Please," I whispered, and tried again. And again. On the third try, the engine coughed, caught, and roared.

I put it in gear and released the throttle. The bike leapt forward, back tire squealing and fishtailing, and the vibration felt like hot hammers pounding up and down my right leg. The lights smeared greasily in my vision, and for a black second I thought that my flesh would fail me.

I blinked, and the world steadied again.

The oncoming vehicle was large and dark, but I couldn't see its details or edges. If it was another tractor-trailer jackknifing across my path, I might not be able to avoid crashing this time.

The oncoming vehicle's lights grew larger, brighter, blazed like insane white suns. . . .

. . . And flashed by me. No attack.

I gasped in a shuddering breath and jammed on the brakes again, bringing the Victory to an unwilling, skidding halt, because in the fraction of a second it had taken for the truck to pass me, I had recognized it. Black and chrome, with red and yellow flames.

Looking back, I saw brake lights blaze red, and heard the juddering shriek as Luis Rocha's truck came to a halt crosswise in the road.

I stripped off the confining helmet, and the cold desert wind chilled my sweating face and fluffed my hair. It was a risk; it was Luis's truck, but that did not mean it was Luis in the driver's seat—and even if it was, the force that had attacked me had used innocents. It could just as easily use him, if it caught him unawares.

For a long second the truck idled, and then Luis Rocha opened the door and stepped down to the road. He didn't seem surprised to see me. Or especially happy. I shut off the Victory's engine, dismounted, and began to roll the motorcycle to the side of the road, limping badly with every step.

Luis, without a single word, came to my side and took hold of the machine. When it was safely out of the way, he turned to me. In the backwash of the truck's headlights he was all shadows and angles, and the flame tattoos along his arms seemed to writhe.

"Leg?" he asked. I nodded. He crouched down and ran a practiced hand from my hip down to my ankle, and I bit my lip to keep from crying out as pressure found pain. "I can't take care of this here. We have to go. Get in the truck."

"My motorcycle—" I couldn't leave it. I needn't have worried; Luis rolled it to the truck, unlatched the back gate, and slid down a built-in ramp. He laid the Victory down in the bed, jumped down, and secured the back again.

"Like I said. Get in the truck."

"There are people hurt—" I could feel their agony and fear battering at me, the way the boy's pain had caught me that day in my apartment. I could feel them crying out for help.

"I know." The resigned look in his eyes, caught in the headlights' glow, was an awful thing. "Help's coming."

He was right. I could hear the rising howl of sirens, and red-and-blue flashes were visible just coming over a distant hill.

One of the wrecks—the tractor-trailer, I thought— shattered in an explosion and blew fire to the sky. I flinched, off-balance, and Luis's hand closed around my scraped, aching right arm.

"Cassiel," he said, "get in the truck. I'm not telling you again."

"You don't need to," I said wearily. "I'm a Djinn. The third time's the charm."

We didn't speak at first. I hated the closed-in metal of the truck cab, but that was less important at the moment than the enormity of the attack that had come against me. I'd seen Djinn wield that kind of force, but this—this hadn't felt like a Djinn. While I didn't doubt there were a few Wardens capable of such things, in terms of pure strength, I didn't think they'd be so . . . obvious.

Then again, Scott Sands had not been a subtle man—but his power was Weather, not Earth.

The first thing that Luis said, after several miles passed beneath the wheels of the truck, was, "Ibby cried all day. I couldn't get her to stop."

She had lost her parents. It hardly seemed odd for a young child to be distressed.

Luis's glance cut to me, hard and dark as an obsidian knife. "She cried because you left."

I shifted so that I was no longer receiving the full glare. "You wanted me to go."

"Yeah. I did. And today I get word that you blew my boss out of a window. What the hell was that? Your idea of subtlety?"

"What did you expect me to do, Luis? Wait at home for your call?"

"Wasn't expecting murder."

"It wasn't murder," I said absently. "He didn't die."

"What?"

"He didn't die. I don't know what happened to him. He jumped, but he never hit the street. It's as if—a Djinn helped him."

"Don't change the subject. You went there to kill him, right?"

"I went to find out what he could tell me. As you would have, if you hadn't needed to care for your niece," I said.

"And what did he say?"

"Not much. Have you ever heard of something called The Ranch?"

"The Ranch," he echoed. "Chicken ranch, dude ranch, ranch dip? What the hell are you talking about?"

"I don't know," I said. "He seemed to think his superiors at The Ranch had ordered him to destroy the office. That is all he told me."

"You suck at interrogation. That doesn't surprise me, by the way."

"I didn't harm him." I thought about it in detail. "Much. Given the circumstances, how would you have handled him to get more answers?"

"What is this, a classroom? Interrogation 101?" But Luis didn't seem to have the same fury inside that he'd carried yesterday. Sharp edges, yes, and a simmering core of resentment, but he did not hate me.

Quite.

"Yes," I said. "That's exactly what it is. I'd like to understand how you would have done it."

"I— Okay, I probably would have gone over there, kicked the crap out of him, and forced him to tell me what was going on." I simply looked at him, and finally he said, "So probably not all that different, I guess."

"No." I felt tired, and my entire right side ached fiercely. "Perhaps you would have done it better."

"Yeah, I kind of doubt I'd have been better at the ass-kicking." Luis's look at me this time was guarded. "You crashed the bike?"

"Not exactly. I had to lay down the motorcycle so a truck would drive over me."

He barked out a laugh, then realized I was serious. "No way. You did?"

"It seemed the easiest way out at the time." I shifted and winced. "I might have been wrong."

Luis kept watching me, flicking his gaze back and forth between me and the dark, largely empty road. We had a five-hour drive back to Albuquerque, barring any surprises. I felt very tired.

"There's a motel up ahead," he said. "Ibby's safe— she's with Angela's mom and her family—so I'm not due back until tomorrow. I need to take a look at your leg."

"It's fine."

"I'm an Earth Warden. I *know* it's broken."

"It is?" I looked down at it, bewildered. I would have thought my body would have been clearer about such an injury.

"Cracked femur, and the more time you spend hobbling around on it, the more damage done. Pretty sure you ripped up some muscles, too." He sounded carefully remote about it, and I felt the warm brush of power, like the faintest touch of sunshine. "All right, if you don't want to stop, let me pull over and take care of it, at least."

I didn't object. The continuing waves of pain were distracting, and they made me feel weak and angry with the weakness. How did humans survive a lifetime of these scars and agonies? It seemed impossible. Did they ever really stop hurting?

We drove on in silence for another mile or two, and then Luis exited into a well-lit but empty rest stop area, though I could not see what was so restful about it; it would be difficult to sleep in the glaring lights, and there were no bathrooms, only a number of battered-looking metal and wood tables and benches. Luis put the truck in park and left the engine running as he unbuckled his seat belt.

"Lean against your door," he told me, "and put your legs up here, on my lap."

With the ache in my right, that was a difficult process, but once it was done there was a simple comfort in having his hands lightly resting on my leather-clad shins. That comfort turned darker and deeper as his fingers lightly brushed up to my knee, then moved up my thigh.

He paused just over the place where the ache was the worst, about midway up the bone. His hand settled there in a pool of heat, and Luis looked up at me. In the dim light of the dashboard, the expression in his eyes was unreadable.

"Hold on to something," he said. "Your hip's actually dislocated. This won't be pleasant, but I have to slip it back into the socket."

I gripped the plastic handle overhead and nodded. Luis took hold of my leg, one hand beneath my thigh, the other gripping below my knee, and without a pause, pushed and twisted. In the middle of the flare of white-hot agony that arced through me, I felt and heard the snap of bone resettling in place.

I let my breath out slowly, and realized that I'd ripped the plastic handle completely out of the roof. I quickly pushed it back in place and secured it with a fast, guilty burst of power. The ache was different now, much more bearable. . . .

And then Luis moved up both hands to encircle my upper thigh, and light moved in a merciless, cruelly beautiful dance through my bones and muscles. It burned. It scorched. My whole body shook in response, and I heard myself give voice to a moan— barely a whisper, but I couldn't stop it.

Luis's hand pressed down, cascading life energy into me, and I felt myself rise to meet it, a wave upon the shore, and the moan purred in the back of my throat, sinful and delicious.

I opened my eyes and saw Luis watching me. His dark eyes were still unreadable, but there was a vulnerability to him now. He *saw* me—not as his brother's human-formed Djinn, not as a burden, but as something else entirely. His hand moved slowly up the sensitive interior of my leg, and even through the layers of denim and leather, I felt it in every nerve.

And then he sat back and left me cold and alone, spiraling down into the breathless dark.

"Better?" His voice was low in his throat, almost

harsh. "Sorry. Sometimes that happens; it's because the nerves—well, whatever. I didn't mean to—anyway. Sorry."

I wasn't sorry at all, but his retreat confused me. I concentrated on slowing my racing pulse. My human body had responded in ways that brought back vivid flashes of sense memory. . . . The dream, the one I thought I'd suppressed. The heat he'd poured into me for the healing should have cooled, but instead I felt it growing and concentrating inside me into a golden liquid glow.

I wanted more. More of his touch.

Luis was no longer looking at me. He faced the floodlit night outside of the front windshield, and his face was tense. Unreadable, yet again. "We should go," he said. "Miles to go, and I don't know about you, but I haven't been to sleep in days." He started the car. "You good to go?"

He was right, of course, but I felt there was something false in it. He'd put up barriers again, strong ones. "Yes," I said, and moved my legs off of his lap. There was still a little pain, but it was nothing like it had been. The warmth persisted. "I'm good to go."

Luis put the truck in gear, and we accelerated out into the night.

Evidently, the fact that I had a driver's license did not convince Luis of my actual driving ability, at least not with his vehicle. He flatly refused to allow me to take the wheel, although he had already admitted his own weariness.

I missed being on my motorcycle. There had been something solitary and wild about it, something I couldn't get from a ride within a vehicle even with the window rolled down. I still felt caged. Trapped.

I still felt the imprint of Luis's hand on my thigh, and now it angered me that I was so weak. *It's only flesh,* I told myself.

But flesh had its own power.

"How did you find me?" I asked Luis at last, when the silence got too thick. The road was long, dark, and almost empty, and I sensed that he was growing very tired. The question snapped him back to alertness. I saw his knuckles whiten as he gripped the steering wheel harder.

"I had an idea where you'd go," he said. "You can't run to the Wardens right now; the Djinn wouldn't have you. So the local Oracle was a safe bet."

I hadn't realized my logic would have been so transparent. "So naturally, you came running to my rescue," I said. My tone was dry and sarcastic, and earned me another glare. Ah, we were back on more familiar footing now.

"No," he said. "I came to get you and take you back to answer questions. I'm a Warden, Cassiel. My brother might have bent the rules for you, but I won't. And I won't have you going on your own Djinn crusade for vengeance, either."

I had not expected that, and perhaps I should have; Luis owed me little, and he had his own life and career to think of. And Isabel. "Did you sense anything about the one who attacked me on the road?"

"Other than Earth powers? Nope. So, there have been three separate attacks—fire, at Manny's office; weather, on the plane; and now earth, on the road. What does that tell you?" Luis didn't wait for my answer. "I'll tell you what it tells me: We've either got an undiscovered triple-threat Warden who can control all the elements, or there's something else going on here. Something bigger than anybody suspects."

"It's more than that," I said. "Manny and I were attacked before that, at a farm." And that power I hadn't been able to identify; it had elements of both weather and earth. Curious.

"Add in the involvement of Magruder and Sands,

and the fact that one's dead and the other one's missing—"

"It's more than just random violence," I finished. "And the shooting—"

"The shooting was my fault," Luis said. "I knew it was dangerous, coming back to town. The Norteños aren't exactly known for their forgive-and-forget attitude." He swallowed hard and blinked rapidly, as if he was holding back a wave of sorrow. "What happened to Manny and Angela is my fault, and I'm going to make it right."

"I do not think it was your fault," I said. "It was mine, as well, if so. As you said, I should have stayed. I should have tried to save lives instead of take them." Manny's empty eyes still haunted me, even more than Angela's. Angela had never had a chance to live, but Manny—I had felt him go, when I was returning from the car crash. I'd felt him *let* go. "If I had tried—"

Luis shook his head slowly. "Too late for any of that," he said. "We made choices. Now we have to live with them. Sucks, but there it is." He took in a deep breath and let it out. "You know, Manny always was the serious one. The hard worker. I was always skipping school, hanging with criminals; he was the one who made our mama proud." Another shake of his head, as if he was trying to deny the truth of his own words. "Doesn't make sense. None of this makes any sense."

I did not tell him that life rarely did; he wouldn't appreciate hearing it, even if it was true. "How did you become a Warden?"

"Didn't it tell you in my file?" He knew I'd studied him. I didn't know if that should feel embarrassing or not. "Yeah, well, I got in trouble. Usual stuff— burglary at first. Thing was, I was breaking into places without the breaking part—I just unlocked doors and went inside. It's easy, you know. And I didn't know it was going to attract attention. I just figured, hey, cool, superpowers. Made me real popular with my homies, at least until the Wardens showed up at my bail hearing, posted for me, and carted me off to the inquisition. I was kind of surprised they didn't kick me right back. I wasn't exactly well behaved. But I guess they saw something I didn't. They put me through school, gave me a job. Two years later, they brought Manny in, too."

He was the younger brother, yet his powers had manifested earlier, and more vividly. I wondered how Manny had felt, trailing behind.

The way he said his brother's name woke a ghost of pain in my chest—there was a certain emptiness in it, and vulnerability. I found myself wanting to take his hand, not to draw power but to give comfort. That was how humans did such things—flesh to flesh.

I was reaching out to him when the next attack descended on us with shocking suddenness.

The lights of Albuquerque blacked out ahead, and I felt the sudden burn of power being released in the physical world. "Luis!" I snapped, and braced myself against the dashboard with one hand. It was good that I did; he slammed hard on the brakes, and I felt a heavy thud from behind as my motorcycle slammed into the cab of the truck. The tires screeched and jittered, but held against a skid.

"Shit," he breathed, and slammed the truck hard into reverse, gave it gas, and whipped it in a fast, reckless turn. "Can you do anything about that? Because I'm a little busy."

He offered me his right hand, steering with his left. I grabbed hold and rose into the aetheric for a look. Night fell away, and the world erupted in a chaos of color. Reds, maroons, oranges, hot flashes and sparks of yellow.

We were in trouble.

"It's coming in!" I shouted. "From the right!"

The passenger's side. I had just enough warning to duck, and the wind hit the truck with so much force that the entire heavy vehicle rocked up on the left two wheels, threatened to overturn, then settled down with a heavy, rattling thump.

A spray of stones, fired at hurricane speed, began pelting us, like bullets from a machine pistol. The window next to me cracked into icy shards, then blew in. I put up a shield as quickly as possible, but even so we were both bleeding and shaken from the attack, and that was only the opening salvo.

"Faster," I said. "It's circling, trying to cut us off."

"This is insane," he said, and somehow held the truck on the road as another gust lashed at us. "What the hell do they *want*?"

"One or both of us dead," I said. "Hold on. I'm going up."

I rose into the aetheric again, scanning the boiling mass of neon colors. There seemed to be no center to it, no weak point to target. *We* were the weak points. I sensed other things from it—a hunger, a blind and furious menace that gave me chills.

Someone hated us on a scale that seemed—even by human standards—insane. I had earned no such enmity during my brief stay in flesh; if Luis had, I could not imagine what he had done to trigger it. But we had to fight it, nevertheless.

Didn't we?

Luis was readying a counterattack, but I hesitated. Something . . . something was not right.

"Wait!" I snapped, as Luis began to strip the rocks and sand from the rushing wind. The theory was good; the wind itself would do damage, but not as much as the hurtling debris. But there was a sense to this that wasn't *right*.

"What?" Luis threw me a wild look. Another gust

slammed into the truck, this one head-on, and the impact was vicious. Cracks formed in the windshield. "Wait for *what*? They'll pound us into scrap!"

I didn't bother to reply. I was busy. Instead of sending power out, I gathered it in, close around us, an armored shield *within* the cab of the truck. Let the metal and glass take the damage for now; I was waiting.

It was a brilliantly focused attack, so tightly wrapped that it punched through my shields like a laser through butter. Aimed not at me, but at Luis.

I lunged forward as he gasped and collapsed forward against the steering wheel. His chest was heaving, his face going dirty-pale.

I had a flash of the singing snap of Manny's bright presence leaving the world, leaving me, and of the exploded meat of his chest. That had been a bullet.

This was pure power, a fist around Luis's struggling, pounding heart. Squeezing.

They were trying to crush the life out of him, and I would fail again, *lose* again.

No. I would *not.*

I batted away the attack with brute force, giving Luis a few precious seconds of recovery time, before it came back, fast as a striking snake. It was almost invisible on the aetheric, a shifting mass of color that blended into the general storm of chaos. Difficult to anticipate.

Difficult to stop.

I couldn't allow them to get a hold on him. Seconds counted in this, and the damage could be mortal, beyond my ability to repair—I didn't know enough about the human body, didn't have the fine surgical instincts of an Earth Warden. My healing of the boy had been lucky, and I'd had no risks; this time, failure would be utter destruction.

I threw myself into the aetheric and put myself in the way of the attack. *Better me. He can heal me after.*

That seemed logical enough, until the attack actually struck me full force.

In the mortal world, I gasped and folded, hands pressed to my chest. The pain was extreme, the panic even worse. Trying to form an effective shield under the assault was near useless; my instincts, my *human* instincts for breath and survival, overrode my logic, made me struggle madly like an animal in a trap.

I felt Luis's hands on me, holding me. "Cassiel!"

I would not fail. I could not allow it. Weakness was a human trait; I was *Djinn*. . . .

I screamed, and the world shattered into knives of agony. *Death. This is death.*

Shadows on the aetheric, and a blazing white outline of a human form in front of me, dazzling my eyes.

Luis. He'd had a chance to prepare himself, while I'd taken the brunt of the attack, and this time, he not only gave me relief from the pain; he struck back, hammering away the assault. He'd done something to shield himself; his heart glowed a brilliant red on the aetheric, and as I watched, the tint spread through his ghostly form, tracing organs, veins, arteries. It tinted his aura into spectrums that reminded me of the hot surface of the sun.

He was *beautiful.* And as I collapsed, shaking and defeated, he stood against them.

Human, and beautiful.

The attack ended not with an explosion, but with a whimper, fading away into mutters and fitful gusts, rattles of pebbles on scarred metal, a final angry spurt of dust.

Silence.

Luis was whispering under his breath, a long monologue in Spanish that I thought was a string of prayers and curses, followed by more prayers. He was shaking, and somehow I was pressed against him, his arms enfolding me.

Breathe. My lungs ached with the effort, but I forced them to work. Bright sparks of pain leapt through my body, the afterimages of what our attackers had done to us, and I knew I was trembling as much as Luis.

"Hey." His voice was low and rough. "You still with me?"

I nodded, unable to speak. My body was sticky with sweat, my hands cold as if they'd been plunged into wet snow. When I swallowed, I tasted bitter salt and blood. I waited for him to release me, but Luis didn't seem inclined to let go. There was something comforting about the warmth of his chest against me, the strength of his arms holding me.

I did not struggle free.

"I'm sorry," I said.

"For what?"

"I couldn't—"

He laughed softly, and his breath brushed my ear. It woke new shivers, pleasurable ones. "You got in the way and gave me time to get it together. You saved my damn life, *chica*. What are you sorry for?"

Not doing it well enough, I supposed. There seemed no logic to that, but there it was, immutable and inexplicable. "I'm sorry about your truck," I said instead.

"Yeah," he sighed. "Damn. Me too. So—did we learn anything from that?"

"They're strong."

"We knew that already."

"They're vicious."

"Knew that too."

I looked up into his face. "They're in Colorado."

"Oh." His arms tightened around me, and his dark eyes widened. So did his smile. "*Didn't* know that."

Chapter 9

I HAD TRACKED the attacker through the aetheric across New Mexico, into mountains to the north. I had lost the trail somewhere near the border, according to the map. I was considering this as we crossed the Albuquerque city limits, but there were no answers to be found on the flimsy paper, which flapped in the wind coming from the shattered passenger's window, and I folded it carefully and put it away.

"Where are we going?" I asked.

"First thing, I'm dropping the truck off at the body shop," Luis said. "Then I'm crashing for about two hours." He paused for a moment, and his voice changed timbre. "I have to go to the funeral home at ten."

Funeral home. An odd combination of words. Homes were for the living, and for a moment I thought about the house—no longer a home—where Manny and Angela and Isabel had lived. Someone else would make it a home, in time, but for now it was a reminder, an empty shell filled with inert, abandoned things.

A place I had once felt happy.

"Should I go with you?" I asked. That earned me another glance, and a moment of silence. "If I shouldn't—"

"It's not that you shouldn't," he said. "It's that we

have to get you cleared by the Wardens and the cops
before you start showing your hot pink head around
town. Know what I mean?"

I did. "How do we do that?"

"I'm working on it. You're going to have to sit
down with a couple of representatives from the Wardens, eventually, but I heard yesterday that some odd
things turned up at Scott's apartment, and the Wardens are looking at that differently."

"And Molly Magruder?"

Luis shrugged. "That one's a little tougher. I don't
know yet, but they said they've got some other leads
on that, too. Anyway, I should find you a hotel; you
dig in and wait for a while."

"I could disguise myself," I said.

"Yeah, you've done a great job so far. *Pink* hair?"

"No one looks at my face." I thought I'd done a
good job. It stung me that he disagreed. "I don't like
to hide away."

"Nobody likes it, but it's the smart thing to do," he
said. He pulled the truck off the road into the parking
lot of a small, cleanly kept motel coated in pink adobe.
"I'll get your bike out of the back, but promise me
you won't go anywhere."

I looked at him, said nothing, and got out of the
truck. Luis shook his head and went around to the
bed of the truck to wrestle the Victory down the ramp,
while I entered the motel office to use my credit card
to buy a room. It was a new experience for me, but
not unpleasant; the clerk was efficient and impersonal,
and the process short. By the time I came out again,
Luis had the motorcycle parked in an empty spot next
to the truck, and I had a chance to survey the damage.

The Victory had come through remarkably un-
scarred. The same couldn't be said for Luis's truck,
which was pitted, dented, and scraped where the paint
hadn't chipped or at least been dulled by the abrasive

scrub of sand. The passenger's window was gone, only jagged fragments remaining. The front windshield was a web of cracks and pits.

Luis was staring at it with folded arms and a miserable expression.

"Man," he said, "knowing you is expensive."

I wanted to say something appropriate, something that would mean I valued his company. Something to recognize the moments in the truck when the two of us had been—different.

Luis continued to look at the truck, and for a moment I caught the sadness in him, the loss, and I knew he was thinking of his brother. The brother he would have to see again soon, in the *funeral home.*

The brother I had failed.

"I want to see Isabel," I said. That made him turn toward me, frowning. "I understand it's a risk. But you said she was asking for me."

"Yeah," he said. "Yeah, she was. But I don't want to put any more of my family in the firing line right now. Do you?"

I shook my head slowly, haunted again by the image of Isabel crouched against the fence as bullets passed overhead to strike her parents. No. I could not risk her. Luis was a target, but so was I, and I could not guarantee the child's safety.

"May I call?" I asked.

Luis took out his cell phone, dialed a number, and turned away to speak in Spanish. After a moment he handed the phone to me.

"Cassie?" Isabel's voice was bright and hopeful, and I felt warmth grow inside me in response.

"Cassiel," I automatically corrected her, but my heart was not in it. "I'm here, Ibby."

"Where are you?"

"Close," I said. "I'm watching over you." I had a sickening memory of saying the same thing to Angela. Empty promises.

"I thought you left us. I thought you went away." Her brightness dissolved into tears. "Mama and Papa can't come home anymore. Can you?"

"Yes," I said softly. "Yes, I can. But, Ibby, you must be patient. I'll see you soon, I promise."

"Okay." She was a brave child, and she mastered her tears into wet snuffles. "I love you, Cassie."

Human words. Human emotion. It felt too large for my chest, this feeling, too heavy with meaning. "Be well," I whispered. "I will watch over you, Isabel." I meant it.

I hung up the phone and handed it back to Luis, whose dark eyes were full of understanding. "She'll break your heart," he said. "I know."

Our fingers brushed, and then I walked away to my small, silent room.

I slept very little, tormented by the memories of Manny and Angela lying dead, by the haunting sounds of Isabel's tears, by the touch of Luis's hands as he healed my injuries. These things were anchors, weighing me down. As a Djinn, I had been weightless, and without ties or cares, and that seemed far away now. Unreachable. All around me, the sounds of the human world roared on, and I found no peace within or without.

Morning found me awake and exhausted. In the light of the bathroom mirror, I was sallow, haggard, and the whites of my eyes were as pink as my hair. I shed my clothing slowly, dropping it piece by piece to the clean tile floor. As human bodies went, mine seemed overly tall, overly thin, barely softened by the rounded breasts and hips. My skin was of a fine, almost featureless texture, and it glowed pale under the harsh lights.

I am Djinn, I told my reflection. My reflection strongly disagreed.

The shower's beating hot water restored me somewhat, and I wearily contemplated the problem of my dirty clothing. I would need to buy new garments eventually. These—even the leathers—had suffered during the night's adventures. I had more, at the apartment the Wardens had provided. . . . But I knew, even without Luis loudly reminding me, that I should not return there. *Home.* It was not, though, and never would be. I had only one home, and it was far away, unreachable.

A careful pulse of power restored my clothes to a wearable state, removing grime, stains, smells, scrapes, and tears. I donned all the required pieces, including the leather, and used the motel's drying device to return my hair to its usual flyaway puffball state.

And I waited, as Luis had instructed. The hours dragged by. I read the holy books provided in the drawers next to the bed, and was both pleased and annoyed—pleased that humans held their history in such high regard, and annoyed by translational inaccuracies.

Television proved to be something I was grateful I could turn off.

When the telephone rang, finally, I grabbed at it with eager relief. "Yes?"

There was a pause, a long one. "Cassiel?" Luis's voice, and yet not his voice at all. I sat up slowly, hardly aware I had done so. There was something tired and awful in his voice. I looked at the clock beside the bed.

It was one in the afternoon. "Luis," I said. "You have been to the funeral home." That combination of words continued to strike me oddly.

"Yeah," he said. His voice sounded slow and deep, as if every word seemed an effort. "About you. The Wardens have bigger problems than you right now, and the Djinn do, too. I've been trying to get anybody, up to Lewis, and it looks like we're on our own."

"I am no longer hunted?"

"Not by the Wardens. There are barely enough of us left in place to hold things together, much less go running around trying fight crime."

"And the police?"

"I pulled a favor from the lead detective on the case—I knew him, from the old days. You're off the hook. There's no body, so they're listing Sands as a missing person." He paused. When his voice returned, it sounded very quiet and very vulnerable. "I picked out coffins. The funeral mass will be in a couple of days."

"Funeral mass," I repeated. "In the church?"

"Yes, in the church, where else would you have one?" he snapped, and I heard the harsh rattle of breath on the phone's speaker. "Sorry. I'm just—me and Manny, we stuck together for a lot of years. Our mother died when we were kids, and Pop went a few years back. It's just us, Angela's family, and a bunch of cousins I barely know in Texas. I'm just feeling alone."

"Can I leave the motel?" I asked. I was aware that I should say—something. But I had no notion of what comfort sounded like, among humans, and I did not think he would welcome it, not from me.

"What? Oh yeah. Yeah, sure. But watch your back." I heard the scrape of metal—the brakes of a large vehicle, I thought—and Luis said, "I'll be at Manny's house. I have to go through things, start figuring out what to do for Ibby."

"Is something wrong with Ibby?"

"It's just that the court's going to have to award guardianship to me for me to keep her. My lawyer says that's just a formality if Angela's parents don't contest it." He didn't sound certain of that. "It'll hurt her if this comes down to a fight."

Once again, I had no wisdom to offer. Something

within me was tired of all the drama, all the emotion, all the *humanity* of it. That part of me continued to whisper, ever louder, *Walk away, Cassiel. You are eternal. They are ghosts in the wind.*

Perhaps they were, but if I walked away, they would haunt me.

"I should go see Isabel," I said. "I promised her."

"Come over here first. I want to go with you."

He sounded so quiet, so unhappy, that I felt it necessary to agree. When the call ended, I slid the room key into an interior pocket of my jacket, locked the door, and left without a backward glance. My motorcycle—still gleaming and largely unmarked—glittered in the sunlight a few spaces down. Keys . . . I searched my jacket pocket, found nothing. They were not in the ignition slot.

They'd fallen out at some point. I smiled slightly, touched my fingertip to the ignition, and willed the machine to life. The engine growled, settled to a low, contented purr, and I realized another thing that I had somehow lost during the evening's festivities: my helmet.

The constant wind tugging at my hair was a new sensation, and I liked it. I liked the blast on my face, the sensation of flying without walls. I attracted stares, of course—why wouldn't I?—but that was no longer an issue. My nerves prickled as I passed a police car, but they gave me only a flat, assessing glance and did not pursue.

I pulled to a stop in front of Manny's house and silenced the engine. The street, as always, seemed quiet. There was rarely anyone to be seen in yards or on the sidewalks, even children. The windows, I realized, were all barred. Doors were blocked by wrought-iron gates.

It was a neighborhood of fortresses and fear.

I knocked on the door, and Luis opened it. He took a single second to look at me, and then nodded and turned away, walking into the living room. I closed the door behind me and followed.

In the bright light slanting in the windows, Luis looked infinitely tired. Older than he had only yesterday. He sat down at the table with a pile of papers and idly shuffled through them.

"I'm looking for their life insurance," he said. "I need to file that for Ibby. Manny told me he had some kind of retirement thing, too. And their bank accounts, I need to freeze those. People sometimes read obits and try to con the banks, steal from the dead." He shook his head. "People." The contempt in his voice was almost worthy of a Djinn.

I reached out to the pile of papers, touched edges, and withdrew three sheets. "Insurance," I said, and laid it in front of him. "Retirement plan. Bank accounts."

Luis stared at me with dark, empty eyes, then nodded. "Thanks."

I sat back, hands in my lap. He fiddled with the papers for a few more minutes, then stood up and walked around the room. It was full of things—things, I realized, that would need to have a future, whether that was with Isabel, with Luis, consigned to destruction, given to others. . . . It was a problem I had never considered. Human lives were lost, but the wreckage they left behind had to be managed. Deconstructed.

Another step deeper into the never-ending grief.

"I'm going to keep their papers, their pictures, that kind of stuff," Luis said. "Anything I think Ibby might want of theirs."

Would that include the small ceramic angels on the shelf above the television, the ones that Angela told me she had collected over the years? Or Manny's books? Or the warm woven throw that trailed fringed edges over the arm of the couch, the one knitted by Angela's mother?

So much. I realized then that Luis had stopped moving, and was staring down at a collection of objects on the battered coffee table in front of the couch.

A book, turned facedown—something Manny had been reading.

A glass with a dried residue in the bottom.

An open bag of animal cookies.

Remote controls scattered haphazardly across an uneven landscape of magazines and newspapers.

Luis collapsed on the couch and put his head in his hands, and his shoulders heaved silently. I felt the storm of emotion from him, dark and heavy.

Walk away, Cassiel. You are not mortal.

I sat down beside him and placed my hand on his back. He didn't speak, and neither did I; the silence stretched for a long time. When he finally raised his head, he took in a deep breath and sat back against the couch cushions. I took my hand away and folded it with its mate in my lap.

"They're gone," he said. "I guess it took me a while to really get it, but they're gone. They're not coming back."

I gathered up the cookies and the glass and took them into the kitchen. The cookies went in the trash, and I filled the glass with hot water. A flash of memory overtook me: Angela, standing here at this sink, washing up dishes from the first evening I'd been welcomed here, to this house.

They're not coming back.

No, they weren't, and the ache of that was like a constant gray storm inside me. A human might have succumbed to tears.

Walk away.

I yanked open the refrigerator door and began to empty the contents into trash bags. The physical sensations helped fuel a growing tide of what I realized was anger. *Anger?* Yes, I was angry at them for abandoning me. For leaving behind Luis and their child.

Angry at my own weakness.

"What are you doing?" Luis asked from the doorway.

"Cleaning," I said flatly, and tossed half-empty bottles of sauces into the bin. The milk was already turning rancid in its carton. "We're here to clean, yes?"

"Not now. Leave it," he said. "I need to think about what I'm going to keep."

"You won't keep any of this," I said, and kept pulling things from the shelves. Leftovers, wrapped in plastic, marked in Angela's clear hand with the dates.

He charged forward, knocking a bottle of Tabasco sauce from my hand, which bounced from the counter onto the hard floor. As it hit, it shattered in a hot red spray. Vinegar stung sharply at my nose and eyes. "Stop!" he yelled. "Just *stop,* dammit! Stop touching things!"

I shoved him backward, and he rushed toward me again. He drove me back against the counter with bruising force, and his hands grabbed my shoulders. I took hold of his shirt, my fingers wrapping into a convulsive fist, and felt a wild, black desire to hurt him, *hurt.* . . .

"Stop," he said, and there was so much despair in the single word that my anger shattered. My fist relaxed, and my hand rested flat against his chest. "Stop, Cassiel. Please stop."

His whole body was pressed against mine, and the wildness in me mutated, twisted, became something else.

I wanted . . .

. . . I didn't know what it was I wanted from him. The conflict in his own expression told me he felt the same, torn in so many directions his self-control was tattering like a flag in a hurricane.

His hands slid from my shoulders up my neck, to cup my face. I could feel every rapid pulse beat in his

veins, every ridge and whorl of the lines in his fingertips.

Luis's eyes were huge and very dark, like midnight
lakes where the unwary drowned alone.

I knew, in that frozen instant, that the next thing
we did would chart the course of our futures, together
and apart. *This is the moment of choice.*

"Stop," I said, and a warning flare, not quite a
shock, passed from my splayed fingers into his chest.

He did, but he didn't retreat, not for a long few
heartbeats. When he did, it was fast and decisive, leaving me there without a word as he stalked to the
kitchen door. His boots crunched shards of glass and
left pale red Tabasco-colored prints in their wake.

I heard him go into another room. Doors opened
and closed, wood banged. I followed his wet footprints
and found him emptying out drawers from a dresser,
tossing the contents onto the neatly made bed. He
barely paused when I appeared behind him. "I'm
going to need some bags in here," he said. "Most of
this has to go in the trash or to some charity."

His voice was his own again—calm, controlled, with
a dark undercurrent of anger traveling beneath the
surface.

I silently fetched him bags, and helped him fill one
bag with underthings and clothing too worn to donate,
one with donations, one with items he thought Isabel
would treasure. That one was the smallest. When he
came across a sealed white garment bag in the corner
of the closet, he took it down and laid it gently on
the bed, unzipping it enough that I could see lace and
white satin.

"Angela's wedding dress," he said. "For Ibby."

I met his gaze. It went on a long time. "Which one
of us do you really think they're trying to kill?" I
asked him. "You or me?" It had assuredly *not* been
only Manny or Angela, or our enemies would have
stopped trying.

The question didn't confuse him. It had been on his own mind, from the lack of surprise in his expression. "I think the more important question is how long is it going to take them to get their power back together to try again." Some of the grief receded in him, which was what I'd intended. "They aimed for you, alone, twice. You do realize that, don't you?"

I nodded. "That might have only been because I am a danger linked with either you or your brother. One or both of you could have been the main target."

"But *why*? What's so special about me or about Manny? He's a—" Luis took a deep, startled breath. "He *was* a good man. He was good at his job, but you know—you know he wasn't a superstar or anything. He was just a guy."

"And you?"

Luis looked away. "I'm not that much, either. I know where I stand. Look, if I'd been any kind of a real threat, they'd have given me a Djinn before the revolt, and I'd be dead now, right?"

"Joanne Baldwin didn't have a Djinn," I said. "At least, not one assigned her by the Wardens. So I don't believe you can make such a claim. Perhaps you don't really know yourself at all."

That got me a very slight smile, an echo of the old Luis. "Who does?"

Indeed.

I cannot speak for Luis, but I stayed alert at all times, ready for any sort of attack, whether magical or physical. I learned that alertness carries a price. By the time we were finished packing the items in the bedroom and marking them, it was late—dark outside.

"You throw out everything in the fridge?" Luis asked at last, sinking wearily down on the stripped mattress. I shrugged. "Guess it's pizza, then."

He called a number taped to the refrigerator's door. He must have realized it was useless to ask me what

I preferred in the area of pizza, because he ordered something called a *combination*, and pulled a couple of beers out of the bottom shelf of the refrigerator, toward the back, that I had left, in case he wanted them. He tossed one to me, and I caught it.

We twisted off the caps and drank in silence. I wondered if he was also waiting for the attack, and feeling the slight, indefinable strain of it.

The pizza came, borne in a sagging cardboard box by an unenthusiastic messenger. Luis paid for it, locked the door, and we sat down together on the couch to eat.

I took the first bite, and it was lucky that I did. My senses were sharper than a human's, mostly because they had received relatively little use, and I tasted the poison immediately. I spat out the bite.

"Don't like the mushrooms?" Luis asked, and was on the verge of putting his own slice into his mouth when I knocked it out of his hand. "Whoa! Okay, you *really* don't like mushrooms."

"*Amanita virosa,*" I said, pointing at the innocent-seeming chunks of mushroom. "Deadly within a day." I moved to point at finely diced white cubes scattered among the chunks of sausage and wheels of pepperoni. "Aconite. Wolfsbane. Very fast acting, difficult to treat. There's more."

Luis had a stunned look on his face as he sank back on the couch, staring at the food. "Somebody poisoned the pizza?"

"The pizza was made correctly," I said. "*Amanita virosa* is genetically very similar to *Agaricus bisporus*, the table mushroom. And I expect that the aconite was converted from garlic. It would be easier to do it from horseradish, of course, but someone spent time changing the toppings with great care."

It took him a moment, but Luis followed my logic. "An Earth Warden did this. Poisoned it by genetically twisting certain ingredients."

"Also by accelerating the decay rate in the meat."

He visibly shuddered. "How the *hell* does somebody think of that?"

"They knew we'd be looking for a direct attack. This was more subtle." It would have worked, too, if I hadn't been possessed of more acute senses than normal. The inside of my mouth tingled, but I knew I hadn't absorbed more than a light dose. "Would you have known?"

"Maybe. I don't know. Probably not right away." Luis looked very shaken. "What about the beer?"

"We'd have felt any attempt to change it while we were here, and I don't taste anything wrong with it." I smiled slightly. "No more than there usually is, with beer."

He responded by picking up his bottle and glugging down several swallows, still staring at the pizza box. "Do you know who it was?" he asked me.

I contemplated the pizza box, touched the damp cardboard, even trailed my fingers over the offending poisonous mushrooms. "No," I finally said. My senses were blunted and imprecise, frustrating. I should have known, should have been able to tell who had done this thing, but trapped as I was, heavy in flesh, the trail went cold.

"All right, that's it," he said. "If I can't trust the food I put in my mouth, avoiding a fight ain't going to work."

I raised my eyebrows. "So?"

"So. We're taking the fight to them."

It wasn't so simple as that. Without knowing who and where, we were moving blind—and with our usual sources of information, through the Wardens, cut off from us, we had little in the way of resources.

While Luis slept, wrapped in an old quilt on the couch, I sat on the floor with a small lit candle and silently called the name of a Djinn, in repetitions of three.

It took me well into the night, and more than one candle, but I finally had a response. The flame flickered, flared, and guttered out in a hiss of molten wax, and darkness fell around me like a heavy cloak.

I didn't move.

When the candle sputtered back to life, a Djinn had appeared across from me.

"Quintus," I said. "Thank you."

He nodded slightly. His eyes glowed with banked fire, and I knew that inviting him here was a dangerous game. He had shown me no special enmity, and had, in fact, saved my life, but that didn't mean he would do it again. Or that he wouldn't have changed sides.

"I'm sorry about Molly," I said. "I didn't kill her."

He didn't blink, and his expression stayed remote and calm. "No," he said. "I know that you didn't. If you had, I'd have ripped you apart and fed you to pigs within the hour."

The venom in him was chilling. So was the fact that he didn't bother to manifest himself completely; his eyes were on a level with mine, but he dissolved into dark gray rolling mist below his waist.

"What do you want, Cassiel? I'm tired of your chanting." Quintus smiled, but it wasn't at all friendly. "Most human calls can't reach us. Yours seems to be especially annoying."

I was glad to know it. It might one day mean my death, if I annoyed them too badly. "Do you know what happened to Molly?"

His eyes narrowed, and it seemed to me that his face sharpened its lines, took on more definition along with more anger. "She was murdered. It was quick and vicious, and I was elsewhere. What more do you want?"

"I want to know how far you traced the killer." I had absolutely no doubts that he'd done so. I'd raced after the car full of gunmen who'd shot down Manny, and if Quintus truly cared for the woman, he'd have done the same.

Seconds passed, thick and ominous. "It's not that simple," he finally said. "Even the Djinn can't fight shadows."

"How far did you trace the attack, Quintus?"

He looked past me, at Luis, who was snoring lightly on the couch. "I traced it to the end."

"What does that—"

"Don't ask me, Cassiel. I can't tell you." Not, I realized, that he *wouldn't*. He *couldn't*. "There is a geas on me."

A geas was a special kind of restraint, one that only a Conduit could apply—or an Oracle, I supposed. It was beyond the power of a normal Djinn, even the mightiest of us.

I had narrowed our pool of suspects considerably— and made it infinitely more dangerous. "We are going to Colorado," I said. "We think the attacks are originating there."

I was careful not to make it a question; a geas would force him to silence in response, or even to a lie. But a statement might pass.

It did. Quintus seemed to relax a fraction. "I hear it's nice this time of year," he said. "Cassiel, be careful. There are more things happening than you can see."

I tried again. "We're going to The Ranch."

Quintus went silent, staring at me. I couldn't sense anything from him, not even a flicker of struggle. The geas was a very strong one, and watchful.

He had, however, confirmed by his very silence what Warden Sands had said—our enemies were at The Ranch.

In Colorado.

Now we just had to find it. According to the maps

I had studied, Colorado contained more than one hundred thousand square miles of land, and much of it was wilderness or ranches.

"Cassiel," Quintus said. "I know you have to do this. If you don't, you'll be killed." He was giving me information, as much as he could. Warning me. "They won't stop coming for you."

I looked toward Luis. "Not only me. And it may touch more than the two of us. It already has." I returned my attention to Quintus quickly, warily, but he hadn't moved. "Our enemies are near a river."

Quintus nodded, but it was very slight. The glow in his eyes intensified, and I thought I saw a flicker go through him.

"Near the border," I said. The flicker intensified. He didn't nod this time. He couldn't. I knew better than to try to push past that point; if it was a truly deep geas, he would attack to defend it.

I wouldn't survive it.

"Don't try to stop us," I said. Quintus stirred, just a little.

"I'm not trying to stop you," he said. "I'm trying to prepare you."

"For what?"

Quintus's presence was flickering like a dying flame. "For the war."

"We're running out of time," I said. "Help us, Quintus. *Try.* Give me something!"

He did try. The flickering intensified, and the outlines of his form blurred and dissolved.

"To find the greatest, look for the least," he blurted. He looked up sharply, toward the darkened ceiling, and screamed in rage and pain, a scream that dissolved into nothing. The candle flickered out again. I quickly relit it, but apart from a discolored burn on the carpet where Quintus had been floating, there was no trace that he'd ever existed.

He'd paid a price—that much was clear—even as

little as he'd said. *The war.* But the war between Djinn
and Wardens—that was over. Wasn't it?

"It has to be," I murmured.

But I was forced to admit that cut off as I was,
orphaned from my own people, I could no longer be
sure of anything.

To find the greatest, look for the least.

It was a clue, but I didn't know what it meant.
When I'd been a Djinn, I would have taken pleasure
in such cryptic comments; I'd have relished the confusion it caused. But Quintus—Quintus had tried very
hard to be very clear.

The geas had prevented it, and punished him.

Look for the least. The least what? The least . . .

The least population?

Colorado was a land of a few population centers,
and much wilderness, but as I studied the maps and
Manny's computer, I thought I found the answer to
the riddle.

Hinsdale County held only 790 people in more than
1,100 square miles, and had the fewest roads.

It was, I thought, not only a place to hide. . . . It
was a fortress made for those who wanted to retreat
from the world.

I blew out the candle and shook Luis awake. He
flailed, trying to get loose from the cocoon he'd fash-
ioned out of the quilt, all too aware that another attack could be coming at any second.

"I think I know where to go," I told him. "Get
ready. We have a long drive ahead."

"Wait." He scrubbed a hand over his face. He
looked very tired. "Tell me first."

He heard me out, in the predawn silence, in the
house his brother had once built a life inside. When I
was done, Luis said, "No."

"No?" I was surprised, to say the least. I'd thought
he understood the urgency.

"We can't drive to Colorado and be back in time

for the funeral," he said. "And I'm not letting Ibby down this time. And I'm not leaving her unprotected while we go off chasing ghosts."

I hadn't thought about that. Now that I had, the weight of it sat like glass in my stomach.

"You're going to have to keep us both safe," Luis said, "until we get Ibby some alternate protection."

I don't know what the look on my face was like, but if it was anything like the frustration that raced through my body, it was no wonder he seemed wary. "Humans," I snapped. I felt energy crackle within me, and for a moment, being balked, I felt truly Djinn once again.

But I knew he was right, as well.

Chapter 10

THE DAMAGE TO Luis's truck was relatively minor, all things considered—cosmetic damage to his meticulously maintained paint job, broken windows, dents. His body shop was run by a man who I thought, at first glance, was a Djinn, but I finally, uneasily, decided was human. His eyes were a very light amber, his skin a darker hue than Luis's, and he had a very unsettling smile.

"Elvis?" Luis responded, when I asked about the man. "He's okay. Hell of a wizard with cars, but not in the actual *wizard* sense or anything."

Strange. Despite Luis's assurances, I still didn't trust the man. I waited next to my motorcycle while Luis settled his bills with the mysterious Elvis, and his truck was driven around from behind the square, rusting building. It looked as flamboyant as ever, with new glass glinting in the windows and a fresh paint job gleaming. Elvis had, it appeared, added some glitter to the yellow center of the flames licking down the sides of the truck.

Luis seemed pleased.

We drove from the repair shop, Luis leading and me following on the Victory, through winding streets and older neighborhoods until he pulled to a stop in the driveway of a plain, square house, finished to a shade of pale pink I liked very much. As Luis got out of the truck and I parked the Victory, the front door banged open, and a small rocket shot out toward us.

Isabel.

She leapt like a cat from the ground into Luis's arms, and he staggered back against the truck. His reaction was exaggerated, but I was fairly certain that the staggering was not. Isabel had momentum on her side.

He buried his face in her long hair, settled her more comfortably in his arms, and then turned toward me. Isabel looked, as well, a pale flash of face, a blinding smile.

"Cassie!" she said. I walked toward them, and she held out her arms. I took her, not sure if it was a natural thing to do. Her weight felt awkward in my arms, but after a moment, it began to feel right as my body found its gravitational center again. She smelled of sweet things—flowers, from the shampoo that had cleaned her hair; syrup, from the pancakes she had been eating. It made her mouth sticky where she kissed me on the cheek. "I'm glad you're back."

"I'm glad to be back also," I said. I didn't correct her about my name, not this time. I studied her at close distance. "How do you feel, Isabel?"

She didn't answer, but her eyes did—they swam with sadness and a child's sudden tears.

"Grandma Sylvia's been making me pancakes," she said. "You want pancakes?"

"Little late for pancakes, kiddo," Luis said, and reclaimed the child from my arms to toss her over his shoulder and head for the door. "Sylvia?" He knocked on the door, and a shadow moved inside. A graying older woman opened the screen and smiled at him— a trembling sort of welcome, and there was a terrible distance in her eyes. She looked like Angela, and she had to stand on tiptoe to kiss Luis's cheek. Her gaze went past him, to me, and her eyes widened.

"That's Cassie," Ibby said proudly, and pointed at me. "Grandma Sylvia, that's Cassie! She's my friend. I told you about her."

"Cassiel," I said, to be sure there was no mistake. "I prefer to be called Cassiel."

Sylvia hesitated, then stepped aside to let me enter. She made sure to give me plenty of space to pass, as if she didn't want to take the risk of brushing against me.

Did I look as forbidding as all that? Or only different?

The front room was a small, dusty parlor filled with old furniture and black-and-white photographs. One had been set out alone on the lace-draped table— Angela, only a few years older than Isabel, wearing a white dress and carrying flowers. There were fresh white roses in a vase on the table next to the photograph, and an ornate religious symbol—a crucifix.

"My daughter," Sylvia said, and nodded at the table. "Angela."

"I know. I knew her," I said.

"Did you." She studied me, and there was a deep mistrust in her expression. "I never saw you around before. I'd remember."

I wondered how much she knew about the Wardens, about what Manny and Luis did. I wondered if she knew about the Djinn, and if so, if she knew about the dangers we represented.

Whatever the case, she clearly wasn't prepared to trust me.

"She was Manny's business partner, Sylvia," Luis said. He let Isabel slide down to her feet. She clung to his leg for a few seconds, then ran off into the kitchen. It seemed impossible that something so small could have such heavy footsteps. "Cassiel's a friend."

Sylvia nodded, but it didn't seem to me to be any sort of agreement.

He gave up, as well. "How's Ibby doing?"

"She slept through the night," Sylvia said. "But I don't know. She's manic like this, and then she cries for hours and calls for you, or her mother and father. Or for *her*." She sent me a look that I could only interpret as a glare. I couldn't think of a reason I should apologize, so I didn't.

Luis cleared his throat. "Sylvia, I made the funeral arrangements. The mass will be on Thursday at eleven. The viewing starts at six tonight." His voice took on a rough edge, and he stopped just for a second to smooth it again. "Do you think Ibby should go?"

"Not to the viewing, no," Sylvia said. "She's too young. Someone should stay here with her." She didn't look at me as she said it, but Luis did, raising his eyebrows.

I raised mine in return.

"Would you?" he asked. "Watch her for a couple of hours?"

"Of course."

Sylvia's back stiffened into a hard line. "Luis, may I speak to you in private?"

He rolled his eyes and followed her into another room. She shut the door, closing me out.

I wandered into the kitchen, where Isabel was dragging her fork through the remaining syrup on her plate. She looked up at me as she licked the fork clean. "Can you make pancakes?" she asked me.

"I don't know," I said. "I've never made them."

"It's easy. I'll show you."

"You already ate pancakes," I reminded her. "I don't think you should eat more. Do you?"

Her shoulders fell into dejected curves. "You're no fun."

As a former Djinn, I felt a bit of satisfaction at that, but it faded quickly. The child was in pain, though she was trying to hide it from me.

"I'm sorry we were gone," I told her. She didn't raise her head. "I know you missed your uncle."

"You, too."

"I know."

"Grandma Sylvia doesn't like you," Ibby said. "She doesn't like you because you're a *gringa* and she thinks you're going to steal me away."

"Steal you? Why would I steal you?"

"Because I'm not safe with *Tío* Luis. She says he's why it happened." *It* being the tragedy that had shattered her life.

The girl's logic was unassailable. "So she thinks I would try to take you away. Why?"

Ibby shrugged. "You're white. The police will like you better. So they'll give me to you. That's what Grandma Sylvia says. She says I'd be better off here, with her."

I had no idea what that had to do with the issue, but I considered carefully before I said, "I wouldn't steal you away, Isabel. You do know that, don't you? I know you love your uncle and your grandmother. I wouldn't take you away."

"Promise?" Ibby looked up, and there were tears shimmering in her eyes.

"I promise."

"Cross your heart."

I looked involuntarily at the crucifix hung on the wall near the door. *Cross your heart* seemed a violent thing to do.

"No, silly, like this." Isabel slid out of her chair, clattered around the table, and guided my hand to touch four compass points around where my mortal heart beat. "There. Now you promised."

She climbed up in my lap, and I stroked her hair slowly as she relaxed against me. She was almost asleep when she said, "Cassie?" It was a slow, dreamy whisper, and I touched my finger to her lips. "I'm scared sometimes."

"So am I. Sometimes," I whispered, very softly. "I won't let anything harm you."

"Cross your heart?"

I did.

When Luis and Sylvia returned, Luis clearly was running short on patience, and Sylvia's expression was as hard as flint. A smile would have struck sparks on her.

"Luis agrees that we'll get my sister Veronica to come and sit with Isabel tonight," Sylvia announced. "You'll want to see Manny and Angela."

She was instructing me, it seemed. I gave her a long, level Djinn stare, and she paled a bit.

"Thank you for your consideration," I said. Isabel had fallen asleep in my arms, a limp, hot weight, and I adjusted her position so that her head rested against my neck. "I will put her to bed."

"I'll come with you," Luis immediately volunteered. Sylvia's lips pursed, but she said nothing as she cleared the syrup-smeared plate, fork, and empty glass from the table.

Isabel didn't wake as I put her down on her child-sized bed—I wondered if it had once been Angela's, as the furnishings seemed faded and used—and Luis showed me how to tuck her in. He kissed the child's forehead gently, and I followed suit. Her skin was as soft as silk under my lips, and I felt a wave of emotion that surprised me.

Tenderness.

"Sylvia doesn't like me because I am a *gringa*," I said to Luis as I straightened, "and because she's afraid I will take Isabel from you."

He seemed surprised by this. I didn't tell him Isabel had been the insightful one and not me. "Yeah, well, with my record the court might not be so thrilled, and it's not like the Wardens are around right now to be character witnesses. Sylvia's saying she wants to be her legal guardian, but that means Ibby has to live here, not come with me when I go off to a new assignment."

"Sylvia wishes to keep her." Luis, I recalled, had been afraid of that. It seemed he was right.

"Not going to happen." Luis brushed the girl's hair back from her face, and I saw the shadow of his brother in him, gentle and devoted. "Sylvia's okay, but she doesn't love the kid like I do. Ibby needs love."

"And Sylvia can't protect her," I said. "You can."

He straightened, looking at me directly, and I looked back. For a moment, neither of us moved or spoke, and then Luis pointed vaguely down the hall. "I should get ready. For the viewing. Listen, if you don't want to go—"

"I'll go," I said. "But we should find someone to watch over Isabel, at least from a distance. Are there any Wardens at all available?"

"Yeah, I can do that. Probably will have to be one of those other guys, the Ma'at. There are three or four of them still in town." He made an *after you* motion, and we closed Isabel's door behind us.

The Muñoz Funeral Home was a long structure, with muted lights and deep carpets and quiet music. We were met at the door by an older man, balding, with small round spectacles perched on his nose. He wore a black suit, like the one Luis had on, and he seemed professionally sad. His doleful expression never changed as he shook Sylvia's hand, then Luis's, then mine.

I had, at Luis's prompting, changed my clothes from pale to dark—a pair of black slacks, a shimmering black shirt, and a fitted jacket. It seemed a fruitless use of power, but I was cautiously pleased with the results of my transformation. I still couldn't willingly alter the structure of my own form, but clothing seemed easier than it had been.

Perhaps—just perhaps—I was learning to use my powers more effectively. My appearance seemed to raise no alarms with the funeral director, at any rate, and I followed Sylvia and Luis down a long hallway, past open and closed doorways. The air smelled strongly of flowers and burning candles.

The funeral director opened a set of doors and preceded us into the room. It was smaller than I had expected, unpleasantly so, and I found myself slowing as I approached the threshold.

Six rows of plain black folding chairs, a cluster of padded armchairs near the back, a table, a book, a pen. Flowers.

The long, sleek forms of open coffins.

I stopped.

Luis and Sylvia kept walking, right to the front, and Luis stayed near Angela's mother as she sobbed, leaning over the casket in which I knew her daughter must lie.

I could not go forward. *There is no need,* the Djinn part of me said. *Their essences are gone from the shells. This is human ritual. You have no part of it.*

The human part of me didn't want to grieve again, and I knew that it would, once I took that last step.

I turned away, walking quickly. Other tragedies were unfolding here, families shattered, bonds broken, promises unkept. *I am not human. I have no part of this. No part.*

I was almost running when I reached the front door.

I stood in the stillness of the evening, watching the last rays of the sun fade behind mountains, and breathing in convulsive gasps.

"Hurts, doesn't it?" someone said from behind me. I turned. I'd heard—sensed—no approach, neither human nor Djinn, and for a moment I saw nothing except shadows.

Then he stepped forward into the fading light. I had not known him in human form, but I recognized the Djinn essence of him immediately. He was a brilliant flame on the aetheric, a burst that exploded out in all directions and immediately hushed itself into utter stillness.

His name was Jonathan, and he was *dead.*

I fell to my knees. I didn't mean to do so, but surprise and awe made it inevitable. *I'm imagining this,* I thought. *Jonathan is dead and gone.*

"Yeah, you keep on telling yourself that, Cassie. Can I call you Cassie? Ah, hell, I'm going to, so get used to it," he said. He looked very, very human at the moment—tall, lean, comfortable in the skin he wore. His hair glinted silver, and his eyes—his eyes were as dark as the hidden moon. "Guys like me don't exactly die. We sort of—get promoted."

Jonathan had held the reins to power for all the Djinn for thousands of years. I had not loved him, but I *had* respected him—if nothing else, because he had commanded respect from Ashan, and Ashan had never been stupid enough to directly challenge him. There was comfort in Jonathan, and there was also dangerous intensity, cleverly concealed by his all-too-human manner.

But he was dead. He had to be dead. We had all felt it. His passing had shattered the entire Djinn world into pieces.

"I don't—" My voice sounded very odd. "I don't understand. You can't be here—"

He flipped that away with a casual gesture. "Yeah, not staying, just passing through. Got things to do. So. How's the world? Never mind, I know the answer. Always teetering on the verge of disaster, right?" He studied me for a second, and extended his hand. "Get up, I don't like people on their knees."

When I accepted the touch of his hand, it felt real. Warm and human. I held it for a moment too long before I dropped it. "Everyone believes you dead."

"Good. Meant that, actually. It was time for me to move on, and there was no way to do it without giving up my spot in the great organizational tree of life. Like I said, I'm just passing through, so I've got no stake in things anymore. But I thought I'd drop in to say hello."

"Why?"

"Why?" he echoed, and his eyebrows quirked up. "Yeah, I see your point; we weren't exactly close. I was the boss, and I was too human for your taste. We call that irony, by the way, down here in the dirt." He let that sink in for a moment, then smiled. "You realized what you've been given yet?"

"Given," I repeated, and I heard flat anger in my voice. "What have I been *given*?" Everything I had once possessed had been ripped away from me. I'd been *given* nothing.

From his thin-edged smile, he knew what I was thinking. "You've been given a chance."

"Chance. What *chance*? I have been cast out, crippled, forced into human skin. I'm hunted and despised. What *chance* is this?"

"Something most Djinn never get," said Jonathan, who had been born in mortal flesh only a few thousand years ago, and yet seemed far older than I. "A chance to learn something completely new. A chance to shed your old life and form yourself in a different body, a different shape, a different direction. You're a blank slate, Cassiel, that's your *chance.*" He didn't blink, and I saw the flicker of stars in his eyes, endless galaxies of them, an eternity of possibilities. "Or just a chance to screw it all up, all over again. Anyway. You're here for a reason."

"I'm here because Ashan cast me out."

He shook his head. "Something bigger than Ashan is in play, Peaches. You'll figure it out. You always did have logic on your side, even if you were as cold as space. You have a battle ahead of you. Just thought

I'd shake your hand while I could, and tell you good luck."

Something rippled in the sky above us, like heat above a road, and Jonathan looked up sharply. His human body flared into light, pure white light, and I sensed the flash of steel-sharp wings as I covered my eyes.

I could see him even through closed lids and concealing fingers—a man-shaped bonfire, coursing with energies I couldn't touch, couldn't even identify.

Jonathan had gone far beyond the Djinn, into something that was legend even to us.

"Got battles of my own to fight," his voice said, in a whisper that came shockingly close to my ear. "Think about what I said, Cassiel. Think about your chance. Remember how it feels to *feel*. It's important."

The light intensified into a burning pressure on my skin, and I turned my back, crying out, as those mighty wings carried the being who had once been the greatest of the Djinn up, out, away.

"Cassiel?"

Luis's voice. I whirled, shaking, and saw him standing in the doorway, watching me with unmistakable concern. There were marks of tears on his face, but he seemed . . . peaceful.

"Something wrong?" he asked. He hadn't seen. Jonathan wasn't visible, not to him.

I couldn't begin to explain. I shook my head and wrapped my arms around myself, trying to control the chill I felt. I had been in the presence of something so great that I'd felt so small beside it, and it made me wonder—it forced the question of what else the Djinn didn't know, couldn't imagine.

Of what I had once been, and might still become. *A chance*, he'd said. But a chance to be what? Do what?

"It's okay," Luis said, and put his hand on my shoulder. "It's good that you cared about them."

Manny. Angela. He thought my tears were for

them—and, in a way, they were, for all the chances wasted, for all that was unknown.

I took in a deep breath and nodded. "I did," I said, and heard the surprise in my voice. "I did care."

Luis put his arm around my shoulders and steered me back into the funeral home, and with his hand in mine, I went to look for the last time on the first two human friends I had known.

I went to say good-byé.

I was surprised by how many people came to the viewing. Greta, the Fire Warden with the scarred face, came to pay her respects and talk quietly with Luis for a moment. She glanced toward where I sat at the back of the room, and for an instant I thought she would speak to me, but she changed course and shook hands instead with Sylvia, who sat remote and quiet near her daughter's coffin.

Some came with flowers. Some cried. All felt uncomfortable here, in the presence of such massive change.

No one spoke to me.

At eight o'clock, the funeral director with the sad face came to me to whisper that it was time to close the viewing.

Luis was shaking hands with the last few visitors when the doors at the back opened again, and five young men walked in—Hispanic, dressed in casual, sloppy clothing. Glaring colors, baggy blue jeans topped by oversized sports team jackets, all for either UNLV or the San Francisco 49ers.

Four of them were nothing: followers. Killers, most assuredly, with jet-black eyes and no hint of conscience behind them.

But it was the one in front I watched.

He was the shortest of the five, slight of build, with a smooth, empty face and the coldest eyes I had seen in a human. Like the others, he had tattoos covering his neck and arms. He was ten years younger than Luis, perhaps more, but there was something unmistakably dangerous about him.

Luis had frozen into stillness at the first sight of the intruders, and now he moved only to keep facing them as they strolled past Sylvia, the funeral director, and the two or three remaining mourners. Luis flicked his gaze quickly to me, and in that look I read a very definite command. I rose from my seat and glided to the others in the room, and gently but without hesitation hurried them toward the doors. Sylvia frowned thunderously at me, but she also understood that something was very wrong.

I closed the doors and locked them from the inside, turned, and crossed my arms over my chest. Three of the newcomers were watching me, assessing what risk I posed; two of them immediately dismissed me. The last of them—smarter than the rest, I thought— continued to keep part of his attention on me.

"Hola," the young leader said to Luis, and bent over Manny's casket to stare. "Holy shit, this your brother? Doesn't look much like you. Then again, the makeup probably don't help. Makes him look like a *puto*. A dead one. *Pinche cabron.*"

Luis didn't move, didn't betray even by a flicker the anger I knew he felt. I could feel it coming off him like heat from a furnace.

"Show some respect," he said. "Leave."

"Respect?" The boy turned slowly in Luis's direction, and his thin smile grew even tighter. "You want to talk to me about respect, *Ene*? You screwed my brother. You ratted him out. You got nothing to say about *respect*."

"Whatever I did to your brother, you killed mine," Luis said. "It's enough. Get out and let us bury them in peace."

The boy sprawled himself over two chairs, completely at ease, and put his feet up on the coffin. "Fuck you and your brother," he said. "We were aiming for you."

Two of the men slipped guns free of their waistbands and held them at their sides. Luis locked eyes with me, and I pushed away from the door.

"My friend asked you to leave," I said. "Please comply."

"Please what? Who is this pasty-faced *gringa* bitch?" The boy didn't wait to hear Luis's response. "Never mind. Just kill her."

The men were turning toward me when I weakened the metal chairs the boy-leader was sitting on. He toppled to the carpet, cursing, and Luis moved forward, grabbed another chair, and hit the first man to point the gun toward me in the back of the head, with stunning force.

I took a running leap and slammed my body into the midsection of the next man, ripped the gun from his hand, and threw it toward Luis. It didn't require much power to disrupt the electrical impulses within the brain of the third man, an interruption just long enough to make him stagger and fall. Luis jumped him and recovered that gun, as well, while I moved to take down the last.

In seconds, it was done. Most of the men were on the floor, their guns in Luis's hands or pockets, and the boy was just struggling up to his knees to find one of the guns aimed directly at him, along with Luis's deadly stare.

He froze.

Luis thumbed back the hammer on the revolver he held. "You need to get your ass out of here before I forget my manners," he said. "Your brother got what he deserved. Mine didn't. You want to keep on going to war, I'll bring it, and you'll be the first one down.

Good thing you're already in a funeral home. Saves time."

"Shoot me," the boy growled. "You better shoot me, 'cause if you don't, you got no idea what we're going to do to you. No place you can go, no place you can hide. You *or* your piece of shit family. Next time we get the kid, too."

Heat flared inside me, sticky and tornado strong, and it was all I could do not to take hold of the boy and take him apart, one bloody scream at a time.

Luis sent me a warning look, one full of unmistakable command to stay still. "Watch them," he ordered, and jerked his chin toward the other men. He tossed me one of the guns. I plucked it from the air and aimed it at the group of angry, hurting men in front of us. The urge to pull the trigger was very, very strong, and they must have sensed their death in the air, because none of them moved.

Luis put the gun he held away in the waistband of his pants. "You got them, Cassiel?"

"Yes," I said softly. "What are you doing?"

"Breaking the law."

I felt the storm of power, even though I was on the edges of it; the gravitational pull of it focused on the boy. Luis seemed to hover, almost floating in the strong currents of it, and then he *lunged.*

He put his hands on the boy's slicked-back hair and his thumbs on the high forehead. The boy opened his mouth, but no scream emerged.

When his knees gave way, Luis followed him down to the floor, still holding the boy's head. Luis's eyes were almost black with power and rage. I kept my focus on the other men. As they realized something was happening to their leader, they decided to rush me. I sank their feet into the concrete floor, and laughed softly as I watched them flail and curse.

Whatever Luis was doing spilled over, out, traveling

in a wave over the men and sending them slumped to
the floor. When that wave finally lapped against me,
I felt my senses slide toward darkness. I took a step
back and braced myself against the door.

It receded. I blinked away the sparkling afterimages.

All the men were down. As I watched, Luis let go
of the boy and went to each of the others, one by
one, to clamp his fingers down on their skulls and
do—*something*.

It took long, long minutes, and I felt his power failing on the last of them. He finished and climbed
slowly, painfully to his feet, then collapsed into one
of the folding chairs.

I edged around the fallen men—still not moving—
and crouched down next to him. The metal of the gun
felt heavy and cold in my hand.

"What did you do?" I asked.

"Changed their minds," he said. "Literally. Wardens can put me away for pulling that kind of shit,
but if I didn't do something, they'd keep coming.
They'd come for Isabel, and I couldn't let that happen.
It was that or kill them, and keep on killing the next
bunch, and the next. Anyway, like I said, the Wardens
got more to worry about than chasing down rule
breakers."

He sounded exhausted. I placed a hand gently on
his shoulder, careful not to draw any more of his
strength away.

"They're not dead?" I asked. They weren't moving.

"Asleep. They'll wake up in the next few minutes.
When they do, they won't remember much. Lolly—
that's the punk-ass son of a bitch in charge of the
Norteños around here—will only remember that we're
even now. Life for a life." Luis wiped sweat from his
forehead with a trembling hand. "And he'll feel guilty.
About Manny and Angela."

"You can do that?"

"Not officially, I can't." He gestured, and I helped him lever himself upright. "Let's get out of here."

I glanced back as I shut the door to the room. The young leader, Lolly, had gotten to his hands and knees. I was afraid for a moment that he would turn and see me and remember, but he seemed transfixed by the coffins that stood just a few feet away.

He stood and walked to Angela, and I saw his hands grip the wooden side. His shoulders began to shake. I couldn't imagine that he had shed tears for the dead in a very long time.

It must have hurt.

I was glad.

Chapter 11

WHAT LUIS HAD just done was a grave breach of the rules of the Wardens, and I understood why; Earth Wardens—the truly powerful ones—could manipulate memory. If it was done subtly enough, the victim might never suspect anything had happened at all.

It was a power that was fearfully easy to abuse, and difficult to detect. Under normal circumstances, I thought that Luis would never have done such a thing, but now, with the Wardens either withdrawn to their own affairs or potential threats . . . he couldn't afford to rely on them for help.

Or me.

"Why didn't you kill them?" I asked Luis. We were out of earshot of Sylvia and the funeral director, who were near the door. Luis shook his head. He was moving slowly, concentrating on the steady motion of his feet, as if it was the most difficult thing in the world at the moment.

"It's a pride thing. You kill a Norteño, you get killed, or everybody near you does. There's no end once you start that. It can roll on for years. Wipe out whole families."

Blood feuds. One of the common threads of human culture, this inability to forget or forgive. It was something they had in common with the Djinn. When I had heard the boy speak of hurting Isabel, I had almost killed him. I wouldn't have hesitated if Luis hadn't been there. I'd have simply ended the threat, with no regard for the consequences. I would have walked away from the resulting war with no thought of guilt.

I had to admit to myself that Luis's way was likely better.

The funeral director stepped into our path and said, in his low, gentle voice, "Is everything all right, Mr. Rocha?"

"Everything's fine," Luis said hoarsely. "My friends got a little carried away by their grief. I'll pay for the damages."

The funeral director's eyes widened, and he moved off down the hall with what might have been unseemly haste. Luis watched him go.

"Another reason not to kill anybody," he said. "Considering the room's booked in my name."

Sylvia stood by the exit, looking sad and angry. She was restlessly crumpling a tissue in her hands, over and over, and she sent Luis a filthy look as we approached.

I tried to remember that she had lost a child, but in that moment, it was difficult.

"You and your *friends*," she said in a low, vicious tone, "had better not show your faces at my daughter's funeral. God help you if you do."

"Sylvia—"

Her eyes glittered, but the tears in them seemed more like armor than grief. "You brought the Norteños *here*? And then you let them *walk away*? What kind of a man are you, you don't defend your own?"

She slammed open the door and stalked away. Luis hurried after her—as much as he was capable at the moment—and opened the passenger's door of the pickup truck. He had to lift her up on the step.

She did not appear grateful.

It was a stiff, silent drive home, with Sylvia sitting rigid between us. In the passing flare of headlights, her expression remained remote and furious. She put away the handkerchief and took out a set of black, polished beads. She kissed the silver crucifix that dangled from it, and then began to work the beds through her fingers, lips moving silently. Rosary beads. I was surprised the custom had not changed from so long ago.

Luis seemed to have no trouble navigating, but I could sense his weariness. He yawned hugely as he parked the big, black truck in front of Sylvia's house, which blazed with warm light, and opened his driver's-side door to descend.

I hopped out and extended my hands to Sylvia. She frowned at me, and then evidently decided that I was less objectionable to her at the moment than Luis.

I lifted her effortlessly and set her feet on the concrete sidewalk. She stepped back, momentarily too amazed to frown, and Luis rounded the hood of the truck. He looked from Sylvia to me and sighed.

"Thanks," he told me. Not as if he meant it. "Sylvia, I'd like to say good night to Isabel. If you don't mind." He hated asking, but seemed to recognize that insisting would only cause the woman to stand more firmly in his way.

Sylvia sent us another distrustful look, and grudgingly nodded. "Don't wake her up if she's asleep," she said. "It's hard enough for her, with the bad dreams."

Sylvia's sister Veronica was in the living room, knitting in the glow of the softly playing television set. She stood up to give Sylvia a hug, and then a slightly more restrained one to Luis. None for me, but Veronica—a large, grandmotherly woman with a kinder face than her sister—nodded and smiled instead.

"She's been very quiet," Veronica said. "I don't think she woke up at all."

Luis moved down the hall, leaving Sylvia to whisper with her sister, and as he reached Isabel's door, I hesitated.

"Stop," I whispered. Luis paused, hand in the air an inch from the knob.

"What?"

I didn't know. There was a feeling—a wrongness. Nothing I could identify, either in the human world or on the aetheric. It was almost as if something had been here and gone, leaving only its acrid, bitter aetheric scent.

"You had a Warden watching the house?"

"Ma'at, like I told you. Yeah, of course."

I shoved Luis out of the way and opened the door myself.

There was no immediate terror leaping to confront me; the room was as we'd left it, only darker. A sparkling night-light glimmered softly against the far wall, casting pink radiance into the corner and across the bed.

The aura was stronger here. *Don't scare the child,* I told myself, and forced myself to move slowly and softly to the bed.

She was a featureless lump beneath the covers. The pink light played out its endless soothing loop, catching the shadows and creases of the blankets.

I slowly pulled them down, and heard Luis's gasp.

The bed held only a stuffed pillow and a rag doll, whose black yarn hair spilled out over the pillow. I put my hand in the hollow where Isabel had been. "Cold," I said. "She's been gone a long time." Perhaps since the first time Veronica had checked on her. I sat back on my heels, studying the bed carefully. There was no sign of a struggle, nothing overturned. No hint on the aetheric of trauma.

Isabel had not been harmed.

Not here.

That maddening ghost of a trace eluded me. I *had*

sensed it before, but I couldn't force the memory to appear. It hovered like a fog at the edges of my awareness, but never came close enough to drag into the light.

My hand remained in the hollow of Isabel's bed, where her body had slept. I could feel each individual fiber of the cool cotton sheet. I could smell the sweet perfume of her hair on the pillow.

Gone.

Luis had moved to the closet and now was conducting a methodical search of the room, calling Isabel's name in a calm, loud tone that grew gradually louder, gradually less calm as each hiding place was eliminated.

His hands were shaking. Not just trembling, but *shaking*, like a man gripped by extreme cold.

After he'd looked beneath the bed, he looked across it at me, and I said, "She's not here, Luis."

His face flushed red, then pale. "She's here. She's hiding, that's all. ISABEL!" He bellowed it this time, got to his feet, and charged out of the room. I heard the sound of his footsteps, his calls, the sounds of doors being opened and shut. Sylvia's strident demands to know what he was doing. Veronica's softer protests.

The screams when Luis finally told them the child was gone.

I stayed there motionless and silent, staring at the dirty rag doll. It was the one the child had been holding the first time I'd seen her in her front yard. One black button eye was missing, and a seam beneath the right arm had given way. Discolored, soft stuffing poked through.

She's gone.

Someone had taken her. It hadn't been the Norteños; I had their scent now, I knew they wouldn't have bothered to abduct a child unless they expected money or blood in response. Lolly had not acted like a man who'd given such orders, though he might have, if pushed. He'd not gone so far, not yet.

Someone else had. Someone with roots in power. A Warden. A Djinn. Someone I had likely touched, possibly even trusted.

They had just made a terrible, terrible mistake in their choice of victims. I had killed for Manny and Angela in a fit of rage and shock. I would do it with cold, measured violence this time, to regain the child.

Outside the room, Sylvia was calling the police. I heard Luis slide down the wall, beaten down this time by his grief, but his grief was different from mine. Mine was a cold, alien thing.

I stood up and retreated to the hallway, where he sat like a broken doll. I crouched down to look into his eyes.

"She's gone," I said, "but I think I know what path we have to follow."

"The Norteños—"

"No. They might have shot into the house, but they're not so stupid as to invite a child-abduction investigation. They would be destroyed by it."

His hands were still violently trembling. "Some predator, then. Some bastard predator."

"No," I said slowly. "I don't think so. I think it had to do with us."

"Us." The flat panic in Luis's eyes receded. "What do you mean, to do with us?"

"Someone wants us stopped; we have ample evidence of that. Together and separately, we've been marked. How better to stop us than to take the child, knowing we both care for her safety?" I willed him to understand me. When I was not certain he did, I reached out and gripped his cold hands in both of mine. "*Luis.* There is a trace of power in that room. Warden or Djinn, I can't tell, but we *must* find out.

Question the one who was supposed to watch over her. Either they were bought off or disabled. We need to know what happened."

His fingers twisted and gripped my wrists, hard.

He pushed me away. I rocked backward, but it's not so easy to overbalance a Djinn, even so little as I now was. My grace seemed to anger him even more.

"This is your fault." He almost spat it in my face. "It started with *you*, you coming here and making trouble. If anything happens to Isabel—"

"If anything happens to Isabel," I said, "I will take my payment in blood and screams. And then you may take yours, from me. I won't fight you. I've done enough harm here already."

Because he was right, of course. This had all started with my arrival. Whatever I had done to trigger these events, trigger them I had; I owed Luis Rocha a debt I could never pay, even before the abduction of his niece.

Someone, somewhere had struck at me, and shattered the lives of everyone standing near me.

That, I could not forgive.

As a Djinn, I could *never* forgive.

Luis was unable to raise the Ma'at who was supposed to be watching Isabel. I couldn't find him on the aetheric.

It was a very bad sign. "He wasn't bought off," Luis said. "Not Jim. No way in hell. He was a friend, and a good one."

He was likely dead, then. Our enemies had assassinated him quietly, without attracting anyone's attention, and then come for the girl. It had been well planned and executed.

It made me wonder why they had not done the same for us.

The police arrived. They were not the same as the

ones who'd been involved in Manny and Angela's shooting, but they made the natural connections—Luis's former gang affiliation, the deaths of Isabel's two parents. Luis was taken away for questioning, although both Sylvia and I insisted he had never been out of our sight long enough to accomplish the abduction of the child.

With the arrival of detectives—a higher order of policemen, I realized, like the difference between Djinn and Oracles—the questions took a personal turn. Luis had arranged to have me cleared of blame in Scott Sands's disappearance, but this was three times in only a few days that I had been standing at the center of a criminal investigation.

I supposed it was natural for them to find this odd, but the feeling grew within me that we were wasting precious time while the police collected their painstaking samples, took photographs, questioned suspects, and conducted a spiral search of the house, the yard, the neighborhood.

"Look, it's still possible the girl could have run away," one of the detectives said to me as I stood on the porch outside, under the glare of portable lights. Yellow tape flapped all around the house. There were news vans now parked at both ends of the street, held back only by the barricades, and Sylvia's neighbors had turned out in force to murmur and gawk. "Did she seem upset?"

"Of course," I replied. "Her parents were killed. But I don't think she's run away."

The detective quirked one perfectly shaped eyebrow. She was a small blonde with a tendency to smirk that irritated me beyond bearing. "Why not?"

"Because she left her suitcase," I said. I had seen it sitting in the corner of the room, covered with pink flowers and Barbie doll stickers. "And she left her doll."

I had succeeded in wiping away her smile. "I see."

"It's possible, if she decided to run away, that she would go home," I said. "But for such a small child, it's too long a walk, even if she knew the way." There were many dangers in the world, predators ready to snatch up the unprotected. I felt sickened by the prospects, but I knew in my heart—what a human feeling— that Ibby had not *gone*. She had been *taken away*.

I had a strong and growing conviction that the police, well-intentioned as they were, could not help us in this, and the longer we stayed here, trying to fit in, the worse things would become. Like the investigators, I knew that trails rapidly went cold, especially such slender trails as I had to follow.

It would be very inconvenient to be jailed as a suspect.

"You don't seem too upset," the detective said to me.

I cocked my head slightly as I thought it over, as I'd often seen humans do. "I don't? I suppose I'm in shock."

"No. Your friend Luis, he's in shock. Grandma Sylvia's in shock. You're not in shock."

"That makes me seem suspicious, I suppose."

"You think?" She smiled again, and it raised alarms all along my spine. "We'll continue this discussion downtown."

She took my arm. Across the yard, I saw Luis, cornered by another detective, notice what was going on. I didn't know what to do—cooperation seemed a waste of time, and violence counterproductive—but Luis reached out, put his hand on the detective's shoulder, and gave him a wide, warm smile. Then he shook hands with the man and came toward me.

"You can't talk to her now, sir," my detective said. Her tone wasn't inviting any arguments, and her grip on my arm was just as firm. "Please go be with your family."

"She is family," Luis said. The detective gave him a look that was so full of incredulity that even I smiled. "Distant relative."

"Yeah? What galaxy?" The detective tugged on my arm again. "Come on, ma'am. Let's go."

"Detective. One moment." Luis was still smiling, warm and wide, and he captured her flat stare with his. "Thank you for all that you're doing to help us." He extended his hand. I knew what he was doing—it was an Earth Warden trick, one of making themselves seem likable and trustworthy—but I could see that it wouldn't work on this woman. She had a streak of distrust as dark as rust through her brittle, bitter aura.

"My job," she said shortly, and added her other hand to push my shoulder. "Move it."

I glanced down at her feet, and whispered into the ground. I was learning, from the carefully controlled way that Luis applied his skills, that for an Earth Warden subtlety was as effective as brute force.

Green grass looped up in ropy strands, lashing her ankles, burying her sensible shoes. When she tried to take a step, she overbalanced, and for a moment she clung closely to me before she let go to crouch down to see what was holding her. "What the *hell*—?"

Luis leaned over, too, placed his hand on her shoulder as if in concern, and I felt the strong pulse of power that slid through her. The grass fell away, but the woman didn't immediately move.

"You've cleared us," he told her in a very quiet tone. "We didn't have anything to do with Ibby's disappearance. You know this to be true. We have somewhere important to go, and you're giving us permission to leave."

I sensed her struggle against him. It was a very close thing, and Luis's strength was very low just now, both in power and in human terms.

I had little enough to add, but I stepped in and added my hand on top of his. He glanced up, acknowledging the infusion of power, and guided it to surgical precision, shaping the woman's response.

Again, it was illegal. The Wardens would have dismissed him for such a use, or taken his powers and left him a crippled shell. But the Wardens had taken their eyes from us, and this was now a fight for more than just survival.

Isabel's life was at stake.

Whatever he did was on too fine a level for me to sense the exact methods, but when he removed his hand, the detective blinked at him, nodded, said, "Fine, thanks for your cooperation. You two can go. I know you're in a hurry."

We walked away together. As we approached the line, one of the officers turned from his post, frowned, and held out his hand to stop us. Luis looked over his shoulder at the detective, who was standing where he'd left her, arms folded. She made an impatient gesture to the perimeter policeman, and we ducked under the fluttering barrier and headed for the street.

We were lucky, I thought, that the news organizations were held back at the end of the street. I saw cameras focusing on us, felt the pressure of their excited attention. It was not pleasant.

I positioned Luis with his back to the cameras, so that he covered me, as well, and said, "You didn't make her trust us?"

"Couldn't," he said. "It's like hypnotism; you can make people follow a path they would have normally gone down, but that detective doesn't trust anybody, and even if she did, she damn sure wouldn't trust me. It was easier to just skip her farther along a track she'd have taken. Anyway, let's get out of here. We don't have too long before she starts looking through her notes and realizes she didn't finish questioning us."

"I could destroy the notes," I offered.

"Cassiel, we *want* the police to help. Just not to put their sights on us. Destroying their notes doesn't get us anywhere." We had arrived at the parked truck, but it was surrounded by forensic technicians who were taking samples. In case, I supposed, we were all lying, the witnesses were all lying, and Luis had abducted Isabel himself. "Crap," Luis muttered. "Well, they're just doing their jobs. Too many to influence."

"It's a foolish waste of time."

"No, it's not," he said soberly. "Statistically, kids get abducted by family members more than strangers. Makes sense. I got no problem with them following every possible lead."

My motorcycle, I noted, was sitting neglected at the curb not far away. Luis noticed it at the same time, and we exchanged a silent look of inquiry, then moved toward it.

"No helmets," I told him, as I straddled the bike.

"Least of my worries right now."

I felt the shift of mass as he climbed on behind me, and then his hands closed on me, low, near my hips. I started the motorcycle. Something about the low growl of it soothed the gnawing fear and anger within me.

Luis shifted his weight to find the balance point, and I eased the bike out into the empty street.

One problem, I realized: we would have to pass through the gauntlet of press clogging both ends of the neighborhood. In the truck we would have had the advantage of height and sealed windows. On the Victory, we didn't even have the relative anonymity of helmets.

"Alley," Luis said in my ear. "That way."

I leaned the bike the way he directed, over a spray of gravel and behind a neighbor's house, and into a narrow paved street filled with overflowing trash cans and refuse.

"Go!" he shouted. "They'll follow us if they can!"

I applied the throttle, and the bike shot forward. Luis's arms tightened around me to hold on, and I accelerated down the alley and into the next at right angles, which spilled into a street. I took the turn fast and accelerated yet again, narrowly beating the light and weaving around a slow-moving van.

"Left here!" Luis shouted, and I crossed three lanes of traffic with the throttle wide open, almost skidding through the turn. "Okay, good, ease off. I think we're okay"

The Victory seemed disappointed to return to its role as mere transportation, but at traffic speeds it glided smoothly, sleek as a shark. We attracted curious glances. I was almost growing used to it.

"Back to your motel," he said. "You get your stuff. I can't guarantee the police won't want to ask us more questions, so it's better we move."

"We need to go," I said. I heard an echo of the Oracle's voice, back in Sedona. *You need to go.*

"Yeah, but where?" he asked. I heard the frustration in him, sensed it in the harshness of his grip on my hips. "How are we going to find her?"

"I think I know a way," I said, and guided the bike back to the motel.

I changed my clothing back from funeral black to pale white riding leathers over a pink long-sleeved shirt. I left the pants dark, though I roughened the fabric weave to denim. My shoes took on the solidity and toughness of riding boots.

I did it almost effortlessly this time, upon walking into the darkened, silent room. By the time I closed the door behind Luis, I'd changed completely. If it surprised him—if he even *noticed*—he said nothing. He sat down on the side of the neatly made bed and said, "What now?"

I opened a drawer near the bed and took out the maps that I had purchased along with the motorcycle. They were tough, encased in plastic, and I had New Mexico and one of several other states, including Colorado.

I unfolded both and flattened them out on the carpet, then took a cross-legged seat on one side. I indicated the other, and Luis folded himself down. "How does this help?" He was impatient and losing his temper. "We don't need maps, we need—"

I grabbed his hand, took a small silver knife from my jacket pocket, and cut his finger with one swift jerk.

"Hey!" he yelped, and tried to pull away. I squeezed the cut. Ruby drops formed and dripped, hitting one map. I moved his finger until the drops were poised over the second drawing. Two drops were sufficient. I released him.

"We need blood," I said. "You and Isabel share a tie of consanguinity. It's not as strong as it would be if we had Manny or Angela's blood, but I think it will do."

He sucked on his cut finger, thinking it over, then slowly nodded. "You're talking about finding similars on the aetheric."

"The Wardens do this?"

"Not with the actual mutilation and bleeding," he said. "Next time, ask before you cut me."

I folded the knife and put it away. "Next time," I said, "I doubt I'll have to ask."

The blood drops were formless blotches on the maps, signifying nothing without the application of will and energy. I held out my hand, and Luis sighed and offered his unwounded one for me to hold.

We focused together on the maps.

What we were doing was, in fact, harder than it might seem; the maps were only a representation of the earth, not the aetheric spirit. If the maps themselves had actually been carried through the distance that was shown, they would appear more fully in the aetheric. In fact, the route I had taken from Albuquerque to Sedona was clearly glowing in Oversight, when I went up to survey our work. The rest of the maps, except for certain parts of the town of Albuquerque, was pale and ghostly—and then Luis touched the map, in the real world, and added all of his experience into its reality, as well.

The map took on depth, dimension, life. A miniature of this section of the world. Luis, like his brother, had traveled widely in this part of the country.

The drops of his blood glowed like fireballs in the aetheric, but their glow would quickly fade as natural decomposition set in. It was an odd thing that the very fuel that drove blood cells—oxygen—was also what corroded them. Already, the iron content was showing a chemical change.

Isabel's connection to Luis was, in mathematical terms, a small percentage. She had half of her father's DNA, half of her mother's; of Manny's DNA, half would be identical to Luis's. The best we could hope for would be a 25 percent connection between the two.

It was still a strong bond. *Like calls to like.* One of the founding principles of the world.

Luis's blood drops glowed brighter, as I bathed them with the essence of the Earth. They rolled very slowly across the plastic, tracing a path in wet trails, from Albuquerque. . . .

. . . Heading north, straight north, winding along the highway that led up to Colorado.

The blood drops on the New Mexico map trembled and stopped moving just before the town of Counselor.

On the other map, the drops showed the same.

"Jicarilla Apache reservation," Luis said. "That's where she is."

The drops—only faintly glowing now on the aetheric—nudged forward another fraction of an inch.

"That's where she is now," I agreed. "But she's moving."

We dropped out of the aetheric, and I wiped the blood from the plastic-coated maps before folding them and placing them in the interior pocket of my jacket.

We studied each other for a long, silent moment, and then Luis said, "You going to be up for this?"

"To finding Isabel? Yes." I was no longer holding his hand, and so had only the smallest access to the aetheric, but the darkness in his aura was very clear. "You aren't."

He blinked. "What?"

"You need rest, Luis. You can't sleep on the motor-cycle. I need for you to be awake and alert."

He shook his head. "No time. Every minute counts, Cassiel. What if—what if they hurt her—" He did not want to think about all the terrible things that could happen to a child, and neither did I.

"If they hurt her," I said, "we will know." I felt that to be true. The bond we had formed was strong enough, and Luis's Earth Warden powers only ampli-fied it. "Luis, you must rest. If you don't, you won't have any power to give me, and this trip will be wasted. We accomplish nothing."

He didn't want to sleep. When I stretched him out on the bed and placed my hand on his forehead, he still fought against the descending darkness. Some-thing in him was too weary to go on—I could sense it—but some other part refused to let go. He'd spent a massive amount of energy in the past twenty-four hours, and I didn't understand his resistance.

His fingers wrapped around my wrist, but he didn't pull my hand away from his forehead. Even at close range, in the dimness, his dark eyes looked like pools of shadow.

"Promise me," he said. "You promise me that you'll get her back even if something happens to me. *Promise.*"

"I will," I said.

"Again."

"I will."

His fingers tightened. *"Again."*

"I will," I said. I bent forward to brush my fingers on his parted lips. "Sleep."

His eyes drifted closed, and his grip loosened on my wrist, falling away.

I had meant to give him only the slightest contact, but his lips felt warm and soft beneath my fingers, and I lingered.

I stayed where I was until I was certain he was asleep, and then I moved to the small, stained armchair near the window. I watched the parking lot. There was little activity, and no one seemed to take an interest in our room.

A thief approached my motorcycle once, looking around to see if anyone was watching; when he tried to roll it away, I softened the asphalt beneath his feet, trapping him, and opened the door. He stared at me, struggling to free himself from what must have seemed to him a nightmare.

"Leave," I told him, and restored the ground beneath his feet. "Don't come back." It seemed I should say something more constructive, perhaps. "And don't steal."

He looked down at his oil-stained athletic shoes and ran.

I went back to the chair, and before dawn came, I slid into a light, dreaming sleep.

I woke up to the smell of brewing coffee and running water. The shower. Luis was bathing. I felt stiff and uncomfortable, but warm enough; I looked down and saw that he had given me a blanket sometime during my rest. I rose, folded the cover, and walked to the coffeepot. I poured two cups and carried them into the bathroom.

Luis was a shadowy form behind the plastic curtain. I set the cup on the countertop.

"Cassiel?" The curtain moved aside, revealing only his face. "What the hell are you doing?"

"Bringing you coffee," I said.

"Yeah, okay, thanks, but—" He sighed. "Privacy's not really a concept for you, is it?"

I gave him a slow, thin smile. "Do you imagine I long to see you naked?"

Put that way, he had no answer. He let the curtain drop back in place.

I leaned against the counter and sipped my coffee, watching the shadowy form move, and when the water shut off, I went back into the bedroom.

Luis dressed quickly. While he was doing so, I washed myself in the overheated bathroom. The cooler air of the bedroom felt good on my damp skin when I walked out, my clothing over my arm.

Naked.

Luis looked, a kind of involuntary inspection, but then he turned his back. I made no comment as I dragged on my underwear and clothing, layer by layer, with the leather on the topmost. "I am not shy," I assured him. "It's not a Djinn trait."

"Yeah," he agreed. "I get that, actually." He sounded very odd. He glanced over his shoulder, saw that I had clothed myself, and faced me again. "We've lost a lot of time."

"No more than we would have if we'd gone as we were, faced our enemies, and lost," I said. "I have her trace now, on the aetheric. I won't lose them again."

Not unless they realized the trick I had used to form the link, and found a way to break it.

I had to hope that they had taken the child for a

reason, because the easiest possible way to sever the link was by killing her.

Luis drained the last of his coffee. "Let's roll."

A quick stop to outfit us both with helmets, and we were on the trail. It was a short enough drive into the Jicarilla reservation. Outside of Albuquerque, the New Mexico landscape edged away into dusty sages, ochers, and reds. There was vegetation, but it was the hardy kind, living on little and surviving much.

I felt an odd kind of kinship with it.

As we traveled, I assessed Luis's condition. He was stronger today, and his reservoir of power had replenished itself. That reservoir, in human Wardens, seeped in from the world around them, a kind of osmosis that I seemed incapable of copying. It would be easier to absorb some of that power through the contact of skin, but I found that if I concentrated and was cautious, I could siphon small amounts even through the shielded contact where his hands held my waist.

I trembled with relief as his warm energy sank through my starved tissues, but I did not think he could feel it. The sensation was likely lost in the road vibration of the Victory as we sped through long, empty miles.

The map had shown us the route that Isabel had followed, but our analysis of alternatives showed us better-paved highways where I could open the throttle on the motorcycle and rocket us along at much higher speeds. Illegal, and therefore a risk, but like Luis, I felt desperate to make better time.

Ibby's captors might be the same who'd launched such vicious attacks against Manny, against me, against Luis. If so, they'd shown little mercy or regard for innocents, and I could not be sure that Isabel's tender age would make any difference to them.

In two hours, we crossed the border into the Jicarilla reservation. There was little to mark it—faded signs and the same harsh country. State Highway 537 led through the heart of it.

I pulled over to the side of the dusty road, into soft sand, to go up into the aetheric. Isabel's position had moved on, but it was not far ahead . . . another two hours at most.

I wondered why our enemies were moving so slowly. Surely a five-year-old child couldn't hold back their progress so drastically.

Unless . . . they meant us to follow. Why attack us, wasting their own energy, when they could force us to waste ours in pursuit, and trap us in the end?

I didn't speak of it to Luis, but I knew his thoughts would have led him to the same conclusions. The technique we had used to track the girl was rare, but not unknown among Earth Wardens; we had perhaps used a less common tactic, but if our opponents were as determined as I expected, they could have planned against it.

And the Jicarilla reservation stretched across the border, from New Mexico into Colorado.

"What are you doing? We need to get moving!" Luis said. He'd taken care of his call of nature, and mine could wait. "Something wrong?"

"I don't know," I said. "How many Wardens between here and the Colorado border?"

"Zero. We're stretched a little thin, you know, and besides, far as I know, there's only one or two left in the entire state. Most of the top rank went to answer Lewis's call on the coast. They're gone now, out of the country."

I turned my head slightly. "Were you asked to go?"

"Yeah." His tone didn't invite further conversation on the subject. "Why are you worried about Wardens all of a sudden?"

I fixed my eyes on the far, shimmering horizon,

where the black ribbon of the road rose up to meet the sky in a vanishing point, and I held out my hand to him. After a hesitation, he took it, and this time, I was the leader rising into the aetheric. We did not go far. We didn't have to.

When we dropped down again, Luis shuddered as he entered his flesh again, and said, "Damn. I was hoping they wouldn't know we were coming."

"So was I," I said. "Helmets."

"Helmets won't help visibility," he pointed out. "You'll be driving blind."

"Put your hand on my back," I said. "On my skin. I can use Oversight if you don't let go."

"You think you can drive like that?"

Blind? Using only the confusing information available on the aetheric to see? Possibly. What choice did I have?

I watched the vanishing point on the horizon grow hazy, then disappear as dirty red smudged the clear blue sky in an uneven, growing line.

What I was showing him in the aetheric was a sandstorm coming. A bad one.

I donned my helmet. It wouldn't keep out everything, but it would do enough to allow me to breathe—unless the plastic broke. I didn't want to consider that possibility. Behind me, I felt Luis adjusting his own helmet, and then his hands slid up under my jacket, tugged my shirt from my trousers, and settled in a warm span on either side of my waist, skin on skin.

The connection snapped tight between us, stronger for the touch, and I took in a deep breath.

"Keep your head down," I told him. "I don't know what else might come out of the dark."

I pressed the throttle and threw sand on the still air, achieved the solid surface of the road, and the Victory dug into the asphalt, growling its challenge. I

edged the speed faster and faster. It reminded me of
old days, of horses thundering toward the enemy lines,
of knights jousting, of a pure, clean purpose. Kill or
die.

The red line on the horizon boiled up and out, like
ink dropped in water. I felt the forces driving it—not
Earth but Weather, the interaction of cold and warm
air creating this deadly and explosive windstorm. In
wetter climates, it would have brought thunder and
rain, but here it only lashed the land, picked up abrasive grit and rubbed it together, building its own energy within the sandstorm.

The first gust of wind danced across the prairie,
heading for us at a right angle. *Tornado*, my mind
named it at first, but I knew that was not right. *Gust-
nado*. It didn't matter what it was called, only that it
hit us broadside in a stinging, powerful rush, and I felt
the back tire of the Victory skid a bit, then grab trac-
tion again. The oncoming wall of sand grew darker as
it came on—still red, but shading now toward brown
as more and more light was blocked. It would blot
out the sun altogether.

"We can't do it!" Luis yelled behind me. I didn't
have the time to answer. It was true: we couldn't possibly affect the entire sandstorm, but I wasn't trying
to. All I wanted was a tunnel through it, a lessening
of the intensity. We could do that. I was certain we
could.

I was certain until the moment I realized how *huge*
the storm truly was. It had looked large from a distance, but it was monstrous now, and still growing
larger. It covered the horizon in red-brown waves, rip-
pling like silk, stretching to the heavens.

A dusty, rattling pickup truck roared up from a side
road, took the turn, and sped past us going the other
direction. I heard the driver shout a warning to us.
He was running.

That was sensible. But on the other side of that wall lay the child we'd come to find, and I wasn't willing to admit defeat. Not yet.

"Stop!" Luis yelled. I barely heard him through the contact of our two helmets, as if we were in the vacuum of outer space instead of safe on the ground. "We can't do it!"

"Hold!" I ordered him. I bent my head, firmed my grip on the Victory, and kept rocketing forward.

We hit the sand, or the sand hit us, with the force of a net stretched across the road. If I had not clung viciously to the motorcycle, we'd have been thrown headlong, likely killed. The Victory skidded, and I tried to right her, but the darkness and screaming sand had no direction, no dimensions. Which way was forward? Even my instincts flailed helplessly. The storm had reached an intensity that crackled with its own energy and power, a half-sentient monster whose only mission was to expand, consume, *grow*. Life, at its most basic.

Oversight helped a little. I drew power through the grip of Luis's hands on my waist and poured it in a laser-straight line through the darkness in the direction I *thought* was north. Even with his power and my ability to amplify and control, I achieved no more than a narrow window in which the sand was merely thick instead of smothering.

I accelerated again, following the line. Around us, the walls of darkness swirled and lashed. The faceplate on my helmet was scratched first, then scoured into fog by the unrelenting blast. I felt a sharp pain in my leg, then another in my shoulder. Rocks. There would be more debris mixed in as the sandstorm's power grew. It could pick up metal, barbwire, wooden posts.

A strand of barbwire could decapitate me as easily as a sword, and for a moment, my courage wavered. *I am going to kill us both.* What would happen to Isabel then?

Ahead, something flickered in the gloom. Oversight was a confusing boil of color, half-recognized patterns, nothing I could identify. . . .

And then, with shocking suddenness, the patterns resolved into gray lines, snapping into angles.

It was a car, and it was heading straight for us.

Chapter 12

I DIDN'T HAVE time to warn Luis, but from the strength with which he was holding on, he was in no danger of slipping from the bike.

I veered sharply, out of our small tunnel of clearer air, into the heart of the storm. I had no choice, and even so it almost made no difference, as I felt the sucking rush of the car's passage, and felt a hiss along the side of my boot where it bumped a passing tire.

I couldn't see it, because here in this lightless hell, there was nothing but screaming wind, burning sand, and false midnight. I had lost directions again, though there was still road beneath my wheels. I had to slow down, uncertain of where the road might end, and I coughed as sand began to filter in around my face-plate, coating my face in acrid dust. Choking me.

Luis was right. We would not survive this.

You're afraid, the Djinn ghost of me whispered. *Like a human.*

And once, I might have found that ridiculous or a matter for contempt. Now I found it a matter of survival. Every nerve in my body screamed in anguish. I wanted to hide, to curl up in a protective ball and wait for this terrible thing to pass me by.

That's your flesh thinking, the Djinn ghost of me said. *That's what they want you to do.* And she was right about that. If this was a Warden-driven storm, it could hover in place, flaying the leather from my back, the skin from my body, like being caught in a sandblaster.

I picked a direction based purely on instinct, and hit the throttle full speed. If I ran off the road into the sand, we'd crash and die in the storm. *I won't*, I told the screaming panic inside me. *I am in control.*

The tires chewed loose gravel in the dark. I took in a gasp, choked, coughed. My mouth was coated with dust.

The handlebars of the Victory danced with hot blue sparks.

I veered left again, off of the shoulder, found the edge by trial and error, and concentrated on short, shallow breaths as we sped into the boiling, punishing darkness.

Something hard and hot slammed into my thigh and dragged loose. Metal, I thought. Wire, most likely.

Faster.

The storm could not last forever. Not even the most powerful Warden, the greatest Djinn, could keep this focus for long. Weather was the most unstable of forces, spinning apart under its own weight.

Oversight showed me nothing, a chaos, an unending sea of flashes and smoke and fog.

And then, dimly, a light.

My scoured, abraded faceplate cracked with a sound like thunder, and the drift of dust behind it became a rushing torrent into my face. I squeezed my aching eyes shut. I was driving blind in any case.

There was no way to draw breath, so I held it, struggling against the impulse to cough.

Almost there. Almost . . .

We burst out of the back side of the sandstorm, into stillness and drifting, smokelike dust. Overhead, the sky was a dull orange, the sun a shriveled dot.

There was no road, only a flatter area of sand.

I skidded the motorcycle to a stop and clawed at my helmet. The buckles seemed frozen in place, but it finally popped free, and as I removed it, the face-plate fell off in two pieces. The plastic was as gray and foggy as the eyes of a corpse.

My helmet, on the front side, had been stripped of paint, reduced to dull gray. A fountain of dirt cascaded out as I dropped it to the road. More dust spilled as I bent my head. I coughed uncontrollably, spitting up dirty mouthfuls, and I finally felt Luis's hands let go of me. I'd have bruises where he'd gripped, I thought, with every finger clearly imprinted.

Luis got off the motorcycle and staggered a few steps as he tried to wrestle off his own helmet. He'd been protected by my body, but even so, when he turned, his face was a muddy mask of sweat and dirt. He coughed and spat, bracing himself with both hands on his knees, and shook his head.

"Can't believe we made it," he croaked. I couldn't speak at all, I discovered. My throat wouldn't cooperate. "You okay?"

I gave him a thumbs-up gesture. Running through my abused body was a rush of warmth, of ecstatic satisfaction.

I had survived. I had forced myself through, and I had *survived*.

As a Djinn, I had never understood how it felt to win against such odds. *It's only adrenaline,* that old part of me scoffed. *Illusion and hormones.*

Behind us, the sandstorm rolled on, howling, black as night. There was nothing we could do to stop its progress, nor was I inclined to try.

I set my face forward, toward Colorado, where Isabel's track still led.

Neither of us could go on for long without some kind of relief. It appeared in the form of a dilapidated,

UNDONE219

barely operating roadside motel just shy of the state line. If it had a name, I didn't see it, only the rusting, flapping sign that said MOTEL, and below that COLOR TV AND AIR-CONDITIONING.

The Victory was coughing as much as I was, and I hoped that it had not been badly damaged by the sandstorm. It had blasted edges, pitted and smoothed, but seemed to have come through relatively unscathed. The same could not be said for me.

I rented a room using gestures and the Warden credit card that bore the name of Leslie Raine. The attendant behind the ancient, cracked counter looked young and far too excited to see a customer. "Y'all were in that sandstorm?" he asked as he hand-cranked a machine to get an imprint of the card. I nodded. "Y'all are lucky to be alive," he said. "Here ya go. Sign here."

I signed where he told me, using the name on the card. The boy was fascinated with my pink hair—still visible, though coated with dirt. "Not from around here," he decided. "Dallas? LA? Las Vegas?"

"Albuquerque," Luis said, and coughed. "Water?"

"Machine out front," the boy said. "Cost you a dollar and a quarter, though. Water fountain right there for free. Well water; no city water." He said it proudly. I raised an eyebrow at Luis, who gave me a mud-caked thin smile in return. As Wardens, we both understood well that *natural* did not equal *safe.* I mutely handed Luis several dollars, and he left to patronize the less risky choice.

The boy looked disappointed in our lack of moral courage. "Okay, then," he said, and handed me a grimy key on an even grimier orange plastic dangle, which was marked with the number 2. "Here you go. A/C's working, clean sheets, adult channel no charge."

I gave him a long stare for that last, and walked out into the brilliant sunlight. Luis was retrieving the last of four cold bottles of water from a sun-faded vending machine. I walked past him to the door that matched the key, opened it, and surveyed our temporary refuge. It wasn't even as much as the motel in which I'd stayed in Albuquerque, but the desk clerk had not lied—there was a bed, neatly made, and once I'd switched the air conditioner on, the blasting breeze was cool. I dropped the key on a table and started shedding layers of clothing on my way to the bathroom, sending cascades of gritty sand down to the carpet. Beneath the layers my skin was filthy and abraded, in places down to the muscle.

I stood under the water for a long time, until what swirled down the drain was clear instead of sandy, and as soon as I stepped out Luis was moving past me, naked, heading in. We said nothing to each other. He averted his eyes from me, and after my first glance, I did him the same. I shook out my clothing and cleaned it with a small burst of power, then did the same for his as the shower continued to run in the bathroom. Fully dressed again, I drank two bottles of water and stared out the motel room's window at the sandstorm, which was proceeding toward the horizon.

I heard the shower shut off, and in a few minutes the rustle of cloth behind me as Luis began to dress. We had said nothing, but there seemed to be communication between us nevertheless. I was acutely aware of him, every movement, and I wondered if he had the same sensation of me.

I handed him a bottle of water, which he thirstily guzzled, and then the second. It was only as he neared the end of that one that Luis said, "You still have the trace?"

I nodded and sipped.

"I've been thinking," he said. "Maybe this isn't about us at all. Maybe it's about Isabel."

That surprised me, and I turned toward him. "How can it be? She's a *child*." My voice had returned, but it was thin and scratchy. I cleared my throat and drank more water.

"Yeah, I know, but hear me out. It seems like they're not in the kidnap-for-ransom business—they haven't called in any kind of demand, not even to get us to back off. They had to have been watching the house to find an opportunity to grab her. So what if all of this has been to grab Ibby, not to kill Manny or Angela or me or you? We're just—"

"Obstacles," I finished softly. "But what value can a five-year-old child hold? Is she even displaying any talents as a Warden?"

"Not yet. Most kids don't until they hit puberty. But it does run in our family." He shrugged. "I started using mine pretty early. Around nine, I think."

I thought back and wondered. It seemed impossible that the attacks would have been designed solely to eliminate potential guardians for the child, but he was right: Taking Isabel seemed to be a primary goal, not a secondary one.

"Then they won't let her go easily," I said. "If they did all this to ensure they could get her."

Luis was watching me, and his expression was tense and grave. "You think they'll kill her?"

"I don't know," I said softly. "I don't know what they want from her."

I turned in the key to the desk clerk ten minutes later, which led to his anxious worry that we had found something wrong with the accommodations, and Luis and I mounted the Victory and resumed the journey.

The trace, on the aetheric, was still there, and still definite. Isabel was ahead of us, but only by an hour. Whatever method of travel they were using to transport her, it was slower than our motorcycle, even double loaded. I opened the throttle, and we began to close the distance.

We rode for almost an hour, and my hunting

instincts—inherited from the Djinn I had been as well as the flesh I wore—bayed for blood. We were maddeningly close, so close that a single fold of the horizon hid her from us.

Careful, the cautious part of me warned. *They'll fight to keep her.*

"Colorado!" Luis shouted as we flashed past a large sign. I didn't care about the boundaries. Isabel's track was only a few miles ahead of us, and I intended to catch them. "Dammit! Cassiel, slow down—cops!"

I saw the cruiser as we flew past it, sitting nose out in a dirt road at the side of the highway. I glanced in my rearview mirror to see if he'd take up the pursuit.

He did.

"Pull over!" Luis was shouting to me now. "You can't outrun them on a straight road; just pull over!"

I slowed. It was hard. My instincts howled to keep on chasing, and although I knew he was right, it seemed wrong to give up so easily.

The cruiser pulled up behind us, and two men got out. One approached us while the other hung back.

"Off the bike, please," the policeman said. He was a large man, solid, with an expression that seemed blankly polite. His eyes were covered by dark sunglasses and shaded by a brimmed hat. My impression of him was one of starch and angles.

I swung my leg over the seat, as did Luis, and once we were off the motorcycle, the policeman drew his weapon and shoved it hard against my chest, right over my fragile human heart.

"Don't move," he said. Luis had frozen, not daring to protest, and that cost us, as well; the other policeman came around the car, grabbed Luis by the collar, and threw him facedown on the hot metal hood of the car.

He put the muzzle of his gun on the back of Luis's neck.

"On the ground," the man who had me said. "Facedown. Do it!"

The asphalt was hot and sticky, but I had little choice. I could resist, but I doubted I could save Luis as well as myself. Too many variables, and I didn't understand this reaction. It seemed out of proportion for a speeding violation.

"Hands!" he demanded. I felt a hard knee in the center of my back, and moved my arms within his reach behind me. He snapped cold metal over my wrists and jerked me up to my knees with a hard pull on the restraints. Pain lanced up my strained shoulders, and I bit down on a wince. "All right, bitch, you've got about one minute to tell me what I want to know. Understand?" He jammed the gun hard at the back of my head. "Understand?"

"Yes," I said. A Fire Warden might have been able to disable the guns. Perhaps it might be possible for an Earth Warden, as well, to warp the metal, but undoing the chemical reaction that fired the bullet was a skill that Luis did not have, and remained elusive to me.

I don't know what question I expected the policeman to ask, but it surprised me when he said, with cold intensity, "Tell me what happened to my son."

I had no idea what he was talking about, and my gaze touched Luis's, where he'd been thrown facedown against the car. His dark hair was damp and clinging to his face. He looked desperate and angry.

Dangerously so.

"What are you talking about?" Luis snapped. "Let her go, man!"

The policeman holding him down pushed harder. "Shut up."

"Yeah, I don't think so! Colorado State Police have cameras in the cars, right? Smile, you jackass, you're busted for brutality!"

"Luis! Enough!" I said, and twisted enough that I could see the edge of the policeman's face, the one holding the gun to my head. "I don't know what you are talking about. Who is your son?"

It was a very dangerous question. I sensed the sick fury building in him, and he was mere seconds from pulling the trigger that would kill me.

"Who's my son?" he repeated. He grabbed a fistful of my pink hair and yanked my head painfully back. "*Who's my son?* You've got to be kidding me."

"Randy," the other cop said. "This guy's got a point. We're exposed out here. You want to get straight answers, we can't do it right here on the side of the road, man."

"Cameras can be smashed," Randy said.

"Maybe so, but passing cars can't."

Randy hesitated, then grabbed the handcuffs and hauled me up to my feet. He shoved me in the direction of the police car as his partner opened the back door and put Luis inside. Luis didn't fight, but as we approached the vehicle the stench of it rolled over me—hot metal, vomit, despair, sweat, blood, stale air, and the reek of plastic—and it was hard not to dig in my feet and resist.

No. I had to learn to deal with this strange problem of mine sometime, and now, with a gun aimed at my head, it seemed a good time to begin.

I told myself it wasn't as bad as I'd thought, once I was inside the police car, but that was a fragile sort of lie that crumbled as soon as the door slammed shut beside me. The air was stifling, and it reeked. I coughed, barely controlling an urge to void my stomach, and tried not to struggle like an animal in a trap.

I am Djinn. This is nothing, nothing, nothing.

No. It was confinement. And confinement was something the Djinn hated.

Officer Randy and his partner got in the vehicle, which rocked to accommodate their weight, and we pulled out onto the road.

"You okay?" Luis asked me in a low voice. I nodded, throat working, unable to speak. I had never liked enclosed vehicles, but this one seemed ever more sinister and confining. "Don't do anything crazy."

"Yeah, listen to your friend," Randy said. We had gone about five miles from where we'd left the Victory, and now he slowed the cruiser and made a right turn on to a barely visible dirt road. The car bounced and rocked along the trail, throwing up showers of dust and rocks.

When we could no longer see the road behind us, he brought the car to a stop and turned off the engine. The *tick-tick-tick* of cooling metal and the constant low chatter from the radio speakers were the only sounds.

"Out," Randy said. His partner gave him a worried look, but complied. He and Randy opened our doors and removed us from the backseat, out into open air again. The hot air fanned the sweat that had trickled down my back, and I shivered.

Randy drew his gun again, staring at me with cool, dust brown eyes. He was a hard man, but I didn't sense real cruelty in him. Desperation, perhaps.

"Now," he said. "Let's start the movie over. Where's my son?"

Luis shook his head. "We don't know what you're talking about, Officer. We really don't."

He stuck the barrel of his gun under Luis's chin, and Luis's eyes squeezed shut to conceal what must have been either rage or fear. He didn't move, but I saw muscles flexing in his tattooed arms.

I, too, was remembering his brother, dead of a bullet.

"I'm going to kill this guy," Randy said, "and then you'll remember what I'm talking about. How's that?"

"If you do, you're a fool," I said, and got the full cold glare. He didn't move the gun away from Luis.

"Explain what's happening. Maybe we can help you. We're also looking for a child. A little girl, Isabel Rocha. She's five years old. She's been abducted from her bed."

That surprised him enough to take his finger away from the trigger and lower the weapon to his side. "What?"

"She's my niece," Luis said raggedly. "My brother and sister died in a drive-by a couple of days ago. Ibby's all I have left." For just that moment, he couldn't conceal the horror and despair of that, and I knew it rang true with the policeman, who took another sharp look at Luis, then at me. Frowning. "Goddammit, you have to believe us!"

It was convincing enough to cause uncertainty in our captor. And the frustration. "A kid," he repeated. "What the hell is going on?"

"Who is your son?" I asked softly. Randy didn't take his gaze from Luis.

"His name is C.T. Calvin Theodore Styles," Randy said. "He's five years old, and he was taken out of his bed three nights ago. Just—gone. No sign of an intruder, no clues."

Randy's partner, who seemed visibly relieved that violence wasn't about to erupt, contributed the rest. "Randy got a call a couple of hours ago," he said. "Came to his personal cell phone, said the one who'd abducted C.T. had left him somewhere to die, and was heading this way."

Randy finally shifted his attention back to me. "The caller said I'd know her by the motorcycle and the pink hair."

"That caller," I replied, "is the one who has your son, and more than likely Isabel. I have nothing to do with it, but they are using you, and me, to slow down pursuit."

Randy kept staring at me. "I get why he's in this," he said. "Family. Why are you?"

It seemed a fair question, and all I could do was shrug, as hard as that was to do with my hands manacled behind my back. "Family," I said. "They're all I have, as well."

That, too, rang true to his lie-sensitive ears, and he exchanged a glance with his partner, who nodded. Without a word between them, they unlocked our handcuffs. Handcuffs, I realized, that either of us could have melted away at any moment . . . and had not. Luis had likely been biding his time, waiting for a strategic moment. I had been—what? Distracted? *Djinn are not distracted.*

"You got a picture of the girl?" the policeman was asking.

"Yeah," Luis said. He dug in his back pocket and flipped photos, stopping on one that showed Manny, Angela, and Isabel in some sort of holiday setting. They were frozen in that moment, happy and glowing. Alive.

It hurt me to look at it. *This is how things are for them. Time is a long road, with tragedy around every turn. They can't go back; they can only bring the past forward with them in fragments and photographs and memories.*

No, not *them.* I was human now, to all intents and purposes. Like them, I was traveling that road now, and time was an enemy: a thief, stealing moments and memories and lives.

Randy—Officer Styles—flipped to Luis's identification card, then examined his other photographs before handing it all back. He was cautious, which reflected well on him. "I'm sorry for your loss," he said. "They look like nice people."

"They were," Luis said. I could tell it was still hard for him to use the past tense of the verb. He put his wallet back in his pocket and sent me a glance. "So where are we? We good now?"

"Yeah," the policeman nodded. "We're good, until

I find out you're shining me on, and then both of you are food for crows if I find out you had anything, *anything* to do with my son's abduction. Clear?"

Luis nodded. "Clear."

Officer Styles's attention turned to me. "Pink, what's your name?"

I almost answered *Cassiel*, but stopped myself. He had been thorough in checking Luis's identity. He'd hardly take my word for it. In answer, I took my own wallet from my jacket pocket and handed it over. He flipped it open to the driver's license. "Leslie Raine," he said, and glanced up at me. "Picture doesn't look much like you."

"Do they ever?" Luis muttered. It was good he answered for me, because I felt stung. I had used a minor amount of power to adjust the photograph to resemble me. Was he implying that I was not skillful at such forgery?

"Huh," Randy said. He studied the photo closely, then me, then the card again.

"I'm albino." Several people had referred to me so; I thought it only fair to adopt the idea. "Perhaps we don't photograph well."

"Don't albinos have pink eyes?"

"Not all of them," I said.

He flipped through the rest of the wallet. Apart from the credit cards that Lewis had provided, there was nothing else. No mementos. No photographs of any kind, saving up memories for empty days.

I wished I had taken some now, not so much to placate the policeman, but to keep Manny's smile vivid in my mind.

He handed everything back. "Kind of a light wallet."

"I'm neat."

"That's not neat, that's OCD," he said. "Okay, I'll buy you guys *might* be legitimate; we already looked you up on the computer in the car. Manny and Angela Rocha, shot dead in their front yard, just like you said. Isabel Rocha, abducted. Got a nice mug shot of *you*, sir, from bad old days."

Luis shrugged. "Reformed," he said.

"Used to be in the Norteños, right? I didn't know that was an option, getting reformed."

"I got a good job."

"Yeah? Doing what?"

"How is this helping to find your son?" I cut in. "Or Isabel?"

Officer Styles took in a breath, held it, and let it out. "It isn't, I guess," he said. "You tell me what you know about this."

It was my turn to exchange a look with *my* partner. Luis, correctly guessing that I did not have enough experience in half-truths to be credible, took the lead. "We got a lead," he said. "Isabel was spotted along this road, heading from New Mexico into Colorado. We were getting close when you stopped us. Look, if you want to come with us . . ."

"Who gave you the lead?"

Luis shook his head. "I can't tell you that. But I promise you, if you let us follow it, we'll do everything we can to get your son back while we look for Ibby."

He meant it, and I knew that Officer Styles sensed it, too. He was on the verge of saying something when his phone rang. He checked the number on the display and said, "My wife." Tension ran dark through his voice. He turned away to speak in low tones, and I did not try to hear what was said. The pain and fear coming from him was palpable, like a sickening fog.

Children, I thought. *What can our enemies want with children?*

So many terrible things.

Randy closed the phone and took a moment staring toward the horizon. When he came back to us, his manner and expression were composed, but that didn't matter. He was far from calm. "Let's go," he said.

"Randy," his partner said. "Everything okay with Leona?"

"She's just anxious. I don't want to tell her—" He shook his head. "I don't want her to know this was a bad lead. She needs a little hope."

It was astonishing, how little it took to change him from a man I needed to battle to a man I wanted to help. Djinn rarely changed their minds, but then, they had scopes of knowledge that humans did not. Human perception, I realized now, was like a prism, reflecting first one facet of a new thing and then another.

It made the matter of trusting someone even more risky. I wondered how they had ever learned to do it at all.

"Can you take us back to the motorcycle?" I asked.

"Why?"

"Because I like my motorcycle."

That seemed to amuse him, but he nodded. "Sure. Why not?"

Back on the Victory, we raced down the road with the patrol car drafting behind us. Luis's hand clasped the bare skin around my middle, sealing the connection between us and allowing me to concentrate on piloting the bike in Oversight as well as reality.

The red, faint trail of Isabel's passage on this land was fading but still present. We were on the track, and we were very, very close. Over the next fold of the road rose the growing shadows of mountains. Desert was rapidly giving way to different landscapes and plants, although the toughest, thorniest bushes continued to make their presence felt.

The air changed gradually, too. We were traveling into different climate bands.

As the sharp mountains began to cut the sky in

hard, black edges, the trace came blindingly clear, in a flare of hot red.

Luis saw it, too. His hand tightened on my waist. I increased speed, flying toward the site. If they intended to fight us, I was ready. Eager for it.

You will not take this from me. Not this.

Over the next ridge, the road fell into a gentle downward slope. There were no roads leading into the underbrush, no obvious settlements or buildings. No sign at all of human civilization here, except for this road built in a clean, straight line through nature.

I slowed, anxiety building inside me. I had expected to see *something*—a car, perhaps, or a building.

There was nothing.

And yet the trail ended here.

I slowed the motorcycle again, this time to a coast, with the engine humming and the tires hissing along the gravel at the side of the road.

I stopped.

"Oh, God," Luis said, and every sound seemed to hang sharp on the clear air. "Where is she?" He sounded as confused and afraid as I felt, and he let go of me and swung his leg over the bike to stride away. He paced like an angry lion, hair blown in a black flag by the whipping winds. Grass bent and whispered its secrets. This flat, open area concealed nothing, but a child might be small enough to be hidden in the grass—

—if the child could not move.

I slowly dismounted the bike and approached Luis, who was stalking the edge of the road, frantically sending out waves of power like radar signals, hoping to get a response.

He did. I heard the sharp intake of his breath, and then he plunged forward, off the road and into the knee-high pale stalks of grass. Insects rose up in confused clouds, disturbed by his passage. I followed him.

Behind me, the police car's doors opened and closed, and I knew the men would be right on my heels.

Luis and I leapfrogged each other, racing through the grasses, both heading for the same point of pulsing red on the aetheric.

When we reached it, there was no sign of a child. No body. No presence at all.

Luis sank down on his haunches near a bare spot in the grasses and held out his hand, palm down, over it. I put my hand on his shoulder, and it popped up in Oversight in hot red.

The soil was darker here.

"What?" Officer Styles barked, as he and his partner stumbled to a halt next to us, looking at—apparently—nothing.

Luis touched his fingers to the soil, and raised them into the light.

Blood, smeared red on his skin.

He rubbed it slowly between his fingers, expression distant and closed even to me.

"It's hers," he said softly. "It's Isabel's."

I knew, with a sinking sensation, that he wasn't wrong.

Something failed inside of him, something that had been tenaciously holding together. His hope was dying here, the precious light of it guttering out like a candle starved of oxygen.

I was on the verge of feeling the same when I became aware of a strange flutter at the edges of my awareness, a kind of red echo.

I let go of Luis's shoulder and stepped away into the grass, hunting for the source of the dissonance.

I found it. It was a plastic bag, the kind used to store blood for reuse in hospitals. It still contained a red film within it. I crouched next to it, studying it carefully.

Isabel's blood was inside of it.

"Over here," I said. Officer Styles was the first to my side.

"Don't touch it," he warned. I nodded. I had no need of touching it, in any case. The presence of the bag itself told me all I needed to know.

They had laid a false trail for us to follow. This was Isabel's blood, taken from her small body, probably while she was unconscious. The bag had held less than a pint. They had sprinkled it along the road, and left a clear trail here, to the spot where they had dumped the rest to draw us in.

I came quickly back to my feet. "Luis," I said sharply. "Be ready. They would have done this for a reason."

He looked up at me with dulled eyes, still rubbing his fingers together. Isabel's blood. He believed she was dead. I showed him the bag, but he seemed not to comprehend.

"They're coming for us," I said. "And she's still—"

I was going to say *alive*, but I didn't have the chance.

There was a low growl from the grass; something leapt at Luis's unprotected back in a dun-colored blur. I heard a chilling roar, one that woke primitive instincts inherited from millions of years of cowering in caves, waiting for predators to attack.

Human instincts, not Djinn.

The beast attacking Luis was a mountain lion, a large one, but I didn't have time to come to his aid. There were other animals closing in, moving with unnatural stealth and focus. Two more mountain lions. Loping in from the north and the south were two large black bears.

"Down!" I screamed at Officer Styles, as a mountain lion prepared to leap at his back. He didn't obey me. Instead, he spun around, gun drawn, and fired. He missed. The mountain lion crashed into him with a vicious snarl and slammed him down on the grass. His partner aimed for the animal's skull.

I knocked his gun aside at the last moment. The report of the shot startled the big cat, and it lifted its head to focus its attention toward the two of us. Huge gray-green eyes fixed on us with terrifying intensity, and it gathered itself for a leap.

"Behind me!" I shouted, and shoved the man into position. "Don't fire!"

The mountain lion launched itself into the air, scimitar-sharp claws extended to disembowel me.

"Get out of the way!" I heard the man behind me yell, but my attention was fully on the animal. Someone was pushing it, controlling it, overriding its self-preservation instincts. These creatures weren't the enemy; they were weapons, confused and terrified beneath the surface fury.

I couldn't condone their deaths, rare as such predators were on the earth since the proliferation of humans. Luis and I could handle them.

It was a risk—a large one—but I slapped my hands down on the creature's skull as it barreled into me, bearing me to the ground with a heavy thump. Soft fur, hard bone, powerful flexing muscles. I saw the flash of teeth. Its claws ripped at the leather covering my chest, and I felt the sting of cuts.

My leather had slowed it, but I had seconds, at best. I poured my power into the creature, not to dominate, but to free its mind from the cage of power that had trapped it. It seemed easier in theory, because the faceless enemy had all the strength of a top-class Earth Warden and all the ruthlessness of a Demon. I slashed at the bonds holding the cat, and it sprang away from me, snarling in terror and confusion.

It leapt past the trembling policeman behind me and vanished into the grass.

Luis's mountain lion lay unconscious on its side, breathing in slow, steady rhythm.

I dragged Officer Styles up to his feet. The four of us formed a square, shoulders touching, as the bears loped closer.

"Next time, put it under," Luis told me. "They'll just grab the animals again once you let go."

He was right. The mountain lion I'd freed from control was veering, turning back toward us at a gliding run. It slowed to a cautious, slow stalk, luminous eyes fixed on me. Its huge paws made almost no sound at all on the grass, but I could hear the low sound of its growl on the cooling air.

They would know my power now. They'd tasted it. I wouldn't be able to be so merciful again without cost. They would kill me if they could. Me, Luis, the two policemen.

All for what? For Isabel? *Why?*

"Cassiel," Luis said, and held out his hand. I hadn't realized that my reserves were sinking, but he was right. I needed power. The golden flow poured into me, waking shivers, and I cut it off as quickly as possible to keep my attention focused outward. "Put them out. Down, if you have to."

I nodded. The policemen had their guns drawn, but unless they were very fine shots I doubted they could bring down any of these animals before being gutted. The bears were charging, one on Luis's side, one on Officer Styles's.

"Go!" Luis shouted, and let go of me. I spun away from him, facing the nearest threat. It was another mountain lion, already in the air. Her muzzle was drawn back, exposing her fearsome sharp teeth, and the roar was meant to freeze me in place.

Instead, I waited until the last instant, stepped aside, and straddled the lion's back to slap my hands on its skull from behind as it landed. She roared again and twisted, but I found the blood vessels I needed, and *squeezed*.

She went limp. Still breathing, but down. I kept her

at that level as I jumped across her body to veer in front of Officer Styles, who had his gun trained on the charging black bear.

This animal was not as large as some, but large enough—at least half a man's weight, all muscle and fury. Black bears were, for the most part, good-tempered, but this one had been driven almost to the edge of madness. He was in terrible pain, and he would savage anything that came within reach of his claws and teeth.

I repeated the trick of knocking out the animal, but this time it was more difficult. I had to concentrate on the mountain lion, as well, and the bear was strong and very, very angry. When it finally collapsed into a messy tangle of broken grass, it was breathing heavily and making a noise that sounded terribly like a moan of fear.

I looked around. Luis had brought down the last mountain lion, and the other bear—cannier than the others—was pacing angrily in jerky paths, charging Luis, then backing away. Never quite committing. That one, I thought, was not fully under our enemy's control.

All in all, we had managed to come out of this well, without unnecessary death.

I should not have been so sure of that.

My first hint of more trouble was from the other policeman—CAVANAUGH, his name tag read—who put a hand on my shoulder and pointed off toward the east. A black smudge of smoke was rising about a hundred feet away. As we watched, it spread into a line, and as the dry grass caught like tinder, flames blazed six feet into the air.

The wind was toward us.

Within seconds, the smoke had reached us, thick and choking. The fire would not be far behind, and grass fires could race faster than a running man. I couldn't leave the animals helpless to burn alive, but if I freed them from control, they would turn on us.

"Run," I snarled to Styles and Cavanaugh. "Get to the car!"

They did not argue. They pelted through the smoke, into the grass, heading in the right direction. I hoped there would be nothing there to meet them, but I had other problems.

Luis coughed wetly as he stumbled to my side. "Gotta go!" he shouted. I nodded.

"Go first!"

He clearly didn't wish to, but he loped into a run and was immediately lost in the thickening smoke. I was coughing now myself, and my nose and eyes were dripping fluids. The air was filthy and thick.

I released the animals all at once, with a snap of power, and three mountain lions and one bear rolled up to their paws.

All oriented on me.

All forced to ignore their natural instincts, which would have taken them from the fire into safety.

They moved to circle me.

I waited until one darted toward me, then dodged and jumped the circle, and *ran*. Not toward the road—I could not be sure that the others had made it to safety yet, and I didn't want to draw an attack to them.

I ran to the north, toward the trees. I fed my muscles on pure golden Earth Warden energy, putting on a burst of speed that kept the mountain lions bounding a few feet behind me. The smoke was blinding, and I felt a blast of heat loom at me from the right, hot enough to sear. I smelled my hair burning, an acrid and stomach-turning stench, and veered to the left as flames flickered and took hold in front of me.

It was no use. The field was fully in flame now, driving me toward the road in a broad, shrinking arc.

Out of desperation, I softened the ground beneath my feet and dropped into a sinkhole of powder-soft sand, plunging grave deep into the earth. I hardened the top as quickly as possible, and felt the thunder as the animals charged on, chasing shadows.

The pressure of the sand and earth around me was intense—cool, insistent, constant. I struggled not to fight it, concentrating instead on holding my breath and staying calm, calm, calm. Seconds ticked by, slow as torture. I counted every pulse beat.

When I could no longer resist the need to struggle for breath, I reversed the process, hardening the sand beneath my feet in stages, and rose from the ground like a dusty, pink-haired Aphrodite. . . .

. . . Into a blackened, stubbled, smoking emptiness like the shores of hell. The fire had passed over me and was sweeping toward the road, leaving smolders and sparks behind, and little else.

There was no sign of the mountain lions or the bears. They had lost me, and continued to race on to the safety of the trees, or veered toward the road.

I felt exhausted, bruised, and smoke soaked as I limped toward the line of flames and black billows. Before I reached it, the last of the grass was consumed to twisted ash, the wind carried sparks across the road, and the field on the other side of the pavement began to burn.

As smoke cleared, blown by the constant wind, I saw that the patrol car was intact, though smoke stained, and so was the Victory. The car doors opened.

Both policemen were safe.

There was no sign of Luis.

Chapter 13

I SEARCHED UNTIL my strength failed, but there was no trace of him. No sign of his body, either. It was dimly possible that he had been caught by the animals and dragged into the trees, but I thought he was too good an Earth Warden to have gone without a trace. And without a fight.

He had simply vanished into thin air, like his niece before him.

And now I was alone.

I had, at least, earned the respect of the two policemen. Styles required no explanations of me; he simply accepted it, perhaps too focused on the enormity of his missing child to care about any abilities Luis and I might have displayed. He would, I thought, find some logical reasons to forget or dismiss it all. Humans were well-practiced in the art of denying what did not fit their neatly ordered view of the world.

His partner Cavanaugh, however, seemed less willing to shrug it off. "But *how* did you take down a cat like that? I mean, it's a friggin' *mountain lion*, not a tabby, and I can't even get my cat to the vet without getting my face clawed off." We were standing at the edge of the road, staring out at the blackened field. I had given up roaming in search of my missing Warden, and simply waited.

What I waited for, I couldn't say. Perhaps I was just tired of losing people.

"It's a simple thing," I said wearily. "Any vet could do it. Pressure points."

"Pressure points?" he echoed, eyebrows rounding in disbelief. "You're kidding. I watch the Discovery Channel, and I never heard of anything like pressure points on a mountain lion. And, anyway, those big cats aren't like African lions—they don't travel in packs like that. It's not natural. And the bears—what the hell was going on? I've never seen black bears attack like that."

"The fire," I said. "Driving animals out into the open."

He was already shaking his head. "Panicked animals keep on running—they don't stop to attack everything in their path. I don't get it, but I don't think I want to, right? This is some kind of CIA thing—you'd tell me but you'd have to kill me?"

And then Officer Styles turned and said, "You're an Earth Warden." I was temporarily surprised into silence. He didn't wait for my answer in any case. "Christ, I can't believe this."

"How do you know of the—"

He made a sharp, angry gesture. "My wife opted out of the Wardens about ten years ago. She was a Fire Warden. They did that surgery on her, the kind that blocks powers."

The world took on a different reality to me in that moment. There *was* a connection: Wardens. *Children of Wardens.* "Has your son displayed any kind of talents?"

"No, of course not. He's *five.*"

Neither Manny nor Angela had referred to Isabel having such abilities, either, and it would be extremely rare for them to manifest so early.

But not impossible. Luis had told me himself that his abilities had begun to make themselves known at an early age.

Styles was watching me closely. "This kid you're chasing, she's his niece. He's a Warden, right?"

"His brother also was," I said. "There is a strong genetic disposition for the abilities to run in families, although it does occur spontaneously, as well." I had studied the phenomenon of Warden abilities in humans for a long time, seeking to discover why they developed, and how to stop them from doing so. I had found no answers.

Officer Cavanaugh was looking at the two of us as if we'd sprouted tentacles. "What in the hell is a Warden? You mean, like a prison warden? Wait, are you talking about those crazy con artists who put on that show for the news in Florida?"

Neither of us paid him any mind. "You think these people—whoever they are—are grabbing Warden kids," Styles said. Muscles jumped along his jawline, as if he were resisting the urge to bite. "My God. How widespread is this?"

"I don't know. The Wardens are—" Secretive. Devious. Embattled. "Not inclined to share their information with those beyond their circle. If there have been other Warden children abducted, the fact that the parents were Wardens would not have been noted in any police reports. We would have to cross-reference lists of Wardens with parents who have reported their children as missing." It was a difficult time for the Wardens, and that made it a perfect time for their enemies to strike. Many parents, if they were off traveling with Lewis Orwell's party, might not even know yet that their children were missing, but I couldn't believe it to be so widespread. This had the feeling of cold, clinical planning, and a laser focus.

Luis could gain access to Warden records. *If he's still alive,* part of me whispered mockingly, but I hushed it. He was alive. I had taken energy from him, and our bond had grown steadily stronger. I would have known if his life had been snuffed out. I had known when Manny . . .

No. He was alive, and had either been taken or followed a trail without me. Or perhaps even both. He could have been lured away and then captured. Not impossible, in all the confusion. He might have even gone willingly, if they had used Isabel to draw him in.

A tremor of rage went through me, burning a red-hot wire trail from the crown of my head to the soles of my feet. Those who had done this—who *continued* to do it—would pay dearly. I had been born into flesh without an instinct for mercy, and what little I had learned had been burned away by this latest affront.

"What can we do?" the other policeman asked. I took a deep breath and deliberately banked the fire inside of me, saving it for a more appropriate time and target.

"You can start by looking through your records," I said. "Any missing or abducted children."

Styles's face could have been formed from concrete. "You got any idea how many of those there are every year?"

"An unpleasantly large number?" I didn't wait for confirmation. "We have little time, Officer Styles. Luis may have no time at all. I must find him and Isabel. I pledge to you that if I find your son, I will bring him back to you safely, but I need to go. Now."

"Go where?" That was a reasonable enough question. I had no reasonable answer.

"Away," I said. "Away from here."

He exchanged another of those looks with his partner, who finally shrugged. "Don't know, man. She could have let us die a couple of times. She didn't. I have to count that in her favor."

Styles's attention returned to me. "I don't trust Wardens," he said. "My wife doesn't trust them. If the Wardens are behind this—"

I could not believe they were. At least, not the official organization. Lewis Orwell and Joanne Baldwin, in particular, would never have condoned it. "I will find out," I said. "I swear that to you."

He nodded and stepped back.

I climbed on the Victory, checked the gauges, and started the engine. I would need gas soon, but for now all I wanted was to get away from the stench of burned grass and defeat.

Officer Styles didn't raise his hand in farewell to me, but I supposed the fact that he also didn't raise a gun was a bit of a triumph.

I went on, heading into Colorado. I was no longer sure my answers lay ahead, but movement, any movement, was better than standing still when there was so little time to waste.

I was five miles down the road when I heard the whisper: Luis's voice, clear as if his lips were beside my ear. "Cassie."

Don't call me that. I sensed a pulse of lazy amusement from him.

"Cassiel."

I brought the motorcycle to a tire-burning halt at the side of the road. The wind had picked up again, whipping dirt in swirls over me. I closed my eyes and concentrated, turning inward. Seeking.

It was his voice, but not his presence. "Luis? Where are you?"

"I'm tied up in the back of a truck," he said. He sounded remarkably slow and calm about it. "Sorry. They grabbed me in the smoke. Not much I could do."

He was lying to me. No Earth Warden would find it difficult to get away from such a situation. Ropes, metal—it was all subject to their power and therefore significantly less effective, unless the enemy also had a Warden focused on preventing his escape.

"You went willingly," I said.

"Busted." He sounded faintly amused about it—and

drugged, perhaps. I was not amused at all. "Look, they suckered us. They set a trap for us. If we want to get to Ibby, we have to let them take us to her. Don't you get it? We have to stop fighting."

"You have no idea what they want from you," I said. "Or what they will do to you. Luis, tell me where you are. *Tell me.*"

"No. Not until I'm ready. I don't want you busting in and blowing everything, and I know you. You're about as subtle as a lead pipe. When I see Isabel, when I know she's safe, I'll signal you."

"How are you doing this?"

"I'm vibrating your eardrum. Old Earth Warden trick for covert operations," Luis said. His tone changed. "Got to go. We're heading north now. Follow us."

And then he was gone, and I heard nothing but the steady, low moan of the wind.

Fool.

I had no choice but to follow his instructions.

I stopped for gas after two more hours of riding and waiting. I heard nothing from Luis, not even that faint and intimate whisper of my name. I wondered if he knew how that had sounded, how *warm.*

I wondered if I had imagined it.

He needs you, part of me said. *That doesn't mean he cares for you. Why should he? You're hardly inviting it.*

It was a foolish thought. There were so many larger things at risk, and it was yet another signal to me that I was sinking ever deeper in the quagmire of humanity. I had to struggle harder, reject these emotions, the pleasures and seductions of this flesh.

I purchased a hot dog at the gas station and ate it while standing next to my motorcycle as the tank filled. I drank a large bottled water before pressing on into the gathering darkness. The road continued to climb, heading from desert to lusher regions, thickening with trees. The stars were already bright, even though the sun hadn't completely slipped behind the branches, and the road was in deep velvet shadows.

At Pagosa Springs, Luis's voice returned to my ear to say that they were still heading north, following the same route I was traveling. "Don't gain on us," he warned. "I don't want to spook them."

I ignored that last, and accelerated.

What traffic there had been fell away. It seemed as if I had the road to myself, traveling endlessly through a cradle of dimly seen mountains that rose to brush stars from the sky. I glimpsed animals on the road—deer, fox, an owl swooping into the hot glow of my headlights to pluck a scurrying mouse from the pavement.

It almost seemed peaceful.

There were no towns, and no turns to take, until I neared the intersection of Highway 160. Luis was silent on the subject of a change in direction, so I continued on, following the twists of the road as it switched northwest, then seemed to reverse directions altogether after the town of Creede. After that, it took another sharp turn, back to the north, avoiding the massive upthrust of mountains.

"Cassiel," Luis whispered, and I involuntarily slowed, surprised again by his sudden appearance inside my skull. "We turned off the main road about five miles before you get to Lake City. We're heading west."

"Are there markers?"

"Look for a leaning dead pine; it's caught in between two others. The turnoff is about ten feet farther on. It's on the left." Luis no longer sounded as casual as he had been, or as confident. "Look, I think—I think they're screwing with my body chemistry. It's subtle, but I think they're making me high, and I can't control my powers as well as I—"

His voice broke up into an earsplitting shriek of

noise. I stopped the motorcycle, clapping my hands to my ears. It didn't help, of course. The metallic scream went on, drilling into my head. Deafening. It seemed to be increasing in power, and I knew that it was only a matter of seconds before it ruptured the fragile skin of my eardrum.

This, at least, I could prevent. It was a relatively simple matter to dampen the vibrations to a low hum of static. Of course, this meant cutting off Luis, as well. Whether it was his own lack of control, as he'd said, or an attack using him as a medium, I couldn't afford the risk of staying open to him just now.

They're making me high, he'd said. I knew, from a small sampling of popular culture and newspapers, that he meant they were giving him drugs—or, more accurately, manufacturing them within his own body. Earth Wardens had trouble healing themselves, even the most powerful of them, and if they were successful in getting past his defenses and poisoning him in that manner, it could be very, very bad.

I didn't dare reach out to him. I needed my concentration all on the road ahead.

He'd given me a small hint, at least, enough to get me on the right trail. I spotted a dead pine matching the description and slowed to a crawl, seeking the trail.

There was none. Not in ten feet, not in twenty. Not at all. I stopped the bike and slowly walked it backward as I studied the rough ground.

They'd erased it. Yes, of course they would. It was something an Earth Warden would find simple, to obscure a trail by growing new plants and moving the earth. Even a Weather Warden could erase all traces using wind and water, but from what I saw before me, I knew an Earth Warden had been behind this obscurement. Some of the saplings seemed green and new, not even weathered by the sun and wind yet.

Some of the dirt, though authentically random in its scatter, seemed freshly distributed.

I spotted the outline of a tire track deep in the brush, and forced a way for myself and the Victory through the tangle. It was at least twenty feet deep, long enough to make me wonder if they had closed the entire trail. I pressed on, ducking to avoid the worst of the stiff branches and needlelike leaves.

The growth suddenly ended, and a dirt road carved itself out of the thin and shadowy moonlight. There were tread marks still fresh in the dust.

My enemies knew I was coming. Even if Luis hadn't warned them, despite his best intentions, they would simply *know*. I had no doubt of that. I would press on as far as they'd allow before it came to conflict.

It didn't take long at all.

I accelerated as the road twisted around a darkly shadowed curve, then another, and as I came out on a straighter section, the trail was blocked by a single, small figure—a boy of Isabel's age, with ragged dark hair and huge eyes. He was wearing a grimy cotton shirt with a garish blue and red design, and small, loose cotton pants. No shoes. His face was smeared with tears, his nose was running, and he looked blank and terrified in the glare of my headlight.

I stopped in a cloud of dust, staring at him. My first impulse was to leave the bike and go to him, but my Djinn instincts tempered my human ones, infused the moment with an ice-cold clarity.

There was no reason for this child to be here, so far from his home, in the middle of the night.

"Is your name C.T.?" I asked. "Calvin Theodore Styles?"

His eyes filled with tears that glittered in my headlight. "Mama?" He sounded lost and very uncertain. He shuffled forward a step. "I want to go home! *I want to go home!*"

His voice rose to a chilling wail, and this time not even my cautious, cold Djinn side could keep me from turning off the motorcycle and dismounting. I approached the child carefully, not wishing to frighten him more than necessary. He was sucking on his thumb, and his eyes seemed the size of the moon that loomed overhead. Silver tears washed clean trails through the grime on his face.

I was halfway to him when the next child appeared. And the next. And the next. All moving silently out of the brush.

Ten, at least, all below the age of ten. Most looked thin and ill-kept, their clothing filthy. Some lacked shoes.

All seemed far too feral for comfort, and they were all armed. Knives, for the most part, but a few had clubs. No projectile weapons, for which I was grateful.

I paused, assessing. They were all around me, coming out of the underbrush in soft, stealthy whispers of leaves and twigs.

"I'm here to help you," I said, in what I hoped was a soothing tone. "Please. My name is Cassiel. Let me help you find your homes."

None of them made a sound, not even the boy who'd wailed so pitifully. The wind through the trees made a hissing sound as the pine needles rubbed together, and I became aware how vast and empty this area was . . . and how alone I had become.

"I am looking for a girl called Isabel," I said. She wasn't here, wasn't among the feral ones. "Ibby. Do you know her?" I focused on the closest child, a girl with short blond hair. "Do you know Isabel?"

She didn't answer. None of them moved, and none blinked. It was odd and—even for a Djinn—unsettling.

C.T.—if he *was* C.T.—was no longer weeping, though tears still trailed down his cheeks. He had assumed the same cold, empty aspect as the other children.

I took a step forward toward him, and they all rushed at me in silence. I jumped, grabbing hold of a low-hanging branch, and pulled my legs up as they slashed at me with silver flashes of blades. A few made grunts of effort, jumping to try to reach me, but they didn't speak, not even to each other.

By some unspoken coordination, two of them bent over to boost up others, who caught hold of lower branches and began to climb toward me. It was a ridiculous situation, hemmed in by *infants*—and yet there was a certain cold logic to it. I would be hesitant to harm these defenseless children, while the enemy—and I knew it *was* our enemy—would not hesitate to spend every small life to hurt me.

They were the perfect shock troops.

As the first child crawled along a branch toward me, mad eyes shining, I shifted my weight and grabbed for her wrist, twisting it. The knife fell like steel leaf.

She raked my arm with her fingernails and bared her teeth.

I had no choice but to sweep her off the branch, stunning her into unconsciousness as I did so. I cushioned her fall on the dirt with a burst of power.

Another was already coming. And another behind him.

These are annoyances, my Djinn side complained. *Deal with them and move on.* And had they been adult humans, I would have done so, but the reluctance to hurt a child was encoded in my helix DNA, and not even Djinn wisdom could counter it. *You'll waste your power fighting this battle. It's what they want.*

I knew that, but I also remembered Officer Styles on the road, the desperation and trauma in his face. The promise I'd made to him.

There were ten children here. Ten families searching for answers and praying for miracles. I couldn't take that hope from them.

I dropped out of the tree, crouched, and began touching the children on the head, one after another. I forced myself to be methodical about it, ignoring their weapons. It worked for the first two. The third scored a long cut along my arm that burned like drips of fire before I sent him unconscious.

The fourth and fifth of the remaining nine went down without injury to themselves or me, but as I turned to the sixth, I felt a blinding cold pain in my side, and looked down to see that C.T. had buried a knife to the hilt in my body.

I slapped my palm down on his forehead, triggering sleep, and he collapsed to the dirt.

That left three still standing. They were two girls and another boy, and they clearly recognized the danger I represented. They stayed farther than arm's length, waiting to see what I would do.

Sink them in the ground.

No. That was my Djinn ghost talking, and I would not do it—first, because it would hurt and terrify them, and second, because I could not afford the burst of power. Not injured.

I eased my weight down to my knees, trying not to gasp as pain arced through my nerves, and reached for the knife in my side. I touched it lightly, diagnosing the wound as best I could. I did not think it had cut any significant blood vessels, but there was damage— intestines cut, a cut to my liver that could be dire if untreated.

I pulled the knife out and somehow did not cry out. Blood dripped from the steel. I held it for a moment, staring at the children who circled me, and then rammed it point first into the ground in front of me.

They rushed me all at once.

Concentrate. My vision blurred, and I blinked away the haze. My hands flashed out, right and left, and brushed sleep into the minds of two of the children. Their falling bodies caused the third to stumble, and his club, aimed for my head, struck my shoulder instead with bruising force. I grabbed it, yanked it away, and pulled him toward me. He struggled in my arms, but I held him still, staring into his empty, wide eyes.

"You," I said softly. "The one who hides behind children. I am coming for *you*."

The boy's mouth opened and he laughed softly. That was no child's laughter. There was too much malice in it, too much knowledge.

Too much madness.

"Come, sister," he said, and his eyes rolled back in his head as he fell to the ground.

He wasn't breathing.

No.

I put my hand over his chest and felt no sign of heartbeat.

My enemy had just killed him casually, from a distance.

"No," I said aloud, and pulled the boy into my lap. *"No."* There was still a feeble flutter of life inside of him, struggling like a bird in a net. "You won't do this."

I put my hand over his heart and closed my eyes. Luis's warnings came back to haunt me—I wasn't trained in this; I could so easily damage the child— but I had no choice. There was no one better qualified to take my place.

I put my fingertips above his heart and forced his heart to pump. Once. Twice. Three times. Each time, I sought for the return of a rhythm, but his system seemed paralyzed, unable to function on its own.

His bloodstream, though sluggishly moving through my efforts, carried little oxygen. None was coming through his lungs. I would have to breathe for him, as well. I pulled in as deep a breath as I could, bent over him, and filled his lungs; the cut on my side stretched and widened, and tears blurred my vision.

My pain didn't matter.

I forced his heart to beat again and again and again. Breathed.

His open eyes stared at me, and there was no shadow of self in them. No hope.

I felt the flutter of life weaken in him, and continued to stimulate his heart in slow, thick beats, an imitation of life, nothing more. . . .

The child's heart suddenly jumped out of rhythm with my prompting, vibrated, and gave a strong beat.

Another.

Another.

He sucked in a breath and let it out in a scream.

I held him against me as he screamed and cried. All around me, the fallen children lay silent. I watched their chests rise and fall, alert for any changes, but my enemy did not bother with their deaths. He—or she—rightly concluded that they presented me with more of a dilemma alive.

I took out my cell phone and checked for a signal. None, of course. This was deep country, off the human track in many ways. I would get no help from the police, not until I could locate a working telephone.

The child put his chubby arms around my neck. I stroked his dirty hair. "What's your name?"

He sniffled wetly. "Will."

"All right, Will, everything is fine now. I'll keep you safe." I would need to bandage my wound. I was losing blood, and it was sapping my strength. The internal damage would have to wait until I could reconnect with Luis or find some other source of aid. "Will, I need you to help me, all right?"

He nodded, but he didn't let go of me.

"I'm going to have to wake up the other children. I will need you to be my helper. When the others wake up, they might be scared, and I need you to be their friend. Can you do that?"

He nodded stoutly, and climbed out of my arms and

stood with his shoulder pressed against mine. Trembling, but upright.

I made certain he was steady enough, and then trailed my fingertips lightly over the forehead of another child, a girl with dark hair and darker skin. She sat up, startled, and began to cry.

"Will," I said. He gave me a doubtful look, but went to the girl and patted her awkwardly on the shoulder.

"It's okay," he said solemnly. "You're okay, Christy."

He knew their names. "Will, is there a girl named Isabel? Do you know her?"

Will continued to pat the weeping Christy on the shoulder. "There are a lot of kids."

That sent a cold ripple through me. "How many?"

"Lots." He likely couldn't count very high, so that was hardly definitive proof, but I had the strong feeling he meant *hundreds*. "I don't know some of the new ones. They just came."

"Came where, Will?"

He and Christy both looked at me as if I was utterly stupid. "The Ranch," they said together.

"And where is The Ranch?"

I heard a click of metal, and an adult voice from the trees said, "You're standing on it, bitch."

It is a custom of human villains, at least in song and story, to take their prisoners back to their secret lair, where the prisoners outwit and destroy the villains.

My enemies were far from fairy tales, and I knew they did not intend to allow me one step farther toward the answers I sought.

The children were loaded into a large four-wheel vehicle and taken away, even Christy and Will, who looked resigned to it all. I felt a pang at seeing C.T. taken yet again, but at least he slept on.

I will keep my promise, I told him. *I will find a way to return you to your family.*

The SUV drove off down the dirt road, leaving me on my knees, my blood dampening the dust around me. I was too weak to resist unnecessarily, so I sat still, hands loosely folded in my lap, as four armed paramilitary guards formed a square around me. The rifles they carried looked lethal indeed. So did the handguns at their hips.

"You're trespassing," one of them said. They all looked oddly interchangeable in the moonlight, thanks to their camouflage jackets and pants and matching caps. One was female, the others male. The speaker was one of the men, tall, with a pleasant tenor voice. I put him on the far side of middle age, from the glints of silver in the close-cropped hair that showed under the cap. "Didn't you see the signs? Trespassers will be shot. That wasn't some kind of bluff."

There had been no signs, but I didn't bother to argue the point. "Who are you?"

"Private citizens defending our land. I think the real question is, who are *you*? You don't exactly fit in around here. Who sent you? FBI? CIA?"

"With pink hair?" one of his fellows snorted. "I'm thinking some kind of private security, private investigator, something like that." He shoved the muzzle of his gun close to my face. "Right? Somebody hire you? You should have taken the money and run."

I didn't answer. All my focus was on keeping the wound in my side from pouring out more of my strength on the thirsty ground.

"Doesn't matter," a third one of them said—the woman, who sounded as practical and cold as all the rest. "She's seen the kids. We have to get rid of her."

"We should ask if they want her as a recruit."

"Come on, you've got to be kidding! She's some kind of Warden; that's the last thing we need. We have to kill her, and do it fast, before more of them show up looking around."

"She followed the first one." That made my drifting attention snap back into focus, and I lifted my head to look at the speaker, who was the older man. The leader of this small group. "She's his backup. So I don't think we have to worry too much about more Wardens calling, especially right now. They're a little busy."

General laughter between the four of them. *The first one.* That had to be Luis. They had Luis here.

If you plan to avoid dying, the Djinn part of me commented coolly, *you should likely do something now.* Because the man standing to my right, the one with the graying hair, was preparing to fire a bullet through my head and put an end to it.

I let go of control of my wound, which responded in a fresh gout of blood, and reached out to the trees with power.

The pine tree branches were firm and springy, perfectly suited to pulling back and releasing. One hit my would-be executioner in the back of the head as his finger tightened on the trigger, and his shot went wild, digging a hole in the ground next to my feet.

I softened the ground beneath their feet, and watched the shock hit as their own weight dragged them down. They flailed as they sank, and two tried to shoot me, but I was already moving, rolling to my feet and limping into the trees. I heard more gunfire behind me, and shouts, and then frantic screams.

Then the ground closed over their heads, and I heard nothing.

I couldn't go far. Black waves of weakness continued to wash over me, until it felt that the ground was softening beneath me, just as it had beneath my enemies. I fell and placed a palm flat on the surface. No, the fault didn't lie in the ground, but in myself.

Human weakness.

I wouldn't get far enough afoot. I needed to leave this place, find help, bring rescue to these children.

I made my stumbling way back to the Victory, only to find that one of the gunshots had exploded a tire and mangled part of the engine. I could have repaired it, if I'd had enough power.

I was using what I had left to keep myself alive.

All that remained of the four who'd tried to kill me were disturbed patches of earth, and a single pale hand breaking the surface. I hardly gave it a glance. My paramilitary friends hadn't appeared from nowhere; they'd likely come in a vehicle, as humans seemed wont to do even for short trips.

I saw a flash of movement in the trees, then a pale, dirty face.

C. T. Styles. He had gotten away.

"Calvin Theodore," I said, and braced myself against the trunk of a nearby pine. I kept my other hand firmly pressed against the wound in my side. "Don't be afraid."

He moved out from behind his concealment but didn't come any closer. There was little expression on his face, and a flatness in his eyes that concerned me.

I said, "Your father sent me, C.T.," and the numbness in him broke, replaced by a flare of hope so bright it was like sunrise. "I need you to help me. Did these people come in a car?"

He shook his head emphatically. My own hopes dimmed as his rose, until he said, "They came in a *truck*. It's a jeep. It's black."

I almost laughed. It wasn't often a human was more precise than a Djinn. "Can you take me there?"

"Sure," C.T. said. He darted forward and held out his hand. I took it. His skin felt fever-warm against mine, but that was only because I was chilled from shock and blood loss. He tugged at my arm to get me started, and we headed in the direction of the cold, rising moon.

"They took everybody in the truck, but I got out the back," he said proudly. "I stayed. I knew you'd help."

I had no breath to spare to praise him. It seemed a long way to this mythical black jeep, and every step poked red-hot knives through my side. My body was sloughing off its shock, and I did not much care for the results. "Wait," I murmured, and pulled C.T. to a stop to lean against a handy boulder. I left black smears against the rock. "How much farther?"

"Not very much. It's right up there," the child said, and tugged my hand. "Right there!"

I allowed him to pull me on. At each rise, he promised me only one more, until my feet were no longer certain of their steps.

At last, I fell, and although I tried to rise, I couldn't.

I collapsed on my back, panting, and saw C.T. lean over me, no expression on his small face.

"I thought you'd never fall down," he said. "Goodbye, lady."

He turned away and left me. I tried to rise again.

The dark rolled in and swept me away.

When I woke, I was being carried—no, dragged. Dragged by the heels, like a carcass, through the dirt. I opened my eyes and made a protest that sounded more like a moan than words—and then I realized that I had spoken in Djinn, not English.

It was now pitch-dark, only thin flickers of light coming through the trees. The moon had moved on without me, but it was far from morning. The air was frigid on my exposed skin.

I kicked feebly, and the one dragging me dropped my foot in surprise. The impact of my heels on the ground sent a searing burn through my side, and I jackknifed into a fetal position in response. I couldn't scream, although I wished to. I could only pant for breath.

I heard a blowing sound, followed by a strange, fast clacking of teeth.

An enormous paw touched my stomach. Even in the dim light, I could see the talons.

The black bear was a shadow in the dark, save for a small glitter of its eyes in the moonlight and a brush of lighter fur around its muzzle.

It was frightened of me, I could see that, and I lay very still. Black bears were not aggressive in the main, and preferred eating plants to people, but that did not mean it wouldn't kill me.

It made that blowing and clacking sound again, and I saw the white flash of teeth this time. It was followed by a long, low moan that lingered like a ghost on the air.

I forced myself not to move as the muzzle dipped and sniffed my face. The bear snorted, shook its huge head, and padded off.

I had been rejected, apparently, as not worth the trouble. After the relief—and, strangely, a touch of annoyance—the trembling set deep into my bones. *I had forgotten that humans were food.* And now so was I. There was something about it that terrified me on levels I had not known existed within me. The Djinn didn't—

I was not a Djinn. I was human, and I was wounded. Predators would be drawn to the blood.

I squirmed around and pressed a hand to my stab wound. Still bleeding. I gritted my teeth, ripped cloth from my shirt, folded it, and jammed it into the open lips of the cut.

I might have cried out. I heard the black bear, not yet so distant, make that long, low moan of fear again. Once the sickening pain and shock passed away, I climbed to my hands and knees and then to my feet.

Backtrack, I told myself. C.T. had deliberately led me astray.

My eyes had adjusted well to the darkness, and I could follow the drag marks, and then the stumbling signs of my progress. Blood smeared on a rock. Dragging footsteps.

It seemed to take forever to return to the road, where my poor, dead Victory lay with its flattened tire. It had leaked gasoline into the dirt from the shattered tank. I limped past it, past the last resting place of my four opponents, and just over the next rise, I found the black jeep that C.T. had so convincingly spoken about.

Keys were in the ignition.

I ransacked the contents of the back of the small truck and found a red cross–marked case filled with useful items. I rebandaged my stab wound, shaking antibiotic powder on it as I did, although I knew full well the bacteria would be inside my system by now. I swallowed painkillers and guzzled a bottle of water I found rolling in the back, then picked up one of the extra weapons. It was small, heavy, and clearly meant to destroy—some sort of machine pistol, with a fully loaded clip. The mechanism seemed simple, as most deadly things were.

I tossed it on the front seat next to me, started the jeep, and followed the trail deeper into the forest.

Chapter 14

THE RANCH—IF that was where I was—seemed endless, and empty. There was little to mark this place as having human residents—no fences, no grazing animals other than deer that bounded away from the road at the sound of the approaching engine. I saw no lights, no structures, no other vehicles.

For all I knew, The Ranch went on for many miles in all directions. Any route I chose, if I left the road, would be utterly random.

But the road had to lead somewhere.

Luis is probably dead, my remorseless Djinn ghost said. *What will you do then? You should walk away now, and save yourself the pain and trouble.*

I glanced at the machine pistol on the seat beside me, and for the first time, answered her directly. "I will not walk away. I will kill them all," I said. "And I will take the children home."

Fine words, fine intentions, but when I topped the last rise and saw the valley, I realized that I could not possibly have enough ammunition to solve the problem that lay before me.

It was a well-lit compound, and by my estimation it covered an area the size of a small town. Tall iron towers ringed the perimeter, and there were two walls, inner and outer, with empty space between them.

It looked like nothing so much as a prison.

Within the walls were square, neatly ordered buildings. Some appeared the size of small houses, and others were as large as schools or city halls. Part of the compound—the *town*—was a parking lot full of vehicles. Trucks, cars, all-terrain vehicles, large vans.

The lights turned night to day not only within the compound, but on every approach.

A line that Manny had once quoted came back to me. "We're gonna need a bigger boat," I murmured. That seemed oddly funny to me at the moment, but that was probably blood loss and the onset of infection.

It hadn't occurred to me that they would be able to detect me at the top of the hill—I'd turned the headlights off—but clearly, I had underestimated my opposition. I heard a wailing alarm rise, and saw people moving down in the compound.

Perhaps it's not for me, I thought, and then the radio fixed to the dashboard of the jeep crackled, and a voice said, "We have an intruder on the ridge in Grid 157, repeat, Grid 157. All units, intercept."

I put the jeep in reverse and backed down the hill, turned it around, and drove as fast as I could the way I had come. The bumps and jounces of the road woke new, special pain from my injuries, but I forced that to the background. Escape was my only viable option. I could worry about my internal bleeding later, if I survived.

I saw a flash of lights behind me. Gaining fast.

Another vehicle crashed out of the trees at right angles to me ahead. I swerved and brushed by it, leaving kisses of paint, and dug the wheels deep in the dirt to pull ahead.

Cassiel?

Luis's voice in my ear. He sounded distant and slow.

"No time," I growled. I checked the rearview mirror. I was leading a minor parade of armed vehicles, and bullets spanged off of the metal of the jeep and splintered trees ahead of me.

Wait . . . don't . . . it's not what you think—

They were trying to kill me, I thought, and so far, my theory seemed quite sound. I shut him out and kept driving, rocked around a sharp turn on two precarious wheels, and less than fifty feet ahead, I saw a row of children standing in my path. It stretched from one side of the road to the other, into the trees.

For just a fatal instant, my Djinn self said, *Keep going.*

I took my foot off the gas and slammed on the brake, bringing the jeep to a shaking, shuddering halt a foot away from the children. They hadn't moved.

I had my hand on the machine pistol, but again, there seemed little use to raising it. I wasn't going to fire, not at a line of children, and they knew it.

C. T. Styles stepped out of the trees and walked up to the driver's side of the jeep.

"You're really strong," he observed. "Most people never make it this far. Come on. I'll take you home."

He'd already led me to die in the woods and be eaten by a bear. I wasn't quite so stupid as to assume he meant me well this time.

Most people never make it this far.

"How do you know how many people make it this far?" I asked him. "You only came here a few days ago."

His dark, innocent eyes grew rounder. "Who told you that?"

"Your father."

C.T. gave me a slow, superior smile. "My dad doesn't know everything. I've been here lots of times. Mom brings me. For training."

Training.

I was certain to my bones that Officer Styles knew nothing about this. Perhaps this time, his wife had been unwilling, or unable, to bring the boy home from his *training*.

Isabel. Had Angela also been sending Isabel here? No, impossible. Manny would have known. It was a distance from Albuquerque; her absences would have been noticed.

C.T. was waiting for my response. I gave him none. He finally dropped his chubby hand and stepped back.

An armed man took his place, holding his weapon steady on me. "Ma'am," he said. "Get out of the truck and leave the gun, or I'll shoot you in the head. Try any tricks, and I'll shoot you in the head. Kill me, and my team will shoot you in the head. Do you understand?"

I did. I let go of the weapon and got out of the jeep. My legs barely supported me, which was helpful, as the soldier kicked the bends of my knees and sent me crashing to the dirt. He yanked my hands behind me and fastened my wrists with thin plastic strips, then pressed the muzzle of the gun against the back of my head again.

"If you mess with your restraints, bullet in the head."

"I am following your theme," I assured him.

I was loaded into the jeep again, this time in the back, with an escort who kept his gun aimed steadily at me.

I had no strength to escape, and, in fact, this time I did not see the advantage in doing so. Below in the camp, there might be medical treatment, rest, and the possibility of finding Isabel. Drawing power from a Warden, maybe even Luis.

The forest held nothing for me now but death, and while that didn't frighten me as much as I'd expected, I did not intend to die a failure.

It offended me that after such a long, powerful life, I should end it with a mortal whimper of defeat.

My interior turmoil had manifested itself in tensed muscles and clenched fists, although I had not realized it until the soldier aiming at my head said, "Stop moving or bullet in the head."

I sighed and relaxed.

The compound was, in fact, larger than I had expected. It had taken time, money, and hard labor to raise the structures and walls. They had learned from their ancestors, I saw—clear open space all around the perimeter fence, where nothing grew, not even grass. I wondered if they used an Earth Warden to tend that barren ground.

The towers evenly spaced around the wall held armed guards—not a surprise, given the convoy that accompanied me. As we traveled into the white glow of the lights, I studied my captor closely. He was nondescript. Medium build, medium coloring that might have owed its origins to any race or country. He wore unmarked camouflage fatigues and sturdy black boots. No jewelry, no markings of any kind, even on the uniform.

"Get your eyes off me," he said. "Or—"

"Bullet in the head," I finished. "You can stop repeating yourself."

He smiled, very slightly, and with no trace of humor. "I don't think so. I think you need the reminder. I *will* kill you."

"I have no doubt."

I turned my attention outward, to where the massive metal gates were slowly opening to allow us passage. Like any good security system, it controlled the flow of traffic, so the gate behind us closed before the one ahead opened, leaving us vulnerable and exposed in the no-man's-land between.

I wondered how I might be able to make use of that. Nothing came to mind, but I was weak, sick, in pain, and had a simmering level of anger that seemed to impair my thinking to a remarkable degree.

The next gate creaked open. *Hydraulics,* I thought. I could work with hydraulics, perhaps.

Just not at the moment.

The guard opened his mouth as I shifted. "Bullet in the head, yes, I know," I said. "Do try to aim for the center of my skull. I would hate to be left clinging to life and force you to waste a second shot."

He shut up.

Inside the compound, the streets were clean and logically organized. Not a soul walked on those pristine streets, though I saw curtains and blinds twitch as we drove past houses and barracks-style buildings with a roar of engines. There was relatively little in the way of greenery, except for a park in the center of the community, with a few tall pines and grass.

Ah. And a playground. I saw the swings, slides, and sandboxes. More proof, as if I needed it, that whatever went on in this military-style outpost, it involved children.

Beyond the park, another building glimmered—not like the others. Pearly white, almost organic in its lines. I only saw it in glimpses, but what I saw disquieted me. There was something that raised echoes inside me, from long ago.

Something that did not belong here.

The jeep came to a halt in front of a nondescript concrete building. "Don't move," my guard said as he climbed out of the vehicle. He never took his eyes away from me. Wisely, he didn't come within my reach, only kept his weapon trained steadily on me while two other soldiers pulled me from the seat and—however unsteadily—upright. I did not offer resistance, or much in the way of assistance, either, since I could hardly manage to walk at the moment.

The concrete building was a prison, and inside were

individual cells, reinforced to the strength of vaults. That, I thought, was designed to prevent the use of Warden powers, but no matter how massive the door, there were always smaller fault points to be found. It was difficult keeping an Earth Warden chained. . . .

I sensed a familiar power signature, and my head, which had been slowly drooping, rose with a snap. "Luis?"

He was in the first vault we passed. I saw the familiar flash of his brown eyes through the narrow slot in the door as we passed. "Cassiel?" His voice sounded slow and uncertain. "You okay?"

"No," I said.

Knowing he was here and alive filled me with a water-sweet relief I had not expected. They locked me into a room next to Luis's cell, and it was grim indeed—plain, seamless floor, plain walls, a stainless steel toilet in the corner, a sink with a water tap. A rolled mattress in the corner.

Nothing else. Nothing at all.

They had not removed the restraints, which begged the baffling question of how they expected me to make use of any of the lavish facilities they'd provided, until I heard the ponderous movement of the locking mechanism rattle, and an Earth Warden stepped into the room.

She was tall, severe, with short brown hair and a pinched mouth, a sharply unpleasant expression that seemed to find me and all I stood for—whatever that might be—in utter contempt. She wore a standard olive green jumpsuit, which fastened with snaps in the front; again, curiously, there was no insignia to be seen. I had always thought humans were compelled to self-identify.

She dropped a neatly packaged bundle to the floor and made a twirling gesture with one finger. "Turn around." I did, a full shuffling turn, coming back to face her. She rolled her eyes. "No, idiot, put your back to me."

"Then be precise," I said.

Once I had my back to her, she advanced with a few quick, light steps, and I felt the plastic straps holding my wrists part with a snap. She stepped away again, holding the remains of my restraints. "All right," she said. "Strip. Everything comes off."

If this was a human effort to make me feel awkward or humiliated, it was doomed to failure. The only issue I found with stripping naked was that it was difficult to bend and stretch without waking new waves of agony from my side. Once I'd managed it—she did not offer help—the Warden walked closer again.

"Raise your arm," she said, and bent to examine the wound in my side. "Nasty. One of our little pets do that to you?"

"Pets," I echoed.

"Rejects," she said. "We still find a use for them. Hold still."

She did not say, *This will hurt*, because I suspected she didn't care. I braced myself against the wall with my other palm, trying desperately not to whimper at the acid wash of agony as she poked and prodded.

At length, she seemed satisfied. "You've got an infection in there," she said. "Damage to your liver, nicked a couple of blood vessels. I'll fix the worst of it. Try not to scream."

She put her hand over the wound, and I learned that not all Earth Wardens who *could* heal *should*. She seemed to have little knowledge of how much pain she caused, and cared even less. In the end, I couldn't stop the scream. It felt as if she had filled the wound track with boiling lava.

Once she'd exacted the price of the scream—which, I realized, she'd been waiting for—the Warden closed up the cut and stepped back to admire her handiwork.

It wasn't neat: A hand-sized patch of reddened, blistered skin, and a knotted scar. "You should consider training," I said. She hadn't given me any power through the contact, hadn't so much as replenished my lost blood supplies. Her healing had, in fact, left me weaker, not stronger, and I believed that was exactly her intent. She'd left me in a position that I would not sicken and die, but I'd be too weak to present an effective threat.

She bared her teeth at me—I would not call it a smile—and kicked the bundle toward me. "Dress," she said. "Unless you prefer to stay naked. I don't really care."

She left, taking my clothing, and the vaultlike door closed behind her. I crouched and picked up the bundle. Unrolled, it contained a paper-thin jumpsuit of brilliant yellow, the color of reflective paint, and a plain pair of cotton underwear. No brassiere, but my body was lean enough that it wasn't an important omission. There were socks, and a pair of flimsy shoes with the word PRISONER printed on the bottoms.

I would have manifested my own clothing, if I'd had power, but I didn't, and I was cold. The vault had a chill to it, like a cave. *Or a crypt.* I imagined them sealing the room and walking away, leaving me to starve alone. A Djinn would have found that frustrating and boring.

A human would find it fatal.

The clothing didn't warm me much, but it made me feel less vulnerable—I supposed I had overestimated how much my human body had influenced me along those lines. A human of this time, this culture, needed coverings to feel safe.

As I unrolled the mattress, I found a folded thin blanket and a small pillow. The blanket I wrapped around me as I paced the room. I could sense Luis's presence, dim and indistinct, on the other side of the wall. If I could touch him . . .

But they had gone to great lengths to be sure I couldn't.

I pressed my hands to the wall, then my forehead. I could feel him there, possibly even making the same attempt at contact.

My eardrums fluttered, and then I heard his voice, in startlingly clear stereo. *Cassiel?*

"Here," I said. I didn't know if he could hear me, but I supposed he could. He had, even on the road. "Are you all right?"

That bitch Warden keeps filling me full of drugs, he said. He sounded angry and unfocused. *Can't keep myself straight. Withdrawal's going to be a bitch. You?*

"She left me weak," I said. "I don't think she found it necessary to drug me." If I could find a way to touch Luis, she'd regret that, at length. "What do you know about these people?"

Nothing, except they've got a pet Earth Warden and some mad building skills. Luis's voice turned dark. *They have Ibby. They told me they'd hurt her if I tried anything.*

Yes, the Earth Warden would definitely have time to regret her actions. "I found C. T. Styles," I said. "Rather, he found me." I explained about the ambush and the odd way the children acted. "I don't believe they are themselves. I think someone is controlling them. Using them."

Why kidnap kids just to run them around like guard dogs? I'm pretty sure there's not a Doberman shortage.

Something the Earth Warden said returned to me. "Rejects," I said. "They're rejects."

Rejects from what?

I didn't know. I suspected that was the question on which so much hinged, including our lives.

Although he tried, Luis lost focus, and our contact

dissolved in eardrum-splitting shrieks and growls of out-of-control vibrations. I stilled it hastily, but I continued to lean against the wall, and I thought that on the other side of the concrete, so did he.

"I don't know if you can still hear me," I said, "but if you can, save your strength. I will do the same."

Practicality dictated that I curl up on the lumpy, uncomfortable mattress and sleep to conserve as much energy as possible.

I dreamed of Isabel, alone in the woods, and a bear.

When I woke, there was a tray being shoved through a slot at the bottom of my vault door. The food did not look appetizing, but that hardly mattered; it wasn't food I craved.

I rolled out of bed, crawled to the slot, and seized the wrist of the man who was pushing the tray inside. He gave a startled yelp that turned to a harsh scream as I attempted to pull power from him.

He was merely human. I got only the lightest tingle of power, not even enough to fuel a single continuing breath, and then he broke my grasp and was gone.

I ate the contents of the meal tray slowly, with great concentration. It would help, but without an infusion of power from a Warden, soon, I would be in real trouble. Unlike a natural human body, mine was not self-sustaining. The equations did not balance, and energy leaked away with every beat of my heart.

All the proteins and carbohydrates on the tray couldn't stop that drain.

Half the day passed in silence. I tried to contact Luis, but he didn't—or couldn't—respond. They might have drugged him even more, to silence him. I still sensed his presence, so I did not think they had removed or killed him.

I grew all too familiar with the confining, featureless space of my cell. Six steps across. Nine steps deep. The ceilings were twice my height, the light fixtures inaccessible behind reinforced panels. There were no windows, only a narrow opening in the door and the slot at the bottom through which the trays came.

Both were bolted shut, with massive vault locks, and I could not summon up enough power to matter against that.

I called on Djinn that I knew, from friend to foe; even an enemy might be an inadvertent ally in this situation. But if anyone could hear my weak calls, they ignored them.

I was alone.

My captors allowed me to wait for two more days, in silence, in growing desperation, before the vault door finally opened, and I was put in heavy chains and taken outside, so weak I could hardly walk.

It was daylight, dazzling bright, and I squeezed my eyes closed against the glare as the soldiers prodded me along. I sensed no Warden abilities in any of them. If I had, I wasn't certain I could have stopped myself from attacking them out of hunger, and that certainly would have ended my fragile human life; the soldiers were deadly serious in their guard duties, and would not have hesitated to shoot.

It was odd even by human standards. There were many people out in the streets—talking, walking to or from some unknown destination. All the rainbow colors of humanity, some dressed in military fatigues, some in simple human dress from a variety of countries. From the park in the central part of the compound came the shrieking laughter of children at play.

No one cast a look toward me, garishly costumed in brilliant yellow, chained, surrounded by armed guards. It was as if I didn't exist at all. I wondered for a few moments if they had placed some sort of Djinn invisibility shield around us, but no—some of the humans passing by *did* see us; they simply and utterly ignored us.

"Move," my guard said, and guided me up the street.

"I want to see Luis Rocha."

"People in hell want air-conditioning," he said, which seemed completely off the topic I had proposed. "You've got a meeting already."

As we came nearer to the main building, the one next to the park, I realized how much larger it was than the others. There were organic lines to the flow of the building's long curves. Where everything else formed squares and angles, this building seemed more grown than constructed, and the material seemed more like mother-of-pearl and bone than wood and stucco.

A Djinn built this, I thought. There were few examples of Djinn artifacts; as a species, we left far less trace than humans on the planet we inhabited. But those that we did make had an unmistakable signature to them, a kind of singing resonance that was visible even to my human-dulled eyes.

I felt a deep surge of unease. The design impressed itself on me, and I realized what it represented: half of the ancient symbol of yin and yang. The park where the children played mirrored the sinuous lines and formed the other half. It had a resonance, as well, a subtle, deep power.

Harmony.

We approached the broad, curving end of the bone house, and a door that gleamed with shifting pearlized color opened without a touch on its surface.

The guards stopped. Their squad leader gestured me on.

I walked up the shallow steps and passed through the portal, into an opulence those outside would hardly imagine possible. The surfaces were breathtaking sweeps of nacre, the colors ranging from ice-cool greens to warm whites. The building had indeed been grown, not built, though there were concessions to human comforts in the form of sleekly rounded furniture, cushions, velvets and furs.

There was a simplicity to it that brought a sense of peace and a terrible kind of stillness. I studied the resonance again, and it was familiar to me. *I know this place.* Yet I'd never been in it before. *I know the one who shaped it.* Yes, that was what troubled me. The Djinn who had formed this exquisite, frightening place was someone I not only knew, but feared on levels I could neither identify nor understand.

I was too exhausted, too weak to *think*.

The door closed. The guards stayed outside. After a moment, the pinch-faced Earth Warden who'd tormented me stepped out of a curtained alcove at the far end of the room.

"This way," she said. She had a silver gun in her hand. "If you try anything, I'll kill you."

Dying seemed almost inevitable, at this point. I hesitated.

"You want to see the girl, don't you? Isabel?"

Something terrible was waiting for me in the direction she wished me to go. I knew it. I felt it in every screaming nerve. *I could not go through that door.* If I did, I would not just die. I would die screaming. I would suffer agonies that I could not begin to imagine, but could feel heavy in the air like poisonous smoke.

She.

The thought brushed across me like a ghost, and I knew it came from my Djinn side, the side that was almost dead now, starved into submission. A mere flutter of resistance.

She waits.

I stared at the Warden without moving. She frowned. "Did you hear me? Move it!"

My eyes rolled back in my head and I collapsed. I didn't try to cushion my fall, didn't try to turn my body, and when my head struck the ground, it struck hard enough to crack bone and split skin. Blood began to trickle past my nose across the pristine pearl floor.

"Goddammit," the Warden sighed. "Just what I needed today—another goddamn epileptic fit."

She came toward me.

I didn't move.

She knelt next to me and put her hand on my hot pink hair, feeling for the fracture.

I opened my eyes, bared my teeth, and dislocated my arm to wrap fingers over her wrist. It was a tenuous hold, but she was startled, and in those vital seconds I ripped power from her in great, bloody swatches, stripping her clean of all aetheric energy. She wasn't as powerful as Luis, but she would serve.

I melted away my chains.

She didn't even have the ability to scream. I held her silent for it, and stared into her wide, agonized eyes, drinking in her pain.

I let her form a word. Just one. "Please . . ."

"I am Djinn," I told her softly. "Do you understand? *Djinn.* And I give you the mercy of the Djinn."

I sealed her mouth with contemptuous ease by stilling her vocal cords; all she was able to produce was a torturous, hoarse buzzing. I put a knee in her back to hold her down and rifled through her pockets. I took the gun, extra clips of bullets, her identification, and a curious medallion holding a silver key.

Then I put the gun to her head, released her vocal cords enough that she could whisper, and said, "Where is the child Isabel Rocha?"

"You Djinn bitch," the Warden wept. "You *hurt me.*"

"And I am not finished," I promised. "Tell me where to find the child."

"Fuck you!"

"I'm not attracted to you," I said. "But if by that you mean you won't help me, then I have no use for you."

I sealed her mouth forever by exploding a blood

vessel in her brain. Relatively painless, and instantly fatal.

It was better than she deserved.

I dragged her body behind a sofa and covered it in silky furs. The bloodstains came up easily, and then I methodically searched the room for a way out.

There was only one.

The way the Warden wanted me to go.

I transformed the neon yellow jumpsuit and prisoner shoes into soft leather trousers and jacket in light pale pink, with war slashes of black. Heavy riding boots.

I moved the curtain aside, expecting another room . . . but it was a hallway, like a long, curving throat. Slick and featureless. There was no sound.

She knows I'm here, I thought. *She's waiting.* My Djinn side refused to say anything, or to give me the name of my fear.

I sensed nothing but cold and ice ahead of me.

I moved on, and as I did, doorways appeared—closed, with no markings. Each felt slightly different beneath my fingers. One was hot enough to blister, even at a brush. One felt damp, and I sensed a vast pressure of water behind it. One was a living grave, rich with the smell of rotting things and the work of scavengers.

What are you looking for, Cassiel? Come. Come ahead.

The voice vibrated in my ears the way Luis's had done, but it was not Luis. It was not any voice I knew. No, it was *every* voice I knew, Djinn or human, a massive and strange chorus of sound.

I stopped where I was, my hand on a closed door, and felt every nerve shrink with fear.

You killed my servant, killer of Djinn.

"She deserved it," I said.

The laughter was the laughter of every murderer.

Mocking, cold, and free of any trace of a soul. *So do you,* the voice said. *For your crimes, murderer of the eternal.*

The nacreous hallway began to close in on me. The pearly layers grew and thickened before my eyes, pushing inward. It would grind me apart. I looked behind and found the way back already closed to me. This structure was the mouth of a hungry predator, and I had no escape but down its throat, the way it wanted me to go. There was something dark and terrible at its heart, waiting to devour.

I took a deep breath and opened the door that stank of earth and rot, and plunged into darkness instead.

If I died here, I would choose my death.

Grave dirt filled my mouth, my nose, my ears. It was heavy and wet on my skin. I knew death intimately, and it tried to push inside me, insistent as a blind worm.

Interesting, the alien voice whispered to me. *But you cannot leave me. I know you now. I will have you.*

I spat it out and pushed through the dirt, swimming in muck, until I fetched up against a hard surface in the darkness. Nacre. The slick, pearly surface had a living structure to it, like bone. Why? Why have this room of grave dirt?

I had no time for riddles.

I blew the wall apart in an explosion of shards, and the house—if one could call it a house—*shrieked.* My strike, even as powerful as it was, had only opened a hole the size of a fist. I battered at it, widening it, and the house fought to close its wound even as I struggled to widen it. The instant I paused, it shrank the gash again.

I rained down destruction until the hole was barely wide enough to pass my shoulders, and then wriggled in. This was the most dangerous moment of all; if my concentration faltered, the house would close the gap and chop me in half or amputate a limb. I could sense the Voice screaming, though I had stilled my eardrums and rendered myself effectively deaf. I'd shut off all other senses, too, save sight. I wanted no sensory attacks to distract me at a critical moment.

The nacre had jagged, knife-sharp edges, and it sliced my skin as I crawled and wiggled through the narrow opening. I felt it shift as I hauled myself through, and for a heart-skipping moment I felt the sharp edges press on my thighs enough to draw blood. It wanted to snap shut. I didn't let it, but it was a very near thing. I hauled my feet free seconds before the nacre mouth snapped closed, gnashing only air.

I was on the white gravel outside of the white house, on the smooth, curving side facing away from the park and the children. I rolled to my feet and began to run, releasing my hold on my senses. I would need every advantage now.

You cannot leave me, Cassiel, killer, destroyer. I have been waiting for you.

This time, the human inhabitants of the compound did not ignore me. I drew shouts, screams, and shots. One bullet grazed my leg, but I dodged the rest, using cover and even the bodies of others. I had little empathy for anyone caught in the cross fire just now. They were only faces, and the terrible thing behind me, the terrible knowledge pressing in on me . . .

What was in that white building, so close to where those children played . . . was nothing less than a monster.

And these adults served it *willingly*.

A squad of armed soldiers came after me, but I was no longer unarmed, thanks to the gun I had taken from the dead Earth Warden. I dropped two men with shots; the others with a burst of power that crippled them, at least temporarily. I had no interest in killing them, but I didn't particularly care if that was the outcome.

"Ibby!" I screamed, turning in a circle. *"Isabel Rocha!"*

I ran on, crying out her name, searching for her individual whisper in all this chaos.

Behind me.

The park.

I reversed course, avoiding the hail of bullets by dodging behind a truck. To get to the park, I would have to go around the bone house, that terrible white place that housed the heart of the monster.

Those hunting me had grown organized in their attacks, and there was little cover left. Even the confused civilians had withdrawn.

I took in a deep breath and dove for the ground. It parted for me like thick water, and I used my body like a dolphin's, pushing against the resistance in sinuous curves.

The bone house extended *down*, into the ground. I sensed its vibration and swam away from it, careful not to touch it.

My breath grew hot in my lungs, rancid and used, and I kicked against the dirt and swam up, tearing my way through the roots of grasses to the surface.

The children were being rounded up in the park. Unlike the rejects I had seen in the forest, dirty and ragged, ill-fed, these were glossy, lovely children in impeccable clothing, all of stainless white.

There were perhaps twenty of them, and they were all under the age of ten.

"Ibby!" I screamed, and one small face came into focus, kindling like a star.

"Cassie!" she shrieked, and threw herself forward, racing toward me.

She was intercepted by one of the adult caregivers, who closed ranks between me and the children. The woman who restrained Isabel was wearing a medallion similar to the one in my pocket, the one that held a silver key.

Ibby stretched out her arms to me, tears streaming down her face, and I aimed the gun at the woman blocking her. "Put her down," I said. There were more soldiers coming now. The tower guards also realized something was wrong, and of a surety, at least two of them could reach me where I stood. I was an easy target.

But I wasn't leaving without the child.

"Put her down," I repeated, "or I'll kill you all."

The woman, wide-eyed, shook her head and held on to the struggling child.

"Your choice," I said, as cold as I had ever been in Djinn form.

I shot her. Isabel shrieked and fell, rolling on the grass. Another adult scooped her up and ran away with her, toward the pearl white building. I saw her chubby arms still reaching out for me, her tear-streaked face desperate, and in that instant I felt the anguish inside me coalesce into true hatred.

No. You will not take the child.

I couldn't stop the instincts she triggered, the fever-ish need to protect her at all costs. I'd kill them all to save her, if I had to, and never look back.

She's my child, the Voice whispered in my ears. *She will never be yours. I will make her one of my warriors, and you and your kind will be wiped from existence, thrown into the darkness where not even memories remain. She will destroy you.*

Isabel disappeared into the door of the white house, which sealed itself against me.

I had to abandon her. It was the hardest thing I had ever done, to turn away, to run with the sick taste of rage and defeat in my mouth.

I darted around buildings, running with as much speed as I could manage. I had no goal now, nothing but the blind desire to live, escape, find another way to get to Isabel. Bullets spanged and cracked around me, and sometimes found their mark. I couldn't heal myself from the wounds, but I could close it off and ignore it for a time, and I did.

It burst upon me, with a blinding jolt, that there *was* still a goal.

I turned toward the prison.

When I reached it, moving so fast I was a blur, there were guards at the door. I barely slowed enough to disable both in screaming agony, then melted the metal outer door.

And then the vault door of the first cell.

Luis Rocha was slumped in a corner, pale and unshaven, barely conscious. His head lolled when I tried to raise him to his feet, and although I could sense the power inside of him, he was blocked from the source by the blanket of drugs circulating in him.

I couldn't heal myself as easily, but I could clear his bloodstream. It was an investment of power, not a cost; as soon as he was cleared, his power began to flow back to me, through our touch.

His hands wrapped around my wrists, and our gazes locked.

"Cassiel," he whispered. "Oh, Christ, what have you *done*?"

I must have looked very different to him.

"Whatever was necessary," I said. I was leaking blood on the floor from wounds I didn't feel. "Stand. We have little time."

He scrambled up. They had also outfitted him in the flimsy yellow jumpsuit and prisoner shoes. I glared at it but decided our power would be better spent toward gaining our escape from this place, before—

The entire building rumbled. Dust sifted from overhead, and the lights flickered.

"Was that you?" Luis asked me. I shook my head. "Me, neither—"

Tree roots exploded up from the floor, cracking concrete. Sharp, jagged roots like daggers, then swords. It happened fast, too fast for us to counter it immediately, and one of the roots erupted under Luis's feet, stabbing through his foot and into his leg.

He screamed and tried to pull free. As I was helping him, another root ripped through the stone floor, thick and strong as a telephone pole, and almost skewered me from below. I stumbled aside. It continued to rise, slamming into the ceiling above and shattering the impact-resistant plastic cover of the lights.

"Go!" Luis screamed at me. I shook my head and pulled his leg free of the root that impaled it, picked him up in my arms, and began to run.

It was only nine steps, I told myself. Nine steps from the back of the room to the door.

I jumped the last three, praying I had guessed right, as a whole forest of roots erupted from the floor and sliced in all directions.

We hit one of the thick, pale structures and bounced—but we bounced *out*, not in. I didn't pause. I hit the ground with both feet and kept running, because the roots followed us, trying to outpace and outflank me. But it was a doomed effort—too much open space, and once we had gained the outside air, too many of their own people in the way to continue an indiscriminate attack.

There was a jeep—possibly the same one that had brought me to this prison in the first place—parked next to the prison building, with the keys dangling in the ignition. I dumped Luis in the seat, climbed behind the wheel, and in seconds we were rocketing for the gate.

I didn't particularly care if adults got out of my way. I hardly slowed as the bumpers sent them flying from the path.

I knew by this time that they would try to use the children to stop me, so it was not a surprise to see those ragged young bodies lined up in front of the gate, only a grim confirmation.

I couldn't stop. Not this time.

"Luis!" I yelled. "Can you open a gap somewhere else?"

He nodded. I pointed.

Where I pointed, the inner wall exploded in a shower of bricks. The children were in the wrong place. One of them tried to scramble in front of us— C. T. Styles.

I slowed just enough to grab the boy by the scruff of his neck and sling him into the jeep on the passenger's side, into Luis's surprised embrace. "Put him out!" I ordered, and then I was testing the jeep's ability to scale a shifting mess of broken wall. The tires slipped; the vehicle tilted—then held and climbed.

Beside me, Luis slapped a hand to the child's forehead and used a burst of power to put him to sleep. "I don't like doing that!" he shouted, which forced me to laugh a little wildly. There was nothing in this I liked. I didn't like the fact that we were in an open vehicle, with gunmen drawing their aim on us, while we slithered across broken bricks into a killing field. I didn't like the fact that I had little chance of surviving this.

I didn't like the gnawing terror of knowing how much I could lose even if I did survive. *Isabel. Luis.* My . . . family.

I glanced over at him, through the blowing fury of my pink hair. He had the sleeping little boy in the crook of one arm and the other braced against the dashboard, and Luis's answering look was full of mad, unbelievable energy.

Just like mine, I suspected.

"Here we go," I said, and the tires bit the barren ground between the walls. I took one hand off the steering wheel and held it out to him, and Luis stopped bracing himself on the dash and instead gave me his hand, his power, his will. There was no conversation between us. None needed.

I pulled power from him and drove it deep under the wall. I softened the ground beneath a long swath.

The wall sagged, but didn't fall. Braced with an internal lacing of steel.

Luis battered at the bricks, but the external wall had been hardened against magical attacks, and now we could feel the dampening influences around us— Weather and Fire were at work, as well as opposing Earth forces.

We weren't going to make it. The jeep was hurtling at the wall at speed. If we hit and it didn't go down, we would die. C.T.'s small body would be smashed by the impact; if Luis and I survived, we'd be easily picked off by the Wardens and soldiers.

The wall *had* to come down. I shook the ground, and the entire structure shuddered and bled dust. Some of the concrete shattered and fell away, revealing a sinister skeleton of iron beneath.

I hit it with a final blast of power a millisecond before the jeep's front grille smashed into the structure with stunning force . . . and in that second, the steel turned translucent, and as we hit it, the crystalline structure exploded into showers of glass.

I ducked instinctively, as did Luis, curving over the unconscious boy on his lap. A shower of shards blew over us, and I felt a hundred hot cuts, but all superficial.

We were lucky. A sharp, daggerlike fragment landed between us and buried itself several inches deep in the plastic and fiber of the edge of Luis's seat. Another few inches and it might have severed an arm, or landed in his skull.

Bullets rang in a hot chatter along the metal. I pressed the accelerator, and we bounced over the remains of the wall and out into the open ground.

"Faster!" Luis yelled.

I knew that. My foot was all the way down, and we were still accelerating, tearing along the rough dirt road that led into the forest.

The forest tried to close against us, but I didn't pause; the Earth Warden back in the compound didn't have time to grow the barricade with any degree of care, and plants forced to cycle into maturity at that rate were naturally fragile. The jeep crushed the saplings trying to block our path, and we sped on.

"Watch for more children!" I snapped, intent on guiding the increasingly loosely steering jeep through the turns. I missed my motorcycle. I wondered if they'd simply abandon it in the woods, leave it to rust. It was a sad end for such a beautiful thing.

If they planned to send the rejected children against us as shock troops, they were unable to get them ahead of us.

We rocketed out of the forest and skidded onto clean, black pavement.

Free.

I looked back as I sped along, going as fast as I dared; there was no sign of pursuit.

No sign at all.

Relief began to creep through my body, slow as poison. I began to feel all the hurts, the cuts, the bullet wounds that disfigured parts of my body. I was battered, but alive.

Luis was alive.

One of the children I'd promised to retrieve was alive. The other . . .

I drew in a ragged breath, startled by a burn of tears in my eyes. *Why am I crying?*

Luis was still holding my hand, though I was not drawing any power from him. It was merely comfort. Human touch.

"Cassie," he said. His touch moved from my palm up my arm, stroked my shoulder, and trailed along my cheeks where tears spilled down. "Big Djinn don't cry."

I laughed madly. "Cassiel," I said. "Cassiel is my name."

And I heard the Voice in my ears, blocking out the world, whisper, *I know your name, Cassiel. I have your heart now, and you will come back to me. You must.*

Chapter 15

OFFICER STYLES MET us just outside of Lake City. I told him to come alone, and not to tell his wife.

He disobeyed both instructions.

Luis had helped with the worst of my injuries—again—but I was bitterly tired now and aching and afraid. Pain, I had discovered, tends to make one afraid, once adrenaline fades. I had never truly understood that before. We sat on a fallen log, in the shadow of a pine tree. C.T. was still unconscious, but sleeping normally. Luis had wrapped him in a blanket he'd found in the back of the jeep.

We were drinking cold bottles of water when the Colorado State Highway Patrol car pulled into the rest stop near our stolen vehicle.

"Heads up," Luis said. "He brought company."

The second person in the car was not, as I'd have assumed, Officer Styles's partner. It was his wife, a fragile little blonde who seemed genuinely relieved and overjoyed to see her sleeping little boy. Officer Styles was grateful, but wary.

I held out my hand to stop Mrs. Styles from approaching, and pointed at the policeman. "You," I said. "Take the boy."

He didn't understand, but he stepped forward and scooped up his son, blanket and all. C.T. murmured sleepily and nestled closer to his father's chest. I felt

Luis relax as the last of the control he'd been exerting slipped away.

"We're in your debt," Officer Styles said. He didn't look happy about it, but that might have been an overload of emotion in a face not equipped to process such extremes. "I can't believe you found him."

"You should know," I said, "that your wife was aware of his location the entire time."

For a second, neither of them moved, and then a breeze shifted the pine tree behind us and skirled up dust from the road, and Officer Styles shifted to stare at his wife. "Leona?"

The pretty little blonde beside him was hardening before my eyes. Her eyes took on a bitter shine, and her smile curdled into something toxic.

She showed that only to me, and only for an instant, before turning toward her husband with a look of wounded innocence. "I don't know what she's talking about! Here, let me hold him."

"Don't," I said, "if you want to see him again. She'll take him. She intends to take him."

Whether he believed me or not, Officer Styles backed up a step as his wife came toward him. "Hold on. Are you saying Leona had something to do with this?"

"I'm saying your wife knows about the compound in the forest," I said. "The Ranch. Isn't that right, Leona? The Ranch, where they collect and train the children."

Luis stirred when the woman cast us a poisonous look. "Cassiel's right," he said. "I saw it myself, man. We were barely able to get C.T. out, and if you let her get her hands on him, I can't swear she won't take him right back. It's some kind of cult thing."

Officer Styles was looking at his wife as if she had turned into an alien creature. "Leona?"

"Give him to me." She held out her arms.

"Answer me. Did you have something to do with this?"

"He's my *son!*"

"He's my son, too!" Styles burst out, and when she tried to grab him, he avoided her rush. "Leona, *stop!* What the hell is wrong with you? How could you—"

"How could I?" Leona's face was alive now, alight with utter fury. "*How could I? After what happened to me? My child isn't going to be mutilated like that.* My child isn't going to be twisted by some group of superior bastards that thinks it knows what's best for the world. *No*, Randy, dammit, I will *not* let that happen to my son!"

"But—it doesn't have to—Lee, he's not even *six* yet!"

"He's already started showing signs. Soon enough, they'd come looking for him. They'd give us a choice, Randy: let them take him away and put him in their special schools, raise him up to be one of *them*, or cut away everything that makes him who he is!" Leona's eyes were mad, I thought. Anguished and mad. "I've lived like that, with half of myself sliced off. It's horrible. It's worse than dying. I won't let it happen to C.T."

"You never said—"

"No, I never said! *You never asked!*" Leona made another grab at the sleeping child, which Randy fended off with his elbow. "This is better for him. I swear it! They'll care for him. They'll train him. He'll serve a higher purpose."

"Yeah," Luis agreed soberly. "News flash, lady: They decided he wasn't good enough for whatever little meritocracy they're running inside that place, so he got to be King of the Rejects, which is like *Oliver Twist* meets *Lord of the Flies*. They were going to kill him, *amiga.* Or at least, they didn't care if he died. One thing about cults: It's all about them, not you."

That stopped Leona's rush, but only for a minute. "You just don't understand. I've seen the future. *She* showed it to me. I know how things will be. *Should* be."

"You're right," I said, and stood up. I ached all over, and watching this travesty of a reunion had turned my heart black. "I don't understand. And I don't care. You took him there, Leona. Why? What did they promise you would happen?"

"They promised me that he'd get to kill Djinn," she said. "Lots of Djinn. *All* the Djinn." She smiled thinly. "That's worth dying for."

I looked at my partner, who seemed not only surprised by this, but more than a little alarmed.

It only confirmed for me what I had sensed within the compound.

I stood up, nodded to Luis, and we walked to the jeep. It had clearly been through a firefight, as had we, and Officer Styles began to realize that now that his son was safely in his arms. "Where are you going?" he asked.

"Things to do," Luis said. He took the driver's seat. "My niece is still in there."

"You're going alone?" Styles clearly thought we were crazy. As we probably were.

"No," Luis said. He fired up the truck as I climbed in on the other side. "I'm going with her."

The hour was just past noon, and the sunlight that filtered through trees struck the road in harsh, glittering lace.

Luis drove fast, but not recklessly. There was an expression on his face that I thought his enemies would not like to see coming in their direction.

"We don't have any chance," I said. "You know that. They are more than prepared for us now."

"I know."

"Then why—".

"You don't think Leona's going to be calling them to warn them?" he asked. "Let them spend all night looking for us. They're good and paranoid about you right now, and we should keep it that way. Don't worry—we're not going back there on our own. You have any allies you can call right now? Anybody we can get on our side?"

I thought it over. "One," I said. "Just one."

"Is it a Djinn?"

I nodded.

"Then that's probably all we'd need, I'd say."

"I can't promise he'll help," I said, "but I can ask."

I had tried calling on Gallan when I'd been in the cell, but I'd been weak and exhausted then, and perhaps he hadn't heard.

I closed my eyes and let the flickering light and steady vibration of road beneath tires lull me into a light trance.

Gallan.

Gallan.

Gallan!

The last call I sent with a burst of true power, and I felt it ripple like a shock wave through the aetheric.

Nothing. There was no response. It seemed eerily silent.

Luis glanced at me. "Well?"

I shook my head. "If he doesn't respond to that, he doesn't intend to respond at all." That disappointed me more than I had expected. I had thought—I had *hoped* that Gallan, of all the Djinn, might still hold a secret regard for me, and be willing to go against the wishes of our mutual lord and master.

But in the end, perhaps he was still Ashan's creature.

A fingertip lightly brushed the curve of my ear. "I'm no one's creature," Gallan's soft voice whispered.

"And you should know that better than anyone, Cassiel."

Luis became aware of Gallan's sudden manifestation in the back of the jeep at the same time that I did, and involuntarily swerved. Gallan—crouching, holding to nothing for support—swayed gracefully with the motion of the vehicle. The wind whipped his long golden hair into a silk war banner. He was dressed in white, all in white, and his eyes were the color of a tropical sea at midnight.

I turned in the seat to look at him, and for just a moment, the full Djinn glory of him blinded me with tears. *This* was what I had lost. What I had once been.

"You came," I said. My voice sounded weak, far too human. "I wasn't sure you would."

Gallan shrugged. "Ashan has other things to concern him," he said. "There are a few of us who have been left to keep watch. And I have been watching, Cassiel."

"I need your help." I glanced at Luis. "*We* need your help. Please, Gallan."

I got a brilliant, cutting smile in return from the Djinn. "*Please.* How very human of you. It's not like you to beg, my love." The smile dimmed quickly. "I will deal with you for this boon."

"We don't need deals," Luis said. "We need help."

"Help comes at a cost. Tell him, Cassiel. Tell him how True Djinn exact their prices."

"Gallan—"

"Tell him."

I glanced at Luis. "True Djinn—you would call them Old Djinn—do nothing without compensation. No favors, no kindnesses. There is always a price, in the end."

"And what's his price?"

Gallan lost his smile altogether. "My price is Cassiel."

"No," Luis snapped, before I could reply. "Not happening. Feel free to fuck off now."

"We need his help!" I said.

"Not if it means your life, we don't." ˙

"I wouldn't kill her," Gallan said, as if the whole concept of killing was beneath him. I knew better. "I have many uses for Cassiel that don't involve her gruesome death. Many pleasant uses, in fact. I think you have imagined them yourself."

The look Luis sent him in the mirror was pure, hot contempt. "So you're a rapist, not a murderer."

Gallan's smile didn't waver. "Not if she consents," he said, and turned his attention to me. "Do you consent, Cassiel? Do you submit yourself to me in exchange for my help in retrieving the child?"

This was a different Gallan than I had known—no, not different; only I was different. His cruelty and capriciousness had been alluring when I'd been a Djinn; I'd only understood the power, not the cost it exacted. I had always found Gallan attractive, always been drawn to him.

I looked into his face now and saw only a cold, calculating predator.

"No," I said. "I don't consent. But you will help us, anyway, Gallan."

He laughed. "Why would I do that?"

"Because you can. Because it's right. Because it's *necessary*."

"I'm not a human," he reminded me almost gently. "Arguments of right and wrong won't sway me."

"They should. We—the True Djinn—have lost that." I remembered what the New Djinn Quintus had said to me. "Long ago, in the beginning, we cared, didn't we? We wished to help. To protect. Now only the New Djinn feel this, and we feel nothing. *Nothing*, Gallan. We amuse ourselves in cruelty and meaningless games. We were better off slaves to the Wardens. At least then we had a purpose."

Gallan—who had been a slave once, where I had not—snarled at me with startling fury. His teeth turned sharp as daggers, and the bones beneath his face shifted to sharper angles. "You were cast out, Cassiel. Don't make it worse."

Luis pulled the jeep off to the side of the road, killed the engine, and turned in his seat to look at Gallan. If he was afraid—and he had to be; no human could look on the face of an angry Djinn and not feel some kind of fear—he hid it well. "Look, either help or don't help. It's your choice. But don't threaten my friend, and don't act like the Djinn hold the keys to the universe. You need us. You need humans; you always have."

"No. We allow humans to exist. We don't need them." Gallan's eyes turned a muddy shade of red. "But you do need *us.* Choose, Cassiel. Do you agree to submit yourself to me or not? Because that's my price. You know I can't change it."

I shook my head. "No, Gallan. I can't."

The angry glow faded from him, and he became almost human now. Almost, but never. "No?"

"You didn't think I'd turn you down?"

"You can't. You need me."

"Not as much as you believe. Good-bye, my friend. We won't meet again."

I turned face forward. My last glimpse of his face showed him startled, round-eyed, and lost.

"The lady said no," Luis said. "Thanks, anyway. Now, if you don't mind, we've got work to do."

Gallan misted away without another word.

For a moment, neither of us spoke, and then Luis said, in carefully neutral tones, "That was awkward."

"That was exceedingly dangerous," I said. "And unproductive." My heart was racing, and I struggled to calm it. My palms felt damp. "He could have killed us."

"He didn't."

"I thought Gallan was the best of the True Djinn. The kindest."

Luis started the truck. "If he's the kindest, I'd hate to see the meanest."

I gave him a look. "You already have."

"Oh," he said, puzzled, and then his frown cleared. "*Oh*. You're talking about you."

"Once," I said, and looked away. "And perhaps still."

We drove past the hidden entrance to The Ranch and on to Lake City, which, though small, was still the largest community in the area. Luis left me to fill the jeep with gas as he went inside to buy food at the small store. When he came back, he pointed down the street, toward a building lit with pink and green neon. "There's a motel," he said. "We could both use a bath and some rest, and I need to use the phone."

"The phone?"

"You called for help," he said. "It's time for me to do the same."

The motel was old, but surprisingly well maintained. The clerk sold us two rooms with an adjoining door, which Luis requested instead of only one; I thought that odd, since we had few secrets now. He handed me my key as we walked outside. "Get cleaned up and eat something." He had gotten a bag of food at the gas station—two sandwiches wrapped in wax paper, some potato chips, some sodas in cans. "I'll leave the door open to my room. Twenty minutes."

I nodded.

Twenty minutes seemed a short time. I washed away grime, dried blood, sand, a thousand tiny irritants in the shower, and used the thin motel shampoo on my hair. I had no clean clothing—again—but I wrapped a blanket around me and opened the door to Luis's room through the connecting passage.

He was on the phone. Like me, he had showered, and his hair was flat against his head, dripping at the ends with beads of water. He had wadded up the neon yellow paper jumpsuit they had given him at The Ranch, and like me, had wrapped himself in a blanket for clothing.

He held the receiver in the crook of his shoulder as he wrote furiously on a piece of cheap paper with a pen provided by the motel. "Yeah? You're sure that's the number? *Gracias*, man. I owe you big time. *Adios.*"

He hung up, ripped off the sheet of paper, and pressed the posts of the phone to end the call. The phone was very old, with a rotary dial, and he fumbled with the unfamiliar operation as he entered a string of numbers.

I sat on the bed and ate my sandwich. It was surprisingly good.

When Luis finished his call—which was conducted largely in Spanish—he hung up and dried his hair with the thin cotton towel slung across the back of the chair. "We've got a couple of hours," he said. "I called in some support."

"Who?"

"Trust me, you don't need to know. But they're sneaky little bastards. And they know how to run an infiltration operation better than just about anybody. They've done it a hundred times, taking down things the Wardens never even noticed. Never *had* to notice, because these guys took care of it before it became a problem."

"The Ma'at," I said. "Yes?"

He seemed surprised I knew. "Yes. Officially, I'm not supposed to know them."

"You called one to watch Isabel."

"Yeah, but he was a friend first, a Ma'at second. These guys aren't any kind of friend, not to me."

I chewed a bite of sandwich. "You admire them."

"Hell, yeah, I admire them. For one thing, they actually learned to work together—Djinn and human—when the Wardens were still stuck on that whole master/slave thing. And what they do isn't brute force, it's subtle." Luis flashed me a smile. "And okay, I dated a girl once who was Ma'at."

I felt a strange surge of antipathy. "Were you speaking to her just now?"

"Mirabel? No. She's off in China, last I heard. I haven't talked to her in years." He studied me through half-closed eyes. "Why?"

I didn't wish to explain, so I didn't, methodically finishing the sandwich and drinking the soda. Luis shrugged and fiddled with the few items on the small desk.

I felt the vibrating disturbance of air a second or two before Luis, and came to my feet, holding the blanket in place, as a shadow thickened and took on form and edges in the corner of the room.

When he stepped from the shadows, Gallan was a changed Djinn. Changed in attire, yes—from brilliant white to neutral gray—but also in other ways.

Most notably, in the way he looked at me.

I held out a warning hand to freeze Luis in place as he gathered his breath for a challenge. Gallan's dark eyes had locked on mine.

"I'm a fool," he said. "Forgive me."

I had never heard Gallan apologize to anyone, not in all the slow turnings of the world. I blinked.

"I saw it," he said. "I went to look at this place you spoke of, this *Ranch.* And I saw it."

"Saw what?" I could hardly hear my own voice over the thundering of my heart, because there was fear in Gallan's eyes, and I had never seen that, either.

"I saw the end of the Djinn." His gaze on mine bored like a diamond-edged drill. "I saw the end of us, Cassiel. I *saw.*"

He swayed. I moved forward as Gallan—a True Djinn, stronger than any human—crumpled slowly to his knees and bent his head.

"We brought this on ourselves," he said. "You were right. *You were right.* I beg your forgiveness."

Luis muttered something under his breath, and said, "Don't trust him."

I didn't. I knew Gallan, and this was not the Djinn I knew. Not *any* Djinn I knew.

"I will help," he said. "I must help you."

I felt a cold hand grip my spine and shake it. "What did you see?"

He shook his head, a violent spasm as if he tried to throw the image of it away and could not. "I can show you," he said, and extended his hand.

I looked at Luis Rocha, who shrugged. "It's your call. I don't trust the guy, but that's probably just me."

I transformed the material of the blanket wrapped around me into cloth—enough to make trousers and a shirt—and took Gallan's hand.

We rose into the aetheric.

Gallan, on this plane, was a shadow, quick and quiet, and I felt heavy and obvious in my human aura. He pulled me with him, heading through a maze of living trees and rocks that gave way to darkness and whispers.

There was no darkness on the aetheric, but it was here, bitter and void of any hint of energy.

We were above the compound called The Ranch.

There were no signs of people, no sources of even electrical power. It was as if every ounce of life had been drained, not just inside the compound, but out. The devastation went on in all directions, stretching almost a mile—death incarnate.

Only the pearl-and-bone yin and the parklike yang remained, glowing in the darkness in white and green.

Pulsing.

Alive.

Hungry.

I felt it pull at us. Gallan backed away, drawing me with him, and rose far up into the aetheric sky until the pulsing, living entity was far below us.

I still felt the drag. So did Gallan. I realized that I was feeling it through him—this thing called to Djinn, lured them.

It ate them.

Gallan was weakening. I took the lead to pull him onward, back toward my mortal body; this time, at least, the anchor of flesh seemed to be an advantage. A salvation.

I crashed back into flesh and opened my eyes to see Gallan still kneeling where he had been, swaying.

He was unraveling.

"I got too close," he said. "Help me, Cassiel."

"Luis!" I grabbed Gallan's arm, but it felt more like mist than flesh, and my fingers sank sickeningly into moistness.

Luis tried, but when he reached out, his hands passed entirely through the Djinn, leaving trails of smoke behind. Gallan's eyes were desperate, his mouth open, but he made no sound now.

He was trapped on the aetheric, and this manifestation was failing.

Fading into smoke.

Gone.

I grabbed Luis's hand and launched us both into the aetheric, trying to follow Gallan's essence, but the darkness disoriented me, whispered to me, taunted and pushed in strange currents.

I heard screams, and the screams of the Djinn are not meant for human ears. I fell back into flesh, and so did Luis.

He was holding me in his arms. I was trembling.

"It eats Djinn," I said numbly. "It ate Gallan. It destroyed *Gallan*."

It was the Voice, the pearl-and-bone yin, the park-like yang. It was the children within it, being used to fuel and enhance a creature that had limitless hunger, an appetite for power and destruction that knew no boundaries.

She, my Djinn side whispered. *Not it. She. You know who she is.*

She had been familiar to me because once, a very long time ago, I had been asked to kill her.

I'd thought I had.

"Pearl," I whispered. "It's *Pearl*."

I collapsed in Luis's arms as the darkness closed in.

When I woke, I was in a bed, sheets and blankets over me. Despite the warm coverings, I felt cold and empty. The room seemed very silent, though I heard voices coming muffled through the wall. The other room, I thought. Luis had put me in my own bed, and he was talking to others next door.

I got up, dressed in my stained leathers, and walked in without knocking. My appearance interrupted Luis as he talked with three others, two men and a woman. The woman, I was surprised to see, was Greta, the Fire Warden from Albuquerque. The others I didn't know, but from their weak auras, they were Ma'at, not Warden.

"Cassiel." Luis's eyes were warm but wary. "How are you?"

I sat down on the bed without an answer. I didn't know how I was. I wasn't sure I would ever know. After an awkward silence, Greta said, "We conducted several flyovers of the compound. The thing is, there's no installation. Nothing like what you described, anyway."

She had printed photographs, which she spread out

on the table. They showed the weathered wreckage of an old farmstead, no modern buildings, no fences, no walls, no houses.

There was no pearl-and-bone building, no living embodiment of yin-yang.

No sign of the compound at all.

"We're still working to get a team in there to do a ground reconnaissance. Luis—is it possible that somehow you were, I don't know, delusional? That the two of you—"

"No," I said. "It is not possible."

Luis wasn't so sure, and he seemed shaken by the suggestion. "Cassiel, they altered my blood chemistry. They could have altered yours, too. Maybe what we saw—"

"What we saw," I said, "was real. The compound was real. The bullets were real. We saved a real child, Luis. That was not illusion."

"Then where is it?" one of the Ma'at asked, and tapped the photos. "Where did it all go?"

I took in a deep breath and let it out slowly. "Luis. I need to talk to you. Only you, alone."

Greta and the Ma'at exchanged looks, then shrugged. Luis moved them to the open door, into my room, and shut it behind them before he turned to look directly at me.

I took a moment before I spoke, because I knew that once I began, he would never look at me so kindly again.

"I need to explain how I came here," I said. "I need to explain why Ashan cast me out. You won't like it."

Luis nodded and settled himself in a chair.

"A long time ago, I became the first Djinn to do murder," I said. The words felt numbing on my lips, like ice. "Another Djinn. Her name was Pearl. You think us cold, I know, but we are the guardians of the Mother, and we have limits. Pearl . . . had none."

Luis leaned forward, intent on my words. "What happened?"

"We had been the first children of the Earth for so long, you know. So many countless, numberless millennia that you cannot even begin to imagine it. Life changed, evolved; we paid little attention to it. Species came and went—and then one arose. One that had awareness, and intelligence, and *understood*." I held his gaze captured in mine. "Not mankind as you know it now. An earlier version, a more peaceful one."

Luis wet his lips. "What did you do?"

"I did nothing," I said. "Pearl found them offensive. She destroyed them. She erased them from the face of the Earth and ripped away everything they were. There are crimes among the Djinn, but that one had no name until that moment—not even as much because of the slaughter, but because of what happened to Pearl in response."

He waited while I gathered my thoughts.

"She . . . went mad," I said. "She tore holes in the fabric of the universe around us that should never be opened, and she could not close them again. She became—other. Alien to us. Ashan sent me to destroy her. It was the first time in our history that one Djinn killed another, you see." I looked away. "She did not defend herself, because she never expected me to strike against her. *It had never happened.*"

Luis was frowning. "But I'm talking about *now*. Not then."

"It is the same," I said. "I destroyed her. I thought I removed her from the world, but there must have been something left. Some seed, some thought, some memory . . . and it grew in secret, in shadow, passed down within the new mankind that arose after her. Now it's here. *Pearl is here.* She's drawing her source power from humans, but her hunger for the Djinn is unlimited. She'll destroy

them. Destroy *us*. What happened to Gallan will
happen to all the Djinn, one at a time. They'll be
drawn in and destroyed.''

Luis swallowed. "Why did Ashan exile you, Cassiel?"

I held his gaze. This moment had been coming all
along. I had dreaded it and feared it, and now it
was here.

"Ashan must have known that Pearl was rising," I
said. "He must have known that the only way to stop
her was to remove her power." Luis's face was slowly
bleaching white. "He ordered me to kill the human
race, but he didn't tell me why."

Ashan never explained. He'd never had to before.
I hadn't guessed his thoughts, or my answer might
have been different. I had thought it was Ashan's
pride and his arrogance. His hatred for the Wardens.

I said, very softly, "He was right."

Luis shook his head. "No. We can fight this. We
can find a way to fight this. We have to."

Tears burned in my eyes—tears of anguish and
shame and fear. "Ashan cast me into human flesh so
that I could understand the risk. So that I would agree
to do what must be done. And now I do. Now I
know."

Luis came off the chair at me so quickly I didn't
think to react. He shoved me back against the wall,
trapped me there with his hands chaining my wrists
against the hard surface. "No," he said. He leaned
his hot, sweating forehead against mine. "No, you
can't believe this. We can beat this, we *can*. We have
to find them. Save Ibby. Stop this from happening."

"How?"

"I don't know! We have to try!"

He was begging me not just with words, but with
the contact of our bodies, with the unspoken primal
warmth that connected us. The power that coursed
from his body into mine.

"Please," he said. "Cassiel. There has to be another answer."

I wanted to believe that. "My people are going to die," I said. "You're asking me to stand by and let it happen."

"I'm asking you to *find another way*."

I broke the grip he had on my wrists with a sharp twist of my arms, but I didn't move away. "You can stop me," I said. "All you have to do is kill me."

That shocked him, drove him back a full step. "What?"

"I'm vulnerable to you. In human flesh, I'm vulnerable. Once I become Djinn again, once Ashan grants me power, you can't stop me. You know that." I wiped tears from my face. "If you want to stop me, kill me. If you don't—"

He lunged forward, hands gripping the sides of my head, but if he meant to hurt me, his touch turned gentle at the last instant. "We'll find a way," he said. "Cassie, we'll find a way."

But as long as I lived, I was a danger not just to him, not just to Isabel, but to every human breathing. I had never thought it would come to this.

I had never imagined Pearl would have survived to bring this darkness back.

"Yes," I said softly. "We'll find a way."

And if I had to do it, I would be Ashan's assassin one last time. He had known that. . . . But what was worse, what frightened me even as a Djinn, was that I knew Ashan better than to think I was his *only* plan.

There were others that would engage at the proper time to fulfill his needs.

Humanity had more enemies than me.

Pearl had moved The Ranch, and she had destroyed everything she didn't need . . . including her followers.

She had taken the children but left behind dead adults, so many bodies strewn across the ground. There was no trace of the compound, the walls, the buildings. She had destroyed *everything*.

The casual power of it was stunning.

I stood on the dry, whispering grass as the Ma'at gathered up bodies, and knew that somewhere she was hiding herself. Gathering her forces. Building her fortress around her.

Waiting.

"I know you can hear me," I said to the wind and the grass. "I know who you are, Pearl. And I won't give up."

I heard the laughter of a million mocking voices.

Will you kill the world to stop me, destroyer of the eternal? Will you commit the sin that cast me out, and destroy yourself, as well?

Luis had said, *We'll find another way.* Luis was real to me now, flesh and bone, and I couldn't simply destroy him. I had lost too much.

Cassiel, Pearl's million voices of the dead whispered. *You already have lost everything. You just don't know it yet.*

I swallowed. "I'm coming for you."

Come ahead, she whispered. *Come ahead, my sister, my murderer. I long for your touch.*

I flinched when Luis's hands landed on my shoulders. He pulled me back into his warmth. "There's nothing here," he said. "Is there?"

"She took the children with her."

"Can you trace them?" Luis raised my chin to meet his eyes. "Cassiel. What do we do now?"

Die, Pearl's voice whispered through the grass.

"We go on," I said. "We find a way."

Luis put his arm around me, and led me back to the jeep.

It was a long drive back to Albuquerque, and I had too much time to think.

Isabel.

The fate of six billion was at stake, but only two of them mattered to me in this moment: Luis and Isabel. *I will find a way.*

. . . To be continued in *Outcast Season: Unknown*

TRACK LIST

As always, music is my muse. Here are the tracks that helped get me through *Outcast Season: Undone*.

"Life Is Beautiful"	Sixx:A.M.
"Three Wishes"	The Pierces
"Mary Jane's Last Dance"	Tom Petty & the Heartbreakers
"Secret"	The Pierces
"Give It Up"	LCD Soundsystem
"Citizen Soldiers"	3 Doors Down
"Your Woman"	White Town
"Hey, Man Nice Shot"	Filter
"Believe"	The Bravery
"I Need to Know"	Tom Petty & the Heartbreakers
"Daft Punk Is Playing at My House"	LCD Soundsystem
"Sloe Gin"	Joe Bonamassa
"Tess Don't Tell"	Ivy
"Mama"	Genesis
"Don't Come Around Here No More"	Tom Petty & the Heartbreakers
"Box Full O' Honey"	Duran Duran
"Last Man Standing"	Duran Duran
"Hunting for Witches"	Bloc Party
"Smalltown Boy"	Bronski Beat
"How Does It Feel"	Eskimo Joe
"The Good Ones"	The Kills
"Falling On"	Finger Eleven
"Ride"	The Vines

"In the Air Tonight"	Phil Collins
"What If I Came Knocking"	John Cougar Mellenkamp
"Ally"	Truth in Fiction
"Electrofog"	Le Charme
"Refugee"	Tom Petty & the Heartbreakers
"Stop Draggin' My Heart Around"	Stevie Nicks & Tom Petty
"On and On"	Nikka Costa
"Everybody Got Their Something"	Nikka Costa
"2Wicky"	Hooverphonic
"Enjoy the Ride" (Feat. Judy Tzuke)	Morcheeba
"Grace"	Miss Kittin
"Saw Something"	Dave Gahan
"Fever"	Stereo MC's

ABOUT THE AUTHOR

Rachel Caine is the author of more than twenty novels, including the Weather Warden series. She was born at White Sands Missile Range, which people who know her say explains a lot. She has been an accountant, a professional musician, and an insurance investigator, and carries on a full-time secret identity in the corporate world. She and her husband, fantasy artist R. Cat Conrad, live in Texas with their iguanas, Popeye and Darwin; a *mali uromastyx* named (appropriately) O'Malley; and a leopard tortise named Shelley (for the poet, of course). Visit her Web site at www.rachelcaine.com.

The Morganville Vampires series

by Rachel Caine

College freshman Claire Danvers has her share of challenges. Like being a genius in a school that favors beauty over brains, battling homicidal girls in her dorm, and finding out that her college town is overrun with the living dead.

Glass Houses
The Dead Girls' Dance
Midnight Alley
Feast of Fools
Lord of Misrule
Carpe Corpus
(coming June 2009)

Available wherever books are sold or at
penguin.com

THE DRESDEN FILES

The *New York Times* bestselling series

by Jim Butcher

"Think *Buffy the Vampire Slayer* starring Philip Marlowe." —*Entertainment Weekly*

STORM FRONT

FOOL MOON

GRAVE PERIL

SUMMER KNIGHT

DEATH MASKS

BLOOD RITES

DEAD BEAT

PROVEN GUILTY

WHITE NIGHT

SMALL FAVOR

Available wherever books are sold or at
penguin.com